# *Sails of Fortune*

To West Jr. High Students,

Christiné Echeverria
Bender

# Sails of Fortune

*by*

## Christine Echeverria Bender

*CAXTON PRESS*
Caldwell, Idaho
2005

Illustrations, including cover art and maps, were created by
artist Sarah Pilar Echeverria.

Published by
*Caxton Press*
312 Main St.
Caldwell, ID 83605


ISBN. 0-87004-449-4

*Caxton Press* is a division of
The Caxton Printers Ltd.

Printed in the United States of America.
172206

*THIS BOOK IS LOVINGLY DEDICATED
TO MY HUSBAND, DOUGLAS F. BENDER.
MAY OUR VOYAGE OF DISCOVERY
AND WONDER NEVER END.*

OTHER BOOKS BY
CHRISTINE ECHEVERRIA BENDER:

*CHALLENGE THE WIND*

# Table of Contents

# *Maps*

# *Acknowledgements*

No work of historical fiction is brought to life solely through the efforts of its author, and *Sails of Fortune* is certainly no exception to this truth. The project was first conceived when a dear family friend named Frank Berria, after learning of the completion of my first novel, *Challenge the Wind*, recommended that I write a book about Elcano. For this suggestion, one of a thousand illustrations of the love that Frank has bestowed upon my family over the years, I am immeasurably grateful. To Frank's wife, Helen Berria, who imparts her warmth, kindness, and assistance with incomparable generosity, I offer my wholehearted thanks for her editorial help with this novel. These two individuals prove that the term "family" must sometimes be broadened beyond the boundaries of blood relations.

Additionally, invaluable throughout the editorial and advisory process were the efforts of my parents Isaac and Phyllis Echeverria, my sisters, Teresa Townsend, Debra Geraghty, Felisa Wood, and Diana Echeverria, as well as Dave and Jean Eiguren, Mark Mollison, Alice Tracy, Dr. Errol Jones, and fellow writer and friend, Lona Rash.

A special tribute is owed to my editor at Caxton Press, Scott Gipson, a business man of both heart and honor with whom it is indeed a pleasure to work.

For the endless encouragement of my sons, Nicholas, Adam, and Gideon, and my daughter, Anna, who also assisted me greatly with editing, I offer a loving embrace, and this book as one of their legacies. To Doug, my partner in life to whom I dedicate *Sails of Fortune*, I give my final and unreserved gratitude.

## *Author's Notes*

Vast and varied sources were utilized in order to depict the characters and events of this epic voyage with historical integrity. Since no comprehensive log books created by either Juan Sebastian de Elcano or Ferdinand Magellan are known to have survived the ages, other accounts, such as that of crewmember Antonio Pigafetta, were relied upon. The nonfiction work of Tim Joyner, which seems to best follow and enhance the writings of F.H.H Guillemard, Hawthorne Daniel, Ian Heath, Ian Cameron, and even Stefan Zweig, proved most helpful. Although Laurence Bergreen's description of the treatment of witnesses during the trial at Port San Julian disagrees with a number of historians, I found that his interpretation best fits the tenor and traditions of those times. Mairin Mitchell's work provided valuable background information into the life and family of Elcano.

*Christine Echeverria Bender*

# A Knife's Handiwork

## 1

September 21, 1519.

Standing still and alone on the last planks of San Lúcar's dimly lit wharf, a darkly cloaked figure fastened his gaze upon the cluster of five ships anchored just offshore. The watcher eased a dagger from his belt as his eyes scanned the vessels with absorbed deliberation, studying them as if intent on memorizing every moon-shadowed block and yardarm, every ghostly line and casting. After several long moments he pulled his gaze lower, crouched down, and brushed his left hand across the graying board at his feet to smooth away loose sand and splinters. Shifting his position slightly to allow the lantern light to fall upon the cleared surface, he lowered his knife and worked its tip into the wood. With practiced skill he began to carve and chip until a letter appeared, and then another.

Mindless of the passing minutes, he paid little heed to the muffled curses and jests that rose from the workers loading wine kegs at the other end of the pier. He did not pause as the knife brought forth words from the letters, and from the words, a pledge. Setting his knife aside, he ran his fingertips over one letter at a time, feeling every corner and curve, binding himself to their meaning with his touch. Only then did he still his hand and blow the shavings away. Taking up his knife and rising, he studied his handiwork.

In letters an inch and a half in height, "For Honor. For Home," stared back at him. Just once he uttered the words aloud. Then, with an acknowledging nod, Juan Sebastian de Elcano returned his knife to its sheath and let the quiet ships draw his attention once again.

As always, the middle ship held his gaze the longest. If fate apportioned him no surprises, it would be upon the decks of the *Concepción* that he would serve as shipmaster for the next twenty-four months. But then, he thought, fate seldom failed to dole out generous shares of the unexpected to those who sailed distant seas, and providence had a good many hours in which to conjure disruption in the course of two whole years.

He had sailed long enough to understand that any voyage could deliver hardship with such consistency that it became as familiar as the shadow of his own ship. But this voyage was like none ever ventured. The risks paralleled the vastness of the distance they were daring to cross. Yet any fears that burdened him were far outweighed by his eagerness to leave the harbor, to depart from the trouble that had haunted his efforts for so long, and to sail toward possibilities even greater than the dangers.

After straining for thirteen months against the wills of time and men, Elcano stood at the verge of his journey's beginning and gradually allowed his senses to overtake his thoughts. He absorbed the fluttering touch of the breeze against his cheeks, then the fishy odors of the wharf, and finally the soft whisperings of the river.

The sound of a single footstep approaching from the far end of the pier suddenly sharpened his hearing. Without turning, he listened more deliberately and heard another soft footfall. Stiffening ever so slightly, he held his body in the same position. He suppressed his breathing, allowing not even the intake of his lungs to interfere with the straining of his ears. The feet advanced unhurriedly, the solid response of the boards beneath their tread revealing the fact that they bore a man of substantial weight. Whoever he was, he was progressing with uncommon slowness and apparent stealth.

Elcano knew that he was the only one at this end of the wharf, the only possible target of the man drawing near. There had already been missing shipments, supply shortages, and simmering discontent among the men that had erupted into a near riot just days ago. An attack on the fleet's officers would fit well with the Portuguese tactics to disrupt the voyage.

Moving his shoulders as little as possible, Elcano reached up and loosened the acorn-shaped clasp at the neck of his cloak. He eased his hand lower, wrapping his fingers around the hilt of a sword he had wielded for fifteen years. At its touch, the nerves of his arm began to hum. As the oncoming footsteps drew nearer, his muscles tightened in readiness. The rest of his body betrayed nothing of his suspicion or his purpose as he gauged the diminishing distance between himself and the suspected assassin. Thirty feet. Twenty. Wait, he told himself. Not yet, not yet.

When he knew that his assailant was no more than three strides away, Elcano suddenly whirled around. In one flowing movement he flung his cape aside, lifted his sword in a hissing, shoulder-high arc, and lunged until the tip of his blade froze three inches from his attacker's throat.

A wordless shout burst from the startled newcomer. He leaped back, jerked his open hands in the air, and yelled, "Hold, Juan Sebastian! Hold!"

Elcano snapped his sword away from the stunned face and took a step toward him. "Blessed Mother! Juan!" He pulled in a couple of breaths then groaned loudly. "Please forgive a foolish friend. I've started imagining evil everywhere, even in your footsteps."

Juan de Elorriaga lowered his hands, took a deep breath of his own, and began to chuckle faintly. "You gave me such a start I didn't even think to draw my own sword." His laughter gathered a little strength when he said, "A good thing, eh? We might have made quick work of one another." At the pained look that crossed Elcano's face, Elorriaga took pity on him. "Ah, we are all too edgy these days. God willing, things will be calmer once we set sail."

Elcano slowly sheathed his sword and retrieved his cape, giving it a snapping shake before draping it back over his shoulders. "I haven't drawn a sword so recklessly since I was thirteen. I almost wish you were not so tolerant with me."

"Oh, I don't intend to let you forget it. I may even send word of this back to your mother."

Elcano allowed himself a smile. "What brought you here so early?"

"Likely the same things that brought you." Pointing at the fleet, Elorriaga said, "I heard the ships calling."

The two men faced the water together and took a moment to do no more than stare out at the gently swaying vessels. Elorriaga's gaze lingered on the largest ship, the *San Antonio*, just as Elcano's attention was once again held by the *Concepción*.

Elorriaga did not turn toward Elcano when he asked, "When, do you think, did your forefathers first take to the sea?"

Elcano gave it a moment's thought. Their shared Basque ancestry spanned so many ages that it was hard to envision a beginning to their ways of life. "Long, long ago. I wonder what their vessels were like."

"They certainly had no ships such as these."

In their early thirties, Elcano and Elorriaga had already faced the dangers and now bore the scars of many excursions. It would have surprised neither of them to know that the other man's thoughts paralleled his own as their minds drifted to the last tasks to be completed before setting sail, and then to their families, and, briefly, to the chance that they may never return.

But the similarity of their thoughts belied the dissimilarity of their physical features. Even from behind and at a fair distance, any man of the fleet would have distinguished each officer from the other.

Elorriaga stood in his predictable stance with his boots spread wide and thumbs tucked inside his jacket, securing themselves to a thick leather belt. A closer look in the daylight would have revealed a strong, clean-shaven face framed by a straight mass of black hair that parted in the middle and fell squarely to his shoulders. His wide swatch of bangs fanned across a well-weathered forehead. When Elorriaga stood upon the *San Antonio's* deck as he did now upon the pier, firm and sturdy as an aged oak, it would not have occurred to his men to question his competence, and even less his orders.

Elcano, comparable to Elorriaga in the dark coloring of his face, eyes, and hair, was an inch taller and somewhat leaner than his friend. He wore finely cut new clothes that he had purchased with the advance of his wages, and the garments complimented his form well. His wavy hair, arched brows, and squarely trimmed beard made his face appear longer than it truly was. Most remarkable of his features, and the one for which he had been rigorously teased in his youth, were eyelashes so long that they brushed the tops of his cheeks with every blink. Elcano's lashes enhanced the fire that flared in his eyes during unguarded moments of excitement or challenge. At such times, his countenance revealed the spirit of a man who might smile in defiance at the first thunderous crack of an oncoming storm.

Still eyeing the ships, Elcano said with feeling, "Such beauties. They've been refitted well." He had purchased all five ships in Lequetio, a village not far from his hometown of Guetaria on the northern coast of Spain. The ships had all given previous service and, though still sturdy, they had shown many signs of wear when they first arrived in Seville.

"Yes, they will serve us well. Just like us, they want nothing better than to be at sea again," said Elorriaga.

Elcano shook his head. "Just like us? What about Juana?"

Elorriaga's thumbs moved to a more comfortable position on his belt and he stared down at the water near their feet. "Sometimes I wonder if it would have been better if I'd chosen only the sea. It would have been easier for Juana."

"Easier perhaps, but not better."

"It's a hard life for a woman, being married to a seaman."

"She would have no one else, if you'll recall. Besides, you were destined to be married."

"Oh, yes? Why me and not you?"

"You know as well as I do."

"Yes, but I need you to remind me."

"My oldest brother is married and has two children, and

5

my next brother is a priest, so the obligations to my family and God have been satisfied. I must find the means to make a household, and this voyage may allow me to do that before I am too old. You now, you are the first-born. You will inherit your family's home, which must be filled with young Elorriagas. That duty required a wife. But it was your wish as well as your duty to marry, and you're only coming on this voyage because you don't want to worry about Juana or your children ever going hungry."

When Elorriaga said nothing in response, Elcano turned to him, understanding. "She'll be all right, Juan. You chose a strong woman. But why are you standing out here talking to me? Go on back to her while there's still a little time."

He shook his head slowly. "No, I'll stay." Elorriaga's voice softened as if he were remembering the intimacies of their last night together. "We said our goodbyes."

Elcano nodded in acceptance.

"I want to ask you something before we sail, Juan Sebastian," Elorriaga said.

"Of course."

"If I don't return from this voyage, if I should die out there, will you deliver the news to Juana?"

Taken aback, Elcano countered, "Don't we have enough to worry us without you speaking aloud of your own death?"

"I've had a feeling for many days now," Elorriaga went on determinedly. "A dark feeling. The situation with the Portuguese isn't getting better."

Elcano lowered his voice. "Which Portuguese? The spies that have plagued us night and day, our own commander, or the other men sailing with us?"

"Well, all of them, I suppose. The captain-general has certainly hired on more of his countrymen than the king allowed. Even if every last one of them is true to the fleet, what about the Portuguese ships that may already be waiting for us to reach open waters? They'll spare no gunpowder once their guns have found us, that's certain. And let's say we're able to avoid all trouble with the Portuguese, you know as well as I that the sea itself is likely to take the lives of every other one of us. It's her way. I'm just saying that if

6

I am one of those she claims, I won't regret my choice to sail, but I'd find comfort now in hearing that you would take the tidings back to my wife."

"All right then. If such a thing happens and it is within my power to tell Juana myself, I will. But this isn't like you, Juan, letting rumors stir up such fears."

"Me? I let rumors stir up fears? Who was the one that drew his sword on a friend a few minutes ago?"

Caught by the truth of this accusation, Elcano smiled and admitted, "Not you."

With a slightly defensive edge, Elorriaga said, "Besides, it's more than a rumor that King Carlos gave the command of this voyage to a Portuguese against the counsel of men with far more experience in such matters than he's gained in his eighteen years of life." He glanced uneasily toward the far end of the pier where three men were unloading crated chickens from a cart. Keeping his voice low, he went on. "Neither is it mere rumor that King Manuel is as outraged at our king as he is at Magellan. If Manuel hadn't so recently married our Princess Eleanor, he would likely have ordered his men to cut the captain-general down in the streets of Seville."

"Quite possibly."

"And while the Portuguese damn Magellan as a traitor, some men of our fleet fear he's still loyal to his homeland. Lord help us, the Portuguese want Magellan dead for betraying their king and some of the Spaniards want him dead because he might betray ours."

Elcano asked, "What about you? Have you come to question the captain-general?"

Slowly, thoughtfully, Elorriaga said, "I find it hard to understand how a man can turn away from his native land, especially in favor of a country that has waged war against it off and on for generations. And Magellan is taking steps that may wound Portugal severely. If we succeed in reaching the Spice Islands, the blow to Portugal's wealth will be so serious that she may never regain her present power. Why would he do this? He's given us no answers. And yet, I've found nothing in his manner to make me question him as an officer and a man of principle. As far as I can judge, he's been genuine in his intentions and tireless in his efforts. Whether I understand it or not, he appears to be devoted to young King Carlos."

It was Elorriaga's turn to ask, "What about you? You've known him a few months longer than I. Have your impressions of him changed after all that's happened?"

Elcano turned to face the ribbon of light just appearing beneath the horizon's gray mantle, a silent herald of the rising sun. "If my first impressions have changed at all," he said, "they've only strengthened. Magellan's the most deliberate man I've ever known. So far, he's been firm, unusually inflexible at times, but fair. He seems unwilling or incapable of using any subtlety when dealing with others, which may explain a good share of the difficulties he's had with our Castilian captains. It's strange how he shows no respect for their nobility even though he is noble himself. He seems more comfortable with common men."

Elorriaga raised an eyebrow and grinned. "Does all that mean you trust him?"

"Yes," Elcano said with a short laugh, "I trust him. And I hope that both of us are good judges of character. Come," he said, throwing his arm across Elorriaga's shoulders and steering him toward shore, "it's nearly dawn. Let's find a hot drink and a place by the fire before the others get to the inn. It will likely be far too long before we share such pleasures again, what with you sailing on that clumsy hulk of a ship rather than with me."

This good-humored challenge sparked the expected rebuttal from Elorriaga, and the two of them headed down the wharf, boasting outrageously about the qualities of their respective vessels.

In the shadow of the knoll-top castle of Duke Medina Sidonia lay the low, rambling Crossbow Inn. By the time the remaining officers of the fleet had crowded into its dining room, and the stragglers from the night before had been nudged out, Elcano's and Elorriaga's flagons were nearly empty. They sat side by side on a bench against the wall, allowing their own excitement to grow with the voices that reverberated throughout the room.

"This bunch won't sit still for a long speech," said Elcano glancing from face to face. "Luckily, Magellan is a man of few words."

When Magellan entered, accompanied as usual by his illegitimate son, Cristóbal Ravelo, and his Malayan slave, Enrique, his manner was notably sober.

"Look at his face," said Elorriaga. "Taking leave of his young wife and babe must not have been an easy thing."

"I heard there's already a second child on the way," said Elcano. "And the voyage is claiming Doña Magellan's brother as well as her husband."

"Ah, yes, Barbosa." Elorriaga took a long drink then said, "The captain-general is bringing a good number of his other relatives along as well. Let's see, he has a cousin captaining the *Santiago*, a great-nephew serving as one of his pages, his natural son acting as a cabin boy, and a brother-in-law and a nephew joining our horde of fumbling supernumeraries."

Few of the trained men had much patience when it came to tolerating the supernumeraries. Little more than high-born passengers, each had agreed to lend an inexpert hand at manning the ships or drawing a sword if either action became necessary. Being neither servant nor sailor, carpenter nor gunner, barber nor caulker, most of the supernumeraries were deemed to be little more than in the way. But if the relative of a powerful official wanted to experience the excitement of a sea voyage, regardless of his lack of training, Elcano knew there was little that a mere shipmaster could do about it, especially when the official happened to be the captain-general, the king, or the pope.

With mischief in his voice, Elcano said, "Yes, a ship can certainly become overcrowded. Which brings to mind, someone mentioned that your captain is sailing with eight personal servants. I told him not even Cartagena would take that many along."

Elorriaga gave Elcano a half-hearted scowl. "You know damned well it's true." Shaking his head, he muttered, "In that, you'd think the man was a bishop himself rather than the illegitimate offspring of one. Still, Bishop Fonseca has seen that his son was well raised. My captain is young but he's a good man. And even if his father is the vice-president of the Supreme Council of the Indies, Cartagena is certainly not the first captain to gain his position through political connections."

"No, he's not alone. Mendoza is captaining the *Victoria* and he's better trained to be a treasurer. Neither Mendoza, Cartagena, nor Quesada has done much sailing into open waters." He nudged Elorriaga with his elbow. "That's why the captain-general hired such exceptional men to master his ships, eh? Heaven knows what he'd do without us."

They both let out a laugh, gaining a prickly look from Magellan and curious glances from a few of the others. Elcano and Elorriaga straightened their faces and moved to the front of the room, resettling themselves just behind their respective captains.

Magellan handed out several sheets of paper to each of the five commanding officers, returned to stand before the fireplace, and waited for the men to quiet down completely.

Not for the first time, Elcano noted the dissimilarity in appearance between the Castilian captains and Magellan. Even dressed in his best clothes the captain-general looked like a well-fed mongrel that had seen a few too many fights. His face bore several small scars and his frame was both short and portly. The shape of his nose proclaimed that it had been broken more than once, and his eyes, though intense and intelligent, were deeply set and thickly lidded. A bushy, gray-streaked beard encircled his weathered face. Rather than displaying the courtly grace and refined bearing of his nearest underlings, an old battle wound to his right knee caused Magellan to walk with a pronounced limp. He spoke with a blunt gruffness that, coming from a lesser man, would have been disdained at court.

Intense and unsmiling, he addressed them now. "Gentlemen, this day has come at last. After mass and confession, we will take to our ships. I do not intend to keep you long. The papers I've just handed to the captain of each ship contain the king's specific orders for this voyage. As you captains can see, His Majesty has been both comprehensive and precise in his instructions."

With a look of mild disbelief, then a cock of his chin toward Elcano, Captain Gaspar de Quesada held the papers to his side so that Elcano could read along with him. As Elcano scanned the pages, he understood his captain's surprise. Seventy-four groupings of regulations!

Magellan lifted the foot of his bad leg up to a stool, crossed his forearms loosely upon his raised knee, and leaned upon them. "I will take the time to emphasize a few of these rules so there will be no mistaking their importance. First, note that by day all ships are to maintain their positions behind the flagship. Every evening the ships are to salute the *Trinidad* and receive any necessary navigational orders. At night, signal lanterns set at the *Trinidad's* stern are to be closely followed. You can read for yourselves the signals that will be used to adjust sails in case of storms or other hazards. It is vital that the fleet stay together at all times."

Waiting just long enough for his silence to underscore his words, Magellan cleared his throat and went on. "The King has ordered that no swearing or gambling is to be allowed aboard ship, and that proper behavior be observed at all times. He also prohibits any women from ever boarding a ship."

While the captain-general addressed a question concerning methods of distributing valuables taken during the voyage, Elcano perused the regulations. Strangely, Magellan had failed to refer to one of the most prominent directives; that the expedition was to avoid landing at any domains currently claimed by Portugal. Perhaps the reason for his silence, Elcano mused, was understandable considering that it was still uncertain whether their destination, the Spice Islands themselves, lay within Portugal's realm. It would hardly have been politically wise of their king to omit such a precaution in an official document, however, given the present state of tension between the two monarchies.

"Finally," Magellan concluded, capturing Elcano's attention once again, "King Carlos particularly points out that the native people of the lands we will visit are to be treated with respect, especially the women. If any force or violence is used against a woman, such an action will be followed by severe punishment. Read over the rest of the rules carefully. Lock them in your memories."

Magellan straightened and clasped his hands behind his back. "Gentlemen, we are embarking on a voyage to fulfill a great vision; to reach the East Indies by sailing westward. For God and King, each man must do his duty to the utmost of his ability. If he does so, we will not fail, regardless of what may lie in our path."

Captain Cartagena, tall, darkly handsome, and clothed in a rich blue fabric generously embroidered with silver thread, rose from a bench at the table nearest Magellan. "Excuse me, Captain-general," he said politely, "but surely we are to be given the details of the route we are to take. I understand that for security purposes the route has not yet been fully divulged, but your captains, masters, and pilots must not be left to sail blindly. The king even specifies," he said, pointing to one of the regulations, "that we are to be given this information upon sailing."

Unperturbed, Magellan asked, "Have we yet set sail, Captain Cartagena? I will hand each captain a sealed description of the first stage of our course just prior to boarding. Any additional information will be provided when it is needed."

Elcano watched Cartagena stiffly retake his seat. Understandably, their route was the cause of great speculation. It was Magellan's claim to know the location of the passage from Brazil to the South Sea, the waterway to the Spiceries, that had convinced King Carlos to support the voyage. The threat of sabotage would make a man carrying such a secret lean toward the side of caution. Withholding this knowledge from the captains at this late stage, however, could also fuel the fear that Magellan was a Portuguese agent after all.

Although he read otherwise on Cartagena's face, Elcano sensed nothing inappropriate in this slight delay in revealing the particulars of their westward journey. It was already known that the first leg of the voyage would consist of sailing the relatively well-traveled stretch of sea to the Canary Islands. Magellan would undoubtedly distribute charts showing his intended route across the Atlantic once they had anchored there.

And perhaps this was only appropriate. After all, the islands that lay off the northern coast of Africa had been granted to Spain under the same treaty that would ultimately decide the destinies of the men now gathered around Elcano at the inn. It would decide who held the right to control the trade of the Spice Islands.

Elcano was just a boy when Columbus sailed back to Spain to announce his discovery of the lands to the west, but he still remembered the excitement it had caused. The question over ownership of what the rulers of Spain and Portugal then thought to be the East Indies instantly stirred the embers of war between them. This smoldering fire slowly grew until the flames of battle appeared unavoidable, but reason was forced upon them by Pope Alexander VI in the form of the far-reaching Treaty of Tordesillas of 1494. With the flurry of a pen, this papal decree divided the world in half by a line of demarcation that ran north and south at a point 370 leagues west of the Cape Verde Islands in the Atlantic Ocean. All lands to the west of this imaginary line were given to Spain, and those to the east, to Portugal.

But the treaty had been unclear on a component that had become more and more vital with the burgeoning of the spice trade; the exact position of the line of demarcation on the other side of the world. No one knew with any precision where Spain's influence ended in the South Sea, and Portugal's began. Although Elcano and his fellow navigators could estimate latitude with fair proximity, the instruments, formulas, and assumptions available to estimate longitude resulted in little better than a rough guess, especially over long distances. In truth, the size of this sea was known only by its mathematically calculated dimensions. Most scholars had concluded that its expanse must be significantly smaller than that of the Atlantic Ocean, but until its measurement could be confirmed, the size of the world and the size of Spain's influence were merely speculative.

As to the temperament of the South Sea, no one could know this until a group of men was willing to be the first to cross it. Elcano was proud to be among that group, but he knew that with only one direction open to them, they must first find a westward passage through the great land mass on the other side of the Atlantic.

Somehow, Magellan had discovered the whereabouts of the passage during his years of sailing around the horn of Africa and on to India, in discussions with other sailors, or while conducting research in the libraries in Lisbon. He had then come to Spain and offered to share his knowledge on behalf of King Carlos. Watching the captain-general closely, Elcano again refused to believe him false in either nature or claim.

"Gentlemen," Magellan said, drawing the attention of all, "I know that during mass each of you will make your peace with God, but I wish to offer a few words before we leave here." His head bent downward and his voice softened as every other head in the room was lowered. "May He who has power over storm, disease, and every manner of calamity be with us throughout this great undertaking. May any of us destined never to return to these shores be taken up into His kingdom. Have mercy on us, oh Lord, in this world and in the next. In the name of the Father, and the Son, and the Holy Ghost. Amen."

Magellan raised his face. "I wish you each a safe journey." Signaling for Enrique and Cristóbal to follow him, he left the room as the other men rose from their seats.

Elorriaga fell into step beside Elcano. "While you're in church don't forget to confess that you almost killed an innocent friend this morning." Ignoring Elcano's huff of protest, Elorriaga continued, "And be sure to include in that list of sins whatever you've been up to with the women of this town."

"Ah, Juan, it's so much easier for a married man to remain pure."

They volleyed taunts until they neared the Church of Nuestra Señora de Barrameda, where their moods grew quieter and more reflective. Elcano thought back to the day before the fleet had left Seville. Upon that day they had attended mass at the church of Santa Maria de La Victoria. Before the altar, their ships' flags had been blessed, and each man had pledged his loyalty to King Carlos. Then each of those under Magellan's command had sworn his faithful obedience to the captain-general.

Today, when Elcano made the sign of the cross upon entering the doors of the church, he wondered how many days would pass before he would pray within such holy walls again. He sidled into a pew, knelt down, again made the sign of the cross, and began to pray. Silently, he asked God to help him and the rest of the men remember the vows given in Seville, to face what lay before them as men of valor. He pleaded for protection against unforeseen dangers, especially the unpredictable power of the ocean. *But if I am destined to die upon this voyage, Holy Father, then please forgive my weaknesses and my sins. Lastly and most importantly, Dear God, please look after my family.*

# Away

## 2

Tough he hid it well, Elcano felt the exhilaration of departure in every nerve as he scrutinized the rigging of the *Concepción* for the third time, searching for any sign of weakness. Seeing none, he turned his heightened attention to the men nearby, and then to those on the foredeck. While studying the proficiency of their actions, he kept his ears alert for a word from Captain Quesada who stood behind him upon the stern deck. His captain in turn awaited the signal from the *Trinidad*.

As last minute adjustments were completed, more sailors migrated to the rails and turned their eyes to the flagship. A few faces looked back toward San Lúcar wearing expressions of fear or longing. Very few families of the seamen lived nearby, but townspeople milled about the shore and the wharf. Elcano searched but did not see Juan Elorriaga's wife in the small crowd, and then he remembered his friend's words, "We said our goodbyes."

One day, Elcano hoped, he would have a wife that loved him enough to weep at his leaving.

"A fine, fine day for our departure, eh, Master Elcano?" said his boatswain, striding up and rubbing his hands together in anticipation. Juan de Acurio's grin spread across the full length of his mustached face and it seemed unwilling to dislodge itself. Five years younger than Elcano, Acurio did even less than usual to rein in his restless energy as he rocked his muscular frame back and forth from his heels to his toes.

"Couldn't be a finer day, Acurio," agreed Elcano. "A man lives for a day such as this."

At a sudden loud clang of metal, Acurio jumped and both

men snapped their heads around. A chagrinned Martin Magellan, the captain-general's younger cousin, was just stepping clear of the ship's three-sided, iron cooking box, which he had just bumped into. Acurio cast a moderated scowl in his direction. By way of apology, Martin offered a nervous bow and moved as smoothly as possible away from the fogon.

"Baggage," Acurio muttered in his Basque tongue, referring not only to Martin but also to the supernumeraries as a whole. "I've never started a trip with more useless baggage." With that proclamation, Acurio resumed his nervous rocking.

Elcano kept his smile hidden. "They will learn their way around the ship soon enough," he responded in Basque. "Breathe in the air, Acurio. Let yourself relax for a change." Speaking in Spanish, he added with confidence, "We have an excellent ship and a strong, willing crew."

"Yes, sir, that we have. Although, when you put all the crews together, we've got more colors and looks than I'd ever thought to see in one fleet. There are mostly Spaniards, of course, and us Basques, but then there are Portuguese, and Italians, Frenchmen, and Greeks."

Elcano nodded. "And the Flemings, Germans, Austrians, and Irishmen."

"And one lone Englishman, sir, the captain-general's master gunner. That slave of his is the only Asian aboard too. Then there's the African slaves and servants, of course. Why, sir, this fleet must have more colors of men than any that ever sailed together before."

"It must indeed, Acurio," Elcano said, then turned his attention back to the flagship.

When the signal came at last, it came without subtlety. Before the banner of King Carlos had been raised more than a few feet above the *Trinidad's* main deck, her bombard and culverin cannons exploded with thunderous roars and great clouds of black smoke. A boisterous cheer rose from the crews and officers of all five ships, two hundred and sixty-five voices unleashing a deep-throated, tuneless song of elation. The sound spread in an instant to shore where the townsfolk waved wildly as they called out their farewells. Little children hopped and screamed with excitement, their voices mingling with the shouts of their parents.

Elcano's heart soared with the din around him. He turned quickly back to Captain Quesada and acknowledged the order to unfurl their sails, then he faced his boatswain again. Grinning, and shouting to be heard, he cried, "To sea, Acurio."

"Banners up! Men aloft!" Acurio bellowed. "Weigh anchors, men! Weigh anchors for God and Spain!"

The fleet began to move. Sails unfurled, sliding down from yardarms and billowing until they proudly, boldly brandished the huge red crosses of St. James, the patron saint of the Spanish realm. The shout "For God and Spain!" echoed from ship to ship as each took her position near the mouth of the Guadalquivir River. The *Trinidad*, her standards flashing gallant colors against a blue sky that seemed only to enhance their brilliance, pulled to the head of the fleet.

Elcano caught a glimpse of Magellan standing high on the flagship's stern deck, his hand holding a velvet hat in place, his eyes aimed ahead. Behind the *Trinidad* and just in front of the *Concepción* sailed the largest ship in the fleet, the *San Antonio*, captained by Juan de Cartagena. Elorriaga stood not far from his captain near the *San Antonio's* aft mizzenmast. He turned back and gave Elcano a brief wave of his beret, then waited a moment to see the salute returned before disappearing on the other side of the *San Antonio's* lateen sail.

Captain Quesada, showing his confidence in the crew of the *Concepción*, appeared to take little notice of the men's efforts as his ship moved into her position as third in line. A little to the port and astern of the *Concepción* sailed Captain Luis de Mendoza's *Victoria*. And lastly, as the smallest of the fleet's ships, the *Santiago* took up the rear position. The *Santiago's* elderly Captain Juan Rodriguez Serrano and several of his crewmembers waved one last time at the figures on shore before easing forward.

*At last*, Elcano thought as his ship gained speed. *At last.*

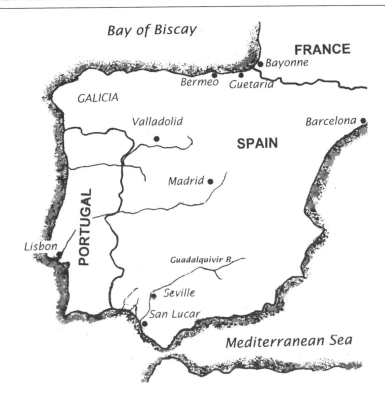

The Guadalquivir River soon spilled the ships into the Atlantic Ocean, where they turned their prows for the first time to the west.

Not a puff of a foul breeze disturbed the fleet on its first day at sea. Few suffered from seasickness, and hopes burned brightly in every breast. The crewmembers performed their duties with willing hands and ready laughs, and Elcano found himself smiling through much of his first watch. It felt good to be at sea again.

The men had already been divided into three divisions, each of which worked a four-hour day watch and, eight hours later, a four-hour night watch. The three groups, in turn, were under the direct commands of the master, the pilot, and the boatswain. This arrangement was unusual in that the captains were not in direct management of the men. But, with the exception of Magellan, their lack of sailing experience made these procedures not merely workable

19

but, in Elcano's opinion, preferable.

As the daylight began to fade and the sand in the *Concepción's* half-hour glass piled ever higher in its clear base, the men of the early night watch waited for the sound of the bell to announce the next call to duty. With several minutes remaining before the change of watch, however, Elcano gave the orders to adjust their sails and approach the flagship. The *Victoria, San Antonio,* and *Santiago* also pulled near to the *Trinidad* in accordance with the king's regulations and, one after the other, each master gave the prescribed salute of, "God save you, Captain-general!"

To every greeting, Magellan replied, "And your captain, yourself, and your crew." Then he said, "Today was a fine beginning, men, a fine beginning. I have no instructions beyond those already in your possession. Heed them well."

They needed only to follow the signals of the flagship's lanterns. That would be easy enough on so calm a night, thought Elcano.

The sea and wind continued to act as amiable companions throughout the next few days, and in very little time even the supernumeraries aboard the *Concepción* fell into the ship's routines. Six days out of San Lúcar, Elcano was standing at the rail of the foredeck, his eyes focusing far ahead of the flagship. Gonçalo Fernandez, the ship's blacksmith, climbed limply up the ladder and leaned over the railing not five feet away. He jumped in surprise when Elcano said, "Breathe deeply, Fernandez. It will help."

"Master Elcano! I didn't see you, sir. I, uh, thank you, sir."

"Not much better today?" Although most of the new men had become tolerant of the ship's movements by now, Elcano had seen this unfortunate passenger retching over the rail on several occasions. His face still looked drawn and exhausted.

"Oh, I feel much better, sir," Fernandez said with pitiable conviction.

"In that case, perhaps you won't deem my news quite as welcome as you would have yesterday."

"News, sir?"

"Do you have a good eye, Fernandez?"

"Why, yes, sir. I've been told that I do."

"Look ahead, then. You may catch a glimpse of Tenerife before the flagship's lookout spots it.

The look of hope that crossed Fernandez's face upon hearing these words was so profound that Elcano stepped closer and pointed out the island's position. "You'll see Teide quite clearly when we get closer."

"Teide, sir?"

"Tenerife's volcano. Unless things have changed since I was last there, it will be rumbling and spewing its poisons, which," he said with a laugh, "will most likely terrify half of our new men. But then, you may be more interested in Santa Cruz."

"Yes, Santa Cruz, sir," Fernandez drew the words out long and low, as he would have whispered a prayer.

"As you know, only those who will be procuring or loading wood and fresh water will be going ashore. But even from the harbor, Santa Cruz is a sight worth seeing, especially for the first time."

"Just being at anchor will be a blessing, sir," said Fernandez. Then he closed his eyes and followed his shipmaster's order to draw in deep gulps of fresh air. He was just pulling in his third breath when the shout of "Land ahead!" rang out from the man near the top of the *Trinidad's* main mast, and hands on all five ships strained their eyes toward the island in the distance.

After its founding in 1494, the settlement of Santa Cruz had quickly become a busy seaport that provided a chance to supply and repair ships before voyaging to the mysterious lands on the other side of the Atlantic. Though the potential delights were many, Magellan's fleet had barely drifted in and lowered their anchors before the officers set selected men to their tasks ashore. The rest of the crews gawked and pointed at the black sand of the beach, the lush forest, and the towering height of a relatively quiet Mount Teide. The only women they saw were those selling fish from a small hut at the end of the wharf, and they appeared to be Spanish.

21

Fernandez had already recovered enough to ask Elcano, "Are there any native women here, sir?"

"No, those not killed by war or the plague were sold into slavery. I've heard they were fair skinned and light haired."

"Truly, sir?"

"So I've heard."

When the shore parties returned with a good supply of water and wood, the fleet moved down the east coast of the island to the port of Monte Rojo, where the men had been told pitch was plentiful.

In the fading light of a tenaciously hot evening, Elcano stood at the shoreline and supervised the loading of the last few kegs of pitch into the *Concepción's* launch. They were ready to push off when Elcano spotted Magellan's skiff rowing toward them from the *Trinidad*, and he had his men await the commander's arrival.

Elcano bowed in greeting as Magellan, Enrique, and Cristóbal jumped from their boat and waded to the dry sand. Enrique stood several paces behind Magellan and his son, keeping his eyes cast downward and his lips silent.

"Good evening, Captain-general," said Elcano. "I hope all is well."

"Well indeed, Master Elcano. Is this the last of the pitch?"

"Yes, sir. We should not be caught short with this new supply."

"Have all costs been well recorded?"

"They have, sir."

"Very good. Then we'll sail within the hour."

Magellan, Elcano, and the rest of the landing party turned at a loud call from the anchored *San Antonio*. "Ship approaching from the north, Captain-general!"

Holding a hand to his forehead to shade his eyes, Magellan continued to watch the ship's advance with scrutiny. "She's Spanish, and she's sailing in haste." With a grunt of surprise, Magellan said, "Why, that's the Barbosa emblem she's flying."

Elcano wondered why Barbosa, the steward of the fortress in Seville, would send a ship to the Canary Islands.

It made no sense, unless the ship had been sent in search of them. But for what purpose? Glancing toward the *Concepción,* then the *Trinidad,* Elcano noticed that several swivel guns were being swung into position, but this precaution was soon proven to be unnecessary. When Barbosa's ship slowed and her men hailed them cordially, Magellan's gunners stood back from the railings.

As sails of the newly arrived ship were being secured and her anchor lowered, Magellan said distractedly, "Master Elcano, I will leave you to your work." Magellan and his companions quickly reboarded their launch, and he ordered, "Row out to meet her, men."

Feeling uneasy at this unexpected visit and wishing he could hear the news that had come for the captain-general, Elcano returned to his own ship and waited impatiently.

Magellan was greeted warmly by the ship's captain, who introduced himself as Lorenzo de Escobar, and they immediately proceeded to Escobar's small cabin.

"You were easier to locate than I had feared, Captain-general, especially after they told me in Santa Cruz that you did not mean to linger here. I could only hope that you had not already set sail."

"We mean to do so within the hour, Captain Escobar."

"Then I will be brief. I have a letter for you from Don Diego Barbosa." Handing the sealed letter to Magellan, he added, "I was instructed to deliver it into your hands without delay."

A sudden look of fear darkened Magellan's rough features. "Is it Beatriz?" he demanded. "My son?"

"No, no, sir. The content of your letter is unknown to me, but your family was well when I departed."

"Praise, God," said Magellan with a relieved sigh.

"Señor Barbosa asked me to carry your reply back to him."

"Very well," said Magellan, and he broke the seal and held the letter to the light of the cabin's lamp.

His forehead furrowed deeply as he read the warning.

23

Word had reached Diego that, before Magellan's departure from Seville, some of the fleet's Castilian captains had whispered their intentions to overthrow their captain-general at the first sign of disloyalty or incompetence. If necessary for the accomplishment of their undertaking, they would kill him.

Magellan swallowed. More slowly, he read the letter again.

Outwardly calm, he said, "May I have paper and ink, Captain?" After receiving these items, Magellan scribbled a brief reply assuring Barbosa that the king would not have chosen Captains Cartagena, Quesada, or Mendoza if he had not had the utmost faith in them. And, he affirmed, as captain-general of the fleet he would make every effort to give these gentlemen no cause for revolt.

As they waited for the ink to dry, Magellan accepted some wine from his host and courteously exchanged general news. The first glass of wine led to a second and Magellan lingered longer than he had originally intended. He at last parted from Escobar with a wish for a safe return to Spain and a request that the captain relay his warmest regards to his family. When Magellan left the ship, countless stars were shining overhead, but the words of the letter pushed to the forefront of his mind and blinded him to the beauty of the heavens.

Back in the launch, Magellan sat still and remote, telling himself that Barbosa could have been misled by Portuguese spies. Knowing Barbosa would try to warn his son-in-law, the agents of King Manuel might simply be making one more attempt to cause ill will between Magellan and his men. Perhaps Barbosa had played right into their hands. On the other hand, the warning might have resulted from nothing more than a harmless remark made in private conversation that had grown more ominous with its passage from mouth to mouth.

And yet, Magellan had seen the distrust in Cartagena's eyes. He was the son of a powerful bishop that had the confidence of the Spanish monarch. Protectively loyal to King Carlos himself, Captain Cartagena was also very ambitious, which was a potentially dangerous combination.

When Magellan reached the flagship he was met by Pilot Major Esteban Gomez, a respected officer and a fellow Portuguese. "All is ready for departure, Captain-general. The other captains wish only to know when they are to come aboard to review the charts with you, sir."

Magellan stared at him for an uncomfortably long moment. "We will set sail immediately after the change of the midnight watch, Pilot Major," he said.

Politely, Gomez informed him, "Sir, the hour has grown late and the watch is to change within moments."

"Yes, and I want no delays before departure."

Gomez's face reflected his startled uncertainty. "But we've been waiting since San Lúcar to receive the details of our course, Captain-general. The king's instructions made it clear that we—"

"As you've already been informed, Pilot Major, the route filed in Seville and approved by the king bears to the south-west until we reach 24° north. I will decide any changes in headings once we pass that point and I will give them to you directly. The rest of the fleet has orders to follow this ship. Now, see that an additional stern lantern is lit before weighing anchor, Pilot Major."

In Gomez's growing disbelief, he blurted out, "Surely, sir, we are to be told the route to Brazil. We could be separated by storm or...the captains and pilots need to know—."

Magellan took a sudden step forward and silenced Gomez with a glare. "For now they need only to know how to follow their flagship. That, I trust they can do!"

Anger sparked in Gomez's eyes, but it was quickly banked. With his jaws tight but his expression controlled, he said, "Yes, Captain-general."

Magellan turned from Gomez's red face and the crew's furtive glances, and climbed clumsily up the narrow steps of the half deck to reach his cabin. Cristóbal followed him to the top of the steps but Magellan motioned the youth away.

Magellan's weak knee buckled as gravity pulled him into his wooden chair. By the light of his lantern, he stared at the wall for several moments. Then, leaning his elbows upon the desktop, he buried his face in his hands. Except for the rhythmic heaving of his chest, he remained quite still. The ringing of the ship's bell announced the change of the watch, and it was followed by the shouted commands to raise anchor and set sail. Magellan listened until he heard a responding demand from one of the other ships, but he did not stir until the *Trinidad* began to move.

As his ship surged forward, Magellan lifted his head and sat formally erect. His body felt the response and his mind imagined the sight as each sail unfurled and stretched to its full expanse under the knowing hands of his crew.

In a matter of days, or weeks at the most, the fleet would pull far away from any lands known to him. Not down the coast of Africa, around its horn, and up to India, but to the west, the mysterious west. The next anchorage he would seek lay across the Atlantic Sea near Brazil, a land possessed by Portugal. He would follow the coast down to the southern Spanish dominions, and sail even farther south, searching for the opportunity to turn again to the west.

And by God, Magellan vowed as he clasped his hands together on top of his desk, *he* would be in command when the passage was found. *He* would guide them through it, and on to the Spice Islands.

The course he had shared with the king and the captains in Seville had indicated that the fleet would turn southwestward just north of the Cape Verde Islands. But what if agents of King Manuel had managed to get wind of their route? To avoid the risk of sailing into the waiting guns of a Portuguese fleet, he had intended to call his officers together before leaving Tenerife to discuss replacing the declared route with one holding to the coast of Africa until they were well below the Cape Verdes. But then he had read Barbosa's letter.

He drummed his fingers on his desk, thinking, evaluating. If one of the captains truly meant him harm, Magellan decided, it was unlikely that the man would be willing to follow him blindly for very long. By keeping his plans to himself, especially their route, perhaps the saboteur could be flushed out. Yes, perhaps.

He limped to the cabinet beside his bunk and took out a chart. Bringing it to his desk, he unrolled it, held down the sides, and studied it closely. Then he reached for his writing instruments. After dipping the quill into ink, heedfully tapping the excess liquid back into the bottle, he touched the quill's tip to the chart, then again, and again, designating by the resulting dotted line their new route across the Atlantic.

When he was satisfied that the ink had dried sufficiently, he rolled the chart up and carefully returned it to its cabinet.

# The Warning

## 3

As the fleet sailed from Tenerife, passing close by the eastward island of Grand Canary, Magellan kept to his cabin more than usual and spoke little on the occasions he chose to emerge. Moving about the ship just before the change of the morning watch, he noted that Gomez and the other officers held themselves courteously aloof as he passed. Some of the hands cast questioning glances at their officers, then murmured uneasily between themselves. Even Cristóbal and Enrique, who seldom left his side, seemed more willing than usual to be sent on errands to different areas of the ship.

When the captain-general appeared on the half deck at midday and summoned Gomez to join him, many of the men moved as inconspicuously as possible to within hearing range. Their stealth was unnecessary, however, for in a voice loud enough to be heard throughout the ship, Magellan ordered, "You will alter our course, Pilot Major, to one bearing due south."

Gomez did not repeat the mistake of probing the wisdom of one of Magellan's commands. He merely bowed in acknowledgement, after which Magellan nodded once and returned to the confines of his cabin, leaving the curiosity of the sailors altogether unsatisfied.

From his window, Magellan kept watch on the *San Antonio* until, reluctantly it seemed, she adjusted her sails and veered to the south to trail them. Not until the *Concepción*, the *Victoria,* and the *Santiago* also fell in line did he leave the window and breathe more easily.

When the crimsons, pinks, and golds of sunset had reached the height of flamboyance, the ships came together to make their previously established salute, and Elcano and the other masters offered their greetings to the captain-general with rigid courtesy. Afterwards, the four ships held their positions as their captains stood waiting to obtain some justifications for not receiving their charts as well as for the unforeseen and unexplained route change. Magellan, seemingly unaware of their expectations, gave a curt command to Gomez to continue on, and turned his back on the other officers and men of the fleet.

Aboard the *Concepción*, Elcano glanced back at Quesada and noted with a shadow of foreboding that his captain's frustrated expression had begun to smolder.

Although the crew of his ship remained outwardly calm the following day, Elcano could feel tension rising subtly with each passing hour. At dusk the ships again drew together and the scene played out, much as it had the night before. But on the third evening out of Tenerife, when still no explanations were offered, the *San Antonio* hung back in obvious protest as the *Trinidad* pulled away from the other four ships. Within the hour, however, as the last of the sun's light left the sky, the *San Antonio* bore down on the flagship under full sails, pulling up beside her just as her lanterns were being lit.

In a powerful voice Captain Cartagena hailed the *Trinidad*.

Gomez came to the flagship's starboard rail at once, his face unable to hide his apprehension.

"Pilot Major," Captain Cartagena called out, "what course are we running?"

"South by southwest, Captain," returned Gomez as the other three ships moved closer in.

Magellan now showed himself on the stern castle and demanded, "What is it, Captain Cartagena?"

"Sir," said Cartagena loudly, standing tall beside the solid Master Elorriaga, "as Inspector General of this fleet it is my duty to ask why our route has been altered without consulting the captains."

In a brittle voice that disseminated far across the water, Magellan said, "I need not explain such decisions to you, Captain."

At this brusque reply, Cartagena flinched noticeably but when he spoke again his voice maintained a level tone. "This new course carries us dangerously close to the Guinea coast, sir, to Portuguese settlements. It also threatens to lengthen our voyage by weeks. As Inspector General I must protest—."

Magellan slammed his hands down upon the rail and cut him off. "As Inspector General you are *second*-in-command, are you not, Captain Cartagena?" Before a response could be given, Magellan shouted, "You, sir, will maintain your position *behind* my ship. You will follow her flags by day and her lanterns by night. *That* is your duty." Angling his head slightly toward Gomez but never taking his eyes from Cartagena, Magellan barked, "Your orders have not changed, Pilot Major. Sail on." With that, he abruptly turned and strode from the rail. Gomez and the *Trinidad's* crew eased away from their rail in uncomfortable silence.

From where Elcano stood on the *Concepción's* foredeck, even by the mellow lights of the *San Antonio's* lanterns he could see the outrage and hostility on Cartagena's face. It was also plain to see Elorriaga's bewilderment and dread, emotions Elcano felt keenly himself.

Standing beside him, Captain Quesada hissed, "What, by all that's holy, is he playing at?"

Having no answer to offer, Elcano could only shake his head.

"Look at Captain Cartagena," said Quesada, staring across the gap of water. "There's the taste of blood in his mouth. It's as if the captain-general put it there purposely." He repeated in frustrated puzzlement, "What is he *playing* at?"

But Elcano knew as well as his captain that this was more than a game. Still, they could do little more than trail the lead ships and await the next move.

For two weeks the fleet endured the heat of an increasingly intense sun as they took advantage of generous winds, sailing between the Cape Verde Islands and Africa's coast, and onward until their path paralleled the land of Guinea. Magellan still gave no indication as to why he continued to hold them to this southward course or how long he intended to do so, and Elcano began to grow as restive as his captain. Conversations between his normally boisterous crew shriveled down to verbal exchanges as small and tight as the few pieces of fruit remaining aboard.

One particularly hot afternoon, the *Concepción's* steward led Elcano down the steps from the main deck and into the belly of the ship. Trying to avoid the filthy bilge water that sloshed at their feet, and breathing in the heavy, fetid air through their open mouths, they came to a stop before a row of kegs.

"That's the one, sir,' said the steward, pointing to a barrel and holding the lantern just above it.

The steward held his breath as Elcano lifted the lid and leaned over to inspect the salted beef inside. When the stench hit Elcano's nose and mouth from such a close range, he let out a harsh grunt and clapped the lid back in place. But he had managed to glimpse inside the dark well of the cask. Reflecting eerily in the lantern's glow, the meat had given off a slimy iridescence. Breathing only in shallow gulps, he said in a tight voice, "Take it up, Campos. Have the men use it as bait."

"At once, sir."

As Campos shouted up to a cabin boy to gain his assistance with the barrel, Elcano saw that the sunlight sifting down from the open hatch was quickly fading. "See that Rochelle has a good look at the other barrels," he ordered as he left the steward, gained the fresh air above deck, and hurriedly made his way to the forecastle.

At first he interpreted the scowl tossed his way by the waiting Quesada as a reprimand for his lateness, but when Elcano reached the railing Quesada jerked his head toward the *Trinidad*, and said, "Trouble's brewing."

Magellan was glaring across at the *San Antonio* as a common seaman trudged to her rail, faced the flagship, and called out, "God save you, Captain-general!" Master Elorriaga remained awkwardly planted in the background, staring at the deck in front of his feet. Captain Cartagena held himself tense and taciturn beside him.

Magellan turned aside and spoke to Gomez, who immediately shouted, "Master Elorriaga!"

Elorriaga's head snapped up and he took one step forward. "Yes, Pilot Major."

"You are to salute your captain-general in the proper manner immediately."

With a movement of his arm that silenced Elorriaga and swept him back to his original place, Cartagena stormed to the rail. "You, Captain-general, have been saluted by my best seaman. If he is not good enough to greet a commander who day after day disobeys the king's orders and leaves his fellow officers in ignorance, I will gladly bring out my cabin boy to address you!"

Gasps escaped from some of the men near Elcano. But Quesada whispered, "Bravo, Cartagena."

Every man in the fleet fixed his eyes on Magellan, anxiously awaiting and fearing his reaction. To their wonder and growing mortification, he gave none whatsoever. As if he'd received neither insult nor challenge, his expression remained unreadable as he spoke again to Gomez and withdrew to the other side of his ship.

All eyes jerked to Cartagena, whose disbelief instantly flared to wrath that reddened his face and narrowed his eyes. He spun around and stormed across the main deck, the look in his eyes scattering men from his path as he made his way to the height of the stern deck. For a moment he halted beside the mizzenmast, then rammed his fist into the treelike spar. Pushing himself away, he moved to the very corner of the stern castle. There he remained, muttering words that Elcano guessed were as dark as the sea before him.

The boatswain of the *Concepción* had come to stand beside Elcano and Quesada to gain a better view of

Cartagena. Elcano turned to him now and said, "Acurio, order the men to return to work, or to their blankets."

Acurio nodded, and said, "Yes, sir," but hesitated.

"There's nothing to be gained by speculation, Acurio," said Elcano with more assurance than he felt. "See to the men."

Nodding once more, Acurio moved to obey.

When he'd left them, Quesada said broodingly, "Well, we shall see whether this night will spark some action from our captain-general. No man can relive such a dare throughout the long hours of darkness and still do nothing."

But Magellan proved Quesada wrong. Nothing was exactly what he chose to do. When another twilight followed a watchful yet uneventful day and the ships came together again, Elcano heard no more predictions from his captain. At the moment when the *San Antonio* was to give her salute, the attention of every man in the fleet was drawn to her main deck, but no one came forward to deliver it. Elorriaga stood back among his crewmen, mute and sweating. Cartagena was nowhere to be seen.

Again, Magellan gave no acknowledgement of the affront, nor did he on the next evening, nor the next, leaving Quesada to conclude, "He's either too weak to act or too blind." Elcano kept his own thoughts silent, but he believed neither of Quesada's assumptions. He merely waited.

When Elcano spotted the skiff from the *Trinidad* approaching the *Concepción* one afternoon, he felt almost relieved. Surely some message was being delivered that would bring the confrontation among the fleet's officers to a head. A rope ladder was tossed over the rail and a ship's clerk climbed aboard. He bowed before Quesada, and asked to speak privately with him, Pilot Juan Lopez Carvalho, and Master Elcano.

Once inside Quesada's cabin, the captain said, "Out with it, then. I don't see you carrying our charts, so what news have you brought?"

"No, sir. No charts. I've been sent to inform you about a difficulty that has arisen aboard the *Victoria*. It requires the attention of the fleet's officers."

"Difficulty? Of what nature?"

"Master Salamón, sir, he has been caught in an unnatural act with one of his young crewmembers."

Quesada muttered in disgust.

"Is there any doubt of his guilt?" Elcano asked.

"No, sir. He was caught in the very act."

Pilot Carvalho demanded, "With whom?"

"An apprentice seamen, sir. Antonio Baresa."

"Damned Sicilian!" Quesada spat. "We should have known better than to let that man master a Spanish ship." He peered closely at the messenger as he impatiently scratched his graying beard. "What has the captain-general to say?"

"He's holding a court martial, sir. All of the senior officers are to meet aboard the flagship in half an hour. He wants the sentence to be passed jointly."

"Very well. Tell the captain-general we will not be late."

The messenger bowed and left them to deliver his news to the remaining ships.

Closing his cabin door again, Quesada shook his head and said, "Now he wants a *joint* decision? Well, it's the life of an officer that's to be decided today, Sicilian or no."

At the appointed time, Elcano and the others gathered on the *Trinidad's* stern castle. Magellan, the four other captains, and Antonio de Coca, the fleet's accountant, sat in wooden chairs while the pilots and shipmasters sat cross-legged on the deck, forming a circle with their superiors. The accused, a pale, heavy-featured man with thin brown hair that fell to just below his jaw line, stood chained before them. Several witnesses, including the thin, dark-haired, young victim stood just outside the ring of officers.

As Elcano expected, the trial was short and decisive. In less than an hour Salamón was found guilty of sodomy.

"You know the penalty for this crime?" Magellan said without emotion.

"I do, sir," said Salamón, raising his gaze.

"Then," said Magellan, his voice softening only slightly, "may God have mercy on your soul. It is fortunate for you, Salamón, that we have two priests sailing with us. You will be able to confess your sins before your execution, which will take place upon our next landing. Be thankful that you are not being condemned to the eternal fire as well as to death."

"For that, sir, I am grateful," Salamón said quietly.

As he was led away, his chains clanked harshly against the wooden deck. Not far behind Salamón, the witnesses shuffled down the steps and disappeared.

Magellan remained seated as he turned to his fellow officers and said, "I thank you for coming, gentlemen. You may all return to your ships."

Before anyone else moved, Cartagena rose quickly to his feet and spoke. "One moment, Captain-general. Since we are all together, I insist that we discuss the fact that you have changed our course without the foreknowledge or consent of the rest of your officers. For the safety of the fleet, we must know your intentions. Just how long do you mean to keep to the south?"

Magellan appeared to become thoughtful, taking his time before offering an answer. At last, he said, "I will hold to the south until I feel we are out of reach of the Portuguese navy."

Clearly suspicious, Cartagena said, "The Portuguese navy?"

"Yes."

Several officers tried to speak at once but Captain Mendoza of the *Victoria* raised his voice above the din. "Captain-general, by running farther south, do we not risk encountering a storm that could force us ashore, onto land *governed* by Portuguese? And Portuguese ships, some of them heavily armed, sail up and down this coast with regularity. Sir, don't such risks pose a greater danger than the possibility of coming upon a handful of ships far offshore?"

"*Not* in my opinion, Captain Mendoza," Magellan said, with such finality that the other officers quieted at once.

Captain Cartagena was the first to regain his voice. Fighting to keep his tone restrained, he said, "Are our opinions not even to be considered, sir?"

Magellan turned darkening eyes upon him. "Not in this."

"Captain-general, a commanding officer's first duty is to safeguard the welfare of his men!"

"That is exactly what I intend to do, Captain Cartagena!"

"When your opinion is outnumbered fourteen to one, you *still* refuse to listen to us?"

"I will trust my own judgment, not yours!"

Cartagena's hands clenched at his sides. "Your judgment, Captain-general, is flawed. Your actions become more suspect with each league we travel. We have given you no cause to shun us from your counsel, yet you continue to do so. I warn you—."

"And I warn you," Magellan said, his voice falling ominously low, "that I too have my suspicions."

"You?" Cartagena demanded with contempt. "Suspicions of what? That we will follow our king's commands rather than your designs? If you continue to flaunt Spain's wishes, to disregard the welfare of this mission, you will find that your commands will no longer be followed!"

Magellan sprang to his feet, grabbed Cartagena by the front of his jacket, and shouted, "Before these witnesses you challenge my authority!" He lifted his head and shouted to Master-at-arms Espinosa, "Arrest this rebel!"

Elcano, Elorriaga, and every other officer on the deck struggled to their feet as armed men pushed forward and seized Cartagena.

"Stop him!" bellowed Cartagena, twisting violently as hands grabbed him. "Quesada, Mendoza, stop him!" Cartagena's thrashing knocked two of his guards to the deck but they quickly regained their feet and their grasps.

"Chain him to the main mast!" Magellan barked to Espinosa.

The other officers shifted and murmured as more armed guards moved between them. Cartagena roared and kicked as manacles were brought forward from a hiding place suspiciously close at hand and locked around his wrists and feet.

"No!" said Elorriaga, taking a step toward his captain, but Elcano grabbed his arm and held him fast just as a guard in front of them unsheathed his sword.

Still writhing and bucking, Cartagena was lifted off his feet and carried down the steps of the stern deck and across and down the steps of the half deck to reach the main deck of the ship. The others followed in jostling rows. As Cartagena's arms were hoisted high above his head and his feet were bound fast to the base of the mainmast, the crewmembers of the flagship gaped in shock and shuddered while shouts of anger and fear rose from the other ships.

Quesada, looking over his shoulder until his eyes met Elcano's, motioned his shipmaster to accompany him, and the two of them pushed forward to reach Magellan as he stood before Cartagena. "Please, Captain-general," Quesada began.

"Take care, Captain Quesada," Magellan warned pointedly. "Do not dare to confront me, or your fate and your hands will be bound with his."

Shooting a glare at the seething Cartagena, wordlessly demanding his silence, Quesada went on. "I do not confront you, Captain-general. I wish only to ask, respectfully, that you take into account that Captain Cartagena is a Castilian nobleman of high birth. I ask you not to shame him and his family by disciplining him in this manner, sir."

"His words were those of a mutineer, Captain Quesada," Magellan said forbiddingly, "and you ask me to treat him with leniency?"

"Captain Cartagena's words were rash and unwise, Captain-general, but I believe he spoke out of concern rather than with any intent to do you harm. Again, I ask you to reconsider his punishment, sir."

Magellan glanced at Cartagena, who now stood as unmoving as the mast he was chained to, and slowly surveyed the eyes of his men.

Captain Mendoza took this opportunity to step forward and bow. "Captain-general, will you please consider releasing Captain Cartagena into my custody. I will hold myself accountable for his conduct."

Magellan let them wait several moments before saying, "Very well. Sergeant-at-arms, release Cartagena from his chains." When this had been done, Magellan approached him. "I relieve you of your command and release you into the care of Captain Mendoza. Do not test the power of my tolerance or my patience again, or you and he will both be punished most severely."

Cartagena clenched his teeth tightly and said nothing.

Facing the group of officers, Magellan called out, "Antonio de Coca!" When Coca came to him, Magellan addressed him directly, "You are the kinsman of the prisoner, his cousin, I believe?"

"Yes, sir."

"Will this relationship prevent you from captaining the *San Antonio* with unquestioning loyalty to me?"

Stunned, Coca forced out, "I, why, no sir."

"So be it. Pilot Major Gomez, have all hands return to their ships and stations at once." This order was immediately relayed and officers hurriedly found their ways to the launches.

Rubbing at his wrists as if to rid them of defilement, Cartagena kept his narrowed eyes aimed straight ahead as he passed Elcano.

Why had Magellan taunted such a man so deliberately, shamed him so absolutely? And what was the motivation behind Magellan's reluctance to share his thoughts about their route? Tormented by his own inability to change or ease the situation, to do anything beyond conjuring up unanswered questions, Elcano let out a soft curse.

Someone bumped into him and he turned to find himself staring at Elorriaga's troubled face. Elcano said quietly, "Have faith, Juan."

"We have yet to turn to the west," Elorriaga muttered, "and already my ship has lost her captain."

Within the hour, great gray clouds began to gather and move toward the ships.

# The Fickle Sea

## 4

Elcano ducked under the foredeck just behind Captain Quesada, pulled off his sopping beret, and wrung some of the water from his hair. Possessing only a fringe of graying bristles around the base of his head, his captain ran a hand briskly over his wet scalp, flinging droplets in every direction. At an arched glance from Quesada, several nearby sailors eased away to find shelter elsewhere.

He asked Elcano sourly, "Have you ever heard of such weather in these latitudes?"

"No, sir, but I've not sailed these waters before," Elcano replied, kicking a pile of coiled rope out of the way to give them more standing room.

"Do you think it will lighten soon?"

"It looks to be growing worse, sir. The wind is already picking up."

When the storm clouds had swept down upon the fleet several days earlier, they had brought with them a constant drizzle but little wind. At first Elcano had turned his face skyward and enjoyed the fresh precipitation. Believing that such a mild rainfall would soon disappear, he had hoped it would distract the men from the edginess they'd shown ever since Cartagena had been relieved of command.

But after days of constant rain, moods grew noticeably more sullen. Huge sheets of canvas, meant to be used for spare sails, began to mold. Clothes sprouted unearned stains and fabric soon deteriorated. Elcano could smell the sour tang of the fungi throughout the ship. They needed the sun to halt the advance of the mold and to cheer the men, but the daystar appeared to be unwilling or unable to pierce through the ceiling of clouds.

Studying the rising swells then squinting to the south, Elcano said, "I suggest we shorten sails, Captain."

"As you know, serving the archbishop has allowed me little exposure to the ways of the sea, Master Elcano. I relinquish the ship's watch to your authority. However, I will remain on deck and observe."

Moments after Elcano called out the orders to trim the sails, the lanterns at the *Trinidad's* stern castle signaled the same instructions.

"Captain," said Elcano, raising his voice to be heard above the wind, "if this storm plays out as I expect, you will be safer in your cabin."

"Understood," said Quesada. "See to the ship, sir."

The clouds began to move; sluggishly at first, and then with building energy and momentum. The sea's surface rolled and swelled higher with each new surge. Less than a mile ahead of the flagship, a flare of lightning in the shape of a huge trident shot down from the clouds, illuminating the sky above the cresting waves with momentary radiance.

Holding to the rail to maintain his balance on the slick deck, Elcano yelled down to Acurio to see that the men tying down the sails were secured by lifelines. Moments later, one of his seamen handed Elcano a section of rope and he tied himself tightly to the railing.

Just below Elcano, Pilot Carvalho stood several feet in front of the tiller on the main deck. Secured to the capstan, Carvalho received Elcano's shouted instructions and barked them to the tiller men. On each side of the tiller, four men braced their bare feet and stiffened their backs to grapple the tiller lines, the ropes jerking and hissing in their calloused fists. While the current pounded with growing force against the *Concepción's* rudder, the seamen strained to hold their ship to the desired heading.

Lightning flashes strengthened and drew nearer, and thunderclaps muted the shouts of the men. The wind whipped the velocity of the pouring rain until it became a battering force. Elcano turned his face from the wind to avoid being stung and choked by the driving deluge.

The first large wave swirled over the ship's port side and splashed across the main deck as men hastened to tighten the lines at their waists and cling to the nearest stout fixture. Several sailors were knocked flat, but many hands grabbed for them and yanked them to their feet.

Elcano swiped the water from his eyes and blinked, trying to keep sight of what lay before the ship. There, like the body of a monstrous serpent, the sea dipped and rose, its movements growing more powerful with every new rush of the wind and current. The *Trinidad* and the *San Antonio* were no more than occasional flickers of lantern light in the dark, slithering sea ahead.

While Elcano continued to call out directions to Carvalho, most of her remaining men were ordered to the hold and the *Concepción* headed straight into the growing swells. Waves crashed upon her decks with greater intensity and frequency, and her prow lifted ever higher to scale them.

Cresting a huge upsurge, the ship seemed to pause upon its very ridge, and Elcano stared down the length of his ship and into the black depths of a seemingly bottomless trough. He bared his teeth and sprayed rain from his lips as he shouted, "Straight on, my lady!" Bending his knees to gain stability as she tilted forward, he rode her downward until her body abruptly leveled and swung up again.

To be certain that his captain had heeded his advice and had sought the protection of his cabin, Elcano glanced over his shoulder. To his surprise, however, Quesada was now fighting to reach his side, and Elcano reached out to help him to the rail.

Quesada cried above the shrieking wind, "Give me a section of rope!"

Sensing that any argument would be futile, Elcano immediately obeyed, and then returned his attention to the dark foaming water that pitched before the prow. Each new bolt of lightning revealed a more unbelievable scene of roiling, crashing sky and sea, and Elcano called out encouragement and adjustments to the men on the deck beneath him.

Together the men of the *Concepción* grappled with the unrelenting storm, sometimes falling or crying out when they'd reached the end of their strength but somehow managing to keep the lights of the *Trinidad* and the *San Antonio* always before them.

When the first group of men at the tiller tired, another bunch was ordered up from the hold, then another, and another. Captain Quesada finally untied his rope and staggered to his cabin. Acurio must have seen his captain's departure because he appeared beside Elcano moments later, holding tightly to the rail but saying not a word. Acurio had relieved Carvalho three hours earlier, but upon the pilot's return to his position near the tiller Acurio had been ordered to get some rest.

"You're not due up here for hours yet," Elcano said in a hoarse voice.

"I'll stay, sir." It was said respectfully, but it was not a request.

Plainly, his boatswain was determined to stay close at hand in case he was needed, and Elcano, sensing that Acurio had come out of genuine concern for him, was moved by this show of devotion. He placed his dripping hand on Acurio's wet shoulder, and squeezed it firmly. "If you mean to stay, tie yourself down. I'd hate to lose you."

Flashing a pleased grin, Acurio immediately obeyed.

Lifting his cracking voice, Elcano yelled to his ship, "Just see what a fine boatswain rides your half deck, lady!"

The two stood shoulder-to-shoulder, withstanding the storm's might until they grew so weary that the violent booms of thunder and blinding bursts of lightning no longer even made them blink. When Elcano's legs suddenly buckled and he fell, he stared at his thighs as if surprised by their betrayal. Grabbing the rail and pulling himself back up, he struggled to maintain his stance.

"Sir, you must rest," insisted Acurio. "Pilot Carvalho and I can direct the ship."

Even as his legs quaked beneath him, Elcano stubbornly remained. In his fatigue he barely noticed when Acurio left his side, until he appeared again with Captain Quesada.

"To my cabin, Master Elcano," ordered the captain. "At once."

Elcano threw an accusing glance at Acurio.

"I said at once," Quesada huffed with added sternness.

Elcano grudgingly nodded and tried to untie his rope, but his hands fumbled helplessly until the captain came to his aid. Casting a more forgiving look at Acurio, Elcano allowed the younger officer to help him to his cabin, but he mumbled about the insubordination of a certain boatswain all the way to his quarters.

As if he'd accepted the storm's onslaught as a personal dare, four more times Elcano reappeared on the half deck after rests far too short, and each time he had to be relieved by Captain Quesada's direct order.

Two hours after midnight on the second day of the tempest's assault, Elcano was at the rail when the ferocity of the storm shifted so abruptly that every man standing was thrown to the planks. When Elcano scrambled to his feet, he heard curses and wails rising from the hold. He could easily picture the frightened faces of those below, especially those of the youngest servants and passengers.

But the squall's new intensity was very short-lived. Elcano, Carvalho, and the men at the tiller had no more than gained their balance and reknotted their tie lines when a torch-like blaze, several feet in height and light blue in color, suddenly exploded to life at the head of each of the three vertical masts. At the brilliant flash of light, Elcano threw his arm across his eyes and let out a sharp cry of pain. Hesitantly, he lowered his arm and squinted his eyes open. He could see nothing. He blinked and rubbed his eyes but everything, everything was completely black. Twice, thunder roared from close by, but he had seen no lightning to foretell its coming. He felt the seething of the wind and sea begin to die away. His ship's movements grew gentler, more stable. Lifting his burning eyes, he could just perceive the bluish illumination running up the masts and rigging, and across the crow's nest and upper yardarms.

Men began to cheer and cry out, "The holy fire!"

"We're safe now, lads!"

"The fire of St. Elmo!"

"Praise God! Praise God!"

Elcano listened to the joyous shouts, and lowered his head in gratitude. When he looked up again, much of the blurriness had cleared from his vision. He could see St. Elmo's fire burning brightly above him.

As the rains eased and finally ceased, the *Concepción* closed in on the *Trinidad* and the *San Antonio*, directing the trailing *Victoria* and *Santiago* to follow her. With the fire of St. Elmo lighting their way, promising by its presence heavenly protection from the storm, the sea slowly settled into a docile roll. The clouds gradually but steadily dispersed. Dawn was not far away.

Elcano made his way on cramping legs to the foredeck. Joined by Quesada, Carvalho, and Acurio along the way, he watched the rising of a resplendent sun.

"Well done, men," said Captain Quesada, his voice betraying his emotion. "Very well done."

Elcano ran his hand over the wet wood on the *Concepción's* prow, closed his still sensitive eyes, and lifted his face. He knew the sun would soon grow torturously hot but, for now, he welcomed its warmth and its reassurance.

Carvalho wrung out the end of his shirt, sighed deeply, and said, "I could sleep for a month."

They all laughed in exhausted agreement. Soon, they turned back to their men and to their duties.

By the time the sun reached its peak, the wind had grown as gentle as a mother's lullaby, and the men took full advantage of the clear day to dry out and repair the sails, clothing, and every other strip of cloth onboard. Not a breath of breeze could be felt by late afternoon and as the ships came to a complete standstill, the armada found itself floating on a sea as lifeless as glass. They'd sailed through raging winds and arrived at a place where there was none at all. How long it would take for the breeze to return, no one could judge.

The wind remained distant that day and the next. As the days and nights continued to pass without change, the meat continued to spoil. Magellan ordered rations to be cut, which sparked incessant grumbling throughout the fleet.

As sharks began to circle the ships in great numbers, Elcano hoped to replace some of their meat with fish flesh. When hooks proved to be of little use, Elcano ordered his men to use gaffs to spear the enormous fish. They were hauled aboard ship flopping, twisting, and gnashing their huge jaws, leaving crewmen to leap out of reach until a fatal blow could be delivered by a harpooner. It did not take long for the hands to tire of the taste of shark meat.

For three scorching, irritable weeks the ships were lapped by weak waves, making no noticeable progress either south or west. Men found too much time to remember that Magellan had ignored the intended route and had brought them to these stagnant waters, and the discontented mumblings grew. Elcano did his best to stifle the crew's disquiet by planting his chair on the half deck, where he sat whittling on a life-like wooden figure of a shark for long stretches at a time.

Occasionally, clouds gathered overhead, but they let loose lukewarm showers that caused the bodies of Pilot Carvalho and several other men to bloat up with prickly heat. The *Concepción's* barber and acting doctor, Hernando de Bustamente, concocted a smelly salve that seemed to give a little relief from the malady's burning itch. Although he did his best to hide it, Elcano chafed with impatience rather than prickly heat, wondering how much longer they'd be held captive in this seemingly limitless pool of slack water.

Then, one morning Elcano awoke with a start as he felt the *Concepción* gently lift and lean forward. He shoved himself upright, hurriedly left the sweltering heat of his cabin, and strode to the half deck's railing.

Quesada was already there, spreading his arms wide and declaring, "A fine strong wind, Master Elcano! Praise the Lord!"

Elcano checked the position of the flagship, already moving rapidly to the southwest. The captain-general had veered westward at last! Elcano took in a huge gulp of air and let it out with satisfaction. "A glorious wind indeed, Captain! If it holds true, we'll make our crossing in record time."

And the wind did hold true.

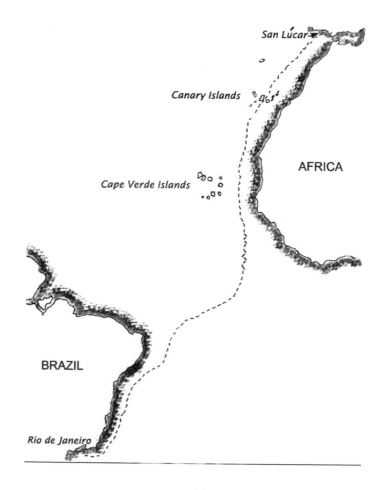

San Lúcar

Canary Islands

Cape Verde Islands

AFRICA

BRAZIL

Rio de Janeiro

Near the end of a day in late November, Elcano was holding a lantern above Bustamente while the barber thoughtfully examined a supernumerary's badly infected foot. Bustamente had just pulled a thin knife from his wooden box of surgical tools and he now began wiping the blade back and forth across his pant leg, signaling that he'd decided to lance the swollen heel. At that moment, to the indescribable relief of the passenger, a shout arose from the *Trinidad's* lookout that stilled Bustamente's hand.

"Land dead ahead!" In a pitch rising with elation, these words were repeated three times.

Elcano and Bustamente hoisted the patient to his feet with such haste that he would have pitched forward if they'd not kept their grips on him. There it was. Brazil. All three of them added their jubilant voices to those of every other man and boy in the flotilla, shouting, "Brazil! Brazil!"

A number of men scrambled up the lines, precariously secured a leg through the nearest rope, and swayed wildly as they waived their arms. They bellowed greetings to the distant shore as if they believed the very trees and sand would answer them with equal enthusiasm. Sailors both young and seasoned jumped and howled, threw their hats in the air, and hugged anyone within reach. In his exuberance, a man fell down the steps of the open hatchway, bumping and cursing. Before Bustamente had even reached the hatch, the fallen man had stormed back up the steps and returned to his carousing with no more than a bloody forehead to attest to the spill.

Acurio found Elcano in the center of the melee and began yipping and dancing a jota around him. The boatswain's manner was so youthful in its lack of restraint and his feet moved with such reckless high spirits that Elcano couldn't help laughing aloud and dancing a step or two himself. With an effort, he brought his own joy under control, and scolded with mock severity, "That's enough of such foolishness, Acurio. Off with you, now. Get those men out of the rigging before they hang themselves." But the gruffness of his words was made wholly ineffective by his wide grin.

"Master Elcano," Acurio said, jerking his head toward the back of the half deck, "Captain's calling for you, sir."

Elcano saw that Quesada and Carvalho were both waving to him, and he did not keep them waiting. When he joined the pair, the captain took Elcano's hand and shook it in both of his own. "Master Elcano, you and Pilot Carvalho have shown yourselves admirably."

Elcano and Carvalho accepted his praise humbly and congratulated him in return.

They sailed closer to land until, less than a mile off their starboard bow, the coastline unveiled its lush beauty as seductively as any temptress, making the strong hearts of the fleet's crewmembers weak with longing and wild with anticipation.

"Well, Pilot," said Captain Quesada, "you are the only one among us to ever set foot upon those shores. You worked there as a trader for several years?"

"Yes, sir, from 1512 to 1516, I helped with the running of a trading post."

"Ah, then you are our expert."

Their discussion was interrupted by Acurio's call. "Captain, the *Trinidad* is signaling."

Drawing the *Concepción* closer to the flagship, Quesada, Elcano, and Carvalho heard Magellan's summons to come aboard. A boat was soon lowered and rowed across the short expanse of water, and these three officers exchanged hearty compliments with Magellan, Pilot Major Esteban Gomez, and the *Trinidad's* Master Giovanni Battista di Polcevera. They all made their way to the captain-general's cabin where Carvalho was asked to recall every detail of Brazil's coastline that might prove helpful in navigating these waters. Afterward, the officers estimated their present position, as well as the distance to their destination of Rio de Janeiro. Charts were amended and enhanced, and notes were scribbled. Finally, Magellan turned the discussion to other matters.

"We have spoken before, Pilot Carvalho, about the nature of the natives in this area. Now, tell us all that you know of them."

"During my years in Brazil the natives were exceedingly friendly, sir, even helpful if the right trinkets were offered."

"But I'd heard that they were cannibals," said Gomez in surprise.

"Oh, that's quite true, Pilot Major. They war constantly against other tribes to obtain captives to eat. They even keep some of the captives for breeding, so that their supply of human flesh is never completely exhausted.

Glances of revulsion circled the room before Gomez asked, "Yet in four years they posed no threat to you?"

"None, sir."

"Were you here when Juan de Solís and some of his men were overrun, and many of them eaten? The survivors said they could do nothing but keep to the ships while their captain and men were butchered and roasted before their eyes."

"Yes, sir, word of that tragedy reached me while I was still here," said Carvalho. "But that incident occurred south of Rio de Janeiro, at Cape Santa Maria. Captain Solís must not have known that he had entered the land of the Querandi. They are a fierce warrior nation. The people in the Rio de Janeiro region are the Tamojos, the Tupinamba, and the Guaranis. I'm confident they will want to trade with us rather than fight us."

Not satisfied, Gomez asked, "What weapons do they possess?

"They use a heavy, seven-foot bow and arrows that are nearly four feet long, sir," said Carvalho.

"How are the arrows tipped?"

"The Tupis use the bones of animals that have been hardened by fire, sir, usually the teeth of sharks. When they fight at closer range, their warriors use a huge, paddle-shaped club they call a tacape. It's only about an inch thick but it has very sharp edges. They can use it either to stun or to behead an enemy. They prefer to stun them, of course. When a captive is brought back to the village, the women and children all participate in the, uh, feasting, sir."

"Any other weapons?" Gomez persisted.

"Yes, sir, the bola. They use it for hunting and in battle. May I, Captain-general," he asked as he motioned toward a quill. Receiving a nod, he dipped the quill in ink and drew on a corner of a chart as he described. "A bola is made from a strip of leather, the tail of which is slightly longer than a man's arm. This tail is attached to two or three shorter strips and at the end of each strip is a round stone wrapped in leather, like this."

Magellan asked, "How is it used?"

Carvalho stood up and demonstrated. "They circle it faster and faster over their heads then let it go. If the throw is accurate, sir, the stones wrap the leather ropes around the neck or the legs of their prey. I should also mention, sir, that they sometimes carry tall shields made from the skins of an animal you may be unfamiliar with, the manatee, or sea cow."

Quesada counted off on his fingers as he said, "Bows, arrows, shields, clubs, and so forth, and you are *confident* that we'll face little danger when we land?"

"Unless things have changed, yes, sir. Not here. These people will not wage war on so strong a party. On the contrary, Captain, they will more likely give us a splendid welcome."

Quesada posed his next question to Magellan. "What of the danger from the Portuguese, sir?"

"If Pilot Carvalho is correct, the Portuguese may present our most serious threat. Fortunately, Portuguese ships travel this coast very seldom. And since Portugal has built no fortress, no permanent settlement, it can be argued that this land has not, as yet, been claimed."

No one voiced, although each of them thought, that this technicality was a fragile argument to rely on, but Quesada did say, "Captain-general, may I ask if you intend to reinstate Captain Cartagena to his command once we land?"

"Cartagena will not resume his former command, when we land or at any other time," he said, effectively ending the subject. "Now, since Pilot Carvalho has sailed these waters before, I'd like him to remain aboard the flagship as we head southward. He will work with Pilot Major Gomez to keep us clear of coastal shoals and reefs, and the rest of the fleet will follow a safer path."

Rather formally, Quesada said, "As you wish, Captain-general."

"Very good. Captain Quesada and Master Elcano, you may return to the *Concepción.*"

As Elcano stepped into their waiting skiff beside Quesada, his captain said, "I'll sorely miss the opportunity to question Carvalho about the natives, especially the women."

Several of the men at the oars nodded in agreement.

# The Unexpected Warrior

## 5

Lazily spreading its rays across the eastern horizon, the sun rose by unhurried degrees to gaze into the boundless mirror of the sea. Fifteen-year-old Pedro de Chindarza, the shortest and most dependable of the three cabin boys aboard the *Concepción*, welcomed the sun's radiance as it reflected off the last crystal grains spilling into the bottom of the sand clock. A moment after the top half had emptied, Chindarza quickly upended the glass before turning away and hurrying to the half deck.

Elcano stood formally waiting and he watched the boy's rapid advance with approval. Here was a young man with the potential to become a commendable officer one day. Chindarza gave him a quick bow, and said, "A fine morning, sir." Upon receiving Elcano's acknowledging nod, the youth took a step forward to better survey the main deck below.

Inhaling deeply, Chindarza broke into a chant that, after seventy-one consecutive days at sea, he often mumbled in his sleep.

> *On deck, on deck, every man of the morning watch,*
> *Get up, get up, sailing men of the Master's watch,*
> *Get on your feet, the sun's awake,*
> *So bold of heart, lively hands of the morning watch!*

Elcano looked on as several exhausted workers from the predawn watch kicked or nudged the awakening stragglers from their sleeping spots and dropped into the empty spaces. A few small puddles of rain from the showers of the night before hastened the wakening of the men as they stepped bare-footed across the damp planks.

Seeing that all was well astir, Elcano was about to go in search of Acurio when Chindarza faced him and asked, "Sir, will it grow much colder as we sail south?

"Yes, Chindarza, much colder. Just how cold will depend on how far south we must travel before we reach the pass."

"But it's the middle of December, Master Elcano. Pardon my asking, sir, but why do we journey farther south at the start of winter rather than waiting for the warmer months?"

"You know how the stars have changed since we crossed the equator? Well, the seasons have changed too. Here, it is early summer, not winter. It is hot this early in the season because we are a thousand miles closer to the equator than we were in Seville."

"The seasons are backward, Master Elcano?"

"To you and me, yes."

Chindarza gave this only a moment's thought before asking what he wanted most to know. "Will we really reach our bay today, sir?"

"We should be there well before noon."

"And when might we all go ashore, sir?"

"We won't know that until we learn what the landing party finds. The natives here may be dangerous. You've heard about the cannibals?"

"Yes, sir, but I've heard many such stories," Chindarza said. "My Uncle Pedro sailed with Captain-general Columbus, as the youngest of Juan de La Cosa's cabin boys. He has told me many stories of the people he encountered on his voyage, even about Caribs that he claimed were cannibals. Señor Bustamente entertains the supernumeraries with similar tales."

"But you assume that there is little truth in them?"

Chindarza hesitated, Elcano's tone making him less certain. "I, well, Señor Bustamente says they wear no clothes at all, sir, not even the women." When Elcano merely lifted his brows, Chindarza's eyes widened and he asked, "Sir, do people here *really* eat the flesh of others?"

"I have not been to this land before but I have read such accounts, and Pilot Carvalho once lived here. He told me it's quite true."

Chindarza stared in amazement. "Which part, sir, the naked women or the cannibals?"

Elcano could not completely hide his grin. "Both parts." Noting how Chindarza's face began to pale, Elcano added, "Chindarza, you can take comfort in the fact that those who have attacked Europeans in the past live far to the south. The natives of Rio de Janeiro are expected to be friendly, but we will take no chances. As I said, we will wait to see what news the landing party brings back before the rest of us leave the ships. Don't you agree that this is only wise?"

"Yes, sir, very wise," said Chindarza, his gaze slipping toward the shoreline.

Elcano was about to leave him again when the boy blurted out, "But, sir, they would be damned forever for such an abominable act. Why would they do such a thing?"

"Not all men believe as we do, Chindarza. These people are not civilized. They are not Christians. They live without clothing, without iron, without education of any kind. And they will likely believe our ways to be as peculiar as we consider theirs."

"But we do nothing as barbaric as *eating* each other," Chindarza persisted, his young face pinched with repugnance.

"No, but perhaps they'd *prefer* that we eat a few of their enemies while we are here." When Chindarza looked back at him with an uneasy frown, Elcano gave up his attempt at humor. "Never mind. Off with you. See to your duties." He left the boy and found Acurio down on the main deck.

Stepping away from the men clustered around the fogon, Acurio said, "The food's so dwindled, sir, it's hardly worth the trouble of sitting down to the kettle."

"Perhaps it's just as well that our stomachs are not full this morning."

With a grimace, Acurio asked, "There's work to be done in the hold then?"

Elcano nodded and led the way, determined to recheck the condition of their depleted stores so that reprovisioning could be done more efficiently once they landed.

When the two officers finally emerged from below decks, the rotten stench of the hold was dispelled by the gentle breeze and replaced by the sweet scent of tropical flowers. Elcano inhaled deeply and let his eyes feast as the fleet eased into a bay of such stunning beauty that many of the hands could utter nothing more intelligible than curses, sighs, and gasps. A high rocky knoll bearing broad vertical streaks of gray and beige guarded the bay. On its lower slopes, a canopy of trees dappled the undergrowth with shade, and exotic blooms blanketed the ground in a vibrant suffusion of color. Bougainvillea pinks and reds accentuated the lushness of the surrounding greenery. Fruits and flowers, familiar to none but Carvalho, flashed their bright hues from under branches and leaves, and filled the air with their intoxicating fragrance.

Passing the stone prominence on their port side, Elcano gained a clear view of deep green hills encircling the arc of a pale beach. Sea birds reeled above the ships while their cousins danced between treetops, giving a festive display of their colors. Their trills and caws blended in a rowdy clamor not entirely unlike the chorus arising from the men. At the base of a peak even higher than the one they had just eased by, anchors found the sea bottom as the men moved to secure the sails.

Elcano leaned upon the stern castle railing and drew it all in. Then he closed his eyes, lowered his head, and thanked God for safely delivering them to such a place.

Quesada was by his side before he'd noticed his coming. "It looks like paradise, does it not?" asked the captain.

"It does indeed, sir."

Pointing, Quesada said, "Look there."

Already the natives were gathering on shore, gesturing toward the ships or racing inland to announce their arrival. A few of them stood beside their longboats. Canoes, Carvalho had called them. Rather than boarding their crafts, however, the Brazilians held their oars at the ready as if awaiting a signal from someone that had not yet arrived.

Elcano's glances at the *Trinidad* and the *San Antonio* revealed that their crews were already adjusting the aims of mounted falconets and culverins. Magellan, evidently confident in the adequacy of these more heavily armed and larger ships, had given no orders for the smaller three vessels to provide additional cover for the landing party. All five ships were well within range of the beach.

Elcano rightly guessed that only crossbows and swords would be taken ashore by the men of the first launches. Carvalho, Gomez, and several other seamen climbed down to the *Trinidad's* skiff and pushed off. The boat from the *San Antonio*, commanded by Master-at-arms Gonzalo Gomez de Espinosa, was not far behind them.

Elcano asked, "Should we ready our boat, Captain?"

"See that no man boards her, but yes, lower it away."

Every eye in the fleet followed the skiffs from the *Trinidad* and the *San Antonio* as they pulled toward shore. They approached tentatively, but before they had come close enough to land, the gathering natives suddenly sang out in loud, chanting voices and began dancing in a manner that suggested both homage and joy.

Elcano heard Carvalho hail the natives in their own tongue, resulting in a sudden hush that was followed a moment later by a roaring salutation. After several more exchanges, Carvalho and Gomez brought their boat all the way to the beach. Carvalho, who had a small canvas bag slung over his shoulder, leaped into the water only to be seized by many hands, lifted onto shoulders, and carried to a circle of men standing near the tree line. Espinosa and several of the armed sailors jumped from the two boats and hurried after them, but it was plain even from Elcano's position on the *Concepción* that the natives were celebrating their arrival rather than threatening it. Before Carvalho had placed a foot on dry land, Gomez and several others were also hefted up and borne by the jostling, cheering crowd to join their leaders.

"Well!" huffed Quesada. "It certainly appears that Carvalho's predictions about a friendly welcome were accurate."

Standing at Elcano's elbow, Chindarza stared at the natives in silent awe.

Elcano also scrutinized the people ashore as Carvalho spoke with them. Few women stood out in the open, but those that were visible wore their black hair long and loose over strongly formed, light brown bodies. The Tupi men were inches taller and noticeably more muscular than were the men of the landing party. More than half of them wore bright swatches of color over their genitals and their buttocks. The rest of them wore nothing at all.

From the bag Carvalho had brought with him, he began to withdraw articles of trade. Elcano's eyes caught the shiny reflection of brass, possibly from a bell or a mirror, as it passed from Carvalho's hand to a man of obvious authority among the native people. More words and items were exchanged. Then, as if some sort of approval had been given, many of the native men turned and raced inland. They soon reappeared with armloads of goods that were loaded into their canoes before the men leaped into their slender crafts and paddled toward the ships.

Canoes, each carrying nearly thirty men, were soon crowding for a place at *Concepción's* side like hungry pups at mealtime. Although small arms had been placed within reach, Elcano could see by the cargos of the canoes and the eager smiles of the rowers that swords would not be needed. The Tupis were allowed to climb up the rope ladders, and they soon thronged the ship.

"Bring a chest of trade goods from the hold, Chindarza," Captain Quesada shouted to the cabin boy.

The natives quickly assembled before Quesada and his box, and a lively round of trading began. Six fowls that resembled chickens were given in exchange for a single fish-hook, a pair of geese for a comb, thirty fish for a pair of scissors, a basket filled with unfamiliar orange-colored potatoes for a bell or a yard of ribbon.

While this bartering was being conducted, Elcano examined the Tupis at close range with a fascination as naked as his visitors' bodies. The natives, speaking and nodding before Quesada and occasionally glancing around the ship, had all shaved the hair from their heads. Not a single body hair marred the surface of the lustrous skin on their muscled limbs and torsos. In marked exception to this smooth effect, their bodies bore intentionally generated scars. Here and there, dark notches of similar length had been scored into the skin of an arm or a chest. Some men possessed foot-long rows of these uniform scars. The man that displayed the greatest number of scars also wore a necklace of what Elcano could not fail to recognize with an inward shudder of disgust: human teeth.

The Tupi faces were broad, and their eyes, a rich brown, but Elcano's engrossment was drawn to the three holes bored into their lower lips through which small round stones hung suspended. He saw that the colorful drapes suspended before their genitalia were made of brilliantly hued feathers, and were secured to woven cotton belts tied around their waists. Shaking his head at such impractical adornments, he turned his concentration to the strange words being passed between them and Carvalho.

Before the trading of food for trinkets had been completed, shouts from the flagship brought Quesada and Elcano to the rail. One of the *Trinidad's* seamen called out, "The captain-general is preparing to land, sir, and he has given permission for one watch from each ship to go ashore. He orders each captain to see that any man allowed ashore is back aboard his ship by nightfall."

Pandemonium erupted on the *Concepción*, where it reigned for several minutes until first Acurio, then Elcano shouted down the cheering men, preventing the most eager from climbing down to the boat. Once a semblance of order had been restored, Quesada handed command of the ship over to Elcano, and then chose seven fortunate men to accompany their captain in the first boat to head for the beach. The Tupi traders boisterously led the way in their canoes.

When the *Concepción's* skiff returned from depositing the first group of men on the beach, it carried Pilot Carvalho back with it. Carvalho's temper flared while he tried to scale the rope ladder against the tide of six men anxiously climbing down. He shoved one eager fellow out of his way with such force that the supernumerary lost his grip on the rope and fell into the water with a loud splash. Amid a roar of laughter, his shipmates hauled him into the boat and the rowers wasted no time in taking up their oars and plying them with vigor.

Pilot Carvalho landed on deck and was heartily greeted by those still aboard. "I can't stay long, men. I've only come to convey an order from the captain-general. No man ashore is to wander out of hearing range of any musket fire from the ships."

Acurio blurted out what was on every mind. "Where are all the women, Pilot? We've seen only a few."

"Calm yourself, Acurio. They're not far off. They've been hiding in the jungle, but they are already returning. Now men, when it's your turn to go ashore you had better not forget my warning about the married women. Though these Brazilian men are more than generous with their daughters, they are fiercely protective of their wives. They won't hesitate to kill a man who molests one of them."

"If we mind that the married women wear their hair bound behind them, like you told us, sir," said Acurio, "trouble should be avoidable."

"Saints above," one of the men yelped, pointing to the beach, and all heads turned.

Hundreds of Tupi women were stepping clear of the trees, and almost all of them were nude. They held back from the seamen on the beach, but their own men encouraged the young women with free flowing hair to draw nearer to the strangers. Trinkets were quickly passed from the Europeans to the Tupi fathers. And as their shipmates gazed on, pairs consisting of a sailor and a girl, and occasionally a sailor and two girls, disappeared into the denseness of the forest.

"Saints above indeed," Acurio said softly.

To Carvalho and Acurio, Elcano muttered, "We're going to have a hell of a time getting the men back on this ship." Before he had finished uttering these words, he noticed dozens of young women being rowed by their male relatives toward the *Concepción* and the other vessels.

"Here they come!" shouted Acurio unnecessarily. Every man was already hanging over the railings and watching them close in.

"Remember the captain-general's orders!" Elcano barked out. "No women aboard ship!" But even he could do little to stop the wave of female flesh that spilled over the rails as canoe after canoe sidled up to their vessel and disembarked its passengers. Short of tossing the women bodily from the ship, which their ever-increasing number would have made difficult at best, there was little he could do.

The women showed little hesitation in presenting themselves before the men, in some cases without the urging of a father or brother. Quite a few, upon finding partners suitable to themselves at a price suitable to their fathers, began to explore every part of the European bodies with their hands.

Elcano, withdrawing himself from the attentions of two girls, yanked Acurio free of another Tupi woman's embrace and hissed, "Tell the men that anyone who dares to copulate on this ship will be refused shore leave!" Acurio turned with the intention of conveying this message only to stumble over the young woman he had just parted from. Calling to bear every ounce of his discipline, he moved her aside and pushed to the center of the main deck. Taking up the ship's bell in one hand and a billet in the other, he bludgeoned the bell until the racket on the ship subsided a little. He then scowled at the men and bawled out Elcano's order.

Immediately, Elcano saw at least three sailors yank up breeches and tie them back in place. Even so, he had little faith that his command would hold for long unless the women were removed from the ship. In a low tone he spoke to Carvalho, still standing at his shoulder. "Pilot, would you," he hesitated uncomfortably, "would you please help the men make arrangements to meet the women of their choice *on shore* as soon as they are given leave. We *must* get these females back in their canoes."

Upon hearing this extraordinary request, Carvalho's eyes shone with mischief. "Of course, Master Elcano." Before he could make good his word, however, a handsome woman, with hair so long it almost brushed the deck, approached with a small boy in tow. She went directly to Carvalho and spoke softly. Carvalho's eyes widened before shifting to the boy. He questioned her for a moment then, turning from the woman and child, he said, "Master Elcano, this is the son I left behind when I returned to Europe years ago."

Elcano noted that Carvalho seemed not the least displeased, then he glanced at the boy. Yes, there was something of Carvalho in his eyes, and his skin was lighter and his nose narrower than was common among his native people.

"His mother asks that I take the boy with me, to live with the gods," said Carvalho.

"The *gods*?"

"Yes, well, it seems there has been a drought throughout the region this summer, and the first rain they've seen in months fell just hours before our arrival. They believe we brought the rain and that we, all of us, that is, are gods."

"And you told them nothing to correct this belief."

Carvalho smiled. "I saw no reason to lower their opinions of us. Their assumptions can only help us with our reprovisioning and—."

"And our entertainment?"

Carvalho flashed an even broader grin. "That too."

"Do you want to keep the boy with you?"

"I do. He's a fine looking lad."

"The youngest cabin boy of the fleet must be twice his age."

"Yes, but there have been cabin boys as young as he on other voyages."

"What is his age?"

"Seven years."

"And his name?"

Carvalho thought for a moment before declaring, "As of today, it will be Juanito Carvalho."

Elcano said with growing impatience, "It's up to Captain Quesada and the captain-general, of course." He raised his eyes to the carousing being enjoyed with growing enthusiasm on every deck. "It appears that more children will be born in the wake of our landing, but I'd prefer that they *not* be conceived aboard the *Concepción*. That would be an unholy and unpleasant irony. Pilot Carvalho, will you please attend to the matter of removing these women?"

Carvalho nodded, tossed his newly claimed son up onto his shoulder, and made his way to the largest cluster of men and girls. Elcano had his hands full fending off females and fathers while he posted trustworthy guards above the closed hatch that led to the hold, and the wine. Next he gathered Acurio and a handful of other stalwart souls to help dislodge the female population from their ship.

Carvalho eventually left them and headed to each of the other ships, where he repeated the captain-general's order about the men keeping close to the beach while ashore. He then returned, rather tardily, to shore and resumed his duties as interpreter for the captain-general.

Hours later, when Captain Quesada made his way back to the *Concepción*, Elcano was granted permission to head for shore. Before he left, though, he was ordered to keep his eyes open for men from the first watch that had failed to reboard at the appointed time.

Of the men who accompanied Elcano to the beach, young Chindarza was the only one who remained close by his side. Luxuriating in the feel of sand beneath their feet, they found Elorriaga lying in the shade with a family of Tupis and being served food by a woman with an infant slung in a woven sack around her neck. A Tupi man, a boy of about Chindarza's age, three younger girls, and an ancient man looked up at their arrival.

Elorriaga beamed. "Juan Sebastian, you've made it ashore at last! Come, sit down. You too, Chindarza. Join us, join us."

Elcano seated himself and politely met the eyes of the woman's husband, then the old Tupi man, and finally those of the youth, nodding to each in a friendly manner.

"This food is straight from heaven," Elorriaga sighed as he bit into a slice of pineapple. "You must try this, try everything. It's all delicious."

"Have you paid them?"

"The mother would take nothing, but I put a pair of scissors into the hand of her husband. He accepted it graciously."

Elcano pulled three fishhooks from the pouch at his belt and gave them to the husband, the old man, and the boy. Then, with great anticipation, he and Chindarza sat down to the first fresh food they had eaten in two and a half months. A meal of fish, sweet potatoes, cashews, roasted tapir, and cassava bread was washed down with sweet, fresh water. While each mouthful disappeared at an amazing rate, groans of appreciation and slurps of approval brought a timid smile to the mother's face. The young girls giggled with unrestrained delight.

When Elorriaga had eaten his fill, he patted his stomach and exclaimed, "If I have a belly ache for a week, it will be worth it!"

"It will at that," said Elcano as he leaned back on his elbows.

Elorriaga eyed him closely. "You've grown too thin, my friend."

"With the shortage of rations, we've all lost a share of our girth. It won't take long to fatten the lot of us back up though, not if we keep eating like this."

Unexpectedly, Chindarza let out a huge belch that produced another peal of laughter from the Tupi girls. He grinned back at them shyly.

As the chuckling died away, Elcano's gaze was captured by the sight of a woman of extraordinary height emerging from the trees. She came toward his group and exchanged a single word with the middle-aged male, meeting Elcano's stare with one just as probing.

Unlike the other Brazilian women Elcano had seen, her hair had been cut so that it fell only to her shoulders. Her belly was flat and her breasts were high and round, indicating that she had never borne or nursed a child. She wore a feathered loin covering similar to that of the warriors, and the lids of her eyes were painted crimson. Four parallel scars, two inches in length and blackened by some kind of dye, descended from high on her left shoulder. For an instant, he speculated on the significance of each scar, but only for an instant. Elcano had never seen such a magnificent combination of primitive strength and beauty.

She kept her eyes on Elcano as she spoke again to the Tupi man.

"Father in heaven," Elorriaga muttered to Elcano. "She looks like she could eat you alive."

"Chindarza, see if you can find Carvalho," said Elcano.

Chindarza got up slowly, as if fearing any sudden movement might cause the wild woman to pounce on him. Once he was several yards away, he spun around and hurried off in search of his pilot.

Words continued to be exchanged between the Tupi woman and the man, perhaps her brother, until the woman with the baby looked at Elcano in surprise, then back at the woman. The man appeared to be trying unsuccessfully to dissuade the woman from some intended act. Even the old man voiced what seemed to be an objection. After a few minutes of this, the woman silenced both men with one slashing motion of her hand. All eyes fell upon Elcano.

Barely moving his lips, Elorriaga said, "Something tells me you're the cause of this family dispute."

Breathlessly, Chindarza ran up behind Elcano and said, "He's coming, sir." The pilot was only a few steps behind the boy, and he greeted the Tupis formally. Carvalho surprised Elcano by speaking directly to the woman, who still held Elcano in her gaze. When Carvalho finally faced Elcano, there were equal shares of amazement, amusement, and admiration in his expression.

"What exactly is going on, Pilot?"

"This woman is a warrior among her people, Master Elcano. Her kind is very rare. She is held in the highest of regard, so high that she has never been forced to accept a man. By choice, she has never married. But now she wants

64

to mate with one of the gods. You seem to be the god of her choosing."

"Tell her that I am no god, Pilot."

"Forgive me, Master Elcano, but that would not be wise."

"Please tell her, Pilot Carvalho."

With a sigh, Carvalho again exchanged words with the woman. She appeared mildly surprised, and then she cast a shrewd smile toward Elcano that seemed to say she knew better. Again, she spoke to Carvalho.

"She's chosen you, Master Elcano. She's a very determined woman. Whatever else I try to tell her, it won't make any difference. Her choice is to be honored."

"And if I refuse her?"

Carvalho shook his head. "It would be a grave insult not only to her, but to her people."

Elcano hesitated. "Since she's a respected warrior, if I go with her are there any special rites, any ah...?" Elcano wanted to kick Elorriaga for chuckling at his discomfort. A little more firmly, he asked, "What are their customs in this regard?"

As amused as Elorriaga, but hiding his mirth a little better, Carvalho said, "She will not take a bite out of you, if that's what you mean." Ignoring Elcano's responding glare, he added, "The customs are not much different here than they are anywhere else, at least not for such things. Just be prepared for her to take the lead, without hesitation or restraint."

Elorriaga said with false gravity, "She'll most likely be too much for you to handle in your weakened state. Perhaps I should offer to take your place."

"I'll manage," Elcano snapped at him, though not at all certain that he could.

As if her patience had reached its limit, the woman stood to her full height. This, Elcano recognized as he too stood, was two inches taller than his own. She stepped across the ring of people and placed her hand upon Elcano's shoulder. Then, lowering her hand to clasp his, she began leading him away from the others. At the edge of the jungle, Elcano

Sails of Fortune

paused only long enough to look back over his shoulder and yell, "Pilot, what's her name?

"It's Akuba," shouted Carvalho. He threw a short laugh at Elcano's disappearing back, and hollered, "It means 'heat'!"


Evening was approaching by the time Elcano retraced his steps to the ocean's edge. Elorriaga, who stood with his hands on his hips while he awaited the return of the *San Antonio's* launch, grinned as he took in Elcano's appearance, and asked, "Did she try to drown you?"

"I went for a swim in the river," Elcano said, brushing his wet hair away from his eyes. "My clothes were so foul that I wore them in with me."

Elorriaga stepped closer and inspected Elcano up and down. "Well, I don't see any pieces missing. What's the bundle under your arm?"

"A hammock." When Elorriaga gave him a suspicious look, Elcano added with a measure of uneasiness, "It was a gift."

"I see. For...services rendered?"

To turn the subject Elcano said, "Just what have *you* been doing while I was away?"

"Exploring, my friend. Did you see their communal houses? I counted over a hundred hammocks in the largest one. These people must never be lonely."

"Akuba showed me the houses when we stopped for the hammock. Is that all you did, explore?"

"I need not reveal all my escapades to you, Juan Sebastian. What about your men, have you had any more luck gathering them up than I've had with mine?"

"Probably not. I'm still three short. If we don't put them to work repairing the ships soon we'll lose half of them to this place."

Elorriaga's skiff arrived and as he waded out to it, he called back, "Considering how exhausted you look, we'll have to put you to work too. We wouldn't want to lose you to that giant beauty."

Gathering the men together proved much more difficult than even Elcano had imagined, especially after Magellan's own brother-in-law, Duarte Barbosa, did not return to the flagship for three days and three nights. To gain control of the spiraling chaos, Magellan ordered Barbosa's arrest and had him locked in chains.

Acurio had just delivered this news to Elcano when they were surprised by the arrival of Captain Quesada and the former captain of the *San Antonio*. Cartagena was brought clumsily aboard the *Concepción* wearing leg and wrist irons.

Elcano met his captain and Cartagena, chained though he was, with a slight bow.

"In my cabin, Master Elcano," Quesada said gruffly.

Once the door was closed, Quesada faced Elcano. "Señor Cartagena has been placed in my custody. Captain Coca and Captain Mendoza mercifully allowed him to be taken ashore for a brief reprieve from his captivity and because of this, Magellan has threatened to maroon Señor Cartagena when the fleet sails from Rio de Janeiro."

Silently cursing Coca and Mendoza for testing Magellan's authority so blatantly, Elcano kept his face blank before the anger of Cartagena and the disgust of his own captain. Calmly, Elcano asked, "What punishments do Captains Coca and Mendoza face, sir?"

"Captain Mendoza was given a stern warning but, since Señor Cartagena had recently been transferred to Captain Coca's custody, he's been relieved of command of the *San Antonio* and replaced with, you won't believe this, replaced with the captain-general's cousin, Álvaro de Mesquita."

"The supernumerary from the *Trinidad*, Captain?" Elcano's voice betrayed his own amazement.

"None other. Pilot Major Gomez should have been given command over Mesquita or anyone else, and he's even Portuguese, if that was the captain-general's motivation. The choice of someone as inexperienced and incapable as Mesquita makes no sense at all."

"You mustn't forget that he's the captain-general's cousin," Cartagena growled.

Quesada went on. "Rather than being granted the captaincy, Gomez is being forced to leave the flagship and to act as Mesquita's pilot. Ha, to act as his wet-nurse is more accurate. Gomez is infuriated by the insult, of course. I tell you, it's as if Magellan is *trying* to cause unrest among his officers."

"I must disagree with you in one respect, Captain Quesada," stated Cartagena. "What the captain-general has done makes perfect sense. He's replaced a rightfully appointed Castilian captain with a man he can easily manipulate. The *San Antonio*, the largest and most powerfully gunned ship in the fleet, is now under the command of a complete incompetent. If Captain Mendoza takes one false step, Magellan will replace him. And do not make the mistake of doubting that you are also under his watchful eye, Captain Quesada. Mark my words, he'll have every captain appointed by the king in chains or at the bottom of the sea before this fleet reaches the Spiceries."

Frowning deeply, Quesada said, "At least we've persuaded Magellan not to leave you behind when we sail, Señor Cartagena. He was not easily convinced."

"As I said, he'll have us all out of the way if we are not careful."

Elcano noticed the repeated omission of the captain-general's title by both men, and from Captain Quesada this breach of naval etiquette was an especially troubling sign.

Captain Quesada rubbed the back of his neck wearily, and shifted the conversation by asking Elcano, "You've heard that Miguel de Rodas has replaced Salamón as pilot of the *Victoria?*"

"Yes, sir. I have."

"At sunrise, I'd like you to accompany me to the flagship to witness Salamón's execution."

"Yes, Captain."

Quesada said, "It's a grim business to be conducted in a place such as this."

Elcano could only agree.

The following morning a review of Salamón's case took no more than five minutes. As Elcano stood among the officers on the *Trinidad's* main deck and the rest of the fleet's personnel looked on, Salamón was led in shackles to the main mast. The rattling of his chains was the only sound to disturb the tight, heavy silence that gripped every ship. Father Pedro de Valderrama, who had already given the condemned man his last rights, blessed him for the final time.

Salamón whispered, "Thank you, Father," before two seamen drew him back, wrapped a leather strap first around his neck and the mast, and then tied the ends of the strap tightly together on the other side of the mast.

Magellan stepped forward and in a level voice said, "Antón Salamón, you have been found guilty of the crime of sodomy and condemned to death. May our God in heaven be merciful to your soul."

As Magellan moved back, Espinosa strode to the side of the mast opposite the prisoner and slid a wooden billet stick between the mast and the knot in the leather strap. Even if Salamón had intended to speak or cry out, he was given no time to do so. On Magellan's signal Espinosa used both of his hands to turn the billet, abruptly tightening the strap around Salamón's neck with the first rotation. The master-at-arms worked swiftly, and Elcano could see that Espinosa was delivering what mercy he could by his quickness. One half-turn, two, three. Almost as if his own air was also being cut off, Elcano unconsciously held his breath.

Salamón's face reddened and swelled, his eyes bulged, and finally his left foot kicked back sharply against the mast as his body jerked in protest.

Men turned away, some moaning involuntarily. Elcano tried to focus on Espinosa's grimacing face and straining arms but he still saw Salamón's body make two violent spasms before slowly slackening, and then ceasing its struggles altogether.

The knot in Elcano's stomach was unwilling to loosen even after Espinosa relaxed his hold on the billet, unwound the leather binding, and allowed Salamón's body to be taken away. It took a long time before Elcano's breathing returned to its former rhythm.

# Dubious Passage

## 6

Word passed from officer to officer that Magellan had set December 27 as their date of departure from Rio de Janeiro, and Elcano responded by keeping his crew vigilant as they scrubbed, repaired, and reprovisioned the *Concepción* in order to meet this deadline. He often saw the captain-general while venturing through the Tupi village or moving among his men at work near the beach, and Magellan never failed to offer a cordial exchange of words before resuming his own activities.

As if it had been no more than a flash of emotion, the discontent felt by the other officers over Magellan's treatment of Cartagena, Coca, and Gomez seemed to have been quickly extinguished. But Elcano could see signs of vexation smoldering in more than a few, and Cartagena's persistent presence near the *Concepción*, even as she was brought ashore to be careened and refurbished, resulted in a constant stirring of the coals.

While ashore, much to Elorriaga's entertainment, Elcano often found Akuba watching him as he oversaw the scraping and recaulking of the *Concepción*. If he accompanied a group of men to gather stores or to meet with other crewmembers, she followed him like a self-appointed guard, even pushing sailors out of her way if they inadvertently usurped her place in line behind him. This proved to be such an embarrassment that Elcano asked Carvalho to explain that she was to stay away from him during his working shifts. Whatever it was that Carvalho conveyed to her, and Elcano strongly suspected it was less than an accurate translation, it only seemed to increase her vigilance as their remaining number of days together steadily diminished.

When Christmas arrived with Elcano so far from his family and lifelong friends, the vast distance between him and home seemed even greater than it really was. Mass was celebrated in the shade of palm and pine trees upon a makeshift altar strewn with flowers, and although many in the congregation wore nothing but feathers and paint to adorn their bodies, the service brought the familiarity and reassurance of Elcano's faith to cheer his homesick heart. After the service, he and Elorriaga managed to sneak into the jungle alone and find a quiet place beside a wide, algae-coated pond that was fed by a tiny cascade of fresh water.

"Look at the size of those lily pads," Elorriaga said as they sat down to admire their surroundings. "They must be four feet across."

"Akuba told me that those pads are sturdy enough to hold a small child."

"You've picked up that much of her language?"

"No, mostly just hand signs."

"You may not know it, my friend, but you're going to miss that woman when we leave."

Elcano smiled. "I know it far too well."

They sat together for nearly an hour, drinking from a bottle of good Jerez wine that Elorriaga had smuggled ashore and brought with them. The minutes passed quickly as they talked of past antics of their brothers, the virtues of their sisters, the guiding strength of their fathers, and the fine cooking of their mothers.

Then, with indulgence and a touch of envy, Elcano listened to Elorriaga's pining for his beloved wife. "She'll be thinking of you today, Juan," Elcano said. "Look toward the time when you'll return to her."

"I do, Juan Sebastian. Every day."

"We'd better get back before they send a party to search for us."

"They'd have better luck if they sent Akuba to search for you," Elorriaga laughed as they got to their feet and made their way back to the beach.

Forty-eight hours later, with many a sigh of reluctance from the men, the ships were ready for departure and at last anchors were weighed. As the wind filled the sails and the fleet began to move, Tupis pushed dozens of canoes into the water and followed after them. Entreating wails arose from a few of the women. Arms lifted and, here and there, tears fell.

With his hand resting on the shoulder of his small half-Tupi son, Carvalho said in surprise to Elcano, "I've never seen this before. They seem to sincerely want us to stay." Little Juanito remained close beside his father, and cried quietly as he waved back to the longboat carrying his weeping mother.

Elcano kept his eyes on Akuba, paddling in one of the canoes close behind the ships. Today she had painted her entire forehead black and had shaped the outline of a red bird upon her right cheek. She paddled with precision even as she kept her focus on him. Her eyes were dry, her head held high.

When the ships began to pull away from the canoes and Elcano raised his hand in farewell, Akuba lifted her paddle with both hands and shouted to him in a clear, proud voice. Before he could ask, Carvalho offered, "She says you are a worthy warrior." Elcano looked back at her and, when she lifted her paddle in one final salute, he waived his beret in the air. He remained at the rail until her canoe, one of the last to turn back, grew smaller and smaller in the distance.

Unnoticed until then, Chindarza too looked back on the scene behind the ship. Noting the youth's mournful expression, Elcano said, "What is it, Chindarza?"

Saying nothing, Chindarza lowered his head.

Perceiving his cabin boy's torment, Elcano said gently, "It is not unusual for a sailor to lose his innocence at a young age, Chindarza. We are mere visitors at each port. You must try not to lose your heart to anyone but the sea until you return home."

Chindarza's head remained down and his hands played restlessly with the hem of his shirt. "Was it not wrong, sir, to be with those women?"

"Ah, my boy. The truth is that we both know it was wrong to take what they offered." Elcano's expression changed subtly, as if his mind were looking back upon a far off memory both tormenting and compelling. When he spoke again, he seemed only distantly aware of Chindarza's presence, and his voice was a stony whisper. "Most things a man chooses to do in this life are deemed to be wrong in the eyes of someone, even when that choice is his only hope of maintaining his honor." After several moments he felt Chindarza's confused eyes focused hard upon him, and with an effort he released the haunting memories from his conscience.

Elcano's face and tone softened. "After your watch has ended, offer your confession to Father Valderrama. Make peace with God and calm your soul."

"Of course, sir. I will."

Lightening his voice even more, Elcano said, "Father Valderrama will undoubtedly expect to see me later today, too. I am one of his most frequent visitors." Clapping Chindarza on his slumped shoulder as they left the rail, Elcano said, "Let's go check with Acurio on how our newly sealed seams are holding up. He's probably been looking for you anyway, needing some chore done that no other man can do half as well."

Chindarza managed a tepid smile.

"As a matter of fact," Elcano said, pausing in mid stride, "I just remembered a special duty I've been meaning to assign to you. Perhaps you've noticed that Pilot Carvalho keeps only a distracted eye on his small son."

Already suspicious, Chindarza said, "Well..."

"Juanito is too young to be allowed full run of the ship now that we're at sea."

"Yes, sir, but—."

"He needs someone as a constant companion, someone who can instruct him in the ways of the *Concepción*."

"But, sir, shouldn't we speak to Pilot Carvalho about this first? Perhaps he doesn't want—."

"I already have, and he agrees that you are just the man to train Juanito."

"Train him, sir?" In spite of Chindarza's best efforts, this had come out as a whine of protest. "Train a small boy?"

"He's young and he speaks little Spanish as yet," Elcano went on, "but he's quick-witted. He'll learn our ways in no time."

"Sir, please, I know nothing about training children."

"Have him help you with your duties. That will be the best way to teach him."

"I'd rather not, sir."

"Chindarza, that's enough!" Elcano seldom had to sharpen his voice with Chindarza, and doing so immediately silenced the youth's protests. "I entrust you with this responsibility because you are the most trustworthy cabin boy in the fleet. Do not disappoint me."

"No, sir," Chindarza said, his cheeks red from the sting of Elcano's reprimand.

"Now, let's go find Acurio."

The time had come for the men to maneuver the fleet southwestward and out of the domain of the Portuguese, whom they had been fortunate enough not to encounter during their thirteen vulnerable days in Rio de Janeiro. Although Magellan still offered no specific information as to the location of the channel to the South Sea, Elcano gained at least some information about a port that lay ahead from Pilot Carvalho. The massacre of the Solis' expedition had taken place four years earlier at a place called Cape Santa Maria. Carvalho believed that this site lay near the same latitude as the horn of Africa, or 34° south, and Elcano and many others began to suspect this cape to be the entrance to the passage.

A close watch was kept on the coastline for any break that might indicate an opening, and every night Magellan asked the ships' pilots to report their estimated position. The winds and weather held fair and, even though every small bay was investigated and charted, within two weeks they had voyaged over a thousand nautical miles.

Their string of uneventful days was unexpectedly broken when an evening squall suddenly arose and slammed into the ships with malicious fury. To avoid being thrown by the wind and waves against the shoal edging the coastline, the flotilla had no choice but to force its way to the open sea. They battled the storm through three watches, until many an exhausted man dropped into the hold or whatever sheltered corner of his ship he could find. When morning finally came, it brought a noticeable lessening of the gales.

With the easing of the wind, Magellan turned the *Trinidad* back toward the west, leading the other ships, or so Elcano thought, to whatever sanctuary the shoreline might offer. But when land was in sight, the flagship curved northward, doubling back up the mist-shrouded coast. Acurio found Elcano on the foredeck and voiced his shipmaster's supposition as well as his own. "If the captain-general is turning back, he's looking for the cape, eh, sir? We may be close."

Near midday, sailing under rumbling clouds and through a veil of whispering showers, the five ships entered a bay so vast that men rushed from their refuges, danced on the decks in the drizzle, and cried out, "The passage! The passage!" No amount of cautioning on the part of Elcano or Quesada could dissuade the men from their certainty that they had arrived at the entrance to the anticipated waterway.

Quesada gave up his attempts to calm the men, saying to Elcano, "This bay must be sixty miles wide. How could it be anything but a strait?"

They lowered their sails, smiling and confident as they followed the *Trinidad* to a sheltered anchorage inside the bay. But while the crewmembers restlessly awaited a signal from the flagship to send a boat ashore, hours passed. With the return of nightfall, the wind and rain began to build again.

Elcano had just joined Carvalho on the water-soaked half deck when Acurio called out, "Looks like the *Victoria's* dragging her anchor, sir!" Hurrying to the rails, the three officers and many of their men watched as the ship drifted with gathering speed toward the *Concepción*. "Stand by the anchor!" Elcano yelled, and seamen leaped to the anchor line. "Chindarza, tell Captain Quesada what's afoot, then get Juanito below," he ordered. The lad spun around, grabbed the hand of the child, and slipped and slid across the water in his haste to reach the captain's cabin.

Over the drumming of the rain and the increasingly vicious wind, Captain Mendoza's shout carried to Elcano. "Drop the second anchor!" With the *Victoria* drawing ever closer, her iron weight seemed to take twice as long as usual to fall and disappear into the water, and Elcano prayed that the anchor would quickly still the oncoming ship. But she kept coming. When no more than thirty feet separated the two vessels, Elcano opened his mouth to order the weighing of the *Concepción's* anchor, and Captain Quesada appeared just in time to witness the *Victoria's* jerking, swinging halt.

In spite of the fierceness of the storm, the men of both ships were breathing a small sigh of relief when someone aboard the *Victoria* hollered out, "Captain Mendoza, the flagship's gone!"

It was so dark and the rain fell with such determination that Elcano could see nothing farther than fifty yards away. The infrequent and distant flashes of lightning provided little light as he squinted into the downpour for any sign of the *Trinidad*. Magellan could not have been clearer in his order to never let the flagship out of their sights, and the officers of all four remaining ships held an immediate council to determine their best course of action.

In the end, it was decided that leaving the safety of the bay would be not only futile but also perilous. They chose to remain where they were. Elcano slept little that long night. If the flagship was lost, so too was the fleet's commander and his singular knowledge of the passage. When Elcano's watch ended, he remained on deck and tried to convince himself of the *Trinidad's* safety.

Sleep had overtaken him just two hours earlier, but Elcano sprang to his feet when he heard, "The *Trinidad*! She's back! She's safe and sound!" He was on the half deck in eight strides. There she was, approaching at good speed and apparently unharmed. To add to Elcano's consolation, the skies were beginning to clear.

The flagship slowed as she sailed closer, and Captain-general Magellan stood upon her stern deck waving back at the men of the fleet. Drawing nearer, Magellan called at the top of his lungs, "What say you, men? Shall we this very day explore waters that no man has yet sailed upon?"

Lusty cries in the affirmative rang out from every ship.

The *Santiago*, the smallest ship with the shallowest draft, and then the *Victoria* led them without delay up the long westward seaway. Although the *Concepción* still held a middle position within the line of five ships, this was the first time she had followed the course set by a ship other than the *Trinidad*. Elcano found himself gazing back often, keenly noting the look of expectancy on the captain-general's craggy face.

With measured caution they proceeded, taking continuous soundings of the water depth along their way. They sailed five miles, then ten, then twenty, and still the channel showed itself to be encouragingly broad with no end in sight. When darkness fell and the ships came to rest along the shallow shore, stories of the fate of Captain Solis and his landing party were intentionally circulated, and the officers had no trouble keeping their men aboard the ships.

During the following two days they traveled thirty more miles up the watercourse, but to Elcano's building apprehension the water level was becoming much shallower. When Captain Quesada ordered an empty bucket to be lowered over the side of the *Concepción* to test the saltiness of the water, Elcano waited impatiently with the rest of his crew until it was hauled back up. Acurio dipped in his hand and slurped the water into his mouth. Rather than spitting it out, he swallowed it, and raised his head with a look of downhearted dismay. "Sir, it tastes like it was drawn from a spring. There's no salt in it at all."

With an effort, Elcano kept his expression calm, but he felt his hopes and confidence in their mission plunge sharply. Every indication pointed to this being no more than a river, a river of previously unimaginable size, but a river rather than a strait nonetheless.

It soon became clear that Magellan was not so easily convinced. While the fleet remained anchored on the north shore, the men were set to work taking on fresh water and repairing the small damage caused by the storms. Heavily armed scouting parties made their way ashore in search of fresh food and information.

Elcano led one such group, and upon his return was surprised to find Magellan and the four captains waiting for him on the beach under the protective guard of two dozen men. Separating from his weary men, Elcano approached his superior officers and bowed.

Magellan asked with little patience, "What have you found, Master Elcano?"

"We scouted nine or ten miles up the shore, Captain-general. The water gradually narrows and becomes even shallower, sir, but we did not see its end."

The disappointment on Magellan's face was quickly masked, but Elcano had seen it long enough to sense how deeply it ran.

"Did you see any natives?"

"We encountered only a small hunting party of four men, and they kept a good distance from us, sir."

Magellan paused, then said in a controlled voice, "Captain Serrano, ready the *Santiago* and make your way farther west. The rest of the fleet will explore the south side of this channel until you return. Take what time you need, but keep your men from landing if at all possible."

Allowing no question or objection to be raised, Magellan immediately turned from the others and boarded his launch. Enrique was beside him before his rowers had reached the skiff.

After he'd gone, the captains and Elcano shifted uneasily until Quesada finally spoke up. "Well, Captain Serrano, I wish you luck, but I'm afraid you will need a miracle to discover that this body of water takes you to the South Sea. Master Elcano," he called, motioning for the ship's master to accompany him.

When they were out of hearing range, Quesada ground out each word, "If that *Portuguese* has been bluffing all along, if he dared to tell our king that he knew the passage to be in this very place, if he was no more than *guessing* or even *outright lying...*"

Elcano lifted his hand to signal caution as their rowers approached. "Captain Quesada, perhaps what we seek lies not far to the south."

Quesada scowled, saying, "It had better."


Charting the southern bank provided few diversions other than the frequent sightings of natives even larger in stature than the Tupis. Carvalho told his shipmates that it was likely that these were the very Querandis that had ambushed the Solís expedition. Magellan quickly passed down an order forbidding the men to land.

One early morning as Elcano, Quesada, and Carvalho bent over Quesada's desk, studying and refining their latest charts, shouts from the men reached them. Leaving the captain's cabin and following the gazes of the crew, they spotted a canoe paddled by a lone native approaching the *San Antonio*. The Querandi drew quite close, stood to his full and impressive height, and in a voice as loud and harsh as that of a bull began to hurl what sounded like insults at them.

"What a magnificent creature," Quesada mused.

Elcano took in the pattern of yellow and black squares painted across his face and the multihued feathers that appeared to have been glued over much of his body. A veritable bouquet of feathers sprouted straight up from his head, bobbing and swaying as if to emphasize his words. Elcano asked, "What's he saying, Pilot?"

Carvalho laughed. "I don't understand many of his words and I doubt you'd want to know the meaning of some of those I can make out, but he's daring us to prove that we are men."

As swiftly as he had come, the warrior turned his canoe around and rejoined his companions on the shore. Much to the surprise of the crews, Magellan called out to them from the *Trinidad*, "Shall we accept his challenge, men?" The response was an eager, thunderous cry.

Under Espinosa's command, both Elcano and Elorriaga joined a hundred men as they quickly armed themselves and made their way ashore. Magellan's order was clear. "Bring some of them back alive."

By the time the first boats landed, however, every Querandi had melted into the cover of the forest. The sailors cautiously breached the edges of the trees but proceeded no farther than a quarter mile into the jungle before they began to fear that they were being led into a trap. Men began to flinch at the slightest snap of a twig or call of a bird. Their tension mounted until Espinosa finally cautioned them to retrace their steps. The landing party steadily retreated to the beach, then back to the ships empty handed.

With the excitement of the short-lived venture ashore already dying away, Elcano's eyes turned again to the west in search of the *Santiago*.

January faded into a February evening before the *Santiago's* sails at last came into view. Elcano's relief that she had not been lost was replaced by disillusionment when he caught sight of the white-haired Captain Serrano's expression of dread. From the *Santiago's* foredeck, Serrano hailed the captain-general, and even from a distance of thirty yards Elcano could perceive Magellan's struggle to hide his reaction to what was then reported.

"Captain-general, this waterway is unquestionably a river. We followed it far enough to dispel all doubt."

Although Captain Quesada was behind Elcano at the stern of the *Concepción*, it was easy to imagine his captain's condemning thoughts. Elcano tried but failed to keep his own mood from darkening, propelled as it was by the ripple of grumbling that flowed through his crew. When Serrano joined Magellan in his cabin aboard the flagship, the volume of the curses and complaints from the men increased noticeably.

Suddenly the sound of fists meeting flesh and bone burst from the decks of the *San Antonio*, silencing the griping of the rest of the fleet. Elcano twisted around in time to see at least six seamen swinging and kicking at each other. Elorriaga's boatswain, Diego Hernandez, leaped among the brawling men, swinging his billet in wide arcs to separate them. Other sailors and supernumeraries stepped in to yank the combatants apart. The whole thing was over in moments. But when the men backed away, their gazes all lowered to the deck and an eerie silence fell over their vessel.

Elorriaga crouched down, disappearing from Elcano's view, then he bellowed out a call to his ship's barber, "Olabarrieta!" The tone of the shout had the men from every ship straining to see what was happening aboard the *San Antonio*.

Accompanied by Captain Mesquita, Olabarrieta had done little more than kneel down before Elorriaga called for Father Calmette.

The men remained rooted, and in the stillness Elcano heard every word spoken by the French priest. "Our Lord in heaven, we ask that you have mercy on his soul, in the name of the Father, the Son, and the Holy Ghost."

Elorriaga stood and removed his beret. He lifted his gaze to the faces of his stricken men, men that only moments before had been brawling. Captain Mesquita shifted uneasily at Elorriaga's side then he went to the rail to address the captain-general, who had been called from his cabin.

"Sir, Seaman Sebastian Olarte is dead."

Magellan's head nodded slowly. "By murder or accident?"

"It was an accident, sir, but the men were fighting."

Rather than asking what had caused the fight, the captain-general said only, "Have the guilty men punished appropriately, Captain Mesquita, and prepare the body for burial at sea."

Mesquita said something to Elorriaga, who immediately faced the crew and demanded, "Which men were fighting?"

Five of them stepped forward.

"Lock them below, Señor Hernandez," said Elorriaga. "Two days without food."

As the subdued prisoners were led off, Magellan lifted his voice again. "All senior officers are to meet me aboard the flagship in half an hour." He left the rail, beckoning Serrano to follow him back to his cabin.

A moment later Elcano was summoned by his captain to the stern deck, where Quesada cast a steely gaze at the *Trinidad* and said, "This death is on his treacherous hands."

When Elcano opened his mouth to speak, Quesada shot his hand up to stop him, and barked in a barely controlled tone, "Don't presume to defend him, Master Elcano. That is one of your own kinsmen lying dead on the deck of the *San Antonio!*"

Elcano stiffened and remained silent under the shadow of the rebuke.

Unrelenting, Quesada said, "Days ago an Irishman fell overboard and drowned, and now we've suffered another death." In a voice suddenly soft and venomous, he said, "Men are dying because of Magellan's lies. He led us here never knowing where the passage was. It probably doesn't exist at all."

At the appointed time Elcano entered Magellan's tensely packed cabin along with Carvalho and Quesada. Magellan held himself before the group with an erect confidence that Elcano suspected of being too rigid to be real.

"Gentlemen," Magellan said, "although this river appeared to be promising, the true passage undoubtedly lies to the south, probably within a few miles. My intention to find it has not been changed in the least by Captain Serrano's news."

"Captain-general," said Captain Quesada, "still you have not shown us the charts of your intended course, the course you described to King Carlos, and so I must ask you, was it here at this river that you anticipated finding the passage?"

Every slightest movement in the cabin stilled.

Magellan did not answer.

Except for the shifting of their eyes, the men remained still as statues.

Finally, Quesada said tightly, "If nothing is known of the lands or seas that lie to the south, I suggest that we revise our plans and set course for the horn of Africa. The winds will be in our favor for much of the journey, and that route is already known to you and a handful of our other men. We can still reach the Spiceries by that route."

"I agree, sir," Captain Mendoza spoke up. "We can still achieve our goal of establishing trade in the Moluccas without wasting any more time hunting for a westward passage."

Captain Mesquita spoke not a word, but Gomez, who had so recently been demoted to serve as his pilot, said, "Sir, the month of February is already well begun. Winter will soon be upon us, and the weather will be felt all the more bitterly if we continue to journey into colder latitudes. What currents and storms await us, we dare not guess. To travel south now would be exceedingly perilous. However, to sail around Africa's horn and up its eastern coast would likely place us in just as dangerous a position given that the Portuguese defend those waters. Therefore, sir, I ask that you consider returning to Spain with what knowledge of this coastline we have already gathered. Once we are back in Seville, we can await the king's appointment of another expedition while these ships are reconditioned and the men well rested."

Captain Serrano studied Magellan as silently as did Captain Mesquita, waiting for a reaction.

Before revealing his thoughts, the captain-general asked, "What of my pilots and shipmasters? What words have you gentlemen to offer?" His gaze swept their faces. "Come, speak your minds."

"Sir," said Elcano, "I suggest that we return to Rio de Janeiro until winter has passed, then we can resume our search for the passage in early spring, when the weather will favor our efforts."

"Captain-general, that is my recommendation also." Elorriaga said

83

Pilot Mafra voiced his preference for returning to Spain before all fell quiet again.

Magellan pursed his lips thoughtfully and said, "There is some wisdom in each of these proposals, but one irrefutable argument against them all. I promised the king to find the passage without delay. I will keep that promise."

Quesada took a step forward, "Sir, we have no reliable information that the passage is anything but illusion. If I am mistaken, if you *do* have dependable knowledge, *now* is the time to show us what your assumptions have been based upon. There is no reason for continuing to withhold whatever evidence you possess."

Facing Quesada squarely, Magellan said with unflinching conviction, "The passage is no illusion, Captain. And we will find it."

Captain Mendoza said, "Please, sir, will you not at least consider Master Elcano's suggestion to winter back in Rio de Janeiro. If we do find the passage we will need our men strong and our stores full."

Several voices rose in concurrence.

Setting his jaw and staring down his fellow officers, Magellan said, "I have heard your proposals, and considered them. We head south at first light. Pray that God is with us and that the channel is close. That is all, gentlemen."

# Tiller and Sail

## 7

The *Trinidad* and the *San Antonio* were the first of the ships to pull free of the river's bottom and glide slowly toward its mouth. Elcano in the *Concepción* was preparing to follow them when he heard voices rising from the decks of the *San Antonio* and glanced ahead.

"We're taking on water, sir!"

"A leak, Master Elorriaga!"

The advancement of the entire fleet was brought to a halt. Repairs that Elcano had first hoped would require only hours ended up absorbing the persistent efforts of the *San Antonio's* crew, and several members of his own, for hours that stretched into two restive days. Adding to his disgruntlement, Elcano found himself to be the unwilling recipient of Captain Quesada's repeated predictions that this delay only foretold of worse troubles to come. When his captain persisted in such gloomy broodings, Elcano found an increasing number of ways to avoid engaging in conversation with him.

At last the *San Antonio* was seaworthy, and the vessels were allowed to flee the river that had brought them such disappointment. Elcano redirected all of his remaining hopes toward the wholly mysterious south.

Both the wind and the weather favored them, and league after league disappeared beneath their keels while Elcano's anxious eyes probed the coast for any indication of an opening. As he recorded every nautical mile, bay, and feature of the shoreline, however, he occasionally caught a troubling glimpse of distant storm clouds that seemed to be building far inland.

The storms seemed to bide their time while the fleet sailed on. When the squalls had gathered their formidable strength, they soared up and across the pampas, racing and tumbling until they burst from the shore to swoop down upon the vulnerable vessels.

Elcano and the men of the fleet braced themselves against the onslaught of the successive storms with grim-faced defiance. Allowing the ships to drift a safer distance from shore and shoals, they threw themselves against the attacking wind and rain, and warred for days to keep from capsizing. On the third terrible night, the *Concepción* was pushed and blown out of sight of the other ships, and her men were forced to labor on alone in the pitching darkness. As Elcano drove himself and his men, he imagined his ship to be a soldier standing wounded and unaided upon a rolling battlefield. But stand she would, he vowed. Stand she would.

Although there was no deviation in the waves or the rain, the next evening's wind did bring a faint change, the first chilling breath of winter. As another night took hold, the rain turned to hail and then sleet, and the men's bare feet began to slip and skid on the icy decks. Bodies already drained of strength fell cursing and grabbing for strong-holds, and then crept to the hold to scavenge for any scrap of canvas to protect their skin from the merciless elements.

Several days more passed before the winds waned enough to permit the *Concepción* and the other ships of the fleet to find each other near the location where they had first been dispersed by the storm. When the ships finally regrouped at a small island, the exhausted men could do no more than wave weakly to their fellow seamen. Elcano's bloodshot eyes looked upon the other ships, with their randomly broken yardarms, missing topmasts, and haggard men, and he thought them a most welcome sight.

Chindarza, standing beside him with his feet wrapped in scraps of canvas and twine and Juanito huddled close by his side, suddenly gave a little lurch and said, "Master Elcano, look ashore! It's crawling with strange birds and beasts."

86

Acurio was just behind them, and he spotted what held the lad's gaze. "Well I'll be. What do you suppose they are, sir?"

"I'm not sure," Elcano said, staring first at the black and white birds waddling on legless feet and diving from shore into the frigid water, then at the sleek black animals with pointed snouts, and fins where legs ought to have been. "The birds look like some kind of geese, but they swim rather than fly," he concluded. "The large black beasts are certainly creatures of the sea. They have faces something like wolves with much smaller ears. And listen to that barking!"

With their attention held by the antics of the sea animals, they barely noticed the six men loading into the flagship's boat and rowing to the island. When the members of the landing party reached shore and the animals scattered before them, Elcano said, "If they're searching for water and wood, they'll be lucky to find either on that rock."

Whatever their original assignment, the shore detail soon turned its efforts to hunting the strange creatures that covered the rocky shore. In no time they had piled a number of carcasses into their boat. Trailing the fleeing animals to the other side of the island, the hunters had just disappeared from view when a squall broke upon the ships with such sudden ferocity that Magellan ordered the fleet to flee before it.

Hours later, at the end of his watch and with the storm still rampaging, Elcano relinquished command of the tossing *Concepción* to her captain and Acurio. Chindarza, who had been on Elcano's watch while Juanito slept in the hold, followed his shipmaster's steps to the captain's cabin. Quesada had been sharing his room with Elcano ever since Cartagena had been installed as a prisoner in Elcano's own small cabin, and it was a welcome sight to the half-frozen man and boy.

Elcano drew off his soaked jacket and handed it to Chindarza, who hung it on one of the seven brass pegs mounted on the wall next to the door. Master Elcano then kicked off his boots and tossed them aside before stripping off the rest of his wet clothes and draping them across the back of a wooden chair. As quickly as his numbed fingers could manage, he accepted the dry shirt that Chindarza held out to him, tugged it over his head, and let its length fall to the middle of his thighs.

Noticing the look of concern on Chindarza's face, he asked, "Something troubling you, Chindarza?"

"It's the men, sir, on the island. In this weather they may be freezing to death."

Wringing out the ends of his wet hair to lessen its dripping onto his shoulders and back, Elcano said, "Yes, lad, that thought hasn't left my mind since we sailed away without them." He looked evenly at the youth. "But they are men of the sea, Chindarza. They understand why we were forced to abandon them, just as you and I would understand if our places were reversed." He rubbed his face wearily, and said, "I have heard that a death brought about by the cold is less cruel than many others. One simply goes to sleep."

"But, Master Elcano, what about the sea wolves?"

"Our men can handle them easily enough."

"But there were so many of them, and it's so dark, sir."

Wishing to remove at least the most brutal of imaginings from the young man's mind, Elcano said, "If they lose their lives, Chindarza, it will be to the cold rather than to those beasts."

Chindarza stared down at the puddles forming around the canvas rags that covered his feet. "Then I will pray that they die painlessly, sir."

"Not that, lad, not yet anyway. Those men are a hearty lot. Pray instead that they have somehow found shelter on that island."

Holding on to this hope, Chindarza said. "Yes, sir. That will be a far better prayer."

Elcano went to his sea chest, pulled out another dry shirt, and tossed it at the boy. "Take off those rags and put this on. You're trembling from head to foot."

Chindarza's terrified eyes spoke as loudly as his startled words. "Oh, sir, forgive me, but I couldn't. Why, if the captain or Acurio saw me in your clothes, sir, they'd have me flailed."

"Nonsense, Chindarza. Anyone who wants to flail you will have to get permission from me first. Excepting the captain, of course. Now, I order you to get into that dry shirt before I start worrying about your survival too." That said, Elcano took off the amulet he always wore and hung it on a small hook protruding from the wall above his bunk. Releasing a low groan, he dropped onto the bed, yanked a cover over him, and threw his right arm over his eyes. Without looking up, he yawned so wide that his jaws creaked, and then uttered, "I'm too tired to set up a cot tonight, Chindarza, but you may sleep in here on the rug. It'll be drier and warmer than most corners of the ship. You can put your own clothes back on when you wake up. They should have shed a few pounds of water by then." When Chindarza still hesitated, Elcano said gruffly, "If I have to repeat myself..."

"Oh no, sir," the boy said, jerking his rope belt loose and tugging off his sodden shirt and pants. Quickly but with painful care to make as little noise as possible, he wrung his clothes out over a copper bucket behind the door and draped them over the back of another chair. With admiration close to awe Chindarza pulled on Elcano's borrowed shirt, a finer shirt than he'd ever hoped to wear. As he caressed a sleeve his roughened fingers reveled in its softness and his mouth widened into a smile. He looked over at his shipmaster, wanting to offer his thanks, but Elcano still lay as he had fallen with his arm across his face.

Chindarza's eyes fell on the amulet that Elcano had just taken off. About an inch in length, it was a thin glass tube encircled with a band of silver at its top and bottom. Engraved in the upper band was a short, thick cross. Chindarza had seen the talisman many times before, but tonight he wondered if it might hold some secret about Master Elcano's past, which the officer seldom chose to speak of.

"Sir?" he said softly.

"Umph?"

"May I ask what your amulet holds inside it, sir?"

Elcano mumbled, "A sliver from a tiller and a patch from a sail."

"From what ship, sir?"

Elcano lowered his arm but kept his eyes closed. "The first ship my grandfather ever sailed on. When he died, my mother gave me his amulet."

"So you would think of him sometimes, sir?"

"So I would never forget him." Elcano pried his eyes halfway open and turned his head to Chindarza. His voice grew gentle with memories. "'Tiller and sail,' he'd say, 'a man needs both to keep moving in the right direction. Stay pointed toward your goals, son, and be willing to work hard enough to reach them.' A wise man, my grandfather."

"Tiller and sail," Chindarza echoed thoughtfully.

"Yes, Chindarza. Now go to sleep."

"Yes, sir."

Chindarza blew out the lantern then curled up on half of the six-foot square rug and pulled the other half over him. He heard Elcano let out a low, satisfied grunt, which was soon followed by ragged snoring.

It took several minutes for the depleted heat of Chindarza's body to rebuild, fill the empty spaces of his cocoon, and completely quiet his shivering. During those minutes he prayed that the six men ashore would somehow be delivered from the wild creatures and the icy rain and wind. As he gradually surrendered his trust to the will of God, his eyes grew heavier and his chest lifted and fell more slowly. When his eyelids would no longer be denied a resting place, his mind wandered back to Rio de Janeiro's pleasing girls and bountiful food. He remembered the feel of hot sand beneath him, and he let out a soft sigh.

Within the rolling ship, accompanied by the external shrieking of the wind and the infrequent shouting of the seamen, Chindarza added his own snores to those of Elcano. Their inharmonious duet filled the cabin and lasted into the depths of the night.

Morning gradually scattered the clouds and cast bright rays of sunshine upon the storm-beaten ships. It muted the wind and calmed the seas just enough for Magellan's argosy to limp back to the island's small bay with the fleeting hope of recovering those they had lost. A thirty-man shore party of sailors, including Acurio and a handful of others from the *Concepción*, lost no time in rowing ashore.

Elcano watched this group's movements as they landed near the abandoned launch and searched around it. Discovering no sign of the missing men, they moved inland, but at a plodding pace that revealed their reluctance to face what they might find at the end of their hunt.

Chindarza stood near Elcano, wrapped in a sheet of canvas to fend off the chilling breeze. "If they had been able, they would have returned to the boat at first light, wouldn't they, sir?"

With little conviction, Elcano said, "Who knows where they might have found shelter? Perhaps it was a hard walk back to the skiff."

As time passed, men began to shake their heads grimly and turn from the rail to go about their regular duties. Elcano, who had not wandered far, caught sight of one dark shape after another climbing the rocks. A moment later he called out, "They're coming!"

The first four men of the search party carried what looked like a trussed up sea wolf. The next group appeared toting a similar bundle. As the rest of their number came into view, four more of the skin-swaddled creatures materialized as upright humans that stumbled toward shore with the aid of a man on each side.

"Some of them are alive!" Chindarza cried. He whirled around to Elcano. "Alive, sir!"

Elcano laughed with relief and said, "By our Holy Mother, Chindarza, as of today I'll never doubt the power of your prayers."

They watched on, Chindarza unable to hold still in his eagerness for Acurio to reboard and explain just how the men had survived.

Wet and cold though he was, Acurio was more than happy to gather the men and officers around him on the sunny deck and voice his tale. "We had a time finding them, I can tell you that much. After circling around and seeing not a sign, a number of the men with me thought the sea wolves had eaten up every trace of the poor bast—," he glanced at the captain, "the poor men. There were so many of the stinking, barking beasts that we had to knock them out of our way just to get through. We were calling out the names of our lost men when all of a sudden hundreds of sea wolves started charging toward the sea and sliding off the rocks. Even after most of them had fled we could see nothing of our missing. We were about to return to launches when, as God in heaven is my witness, one of our lost men rose right up from amidst the rocks that the sea wolves had just left."

The listeners gasped, "No!"

"Amidst the sea wolves!"

"Merde!"

Acurio nodded and scanned the tightly huddling circle of his bedraggled companions. "He rose up, I say, and then another, and another. We gathered around these three, and one of them lifted his arm and pointed at the mouth of a low cave just paces away. We'd passed within sight of the place before but we'd not seen it. Well, we made our way inside the cave and there we found our other three men all snuggled up against the bodies of more sea wolves!"

"The clever devils!"

"How is it they weren't killed and eaten, sir?"

"The way I see it," Acurio said, leaning forward, "by wrapping themselves up in the skins they'd taken when they first landed, they fooled those sea wolves into thinking they were some of their own kind. Those monsters let the men bed right down with them! It was something to see, I tell you. And whew! Their stench was mighty enough to strip pitch from a hull."

Not a voice disclaimed this announcement since potent evidence of its truth emanated from Acurio and every man who'd accompanied him ashore.

Captain Quesada asked, "Then they're *all* alive?"

"Yes, sir. The *Trinidad's* doctor may be applying his saw to a frozen foot or two, but I'd wager that every man will live."

"Praise our Lord," said Chindarza.

"Amen," several others responded.

"Amen indeed," Elcano said as he met Chindarza's smile.

The conversation was cut short when a few men jumped to their feet and requested to go ashore to hunt the sea wolves. Quesada turned to Elcano and Carvalho. "We could certainly use the skins to make some decent shoes and cloaks." This was vigorously agreed upon, and Elcano permitted Chindarza to join Acurio's new landing party.

The other ships followed the *Concepción's* lead and the island was soon swarming with seamen. Their eagerness turned to acute disappointment when they discovered that all of the sea wolves had taken to the waters and were showing no inclination toward returning. In the end, the hunters had to satisfy themselves with bringing only penguin meat and skins back to their ships.

This fresh meat was tossed into the pot and heartily celebrated by their shipmates. Much to the pleasure and entertainment of the crew, Chindarza had returned to the ship with two live penguins. These strange birds were immediately caged and placed in the middle of the main deck, where they were named, fed, and studied by all. The skins of the less fortunate penguins, after being tanned by untrained hands, made only the flimsiest of footwear and proved too thin to serve well as any other type of outer clothing.

As the fleet left the island and was again accosted by storms, the disintegration of the shoddy shoes seemed to keep pace with the decline of morale among the men. To add to their discontent, headwinds built in power until they were forceful enough to drive the fleet backward, and the assaulting cold intensified to crack and tear the skin of the hands straining to keep the ships afloat.

On one howling night while Elcano guided his ship from the half deck, a savage wind broke upon him so suddenly that it knocked him backwards against the planking. For an instant he lay there stunned, his eyes wide as they watched the stern castle's railing and spindles suddenly shatter and fly into the air. He coiled into a tight ball just before a shower of splintered wood crashed down upon him, driving shards through his clothing and skin.

He managed to crawl and stumble halfway to the captain's cabin before Acurio reached him. Helping Elcano to the captain's cabin and receiving assurances that no major injuries had been sustained, Acurio took over what remained of the watch.

Leaning against the door for a moment, Elcano gingerly removed his cloak and then the rest of his clothing. Quesada got up from his bed and lit a second lamp as Elcano draped a blanket around his cold shoulders and sank into a chair. Carefully, he reached down and pulled out a short, thin piece of wood protruding from his thigh, markedly increasing the amount of blood flowing from it.

Seeing this, Quesada went to a cabinet, drew out a handkerchief, and handed it to Elcano. "Shall I call for Bustamente?"

"No thank you, sir. None of these is serious," he said, yet he sucked in his breath as he extracted an inch long sliver from his left forearm. "I'd be grateful for the use of a needle though, sir."

After handing Elcano a large needle, Quesada filled a glass with port and set it at his elbow, and then watched Elcano methodically dig out one splinter after another.

"May I assist you?"

"I'm managing, sir. But thank you."

"The watch will soon be changing. I'll have Bustamente take a look at you when it does."

This time it was not a request and Elcano offered no objection as he concentrated on the resisting slivers. When he had removed every sizable one that he could reach, he paused to take a long drink from his cup.

Quesada had been silent for several minutes, but now he said harshly, "Curse him!"

When Elcano met his eyes, he needed no explanation as to whom he referred.

"What do you say about him now, Cano?"

It was the first time Quesada had used his informal name in months. "Sir, I'll admit, I'd surrender all my worldly goods to be back in Rio de Janeiro right now."

"He refused to listen to yours or any other suggestion. He cares *nothing* for the rest of us."

Uncomfortable with the intensity of Quesada's bitterness, Elcano said, "Well, sir, the captain-general has done all of the navigating through these many weeks. He's led us through storms that we might not have survived otherwise." When Quesada made no reply, he added, "They say he sleeps less than anyone else on his ship, eats only what his men eat, and bears the cold for hour upon hour. I've even heard that he remains cheerful regardless of the hardships."

"Cheerful!" Quesada exploded. "How dare he be cheerful when we are freezing to death! Our men haven't had a hot meal in three weeks. They have no clothing heavy enough to keep out the wet or the cold. Many of them have been pledging to join a *monastery* if they'll only be delivered from these accursed storms. Imagine!"

"Sir—."

"You know how our stores are dwindling. He drives us on and on down a coastline so desolate that we've seen no natives for six weeks. And to what end do we follow him? The passage? Did we find his precious passage within a *few* miles of the river, as he claimed we would? A few miles! We've sailed a *thousand* miles since then. Two months of storm, and cold, and *nothing* to show for it but weak men and damaged ships!" He cursed, and struggled to rein in his rage.

Unable to dispute any of this, Elcano simply said, "We have no choice but to follow him, sir."

Quesada placed his hands on the small table that stood between them and leaned closer. "Señor Cartagena and I agree that the time is coming when he *must* listen to reason. It's nearly the end of March, barely the beginning of winter here, and I hate to think what the elements will feel like in a month or two. Soon we'll have reached 49° south. Even Magellan can't intend to continue until we hit solid ice. He has to turn back. If he doesn't, many more men will die."

This last statement was voiced with such heavy sadness that Elcano could think of nothing else to say. Silently, he lifted his cup again. Before he finished his port, Quesada left him and sent Bustamente and Chindarza back to bind the worst of Elcano's cuts.

Hours later Elcano was sleeping like a corpse when he was roused by Chindarza and Juanito. "What?" he grumbled, his body aching and his eyes feeling like they'd been tarred shut.

"Master Elcano, we've found a bay!" Chindarza said.

"A bay!" chirped Juanito.

Elcano rubbed his eyelids open and sat up with a groan. "A bay, you say?" He glanced at the bandages around his thigh and his elbow, and was relieved to see that no blood had soaked through them. After flexing his sore muscles a couple of times, he got to his feet. "All right, all right. Off with you. I'll meet you on deck."

From behind sputtering clouds, the early sun glowed dimly upon the three that joined their crewmen on the stern deck as the ship sailed between bluffs towering a hundred feet above the entrance of a narrowing inlet. With every man and boy gawking at the shorelines, the fleet crept forward another half-mile, passing into a harbor where the tide still pulled roughly at the ships.

Elcano scanned the bleakness of the low hills and crags in the morning gloom. He knew that the ships couldn't sail much farther in their weather-beaten condition, but this cold, unwelcoming place was a weak comparison to the haven that Rio de Janeiro had offered. Turning toward his men, he saw disheartenment so raw that his empathy with them overshadowed much of his relief at reaching a moorage, any moorage, alive.

It was hard not to remember that, according to Magellan's promises, they should have been partaking of the comforts and wealth of the Molucca Islands by now. They should have been loading their ships with spices and silks, enjoying the bodies of the exotic island women, and feasting at heavily laden tables. Instead, they must face surviving the winter in an icy, uninhabited bay, repairing storm-torn ships in the bitter cold and eating only enough to keep them working. Worst of all, their hopes of ever finding the pass, of ever reaching the Moluccas had dwindled along with their stores of food. In the eyes of more men than he would have guessed, he saw a deadly fear.

When Captain Quesada approached, he softly voiced what Elcano knew to be the thought held by many of his crewmates. "He'll kill us all before he's through."

Weary hands worked the lines to lower the anchors, and boats were sent ashore to scout for provisions. The ships' stores were ferried ashore and the groundwork was laid for the construction of winter shelters. Men had barely learned the name that Magellan had chosen for their port before they were cursing it. San Julian.

That evening Magellan called his officers together before the provisions that stood in stacks and rows at the beaches inner edge. "Gentlemen, look at our foodstuffs. I've taken an inventory and it appears that much of what we paid for in Seville was delivered at a shortage. We were cheated. To this extent, the sabotage of our enemies was successful."

Exclamations and grumbling erupted but Magellan held up his hands for silence and it was gradually given. "I understand your anger, but such treachery will not bring about the failure of this expedition. It will simply require us to take immediate action. We have no choice but to cut our food rations in half."

"In half!" Captain Quesada roared. "Our men are drained of strength. They need *more* food, not less!"

Captain Mendoza's voice was lower in volume but just as urgent in tone. "Captain-general, we still have enough food to return to Spain. Our men have suffered enough hardship without asking this of them. The time has come to turn back."

"Yes, sir," Pilot Mendes put in, "I recommend returning to Spain immediately after we've made our repairs."

Magellan waited for them to quiet. Then, in a steady voice, he said, "I will not return to the king until our mission has been fulfilled."

"In that case, sir," said Elcano, "may we take refuge for the winter in Rio de Janeiro rather than here?"

"Has it not occurred to you, Master Elcano, that the Portuguese may well have heard of our previous stay in that port by now? They would love nothing better than for us to sail back into their grasps."

"But, sir, wouldn't that risk be less—."

Quesada cut him off by shouting, "It's absolute madness to continue under these conditions!"

All voices abruptly hushed. Magellan's eyes became hard and imperious. "I believe in the strength and forbearance of our men. They will not only survive the winter here, they will give us cause to praise their efforts when we set sail for the Spiceries in the spring. My order to remain in Port San Julian is final. It is your duty, gentlemen, to carry it out." With a wave of his hand to the officers of the *Trinidad*, he strode in his limping gate away from the others.

Quesada's eyes touched on Elcano before turning to Captain Mendoza. The three drifted away from the rest of the officers until they had reached a safe distance. Quesada said just above a whisper, "We will meet with Captain Cartagena aboard the *Concepción* an hour after nightfall."

Hearing this restoration of Cartagena's previous title of authority, Elcano felt a slight twisting of his gut.

# Easter Night

## 8

Made even darker by the clouds that eclipsed the moon and the stars, night's blanket concealed the *Victoria's* launch as it rowed quietly toward the *Concepción*. Once there, Captain Mendoza scaled the rope ladder and headed straight to the captain's cabin. Cartagena, Elcano, and Captain Quesada were already waiting. Pilot Carvalho, a Portuguese, was notably absent.

After softly bolting the door, Quesada said, "Welcome, Captain," and offered Mendoza a chair beside his own. "Let's speak directly to the point, gentlemen," said Quesada. "We have met here to discuss how to deal with Magellan. First, allow me to restate our situation. Tomorrow is Easter Sunday and we will spend it aboard crippled ships in a desolate land that lies farther to the south than any craft has ever sailed. We have labored for over nine months under the command of a Portuguese captain-general that from the time we left the Canary Islands has refused to follow the king's designated sailing route. He has blatantly and repeatedly disregarded the royal order to keep his captains informed of any route changes and to consult with them on significant matters related to this voyage.

"When Magellan was confronted because of his actions, Captain Cartagena was arrested and humiliated as if he were a traitor. Now, and I no longer have any doubt of this, he has led us far beyond the place where he told the king we would find the westward passage. He *doesn't know* where it is, which likely means that there really is no such channel. As some of us have suspected all along, he may well have planned this expedition to *confirm that no such passage exists* rather than to sail to the Moluccas. I don't have to tell you what a boon such a confirmation would give to Portugal or what a blow it would deliver to Spain."

Cartagena lifted a hand to Quesada, who nodded for him to speak. "As inexcusable as his treatment of me has been, his reason was clearly to replace me with a man of his choosing. But now he orders all of us to winter in this miserable place because he must avoid returning to Spain. If he does not find this questionable passage, he will be proven false. So he *must* find it or wait for a chance to replace all of us Spanish officers with Portuguese puppets."

"We three," said Mendoza, indicating himself, Cartagena and Captain Quesada, "have been chosen personally by King Carlos to serve not only as captains, but as the fleet's treasurer and her inspector general. These positions of trust and responsibility were neither assigned nor accepted lightly. It is our sworn duty to protect our ships, our men, and the integrity of this voyage. He has already cost us the lives of three men and has jeopardized all of our crews. We are obligated to take action before he causes an all-out uprising."

In the pause that followed, Quesada noticed Elcano's silence and he said to him, "Speak up, Cano. What have you to say?"

"Captain, I wish to know what action you are proposing."

Cartagena answered for him. "We mean to take the command of the *San Antonio* away from that imposter, Mesquita, and to restore it to a captain rightfully appointed by the king. When we once again hold the majority of the ships, we will present Magellan with a petition demanding that he disclose the details of his proposed route. If, as we all believe, his route is nothing but a pretense, he will be exposed for what he is; a traitor to the Spanish Crown."

"And then, sir?" Elcano asked quietly.

"If he declines our petition, we, as designees of King Carlos and under the maritime Laws of Rhodes and Oleron, are clearly entitled to refuse to sail under his command. We will be within our rights to replace him as captain-general with one of our own. If he refuses either to return to Spain or to step down, we will arrest him and take him back for trial."

Elcano shot Cartagena a startled look, but Quesada added smoothly, "None of us believes that this will be necessary. Magellan is no fool. He will agree to turn back toward Spain when we make it clear that we no longer accept his ruse. Yes, he'll deem that preferable to surrendering his command. Most likely he'll make it appear to the men that it is his idea to head back. When we land in Spain, he may try to escape or he may attempt to convince the king that he was given false information about the passage and that none of this was his fault."

Elcano asked, "What if the passage truly does exist, sir, just farther to the south?"

Cartagena flared. "If a passage lies to the south, another expedition will find it, one that hasn't been deceived, manipulated, and recklessly endangered by a foreigner! Master Elcano, need I remind you that your first loyalty is to your king? Your second is to your captain. You, of all men, should know this."

Elcano felt the sting of his words, felt the shame of his past surge to life. His cheeks burned as he said tightly, "Yes, sir. I know this well."

"Then you also know that it is your duty not only to obey our orders but to persuade others to act with us," Cartagena pushed on. "It will take the actions of a majority of the fleet for our endeavor to fall within the law, and for it to succeed. We already have the *Concepción* and the *Victoria*. We need the *San Antonio*. Tomorrow, after midnight, we will board her and take her back. Many of my men are still loyal to me. I need only send word to Coca to be ready."

Quesada's tone became persuasive, "Master Elcano, we need you to speak to our men and to your friend, Elorriaga."

"I believe he will stand with us," said Cartagena. "Before my command was stolen, he served me well. Still, he is independent in his thinking and may need to be reminded of his duty."

Elcano asked Quesada pointedly, "We mean only to present our petition and to take actions within the law, sir?"

"We will stay within our rights and hold to the bonds of our duty," Cartagena cut in again. "You must speak to Elorriaga tomorrow after Easter mass. Neither Captain Mendoza nor Captain Quesada will be attending the service. They will also be absent from the dinner that the captain-general has invited them to attend aboard the *Trinidad*. Their failure to appear will serve as a warning that we mean to have our voices heeded when next we meet. With the majority of the fleet behind us, he will have no choice but to consult in good faith, and to reveal his empty hand."

Elcano cast a questioning glance at Quesada.

"You've heard my orders, Cano."

Elcano lowered his eyes and nodded twice.

"Good," said Cartagena, rising. "If all goes well tomorrow, gentlemen, we'll be sailing for home the day afterward. Now, someone had better put these damned shackles back on before any of the men sees me without them."


During the morning service, Magellan gave no sign of noticing the absence of Captains Quesada and Mendoza. Afterward Elorriaga and Elcano ambled off together down the chilly, inhospitable beach.

Elorriaga studied his friend in silence until they had walked a good distance from the others, then he asked, "What's afoot? Where is your captain?"

Watching Elorriaga's face cloud with each new revelation, Elcano told him everything that was about to unfold.

At last Elorriaga demanded gruffly, "You've agreed to be a part of all this?"

"I swore an oath of loyalty to our king."

Struggling to keep his voice down, Elorriaga said, "You swore an oath of loyalty to the captain-general as well."

"Of the two, who should take precedence over the other?"

Elorriaga quieted at this question, considering. "In the end, we must first obey the wishes of our own ship's captain. He is our immediate commander."

"Señor Cartagena was your first captain."

"But he is my captain no longer."

"You would follow Mesquita, knowing his incompetence better than any of us?"

With sad resignation, Elorriaga said, "Juan Sebastian, he is still my captain."

In a tone that matched Elorriaga's, Elcano said, "And Captain Quesada is mine."

"Then our separate paths are chosen."

"Yes, I guess they are."

Elorriaga gave a kick to the sand at his feet. "Damn the quarrels of proud men."

"We may all be damned if this isn't resolved with calm heads rather than the waving of swords."

"Yes, let's pray it doesn't come to violence."

"I already have prayed, and will continue to do so."

Their eyes met and held once more. "May God keep you safe," said Elorriaga.

"And you, my friend."

They parted with reluctance, rejoining their respective parties that had already begun boarding the launches.


The men were kept aboard the ships for the remainder of the day. Shellfish that had been gathered the afternoon before and fresh sea wolf meat were served as an Easter feast. But even as they savored these rich foods, Elcano noticed the men glancing at him and Quesada uneasily and muttering in low voices. As if they were watching the first flashes of lightning of a gathering storm, he knew they sensed and dreaded the impending clash between their leaders. When night fell at last and no tempest of wills had yet descended upon them, many took to their blankets with a sigh of relief.

Before long, however, men on the decks of the *Concepción* were tapped on the back and beckoned to follow Acurio to the half deck. Some were surprised to see Cartagena standing fully armed before them. Many were not. While the ship's launch was being made ready, the seaman blackened their faces with charcoal and took up their weapons.

Captain Quesada turned to Elcano and Acurio. "Watch over the ship. I know I leave her in good hands."

"Sir—," Elcano began, but Quesada stopped him.

"I know what you would say, Cano, but the time has passed for talking. We must follow the instructions of our king. We must protect the lives of our men. Be prepared for any response."

Quesada, Cartagena, and their coal-faced men loaded into a longboat with oars muffled by skins, and pushed off into the clammy fog. They were lost from Elcano's sight almost immediately.

"I fear the lust for vengeance that is in Señor Cartagena's eyes, sir," whispered Acurio.

Elcano had noticed it too, and he now strained to hear something, anything beyond the rail where they stood. All was eerily silent, as if the sea itself had been hushed.

When the launch touched against the side of the *San Antonio*, it was joined moments later by the *Victoria's* skiff, whose captain had remained aboard his ship according to plan. A password was whispered to Antonio de Coca, waiting on the deck above them. Without further words, the boarders nimbly scaled the ropes and eased themselves over the main deck's railing. A few men that had been sleeping in quiet corners stirred, but they were immediately silenced by ready swords and the hissed message, "Captain Cartagena is reclaiming his ship." Two men from the boarding party hurried to guard the *San Antonio's* armory while the others slipped down into the hold where most of the hands were wrapped in their sleeping blankets. Caught unaware, no resistance was offered from those below decks.

Cartagena, Quesada, and several of their men loped to the captain's cabin and threw open the door to startle a slumbering Mesquita. At the intrusion, he bolted upright in his bunk and demanded groggily, "What is it!" He was grabbed, hauled from his bed and held fast by two men.

"We have taken the ship," said Cartagena icily, "and now, you. Will you agree to follow my command?"

"Your command! The devil take you all!"

Cartagena smiled with approval. "Shackle him. Lock him in the clerk's cabin."

His guards complied so swiftly that Mesquita was given no time to oppose them. Amid the rattle of chains and curses of protest, they shoved him into the smaller abutting cabin.

"You three, stand guard," Cartagena ordered, pointing out the men.

He and Quesada hastened back to the half deck where they heard the approach of a determined, angry voice. Quesada whirled around and confronted the newly awakened Elorriaga, who stormed toward him armed with nothing more than the ferocity in his eyes.

"Captain Quesada!" Elorriaga barked, his chest heaving and his feet planting themselves not three feet in front of Quesada. "In the name of God and King I demand that you release our captain and return to your own ship!"

"Keep quiet, Elorriaga, and you won't be harmed!"

"Where's Captain Mesquita?" Elorriaga raised his voice to a shout, "Captain? Captain Mesquita?"

A ring of men from the *Concepción* closed around the officers, their hands clasping the hilts of their swords. Glaring at Elorriaga, Quesada snarled, "Are we to be thwarted by this idiot?"

The *San Antonio's* boatswain tried to edge forward to stand beside Elorriaga, but his shipmaster pushed him back and snapped. "Arm the men, Hernandez. Free the captain at once." But Hernandez was seized before he could either move or speak. Elorriaga's eyes bored into Quesada. "You will not take this ship!"

"I already have," said Quesada.

"This is treason! Treason!" Elorriaga thundered, taking a step toward him.

Quesada moved so swiftly that only a reflecting flash of lantern light revealed the dagger he snatched from his belt and thrust at Elorriaga's throat. Elorriaga jerked back and to the side in an effort to evade the strike, then grunted in pain as the knife bit into his chest two inches above his heart. Amid stunned gasps and cries from the *San Antonio's* crew, Elorriaga called out once more, "Treason!" In answer, Quesada raised the knife again.

Unarmed as he was, Elorriaga could do nothing but back into the corner against the rail and raise his arms to protect his neck and chest from the coming blow. The plunging knife sliced deep into his right arm, severing skin, muscle, and tendon. Even as Elorriaga yelled out in rage and pain, the dagger came down again and ripped into his left arm. The blade rose and fell again and again, until Elorriaga stumbled to his left and his slashed and bleeding arms fell helplessly to his sides, leaving an open target. Quesada did not hesitate. Drawing his arm back, he drove his blade deep into Elorriaga's belly.

Elorriaga groaned but stared in angry defiance, holding Quesada's fevered gaze even as he fell forward and the knife was pulled from his body.

Hernandez, whose shouted pleas to stop the attack had been ignored, jerked free of his captors and dropped to Elorriaga's side. A handful of his shipmates pressed forward to help him while others glanced about in search of a weapon.

Still grasping the bloody knife in his hand, Quesada hissed to his men, "Keep your swords drawn, and cut down any man who moves against us." When he turned to Cartagena, his fellow conspirator's face revealed a dreadful resignation. "Secure the ship," Quesada ordered his men, and they jumped to obey.

The *San Antonio's* three Portuguese crewmen were soon shackled and tossed into the hold. With Mesquita chained in the clerk's cabin, and Elorriaga's blood forming an expanding pool of crimson on the planks of the half deck in spite of Hernandez's efforts to stop the flow, Quesada's demand was quickly met. As soon as he received assurances that all was under control, Quesada had his men bring Pilot Mafra before his old captain.

Juan Rodríguez de Mafra stood rigid but unfettered in front of Cartagena, who said, "Pilot, you once served me loyally. I expect you to show Captain Quesada the same constancy. For now, he will oversee the commands of the *San Antonio*, the *Concepción*, and the *Victoria*."

Mafra addressed Quesada stonily, giving sharp precision to each of his words. "Forgive me, sir, but after what has befallen Master Elorriaga, I am unable to comply with your commands."

Showing neither surprise nor disappointment, Cartagena waved a hand at Mafra's two guards. "Take him below and chain him with the others."

Quesada turned to head toward Mesquita's cabin and noticed Hernandez still clumsily attending to his wounded shipmaster. To a group of men standing close by, Quesada said, "Take Master Elorriaga to his cabin and let the ship's barber see to him."

Leading Cartagena to the captain's cabin and shutting the door, Quesada said, "Now that Elorriaga and Mafra are of no use to us, we need help sailing this ship. Is there any chance that Hernandez will cooperate?"

"He's as faithful to Elorriaga as an old dog." Allowing some of his dissatisfaction to show, Cartagena stared penetratingly and said, "Your attack on Elorriaga has made our task much more difficult."

Quesada bristled at the rebuke. "You saw what happened. I had to silence him before he brought the whole fleet down upon us."

"Enough. It's done. As you said, we need help sailing the *San Antonio*." They both considered their options for several moments.

Thinking aloud, Quesada mumbled, "The *San Antonio's* men seem willing to trust neither of us now. They admire Elcano, and they know he's Elorriaga's friend. They're not as likely to blame him for what has happened here. Yes, with his experience..." His voice trailed off, but returned with conviction as he looked over at Cartagena. "We'll bring Elcano over to master this ship, let him command it even. He's the best choice under the circumstances. Elcano will hate leaving the *Concepción*, but he'll follow my orders. I'll remain here but in the background."

"But Elcano *is* Elorriaga's friend. I don't doubt his present allegiance to you, but he'll soon learn that it was you who attacked Elorriaga."

"Once Elcano is here, he'll understand that he has no choice but to carry out our plan."

"Perhaps, but we must keep what's happened to Elorriaga from him for as long as possible. For now it would be best to tell him only that the officers are locked in the small cabins and in the hold. I'll bring Hernandez back to the *Concepción* to keep him from rousing the *San Antonio's* men. And I want Acurio to remain with me."

"Elcano won't like that either, but yes. You'll need Acurio to act as shipmaster during Elcano's absence."

They carried out this proposal at once by sending out a skiff to bring Elcano over to the *San Antonio*. In the meantime, Quesada ordered the steward to open the stores of food and let the men eat as much as they wanted. Initially refusing to do so, Steward Gopeguy was threatened and shoved until he pried open the lids of barrel after barrel of the horded supplies. Men and boys snatched up the sea biscuits and salted meat, and wolfed them down. Wine too was doled out, but in measures deemed just enough to sway the men's moods. And all the while, the crewmembers were warned to keep their voices low. Those who failed or forgot to heed this warning were quickly silenced by a sharp blow with a ship's billet.

Elcano heard nothing suspicious until his launch drew to within twenty feet of the *San Antonio*. He boarded the ship wondering why so many men were moving about, and his expression hardened to grimness when he saw them filling their arms with more food than they could carry and dropping precious handfuls here and there about the deck.

"Where is Captain Quesada?" he demanded of the first seaman he saw. In answer, several arms lifted and pointed to the captain's cabin. Elcano spotted Gopeguy standing over the barrels, and strode over to him. Raising his voice just loud enough for most of the sailors to hear, he said, "Steward, if any man has taken one *crumb* more than he is able to eat within five minutes, he is to return the excess at once or you are to report his name directly to me. Is that clear?"

Visibly relieved, Gopeguy said, "Yes sir," and immediately went in search of parchment and pen.

As Elcano left the main deck, men were already moving to replenish the barrels. Climbing distractedly to Mesquita's cabin, he found Quesada and Cartagena deep in conversation, but they quieted at once when he stepped through the open doorway.

He offered a quick bow and said, "Sirs, the men in the launch brought me little word except that I am to assume command of this ship. Is this true?"

"For the present, yes," said Quesada.

"I don't understand, Captain."

"It's quite simple. We feel that the crew of the *San Antonio* will more readily follow your commands than ours."

"But I'm needed aboard the *Concepción*, sir."

"You are needed here more. Until you are told otherwise, Cano, you will master the *San Antonio*. I order you to do so for the good of the fleet."

Elcano studied Quesada's face, then Cartagena's. "What has happened, sir, that would warrant such an order?"

Quesada stated more firmly. "We have little time for further explanations. Señor Cartagena must leave at once for the *Concepción*. I have work to attend to in this cabin and you have this ship to command. See to it at once."

Cartagena immediately headed for the launch and Quesada closed the door behind Elcano, leaving him to stand outside and wrestle with a greater number of questions than he had brought with him aboard the *San Antonio*.

In only moments, however, Gopeguy quietly scaled the steps to the half deck and cautiously approached Elcano.

"What is it Gopeguy?"

The steward glanced around, then murmured, "Look to your left, sir, on the deck in the corner."

Elcano's glaze swept to the dark spill for the first time. Taking a lantern from its hook on the wall, he drew nearer and crouched down beside the puddle. He touched two fingers to it, rubbed them with his thumb, and then brought his hand close to the lantern. When he straightened again, he hesitated before asking, "Whose?"

"Master Elorriaga's, sir."

The lantern twitched in Elcano's hand and the words echoed in his head like the tolling of a bell. At the same time, the smell of the blood rose to his nostrils and his stomach knotted. Forcing himself, he asked, "Is he dead?"

"Not yet, sir, but he's badly wounded."

Elcano stared straight ahead, seeing nothing, then very slowly turned his eyes toward the door to the captain's cabin. He did not step toward it even when Gopeguy said, "It was him that did it, sir. Captain Quesada himself. Master Elorriaga wasn't even armed."

Snapping his gaze back to Gopeguy, Elcano's face darkened and his breathing deepened until he suddenly lurched toward Quesada's cabin. A pace before it he jerked himself to a halt, took three heaving breaths to gain control, then pivoted and reached the steward in two long strides. Grasping Gopeguy by the arm, he demanded, "Where is he now?"

"In his cabin, sir. Our barber did what he could to care for him, sir, but Father Calmette thought it best to give him his last rites. They're both with him now."

Elcano released his hold and let his hand fall to his side. "Is he conscious?"

"Only for a short time now and again, sir."

"Where was he wounded?"

"His arms, his chest, and his belly, sir.'

Silently groaning, Elcano lowered his head. After a few moments had passed, he said hollowly, "It may give him little comfort now but, if he wakens, tell him that I am here. And if he calls for me or...worsens, send for me at once."

"Yes, sir."

When Gopeguy hesitated in departing, Elcano looked up and asked, "Was anyone else wounded?"

"No, sir. Just Master Elorriaga."

Elcano said barely above a whisper, "Just Master Elorriaga."

Bender

"I...I'm sorry, sir."

"Go to him now, Gopeguy."

With a nod, the steward left him.

Moving to the rail, Elcano forced his lungs to draw in the soggy air. He lifted his face to the murky sky and silently cursed Quesada, then he cursed himself, and then every man ever born to the sea. Bitterly, he muttered, "We're bloody, bloody fools, all of us. We hoped to bring reason to a perilous cause, and what have we done?"

With another breath he whispered, "Juan," closed his eyes, and began to pray.

The sounds of the men on the main deck below finally brought his thoughts back to the *San Antonio* and compelled him to consider what must be done. He was in command of a rebellious ship aboard which his good friend had been wounded, perhaps fatally, by his superior officer, a superior officer he was still duty-bound to obey.

Elcano understood that Elorriaga's wounding had triggered much more than his personal anguish. It had all but erased any chance for a peaceful discussion with Magellan. There was little telling how the captain-general would react once he learned of the violence brought against one of his favorite officers. When their activities became known, Magellan might even open fire on them. Although it was hard to believe that Magellan would respond with so little restraint, especially since the *San Antonio* possessed the greatest firepower in the fleet, Quesada and Cartagena had left Elcano no choice but to prepare for the worst.

Pushing away from the rail, Elcano ordered the ship's cabin boys to clean up the stain of blood. Next he had the men ready the cannons and guns, and train them on the *Trinidad* at the mouth of the harbor. So far no sign had been given that the other ships, still muffled and shrouded by the fog, were aware of what had taken place aboard the *San Antonio*. Morning would be soon enough for Magellan to learn that three of his five ships were held by men willing to use force in order to have a voice in the destiny of this voyage.

Quesada made no appearance and for that much Elcano was grateful. He was not yet certain he could maintain mastery of himself in the man's presence, and the last thing the fleet needed now was more violence among its officers. Once all was ready, he ordered most of the crew to their rest while he paced the stern deck with troubled steps.

The waiting for any word from Gopeguy, for the sun's light to reveal the outcome of this Easter night's work, and for an answer to what he should have done to prevent Elorriaga's wounding; this was a terrible penance.

# Chained

## 9

After a night burdened with a year's misgivings, Elcano watched the sun's first light sift through a misty shroud of loose clouds. The fog slowly thinned and ascended, allowing just enough visibility to behold the flagship's launch rowing away from the *Trinidad* and heading directly toward him. As the sailors in the boat drew near the *San Antonio*, Elcano held himself back from their view and read their faces, saying to himself, "They don't know."

Without showing the slightest sign of wariness, they pulled close in and a heavily bundled man called out to the hands above, "Well lads, who's to come ashore to gather water this morning? Why aren't they boarded and ready at their oars?"

A seaman leaned over the ship's rail and said, "You men are to tell your commander that Captain Gaspar de Quesada now oversees the authority of the *San Antonio*, the *Victoria*, and the *Concepción*. No further orders will be taken from the captain-general until he agrees to meet in good faith with the other captains."

Stunned speechless for an instant, the men in the skiff quickly recovered themselves enough to grasp their oars and heave away. As they rowed back toward their mother ship rather than to shore, Elcano could feel the eyes of his crew, some hostile, some fearful, and some steadfast, turn toward him. Their gazes drifted away, however, when Quesada came to stand beside him.

Elcano's muscles stiffened and it took a moment and a great effort to ease them. He faced his commanding officer only when he was confident that he could do so with an outward look of control.

Without meeting his eyes, Quesada said, "I have been drafting a message for the captain-general that I wish you to read. It will be delivered to Captains Mendoza and Cartagena for their signatures, then on to Magellan."

Elcano's implacable silence was more powerful than any words he might have uttered.

Quesada shifted uneasily, and finally said, "The letter is on my desk."

Before Quesada could leave, Elcano stepped beside him and said, "One moment, sir." Then he called to a nearby hand, "Bring us news of Master Elorriaga." Neither officer moved or spoke until Gopeguy came to them on weary legs.

After offering a short bow, the steward said, "Sirs, Master Elorriaga still lives, but he lies pale as death and his breathing is feeble. He's lost more blood than I ever conceived a body could hold."

Elcano said, "As long as he breathes, we may yet hope, Gopeguy. See that he's well tended, and that his caretakers know to report to me at the change of every watch. Now get some rest."

"Yes, sir. Thank you, sir."

"And, Gopeguy," Elcano added, "the stain of blood on the half deck can yet be seen. Now that we have the daylight, the cabin boys are to remove it completely."

"I'll set them to it at once, sir."

Without addressing Quesada, Elcano slowly pivoted and directed his steps to the captain's cabin. Once there, he unclenched his fists, threw off his damp cloak, and picked up Quesada's letter. Frowning, he scanned the lines that enumerated the occasions upon which Magellan had failed to follow the king's instructions and the resulting sufferings of the officers and men. Quesada explained that they had resorted to taking the ships to ensure that the welfare of the men and the council of the officers would be attended to in the future. If Magellan agreed from this day hence to follow the orders of the king, every man would faithfully obey him.

The letter could not have sounded more reasonable, but Quesada's words were now tainted with Elorriaga's blood.

Did Quesada hope that Magellan, once he learned of it, would ignore this fact? On the other hand, Quesada was at least trying to resolve their situation without resorting to full-fledged war. If it came to that, Elcano knew there would be no victors, only survivors.

Letting the paper fall to the desk, he rubbed his hands over his cold, tired face. If it was true that God blessed fools, as his mother often claimed, his prayers of the night before had at least a chance of being heard. He moved to the rumpled bunk and rolled onto it, surrendering his bruised and exhausted mind and body to a sleep that would no longer be denied. He did not stir when Quesada came in, sealed and wrapped the letter, and departed with it.

Hours later, however, Elcano was awakened when Quesada reentered the room calling his name and clasping another letter in his hand. Holding it up, he said, "This is Magellan's response. He's invited the captains to his ship to talk." He gave a short, skeptical laugh. "Does he think we've forgotten how he snared Cartagena? Still, there's a chance he may be willing to talk."

Elcano, his body feeling as if it were anchored to the bunk, pushed to a sitting position and peered in the direction of the desk as Quesada scribbled an answering note.

"There. I've requested that he meet with us here. We shall see if he was merely setting a trap or if he's willing to listen to reason." Quesada folded and sealed the letter before leaving as abruptly as he had come.

Elcano eased himself up from the bed to see to the ship. As the daylight hours passed, he saw the San Antonio's launch row to the *Concepción* and back, then to the *Victoria* and back. After each return, Quesada went to his cabin and later emerged with a slightly revised letter.

The men in the *San Antonio's* launch, already hungry and cold, pushed off yet again to deliver the latest letter to the *Trinidad*. The sea was swelling and the wind strengthening as they pulled hard against the oars to cross the bay and reach the flagship. Once they finally grabbed hold of the lines at her side, they were again ordered to wait for a reply. A short time later, word was passed down that they were welcome to board and have a warm bite to eat while the captain-general was writing. No one hesitated.

They were greeted on deck with a generous cup of wine and the best meal they'd eaten in months. While they supped, they were wrapped in dry blankets and sheltered under the eave of the foredeck, where their cups were filled again and again. To their amazement, they had no more than emptied their plates before being invited to the captain-general's own cabin, and they all found him to be the most congenial of hosts. Within minutes they were drinking his fine port and telling him all about the overthrow of the *San Antonio*, about the wounding of poor Master Elorriaga, and about how many men were still loyal to him. The drink continued to flow so freely that they soon grew drowsy and could think of no reason to turn down the good captain-general's offer to take a short rest there aboard his ship that evening.

The dusk deepened while the *Trinidad's* guests were helped below to find a place to sleep, a sleep so sound that none of them stirred as the men on the main deck quietly moved their launch to the side of the *Trinidad* that could not be seen from the decks of the *San Antonio*.

It was not long before it had grown dark enough to conceal Master-at-arms Espinosa and three of his mariners as they boarded the *Trinidad's* skiff and rowed toward the *Victoria* rather than the waiting *San Antonio*.

Not until they were within forty yards did a call of, "Stand away!" come from the *Victoria's* lookout to foretell her crew of Espinosa's arrival.

Espinosa's men lifted their oars. Keeping his voice down, Espinosa said, "I have a message from the captain-general for Captain Mendoza."

Mendoza appeared at the rail. "Hand your message to one of my men, Espinosa."

In a surprised tone, Espinosa said, "Do sixty strong men and an able captain have anything to fear from so small a party, sir?"

"Hand up your message or move off," Mendoza warned.

"Forgive me, Captain, but I was ordered to surrender a letter into your hands only, and in private."

Mendoza paused, considering the practical reasons for such an order. "Are you armed?"

Espinosa and his companions opened their cloaks wide, revealing nothing but an empty belt and clothing.

"Very well then, but only two of you may come aboard."

Espinosa and one of his men scaled the ropes to the ship's main deck, and proceeded to the captain's cabin. When three of Mendoza's men moved to follow them inside, Espinosa cleared his throat, "I'm sorry, Captain, but I have been given authority to relay certain...offers that must not be shared with your men until an agreement has been reached. The offers are very tenuous in nature."

Mendoza studied his visitor. "I understand," he said at last. "You men, wait outside."

With the closing of the door, Espinosa took from his jacket an oilskin wrapped letter, and handed it to Mendoza.

The captain's eyes moved across the few lines and a sneer began to form on his mouth. "So now it is just I who is being asked to come to the flagship. I already know of the invitation he sent to Captain Quesada. The captain-general should know that I am no more likely to be caught in so obvious a trap than he is."

Shaking his head in disappointment, Espinosa accepted the paper and tucked it back into his jacket.

Mendoza said, "Tell your master that if he intends—."

Espinosa's right hand darted to the back of his belt as he leaped behind Mendoza, grabbed a handful of his hair, wrenched his head far back, and drove a dagger deep into his throat. The master-at-arms yanked his blade free but held the captain's head pinned back, and Espinosa's companion thrust his knife up between Mendoza's throat and chin. The power behind the thrust forced the blade through his skin, tongue, cartilage, and brain until its tip imbedded itself into his skull.

Without releasing his hold on Mendoza's hair, Espinosa lunged back to avoid the fountain of blood that spewed from the gored neck. He then lowered the body of his former superior officer, a captain appointed by the king himself, with more gentleness than he would have used if he'd been handling glass. After motioning for the sailor to guard the door, Espinosa paused just long enough to close Mendoza's eyes, and whisper, "Your words were most unwise, Captain. He caught you in his trap after all."

Taking up a lantern, Espinosa passed it back and forth across the cabin window that faced the *Trinidad*. He lowered the lantern and squinted in that direction for several moments, and at last mouthed the words to his blood-stained accomplice, "They're coming."

To avoid raising the suspicions of the guards outside the door, Espinosa spoke in undertones, as if still in conversation with Mendoza. He glanced often out the window to gauge the progress of the advancing longboat, and silently relayed its distance to his fellow assassin.

Although it seemed otherwise to those who shared the dead man's cabin, the launch from the *Trinidad* arrived within only a few minutes. Just as Magellan's brother-in-law, Duarte Barbosa, and his fifteen men clambered to the *Victoria's* main deck, Espinosa snatched up Mendoza's sword and burst through his doorway, shouting, "Captain Mendoza is dead! Long live the king and death to all traitors! Who stands with Captain-general Magellan?"

Caught unprepared by the *Trinidad's* sword waving forces, and even more so by the news of their captain's death, the crew the *Victoria* surrendered without a struggle.

Aboard the *San Antonio* Elcano was awakened from sleep, this time by a cabin boy rather than Quesada. Unwilling to shake the shipmaster even in his excitement, the boy repeatedly called his name. "Please, Master Elcano, Captain Quesada is asking for you! Something's wrong aboard the *Victoria!*"

Elcano got up swaying on his feet and rubbing hard at his eyes. "All right, boy. Go along. I'll be on your heels." He grabbed his cloak, tossed it over his shoulders, and leaned into the cold wind that blasted him as he left the cabin.

Elcano found Quesada waiting for him in the corner of the stern deck farthest from the aft lanterns.

In a voice made dreadful by its finality, the captain said, "He's taken the *Victoria*."

Even as these words were being uttered, Elcano looked helplessly on as the *Victoria* settled into position between the *Trinidad* and the *Santiago*. The three ships now effectively blocked the exit to the harbor. Their gun ports gaped open and ready.

Quesada's voice became chillingly distant, almost philosophical. "Have you ever played the game of chess, Cano?"

"How could Mendoza have been so easily taken? How?"

"If we were playing chess now, Magellan and I, he would be saying 'check'. He has us. Unless we are willing to expend the lives of many men, he has us."

Elcano's eyes skimmed across the faces of the men and boys that also lined the rails to stare uncertainly out at the challenging three ships. The thought of them torn and bleeding like Elorriaga made him demand, "Surely, that is not your intention."

Quesada gave him a sad, painful smile. "My intentions are still forming. But if we surrender our arms there's no telling what Magellan will devise as our punishment. For me, because of Elorriaga and my leadership in this, it will be harsh. I need to speak with Cartagena and Coca before I decide our next move."

"Do you think he's killed Captain Mendoza, sir?"

"Do *you*?"

Elcano looked again toward the *Victoria*, searching her frame as if she alone could give them an answer. Then at last, he said, "Yes."

"Cano," said Quesada, "send someone to the *Concepción* for Captain Cartagena. We may have little time."

Quesada met with Cartagena, Coca, and Elcano in the captain's cabin only briefly before he ordered Mesquita to be brought from the clerk's cabin. The former captain of the *San Antonio* was seated and unchained. Quesada dismissed the guards and said, "I've brought you here to ask you to speak to the captain-general for the survival of the fleet. Since he is your cousin, he may listen to you."

Mesquita stared at him incredulously. "The survival of the fleet? After you've taken my ship, wounded my shipmaster, and shackled me like a criminal? I'll see every one of you hanged!"

Quesada slapped his hand upon the desk. "Think, man! Before you refuse, think what Magellan might do if he is not made to see reason. The survival of the fleet *is* at stake. If he reacts savagely, what will it mean to our chances of reaching the Moluccas or of returning to Spain? What if he decides to have all of us executed? What then? How will the rest of you survive when even more men turn against you? And if by some miracle you do return to Spain, what manner of reception will you receive once the king learns that Magellan has killed his Spanish officers? He will know that it was brought about by ruthlessness and treachery, and not every seaman will fail to tell what has really happened on this voyage."

Mesquita straightened in his chair. "You deceive yourself, Captain, if you believe he will listen to me over his own council. Even if I were willing, it would be useless for me to try to convince him of anything."

"I ask you to reconsider."

"I will not."

Quesada yelled for the guards, and Mesquita was chained again and led away. The wind began to howl outside as Quesada's gaze touched upon each of the others. "Our choices are few; surrender or try to break through his blockade and sail for home." All were silent until Quesada went on, "I say we try to ease past them. We will tell Mesquita that we've decided to accept Magellan's offer to talk aboard the flagship. We'll approach as if we intend to anchor close to the *Trinidad*, and we'll position Mesquita at the prow to tell them to hold their fire. If we have a chance for flight as we near them, we'll take it."

Elcano asked, "And if there is no chance for flight, sir?"

"Then we must be prepared to fight."

Cartagena said, "I agree."

120

Quesada looked at Coca, who hesitated, then at Elcano.

Slowly, Elcano said, "If escape is not possible without loosening our guns against our own countrymen, I advise that we abandon our plans."

Quesada said, "Do you mean that we should surrender?"

Elcano's gaze did not waver. "I do, sir."

Quesada pursed his lips, tapped on his table, then rose from his chair. "Thank you for your thoughts, gentlemen. I will consider them, but it is my responsibility to lead you tomorrow in whatever action I deem best. We have several hours before dawn. Use them well to prepare for whatever may come."

Elcano already knew where he would head after he left the cabin, and he wasted no time before taking up a lantern and making his way to Elorriaga's room. He'd received reports on Elorriaga's condition regularly and had prepared himself for what his friend's appearance would be. Even so, as he stood over Elorriaga's blanketed body and shiny, pale face, he felt his heart tighten. For a terrible moment, Elcano could see no rising or falling of his friend's chest, and he glanced quickly at Gopeguy sitting beside the bunk.

"He is still with us, sir," said the steward gently.

Elcano lifted the blankets and his nose was met by the smell of blood, sweat, and the first hint of contamination. Breathing shallowly, he examined the stitched lacerations on Elorriaga's chest and abdomen, and the bandages that enwrapped both forearms. Only traces of red seeped from the wounds and through the cloth. The care of Gopeguy and the others was obvious, as obvious as the death that hung in the air around him. Elcano replaced the blankets, and leaned close to Elorriaga's ear. "Juan, it's Juan Sebastian."

There was no response other than a soft groan.

"Juan, I've come to see you," he tried again, but his thickening voice cracked. He closed his eyes and lowered his forehead to the bunk by Elorriaga's shoulder.

Gopeguy rose and left him to whatever comfort privacy might give him.

Elcano lifted his red eyes and whispered, "Juan, you must not die."

There was a small movement under the covers, as Elorriaga, his eyes still closed, tried to lift his hand. Weakly, he moaned in pain.

Elcano's words came out in a rush as he touched Elorriaga's shoulder. "Don't move, Juan. Please, don't move. There now. There. Rest again."

Elcano said no more to Elorriaga. Instead he took up a conversation with God, asking for the survival of his friend.

Gopeguy rejoined them before long to sit in silence with Elcano. The steward's eyes grew heavier as he slumped down in his chair, and at last he began to snore.

Elcano was still awake when the *San Antonio* abruptly shifted and began to move. Stumbling to his feet and outside into the darkness, he almost collided with Coca, who grabbed his arm, shouting, "The anchor line has snapped and the current's driving us straight for the flagship! Arm the men at once!"

Whirling around to stare at the lights on the *Trinidad's* decks, Elcano saw that a third of the distance that had separated the ships had already disappeared. A mere two hundred yards now lay between them. Elcano raced toward the foredeck and called out, "Lower the other anchors!" But one of the hands appeared before him, holding the sheered end of an anchor line and saying, "Two of the three lines have been cut, sir. With this current, the last line won't hold long enough to slow her."

"Rig another anchor! Use cannon balls if you have to, but stop this ship!"

Elcano swept the decks with his gaze and spotted Quesada emerging from the storeroom wearing armor that covered him from his feet to his neck. Hurrying forward, Elcano demanded, "Captain, was it your order to arm the men?"

"It was."

Elcano stole another glance toward the *Trinidad*, now no more than a hundred fifty yards ahead. "We will not escape, sir. We can't raise the sails and gather enough speed to avoid the worst of their guns and we can't stop our movement before we reach them. Arming the men will only doom them and this ship."

For three seconds Quesada's eyes held him. "All right, Cano. I alone will be armed. I am the one who has brought us to this. Look after the men."

"But, sir, you'll make a target of yourself. You'll have no chance—."

Quesada gave him a shove toward the foredeck. "Go, Cano. Get Mesquita up there to hold off their fire. Tell him we mean only to anchor next to the *Trinidad*."

Leaving him at a run, in moments Elcano had two men standing beside Mesquita as he frantically waived and yelled across the water to the doubled watch of the flagship, "Hold your fire! Hold your fire!" Elcano hurried back to the main deck and stood before the storage room that held their arms, turning away men who held out their hands for a sword or a spear.

Despite attempts to slow the *San Antonio*, she was drawing ever nearer to the flagship. Elcano's dread rose as he watched some of the *Trinidad's* gunners descend into the hold to man their large cannons while the rest turned the swivel guns mounted on the upper decks toward the *San Antonio*. Lancers and crossbow archers lined up along the rails as other crewmembers stood behind them readying grappling lines.

More men of the *San Antonio* added their voices to Mesquita's, and others turned to Quesada who now stood exposed and unyielding on the stern deck. One of the gunners called out to him, begging to be allowed to ready the cannons. With his wispy hair ruffling in the wind, Quesada's only response was to yell, "Stand brave, men! Offer no resistance!"

But as the cries begging the flagship to hold her fire rose to a panicked pitch, they were suddenly silenced by the booming roar of cannons. Elcano threw himself to the deck as wood exploded from the *San Antonio's* hull and rained down upon them. Elcano had commanded gunner squads for years and, even amid the cursing and screaming of the men around him, he recognized that Magellan had used only his light artillery. The captain-general was warning them, forcefully, but he had not meant to sink them.

From below decks, Elcano heard the startled cry of the *San Antonio's* Pilot Mafra, then shouts from the other men chained below. Elcano had just managed to gain his feet when another round of shots slammed the ship, forcing him to his knees.

"Stay down! Stay down!" he shouted. He bent low and struggled over the debris in an effort to help the wounded and frightened away from the rail. Six feet from his goal, he was thrown back as the ship was hit by another cannon blast. "Enough!" he bellowed in rage, rising to his full height and squaring to face the *Trinidad*. In one fleeting moment, through the clouds of gun smoke, he saw the spears leap from the hands of the flagship's lancers. He had only time enough to yell out, "Take cover!" before he leaped back behind the mast. The arcing missiles descended like diving eagles, but noticeably few found a human mark.

Elcano looked back and caught sight of Quesada, still standing alone on the stern deck. Most of the spears had been directed at him, but his armor and shield had deflected those that had been aimed with accuracy. Surrounded by tall shafts, he raised his sword high in defiance.

As the *San Antonio* drew abreast of the flagship, the *Trinidad's* grapplers let their hooks fly. Elcano and the crew stood well back from the rail as the hooks fell and grabbed hold.

"Stand steady, men," he said. "Show them you bear no arms."

Men tripped and tumbled over one another, clustering as armed men vaulted to the decks.

Elcano stood rigid and silent as he was quickly surrounded and swords were thrust at his chest. He looked up to see Quesada lower his lance and his shield, then submit to being dragged to the main deck and shoved toward Elcano, where the two were soon joined by Coca.

Espinosa faced the seamen and shouted, "To whom do you pledge your loyalty?" He was answered by a howl of, "For King Carlos and the Captain-general!" Some of the crew of the *San Antonio* grabbed men they had stood beside moments before, and held them fast.

When shackles were brought forward, Elcano forced himself not to struggle as the metal was clasped around his wrists and ankles, and the locking pins were driven home.

The morning sun rose bleak and damning as it glinted off the steel swords of the captors and the iron chains of the captives. Elcano and the others were jostled across planks and pushed onto the *Trinidad's* main deck. Magellan stood above them on the half deck and surveyed the group with unnerving coldness. A launch had already been dispatched to the *Concepción* and little time passed before Cartagena was standing shackled among the prisoners. Elcano felt what little hope remained to him dwindle as accusations and denials were flung between the ships and Espinosa's men weeded out the last of the suspected mutineers.

Magellan remained silent and detached until Espinosa looked up at him and announced, "Captain-general, the ships and crews are yours!"

Limping even more heavily than usual, Magellan descended the steps, and his expression was venomous as he approached Captain Quesada. Without a word, he raised his arm and slapped Quesada so hard that his face snapped sideways. Stunned only momentarily, Quesada made a lunge at Magellan but was jerked backward and wrestled to his knees by his guards. The captain-general stepped to Cartagena next, cuffing the bishop's son with no less force. Coca was given the same insult before Magellan moved to stand before Elcano.

Standing four inches taller than Magellan, Elcano fixed his gaze upon the *San Antonio's* rigging and waited with his jaws locked tight. But Magellan hesitated. A moment passed and then another. Elcano lowered his glance slightly, and realized too late that this is what the captain-general had been waiting for. Once their eyes met, Magellan's hand reared back and collided with Elcano's cheek, splitting the edge of his lower lip with the blow. Elcano managed to recover the stiffness of his stance but not before a short, low growl had escaped his lips.

Magellan passed on down the lines of men, some forty in all, reddening each cheek and devastating each man's pride. There was a cold fury in the force of Magellan's continuing assault, unrelenting even to the pain he inflicted upon his own hand. Hearing this, understanding it, Elcano touched his tongue to the corner of his bleeding mouth, and his mind chilled with foresight. *This is no more than a taste of what will come.*

# Blade of Inquisition

## 10

Although the sun's heat managed to lessen the bite of the frigid air, it did little to warm the cold expressions on the faces of the men sitting behind the table on the *Trinidad's* main deck. With Magellan seated off to the side, Mesquita leaned forward between two clerks and announced, "This inquisition is commenced in the name of His Majesty, King Carlos of Spain to prove the cases of treason against the men bound before us."

Elcano had said very little since his arrest several hours earlier. The chains around his wrists and ankles seemed to have locked his ability to speak somewhere deep inside his body. As he sat cross-legged on the deck beside Quesada and watched Mesquita's barely concealed thirst for vengeance, Elcano knew that words could do him little good now. As his gaze shifted to Magellan, he perceived that the captain-general wanted something more useful than revenge. He intended to inflict enough pain and horror to insure the men's obedience in the future.

As if to confirm this supposition, several men came up from the hold carrying Mendoza's stinking corpse and wrapped it in chains. They tied a rope around the shackles at the ankles, threw the rope over the main yardarm, and raised the body until it hung swaying upside down, the slashed neck gaping wide. Despite their helplessness and fear, the sight of a Spanish Christian nobleman being treated with such deliberate disregard for decency roused the prisoners to a muttering mob.

Magellan's face was as unreadable as an iron mask. Mesquita, however, allowed his pleasure at the mutineers' reactions to show. "The inquisition of Luis de Mendoza, former captain of the *Victoria* and treasurer of the fleet, will now begin."

Witnesses were called. Questions were asked. Notes were taken. The conclusion was reached. Mesquita stood and addressed Magellan, "Captain-general, the accused has been found guilty of treason and his penalty has been decided. With your approval, Luis de Mendoza will now be decapitated and quartered. His remains will be spitted on a pike to serve as a warning to all who would ever again consider taking such evil actions." Magellan merely nodded.

Elcano tried to distance his mind as Mendoza's body was lowered, unchained, and laid out upon a wide plank. Taking up his position beside it, Espinosa raised his sword high and sliced downward with a blow that severed Mendoza's head from what remained of his mangled neck. Men then secured the ankles to the rear capstan and the wrists to a similar device forward, components of the ship that had previously been used for no more grisly a purpose than to heft heavy loads to her decks. A few of Espinosa's men gathered around each capstan, took hold of the protruding spokes, and heaved. Elcano closed his eyes as the ropes pulled tighter and tighter, and the arms and legs wrenched free of the torso.

Hesitant hands gathered up the ghastly remains, placed them in a canvas bag, and rowed to shore. There, in a huge pot, they parboiled the body segments in water treated with herbs to preserve the flesh and discourage the birds. When the smell of this brew reached Elcano, he lowered his head and covered his nose and mouth with his sleeve. Just before sunset, Elcano watched through sickened eyes as what was left of Captain Luis de Mendoza was spitted upon a pike, his head mounted at the top with his face pointed squarely at the ships.

Along with the rest of the prisoners, Elcano was herded below, where the nightmares of this day would provide ghostly company throughout the night. But as he fought to forget what stared at him from the beach, and that the morning would bring the first day of inquisitions for the living, Elcano found the strength to thank God that neither

Acurio nor Chindarza had been among those arrested. They had been safely aboard the *Concepción* and, so far, had not been implicated. For himself and his companions, he asked that courage be granted at the moment Espinosa swung his sword.

Early the next day, with Mendoza's sightless head clearly visible ashore, Elcano sat shivering on deck while the men of lowest rank were brought forward to testify against their shipmates and officers, some willingly and some with great reluctance. Those foolish enough or honorable enough to withhold anything that Mesquita demanded as evidence soon reconsidered. Things seemed to be proceeding closely to Mesquita's plans until Father Calmette was led before the tribunal. Even Cristóbal, Magellan's own son, cast an uneasy look at the captain-general, but Magellan did not meet his eyes.

"Father Calmette," Mesquita said, his voice severe with condemnation, "up to now you have withheld information that you learned while hearing the confessions of these men. Had that information been brought to the attention of the captain-general, this mutiny might well have been prevented. In failing to be forthcoming, you have committed treason against your king. I order you now to reveal all that you were told regarding the plotted overthrow of the authority of this fleet."

Father Calmette, diminutive in stature and serious in nature, said, "I respectfully decline, Captain Mesquita. My holy vows forbid me to reveal what is uttered during the sacrament of confession. To do so would condemn my soul to eternal damnation."

"If you refuse to answer, Father, you will be subjected to torture. We will use the strappado. Do you understand?"

It was plain by the stunned look on the priest's face that he understood perfectly. Although Elcano had also heard of this torture, he found it difficult to believe that even Mesquita would resort to inflicting such pain upon their priest.

Mesquita resumed. "Now tell me, Father Calmette, when Captain Quesada—."

"Forgive me, Captain Mesquita, but I *cannot* tell you what has been confessed to me."

Mesquita glanced at Magellan, but the captain-general's gaze drifted to the opposite shore of the harbor. After a slight hesitation, Mesquita motioned to Espinosa, who commanded two of his men to step forward. Trying to hide their uneasiness at laying hold of a priest, these two hastily tossed a rope over a yardarm and tied it to the chains that bound Father Calmette's hands behind his back. Several prisoners called out, asking for mercy on the priest's behalf, but at Mesquita's signal the rope was pulled until Father Calmette's arms were lifted so high that his head was bent far forward and his feet were nearly drawn from the floor. He stifled an exclamation of pain and stood panting and grimacing before his interrogator.

Elcano suddenly shouted his outrage and tried to stand but he was immediately knocked sideways by the force of a well-aimed club. Other voices yelled out and several more men struggled to gain their feet, but they too were beaten back down by their guards.

Mesquita pretended to ignore the disturbances. "Are you now ready to answer my questions, Father?"

With a look of despair, Father Calmette shook his head.

The rope was raised again, lifting the priest three feet off the deck. One prisoner managed to gain his feet in a futile attempt to help his priest but he was clubbed unconscious before he had taken two steps.

"Now, Father?" demanded Mesquita.

Gasping, his face reddening, the priest again shook his head.

With his head pounding from the clubbing he'd received, Elcano watched in horror as Espinosa's seamen hoisted Father Calmette three feet higher, and then suddenly loosened their grips on the rope. Just before his feet could hit the deck, Father Calmette was jerked to a vicious stop. As his arm joints wrenched and his muscles and tendons tore, a piercing cry of pain broke from him.

The scream was still echoing in the ears of the stricken witnesses when Magellan quickly approached Mesquita, whispered insistently in his ear, and then withdrew to his former spot.

Mesquita shifted in his chair as if he were less than pleased. "If any accused man wishes to disclose for himself what he confessed to Father Calmette, I will hear him now."

Most of the men, including Elcano and Quesada, quickly voiced their willingness to make such a disclosure, and their names were recorded. Their priest was lowered to the deck, where he crumpled to the boards, his arms unable to move. The guards untied his ropes and allowed his shipmates to draw him back into their midst, muttering words of comfort and prayer.

But Captain Mesquita's vengeance had not yet run its course. Andrés de San Martin, the astrologer of the fleet and the pilot of the *San Antonio*, gave such unacceptable testimony that Mesquita ordered the stages of torture to advance far beyond the level that Father Calmette had endured. In the end, cannon balls were tied to San Martin's feet, thereby wrenching every major joint and spreading the pain throughout his entire body. In the end, Elcano knew that San Martin was whispering, "Yes, yes," to damning questions his mind could no longer even follow.

The last to feel the strappado's grip was a seaman named Hernando de Morales. His torture was even more severe than San Martin's. When Mesquita finally allowed Morales to be brought down Elcano could see that, although the seaman was still breathing, no man could live long after being subjected to such torment.

By the time they unbound Morales' ropes, the evening was darkening into brooding grays and browns, as if the very earth and sky felt the day's malevolence. Elcano and the other prisoners were returned to the hold, where they again faced another night filled with images and dreams so terrible that sleep was a thing to dread. The whisperings of Mendoza's ghost, the cries and moans of the men who had been tortured, and the prayers of those who had yet to testify kept Elcano awake for a long time. An anguished sleep finally overtook him but he awoke before dawn, and muttered with dread, "Today, I will be called."

Soon he found himself standing before the tribunal, the left side of his face swollen and red from the blow he'd received the day before, and he began. "The events that have led up to this trial were not meant to result in a bloody rebellion. On the contrary, the actions were taken with the objective of *forestalling* harm and safeguarding the lives and wellbeing of the men of this fleet. As for myself, I wish only to say that I acted according to the orders of my commanding officer and according to my conscience as to my duties to our king."

Mesquita's disdain was palpable throughout his questioning, but Elcano held nothing back. He had no doubt that he would be found guilty yet he retained the hope that the record of his testimony would survive him and return to Spain to speak in his stead. Someday, if his final words were read by an objective authority, perhaps the dishonor brought to his family by his condemnation would be lessened.

The questioning stretched on, covering every detail and motive except those surrounding one important action. Since he had not been aboard the *San Antonio* when Elorriaga had been wounded, he was spared giving testimony about Quesada's participation in this. Elcano's legs felt as if they were about to buckle when he was at last allowed to sit down again.

The other officers were also interrogated. Even Elorriaga, ashen and weak-voiced, was carried from a cabin still wrapped in his blankets. As Elorriaga was borne past the prisoners, his searching eyes found Elcano near the front of the crowd of faces. As their gazes met, Elorriaga's expression held only an overwhelming sadness. He was placed in a chair before Mesquita and supported on each side by a seaman. His questioning did not last long, but his testimony left no doubt as to Quesada's exact role in the takeover of his ship.

When Elorriaga finished, he was returned to his cabin and the tribunal turned to their last witness, Quesada. Although it was only mid-afternoon, Mesquita surprised everyone there by saying, "This court will conduct its final interrogation tomorrow. Guards, take the prisoners away."

Below decks, Quesada made his way to Elcano and sat upon a barrel beside him. "Well," said Quesada, "if we are to die tomorrow at least this will be our last night in this squalid hold."

Elcano could not manage even a weak smile.

"The sentencing will come tomorrow."

Elcano nodded, as certain of the outcome as Quesada.

Quesada grew quiet for a moment, and then said softly, "You have been loyal to me, Cano. I thank you for that, and I deeply regret that it has all come to this."

Elcano knew this to be true, and he held back the words of reproach he might have spoken. Instead, he said, "Yes, sir."

"Are you afraid of tomorrow? Of the death it will bring?"

"I have certainly not led a sinless life, sir, but now that my time is ending I find that it is shame that I fear more than death.

With a nod of understanding, Quesada said, "Tell me, Cano, if they do to our bodies what they did to Mendoza's, do you think we will have any chance of reaching heaven? It haunts me to think that we may be denied paradise because of such mutilation."

"Sir, I am not willing to believe that our souls are forever damned because of the actions of other men."

Quesada sighed, "That gives me comfort, Cano. It gives me hope."

Thinking of Chindarza, Acurio, and the others aboard the *Concepción*, Elcano asked, "Do you think the rest of the fleet will ever reach the Spice Islands, sir?"

"With Barbosa captaining the *Victoria* and Mesquita back on *San Antonio*? There's little possibility that they can even make it back to Spain. But if Magellan does reach the Spiceries, he'd be an imbecile not to stay there. Once King Carlos discovers what Magellan has done here, he may well send assassins after him. Portugal would be too close a hiding place."

Elcano's mind turned to what weighed on it most. "Have you thought about writing to your family, sir?"

"If I left a letter, I doubt Magellan would have it delivered, but perhaps it's worth a try."

"Yes, sir, I believe it is."

The commander of the watch granted their request for paper and ink, and Elcano, Quesada, Cartagena, Coca, and a handful of others gathered their thoughts as they awaited their chance to use the quill and a sheet of parchment. When these tools were eventually passed to Elcano, he was surprised to realize that he felt almost at peace. He took his time with the letter to his mother, whom he recognized more clearly than ever before as a woman of wisdom and character. Thinking all the way back to when he was small, picturing her telling stories and singing to him, bandaging his small hurts and listening to his imaginings, trying to hide her sadness each time he sailed away from her, he understood the depth of the love she had always held for him.

The quill scratched across the page as he briefly detailed the actions for which he was being condemned, and his reasons for taking them. He assured her that he was not afraid but that he regretted not being able to see her and his siblings again. In simple but sincere words, he relayed his pride at being her son, and expressed his confidence that she and his older brothers would look after the family well. He closed by asking her to remember him as a loving son.

Passing the inkbottle on to waiting hands, he watched the ink dry on the page in his lap and wished he could have said something that would have given her more comfort. He also wished that he had been given the chance to say farewell to the remainder of the *Concepción's* crew and, he admitted, to the ship herself. With the understanding that this night's sleep would be his last, he closed his eyes and surrendered to the heavy darkness.

Quesada was sitting beside him when he awoke, and he asked thoughtfully, "What is the date, Cano?"

It took a moment for Elcano to reconstruct it. "April 7, sir."

"Ah yes. When April comes to Castile, spring is just beginning to bare her beauty. Here, it is nothing but ugliness. I am ready to leave this place, Cano. Yes, it is time. Listen now, they are coming for us."

The wind gnawed at the exposed skin of the ragged men as they plodded up the steps from below. Quesada was pushed forward and Mesquita began his questioning at once. After enough evidence had been gathered to satisfy Mesquita, he announced the guilt of the accused and ordered all of the prisoners to rise. When this was obeyed, he loudly read the names of each of the forty men from a list he held before him.

"These men," he said, "are hereby found guilty of treason against the Crown of Spain. In punishment for this crime, each of them is condemned to die."

Some of the nearby onlookers raised their voices in agreement, but a number of them, most noticeably those aboard the *Concepción*, broke out in violent objection. Here and there men from the other ships muttered senselessly or stood in shocked silence. But every voice hushed when Mesquita lifted his arms and shouted, "You have heard the sentence of this court of inquisition. Any man who interferes with it will find himself joining the condemned." He then called out, "Gaspar de Quesada, step forward!"

Quesada rose to his feet and walked to Mesquita with as much dignity as his shackles allowed. The grumbling started up again and quickly increased in volume. One of the forty ill-fated men shouted, "No!" and knocked down a guard in an effort to reach the captain. But Quesada spun around and yelled above the rest, "Hold fast, men!" Movement stilled as suddenly as a breath being caught. "Heed well my final order. I am resigned to this fate, unjust as it is. We must each face what will come with the pride of a true Spaniard." Quesada let his gaze sweep over the faces of his men one last time before facing around and holding himself in readiness.

Mesquita lifted his voice again. "The court has decided to show leniency to any prisoner who agrees to carry out the sentence passed against this man. One among you who is willing to serve as executioner will thereby save his own life. All those who are so willing, step forward."

No one moved or spoke.

"Understand me," Mesquita said more loudly. "We will spare the life of any man who will now step forward and carry out this single execution."

Only the wind stirred and whispered. The prisoners sat still and mute as stones.

*So,* Elcano thought, *there is your answer.* Those condemned with Quesada were willing to die with him rather than kill him. And of those that were neither doomed nor wearing chains, not even Espinosa was willing to execute Captain Quesada publicly. Even the master-at-arms knew that anyone other than the king and members of the royal council that dared to carry out capital punishment against a Spanish nobleman risked being found guilty of a crime that carried its own death penalty.

Mesquita's impatience grew as he scanned the noncompliant faces before him. His sweeping glance instantly stilled when he noticed the misery in the eyes of Quesada's foster brother and personal secretary, Luis Molino. "You," he barked, pointing at Molino, "you will receive the clemency."

Molino's stunned gasp was immediately followed by pleas for mercy and shouts of refusal, but these were ignored as two guards grabbed him and hauled him forward. He fell to his knees between Mesquita and Quesada, begging to be released from this order. At a signal from Mesquita, Molino was silenced by several blows inflicted by Espinoza's men. When the beating ended, Molino's head drooped in surrender, and the shackles at his hands and feet were removed.

Guards cleared the captives away from a section of deck, and then they took hold of Quesada. Captain Quesada tried to shrug their hands from his shoulders but he was dragged to the empty space on the deck and forced to his knees.

Molino was shoved to Quesada's side and the hilt of a sword was trust into his hands. "Forgive me, Gaspar," he cried. "Forgive me, brother!"

Quesada stared straight ahead, neither looking at nor speaking to Molino.

Elcano's eyes darted from Quesada to the block being set two feet before him, and then back to Quesada. This man had wounded Elorriaga. He had also been Elcano's captain, the man whose commands he had followed, and the man he now followed to his death.

Quesada leaned forward and placed his neck upon the block. Men pulled his arms to the side and held him down.

"Molino, it is time," said Mesquita, his harsh voice betrayed by a slight quiver.

Grasping the sword as tears spilled from his eyes, Molino whispered again, "Forgive me."

Quesada said nothing.

Weeping openly now, Molino lifted the sword high. But he stiffened and could not bring himself to lower it.

"Now!" shouted Mesquita.

A sob escaped Molino but the sword remained motionless.

Seeing Quesada trembling, sensing what it was costing him to keep from struggling, Elcano silently ordered, "Now you fool! Now! Now!"

Molino suddenly seemed to understand the terror he was prolonging. He sucked in a breath and released a deep-throated cry, slashing the sword downward with all his strength.

With an effort Elcano aimed his eyes at Molino's tormented face, but with his sight directed away from the blade, his hearing was acutely heightened. Elcano heard every detail as the sword sliced through the air, cleaved through bone and tissue, and bit into the wooden block. Elcano's shoulders jerked and his gaze involuntarily fell when he heard Quesada's head and body drop separately to the deck. His stare fixed itself unmercifully on Quesada's upturned face.

Molino stumbled backwards. He fell and crept away to a far corner of the deck, where he covered his head and moaned.

137

Espinosa's men moved forward at once and tied Quesada's arms and legs with the ropes of the two capstans. Replicating the dismemberment of Mendoza's body, Quesada's limbs were stretched until they were at last torn loose. The gruesome pieces that had so recently formed a living man were bagged, taken ashore, parboiled, and spiked. Not until two sets of unseeing eye sockets stared out at the ships were the men made to face Mesquita once again.

But now Magellan stepped in front of Mesquita, and said, "Although the king has granted me absolute authority over the life and limb of every man under my command, and although each of you has been formally sentenced to death by this court of inquisition, I have decided to commute the sentences of each of you."

An unintelligible cry of despair escaped Molino's lips as glances of hope and suspicion leaped between the others.

"Rather than death," Magellan went on, "your sentences shall be reduced to hard labor for the duration of our stay in this port. To all of you will fall the duty of repairing the ships. You will remain in shackles during the length of this term. If any man shows the least sign of mutinous behavior, his death sentence will be immediately reinstated."

Turning to Mesquita, he said, "Captain, set them to work at once."

As Magellan climbed to his cabin, Elcano grimly imagined what the long months ahead would hold, and his resentment deepened. *It would have been better if you had killed me today.*

That night, pain-ridden though he was, Father Calmette insisted on leading the men in prayers for the soul of the late Captain Quesada. Elcano, his hands and feet already half-frozen and his muscles strained to the point of exhaustion, chose to pray for those living this earthly hell rather than for the dead.


During the days and weeks that followed, the free men were put to work on shore erecting wooden huts for the stor-

138

age of goods and the shelter of men, as well as a stone smithy to rework their weapons, tools, and ship castings. Elcano and the other prisoners labored in and near the icy water not far from the hideous remnants of their dead captains.

Reluctantly at first, Elcano accepted his men's request to organize and oversee their tasks, but he kept himself quiet and aloof from them all. After the ships were unloaded down to the last bar of ballast, men in ragged clothes pumped the putrid bilge water from the holds. In turn, each vessel was brought to the shoreline to be careened, first on one side then the other, enabling the men to use brushes and strong vinegar to cleanse the interior, then to scrape, repair, caulk, and tar the hull.

The land crews made good progress and by the twelfth night ashore, Elcano and the prisoners, comprising the last group to be given shelter, were led into a hut with a smoky fire burning in its center. After some shoving and jostling for places, split and bleeding hands and feet were thrust toward the heat. Many an "ah" and even a weary smile or two circled the crackling blaze.

One of the fleet's hunters soon entered the hut and dropped a large chunk of meat into the pot at the edge of the fire. "Here's some real food, men. I've not yet tasted it myself but it comes from an animal that looks like a long-necked, long-legged sheep. We had a time getting close enough to bring one down, I can tell you. Some of the hides are being cured right now. If anything will help keep off this damned cold, they will. These creatures have the thickest wool I've ever seen."

The shelter, the fire, and the prospects of decent food and warm clothing enlivened the men that night. But though Elcano sat among those that smiled and sighed at such comforts, his face remained hardened and he kept his thoughts to himself.

Acurio and Chindarza were given no opportunity to approach their former shipmaster, and Elcano missed their company keenly. Near the end of the third week, as he squatted down to inspect a plank that had just been refitted against the *Santiago's* keel, he felt a tap on his shoulder. Turning, he found Chindarza standing beside a small barrel, accompanied by little Juanito and a cabin boy from the *San Antonio* by the name of Juan de Zubileta. Although they still wore clothing much too thin for their surroundings, the feet of each boy were covered in roughly stitched boots made from the hides of what the hunters had taken to calling wooly mules.

Although Chindarza was being watched from the edge of the beach, he didn't hide his happiness at seeing Elcano. "Here's some water for you and the men, sir."

Elcano accepted the cup held out to him, but he shook his head and said softly, "I am no longer an officer, Chindarza. My rank is now lower than your own. You must no longer address me as 'sir'. Others will punish you for doing so."

Straightening his shoulders slightly, Chindarza said, "Even the lake water here is briny, *sir*, but we drew it just an hour ago."

Moved by such a show of allegiance, Elcano nodded and took a drink. Lowering his cup, he said, "I see that you have an able crew today, Chindarza." Zubileta and Juanito both stood a little taller, and this small gesture brought a subtle smile to Elcano's face. "The men are thirsty. See that each one gets his share."

"Yes, sir," all three said at once, and proceeded to move among the prisoners with their cups.

While Zubileta and Juanito were scooping up water from the barrel for the last of the men, Chindarza casually motioned Elcano a few steps away. Glancing at the guards to confirm that he was not being closely watched, Chindarza turned his back to them, drew a small piece of dried fish from inside his shirt, and handed it to Elcano. "From Acurio," he said.

"Chindarza," Elcano said, hesitating before slipping the food into his own shirt, "you should not take such risks, nor should Acurio."

"No, sir."

"I'm sincere in this. Don't do it again."

"But, sir, I must follow Acurio's orders."

Elcano could see the hint of a grin behind Chindarza's straight face, so he stiffened his voice. "Will you still honor my wishes, Chindarza?"

The smile faded from Chindarza's eyes. "Yes, sir."

"Then tell Acurio not to send me food. It's too dangerous, for both of you."

"I will tell him, sir."

"Good." He reached out and clasped the boy's arm. "And, Chindarza, I thank you, both of you."

As Elcano and the other men returned to their work and Chindarza was just recapping the water barrel, Juanito suddenly tugged hard on his arm and said, "Look, Chindarza!"

Squinting in the direction that Juanito was pointing, Chindarza eye's widened and he shouted to Elcano, "Sir, someone's in the water! It, it looks like Baresa!"

Heads jerked up and scanned the bay. Their guards took off running down the beach, leaving the prisoners clanking and tripping in their irons as they struggled away from the ship to get a better view.

Elcano saw that it was indeed Antonio Baresa, the young Genoese whom the late Master Salamón had sodomized many months ago. Baresa was already up to his chest in water cold enough to kill him within minutes. Taking a deep breath, Elcano bellowed, "Baresa! Come back to shore!" Other voices were raised, beckoning, ordering, and begging, but the youth never turned around. As if his feet had been swept out from under him, Baresa's head went under, reappeared for an instant with his arms grasping at the water, then disappeared again below the surface.

With his fists clenched at his sides, Chindarza whispered, "Come up, come up!"

A dozen sailors shoved a boat from the sand, grasped the oars, and sped away. But the tide rose and fell, rose and fell, and the water's gray-blue surface remained otherwise undisturbed. There was no reappearance of the dark-haired apprentice seaman. The men in the boat searched on, not knowing that it would be more than a month before the greedy sea would relinquish Baresa's body to the shore.

As hope faded, one of Mesquita's men ordered them back to work. Trudging along beside Elcano, Chindarza expressed what many of them had been asking themselves. "Why would he do such a thing, sir? How *could* he damn his soul forever?" The other boys and several men, as stricken as Chindarza, also waited for Elcano's answer.

"God alone knows for certain, but you have seen how some of the men have treated him since Master Salamón was executed. Perhaps Baresa could no longer bear their insults, especially in so harsh a place as this."

Juanito began to cry. "This bad place! Very bad."

Elcano stopped and crouched down to the small boy's height. "Yes, this is a bad place, but we must be strong for one another even here. Chindarza needs you to be brave, Juanito, like the warriors of your people. If you are not, you can be of little help to him."

"I be b-b-brave," Juanito sniffled.

Elcano stood up slowly and studied the young faces around him. He thought of Elorriaga, still clinging to life, and of those fighting against illness and frostbite. Comparing his own courage to theirs, he felt a stab of shame. "Yes, Juanito," he said, "we all will be brave."

# Port San Julian

## 11

"**G**iven the chance, I would kill him with my bare hands," said Cartagena, huddling near Father Calmette at the edge of their hut's dying fire. He lifted raw, grimy hands to display his cuts and torn nails, and gave a dark laugh. "Who'd believe these hands belong to a man of Spanish nobility? If I were to use them on Mesquita, I'd dirty his Portuguese neck. That just might give me as much pleasure as squeezing the last breath out of him."

Father Calmette, whose body if not his mind had nearly recovered from Mesquita's tortures, scanned the pack of men sleeping around them. He said softly, "You'd be doing God's work, but you'll not be given the chance. Mesquita knows how much he is hated. He watches. We must keep trying to convince the men to act with us."

Cartagena nodded. "It's hard to believe more of us haven't died. Who would think men could toil so long on so few mouthfuls of food?"

"I've heard we'd be given even less and be beaten even more if the captain-general hadn't stepped in more than once."

"The captain-general!" Cartagena spat. "Wasn't it he who put Mesquita in charge of us?"

"Yes, yes, I meant only to say that he has stayed Mesquita's hand when that demon would have killed us all long ago."

"Because of those two, several men have already frozen and starved to death. None of us will survive if we don't act soon." Cartagena lay back wearily and draped his forearm over his eyes.

Lying as still as those sleeping around him, Elcano was grateful when Cartagena and Father Calmette quieted at last. Almost daily these two attempted to convince the men to rebel, and they generally started with Elcano and Coca. But they no longer had the power to command Elcano. He and Coca ignored their pleas. What they plotted was madness. Their efforts would be better spent on the ships, at least one of which was finally refitted. Elcano was surprised at the pride he felt in the fact that the small and swift *Santiago* was not only ready, she was sailing south today to scout the coastline ahead.

Chindarza had brought him word that Magellan was growing more and more concerned about the hunters' inability to bring in enough food or furs, and he was sending Serrano in search of the passage, or at least a more bountiful harbor. With the daylight hours dwindling to a precious few per day and the snow creeping ever nearer to the ocean's edge, the bodies of the men needed more nourishment to battle the cold.

When their morning guards arrived, the prisoners shambled from the hut to the beach as usual. But today Elcano paused in his work long enough to watch the *Santiago* set off, and allowed himself a small thrill of hope that her exploration would be successful. As her sails disappeared down the coast, a man beside him said, "By God, I'd not want to face these wicked seas alone."

Turning to their latest task of resealing the *Trinidad's* underbelly, the chained men gathered around a huge bubbling pot of tar as Elcano distributed buckets and brushes. Before half the buckets had been filled, the men in line stirred uneasily and someone muttered softly, "There's trouble coming."

Elcano turned around as eight armed men brushed past him and took hold of Father Calmette and Cartagena. Struggling for only a moment, Cartagena shouted, "What's this? Explain yourselves!" as he was forcefully led away. The priest, mute with terror, marched without resistance toward Mesquita's hut.

"The rest of you, go on about your work," the last of the retreating guards ordered.

"The fools," whispered Coca to Elcano. "It was only a matter of time before one of the men reported their scheming."

At Elcano's probing gaze, Coca turned away and resumed his place in the tar kettle line.

That afternoon Chindarza again was able to bring water to Elcano and the other prisoners. With the first dipping of a cup, the boy said, "Señor Cartagena and Father Calmette have already been tried and convicted, sir. They're to be marooned when we sail from here."

Coca, who had leaned in close to hear the news, said, "So, Magellan won't order the killing of the bishop's son even now. Nor will he stain his soul with the blood of a priest. Yet he'll doom them both. What chances do two such as they have to survive here? A quick death would have been more merciful."

One of the men muttered scornfully, "Mercy ain't exactly the captain-general's favorite word."

"We'd best get this tar applied before the guards unbelt their lashes," Elcano said.

Although Elcano hoped to hear of her return each day, an entire colorless month dragged by without a word or sign of the *Santiago*. Nothing disrupted the bleakness of his existence or the lessening of his fragile expectations except the brief visits from Chindarza and the occasional sounds of music. Sometimes, drifting to him from a nearby hut at the close of the day, he heard a voice lifting in a sad song, a lute being softly strummed, or a flute whirring in slow, delicate runs. During such moments, he held absolutely still, allowing his hungry ears and abused spirit to capture every note.

While the consecutive dawns brought no relief from the cold or the toil, at least Elcano's duties were now being carried out aboard his beloved and nearly repaired ship. He was helping to heave the *Concepción's* cannons back into position, his hands stinging from the bite of the frosty metal, when he heard excited shouts coming from the men on her decks above. Hurriedly securing the cannons in place, he stepped to the nearest gunport and peered outside.

"A native," exclaimed Coca, who stood at the next port, "and he's seven feet tall if he's an inch!"

Elcano let out a low whistle when he caught sight of a huge Indian bellowing an erratic song while dancing and whirling in circles on the beach. Every few moments the giant paused to grab a handful of sand and throw it in the air over his head so that it fell back into his upturned face. Then the prancing and singing recommenced.

Evidently the captain-general had also noticed the visitor, because Elcano saw a seaman rowing the *Trinidad's* skiff to the mainland with the obvious intention of making contact with the giant. The boat soon landed and the sailor, doing a fair job of hiding his fear as he neared the wild man that doubled him in size, began imitating the bizarre dance movements.

Elcano, still watching from the gunport, said, "By all that's holy, it's working. He's moving toward the skiff. He's getting in! Let's go above, men." Their guards were so captivated by the monstrous stranger that they didn't seem to notice when the prisoners crept from the hold to find better viewing places. Elcano and the others stared spellbound as the native was rowed to within twenty feet of them.

His heavy, fur cape had been flung back when he had grasped the sides of the boat, revealing that he wore nothing underneath but a genital binding and fur boots. A thick ring of red encircled his large face, and dark yellow paint bordered his eyes. Each cheek bore a red shape that resembled a human heart. His head appeared to have been plucked nearly clean of hair, and the lock that remained had been painted white. A thin cloth band was wrapped around his head and a short, heavy bow hung from his shoulder.

Elcano pulled his gaze away just long enough to scan the beach. There was another native, but this one held himself back near the trees, evidently waiting to see what would happen to his friend.

The boat rowed to the refurbished *Trinidad* anchored at a small islet nearby and the giant climbed aboard. Elcano watched Magellan greet him with hand signals of welcome and friendship.

Coca said in a low voice, "Look how he towers over Magellan. He could eat him in three bites!"

As if the same thought had crossed the captain-general's mind, the Indian was handed a food basket containing what the watchers guessed to be sea biscuits. After sniffing then gobbling down its contents, the native was offered a bucket of water, which was emptied as quickly as he had depleted the basket of biscuits. Something glinted briefly as it was presented by Magellan to the visitor. Glancing closely at the gift, the giant sprang back in fear, unintentionally knocking down four of Magellan's men.

Elcano gave a short chuckle. "One of our mirrors, I'll wager. There, he's looking again, growing braver by the minute."

Other gifts were bestowed before the giant reboarded the skiff and returned to shore. His tribesman waited until he'd landed and the boat had pulled away before striding toward him to learn of his encounter. After words were exchanged and the gifts were displayed, the companion spun around and raced back into the trees. Not long afterward, eighteen men and women stepped into the open.

"Feast your eyes, lads!" a man gasped beside Elcano. "Have you ever seen such breasts? Why, one of them could satisfy four babes."

"Or men!" someone howled.

"They're painted as wild as their warriors!"

"They're certainly plumper than the males, and a head shorter."

"They've probably grown plump eating man flesh, lads!"

Elcano was too fascinated to pay heed to the seamen. Instead of carrying only weapons, the women were laden with heavily filled baskets strapped to their heads. Four of the women led a young beast, much like the wooly mules the sailors had seen earlier, but bearing a shorter, reddish brown fur. These newly arrived natives lowered their baskets and began to dance and sing as their leader had done, repeatedly pointing at the ships and then to the heavens.

"They must think we came from the sky," said Coca.

Several of Magellan's men now ventured ashore, including Juan Carvalho. The leader of the natives came forward and presented Carvalho with the contents of their baskets. Scooping his hand into one, Carvalho lifted a handful of what appeared to be flour, and let it sift through his fingers and back into the basket. He waved his hand toward the small beasts and a native shouted, "Guanaco," then gathered the lead ropes and placed them in Carvalho's hands.

Through signs, the Indians now seemed to be inviting the Europeans to hunt with them. After this request was relayed to Magellan and his permission was granted, Elcano watched two parties comprised of natives, Europeans, and two of the young guanacos disappear into the swampy hills behind the sailors' huts.

"There are women in this God-forsaken place," one of the prisoners muttered as if still trying to convince himself. "Women."

Not for the likes of you," a guard laughed harshly. "Even without shackles on, a man ought to think twice before testing a female who'd prefer eating him raw to bedding him. Now, that's enough gawking. Back to it! This ship won't finish mending herself."

But their repair work was interrupted almost at once when orders were issued to move the men and diminishing supplies back to the ships. No one had forgotten the fate of the Solis party. With the appearance of the wild men, Magellan clearly deemed it unsafe for any of his men to sleep ashore.

During the shuffling activities of the day, the prisoners had made several trips to each ship and Elcano now found himself among a boatload of men taking three of the Indian baskets to the *Trinidad*. He knew that Elorriaga had already been taken aboard the flagship and, although he had repeatedly received word that his friend's condition had not changed, Elcano realized that this errand might offer an opportunity to see him. As they drew near the ship, Elcano decided to take that chance. When one of the

*Trinidad's* hands reached down for the baskets, Elcano said, "These are heavy. I'll bring them up."

Waved aboard, Elcano kept his eyes downcast as he made his way as briskly and quietly as his chains would allow. He had almost reached the officers' cabins when Magellan suddenly opened his door and jerked to a halt in front of him. They stared at one another. Boatswain Francisco Albo noticed Elcano for the first time, took a step toward the half deck, and called out, "Captain-general, may I be of assistance?"

After a moment's pause, Magellan held up his hand and said, "I think not." Another moment of scrutiny passed between them before he said gruffly to Elcano, "You may stow those baskets below."

Elcano forced himself to steady his breathing, to guard his features, to bank the fire in his eyes At last he said, "Sir, may I see Master Elorriaga?"

Magellan's harsh expression eased slightly. "Is that why you are here, to see him?"

"It is, sir. I have not spoken to him since...since Easter."

Magellan considered, and said slowly, "Stow the baskets in the hold, then you may see your friend."

Uncertain that he could trust what he had just heard, Elcano asked, "I may see him, sir?"

"Not for long. He's very weak. He's in the clerk's cabin," said Magellan. He limped away and climbed down to Albo on the main deck.

Elcano took the baskets below and quickly returned to open the door of the small room. Compelling himself to ignore the smell, he knelt beside the cot and looked upon Elorriaga's features, so sunken and lifeless. "Juan," Elcano whispered, reaching out and touching Elorriaga's forehead. "Juan it's—". A surge of grief rose up and hit him like a physical blow. Suddenly he could only breathe in short gasps. He let out a sharp moan and buried his face in the blanket, choking out, "Cold as death because of me."

With little hope, Elcano lifted tormented eyes and begged, "Please, Juan, you must not die. Soon we'll leave here. We'll find the passage and sail north to where it's warm. You'll grow strong again. Think of Juana. You must live to see Juana! Please, Juan. Please."

When Elcano's head fell again to the covers, he surrendered at last to the misery he'd long suppressed and, muttering his friend's name, he let his tears overtake him.

As if from the recesses of his mind, Elcano seemed to hear someone whisper, "Do not cry for me." When these words came again, a little stronger, he raised his dirt-streaked face and quieted.

Elorriaga's half-opened eyes were upon him, and they were soft with compassion. "Do not cry, my friend," he said in the gentlest whisper of his old voice.

"Oh, Juan, when you didn't awaken, I feared you..."

"Soon. They wouldn't let me see you, Juan Sebastian." The shadow of a smile crossed his face. "I should have known you'd find a way to get to me." He opened his eyes wider and focused them more closely on Elcano's face. "They've been starving you," he accused.

"No, no. They give me more than enough."

"I must tell you something," Elorriaga said, his voice already weakening. "You remember your promise to me?"

"Yes, Juan," Elcano said, knowing well the promise to which he referred.

"Listen to me now. I release you from it. I bid you to let someone else go to Juana and tell her of my death."

"After so long a fight, must you give up all hope of seeing her again?"

"There has been little hope since the first night. I think I have only been waiting to see you." He took a rasping breath to gather his ebbing strength. "In return for releasing you of one promise, I must ask you for another. Promise me that you will stop blaming yourself for what has happened to me. It was not of your doing."

"Juan, I—."

"Promise me quickly. I hear someone coming."

"I promise to try."

Satisfied, Elorriaga said, "You must return for both of us now. You must live through whatever comes, Juan

150

Sebastian, *whatever* comes, and return to your family. My soul will rest easier if you do."

The door opened and a seaman said to Elcano, "The captain-general orders you to return to your boat."

Elcano touched Elorriaga's shoulder and held his gaze. "Go with God, Juan."

"And with you, my friend."


That night the prisoners were lodged aboard the *Concepción* under Barbosa's vigilant eye. When an allowance of fresh meat was delivered to the prisoners, it was eagerly plopped into the water of the cooking pot, which was immediately placed over the fire. Elcano had been even quieter than usual since seeing Elorriaga, but he now asked, "What meat is this? A gift from the natives?"

"Our own hunters brought down one of the guanacos," said a guard. "*This* is from the natives. Toss some into the kettle. I've not yet tasted it, but they say it works to thicken the broth." He hunkered down near Elcano and said, "Would any of you care to hear of the hunt?" Heads were nodding as he settled in to share his story.

"Well, our men were mighty wary of the giants, but with food being as scant as it is, the captain-general sent them off to hunt together, and off they went. Them Patagonian warriors—the captain-general's named them Patagonians on account of their big feet—they're crafty devils. As I heard it, they took them two young guanacos they'd captured earlier and tied them to a scrubby tree. In no time at all the critters started to bawling, and their cries tempted four adult animals to within range of our lads' arrows. Now that we know that trick, our hunters should be bringing in more meat and furs. That is, so long as the Patagonians don't start any trouble."

Elcano's mind had caught and held on to the prospect of furs for warm clothing. How long had it been since he'd been truly warm? Every day the icy sting of the metal rings around his wrists and ankles seeped more deeply into the bones of his hands, feet, and legs, settling most painfully in his fingers, toes, knees, and hips. Even the small fire in their hut had done little to relieve the ache's intensity. The aching had grown so terrible and so constant that it was hard to imagine the possibility of living without it. As he held his crusty hands out to glowing coals in the fogon's sandy bed, Elcano decided that after his meal he would climb down into the hold and try to dream of warm clothes.

Although significant repairs were still needed aboard the *Victoria* and the *San Antonio*, even these ships had been made stable enough to be returned to the water where the men could work with less risk of a surprise attack from the natives. In spite of a general uneasiness caused by their presence, however, the Patagonians provided a much-needed topic of gossip and speculation while the fleet awaited the return of the *Santiago*.

One particularly friendly native mingled with the sailors so readily that by the end of a week he could recite a few simple prayers in Spanish. In recognition of this achievement, he was baptized by Father Valderrama and presented with many gifts. Before leaving them, this newly christened Indian gave Magellan an adult guanaco, which was added to the cooking pots and enjoyed by many.

Rather than the abundance of meat and clothing that Elcano continued to hope for, the next sun's turning brought unlooked for visitors. Near dusk, just as he and his men were putting away their tools Elcano heard the scrambling of feet above him on the *San Antonio's* fore and main decks, followed by someone shouting, "Over there, Captain Mesquita!"

"What is it?"

"It looks like a ghost, sir!"

"It *does* look like a ghost, sir!"

"Silence, you oafs. It's as human as you are."

Elcano and the other prisoners scrambled up the stairs, their chains clanking and jingling as they went. He made his way to the rail, careful to stay a safe distance from Mesquita.

"He won't make it much further, sir."

"Maybe it's a sick Patagonian, sir."

"He's got shredded breeches still clinging to him."

"Why, sir, it looks like Garcia!"

"From the *Santiago*?"

"Yes, sir."

"There's another one, sir!"

"Get to the boats! Hurry, before the natives spot them!"

As the skiff pushed away from the ship, Mesquita called over his shoulder, "Pilot Mafra, signal the captain-general!"

Minutes later, two men weighing little more than skeletons were lifted to the deck of the *San Antonio*, where they were wrapped in blankets and given warm broth to drink.

"Is it you, Garcia?" said Mesquita.

A feeble nod was the only response.

"The other one's Pierre Gascon, sir," Mafra supplied.

Mesquita looked from one man to the other and asked, "The *Santiago*?"

Garcia managed to keep his red eyes open long enough to mouth a single word with his tattered lips. "Lost."

A fearful and grieving murmur moved among the men.

"Carry them to my cabin," Mesquita ordered, and Garcia and Gascon were lifted with gentle hands and taken away.

Elcano stared off to the south and wondered if anyone else had survived, wondered how the *Santiago* had gone down, and wondered if a similar fate awaited them all in that unknown sea. Soon afterward, a grim-faced Magellan boarded and went directly to Mesquita's quarters to question the men from the *Santiago*.

After a sheltered night's sleep and two meals of broth, sea biscuits, and a good measure of wine, Garcia and Gascon were able to tell their story more fully. One of the *San Antonio's* caulkers that had been working along side the prisoners for days, Pedro de Bilbao, came below decks and passed along the news to Elcano.

"They sailed some seventy miles south to a river whose mouth spans well over two miles," said Bilbao. "On the feast of the Holy Cross Captain Serrano landed at a place he named Santa Cruz. The sea wolves and sea geese are plentiful there, Garcia says. He and the others explored the area and then stayed long enough to restock their food. After sixteen days, they weighed anchor and were heading farther south when they were struck by a squall that was bad enough to rip their spars loose and even carry off their rudder. Captain Serrano rigged new sails in such a way that they sailed the *Santiago* back to shore *bow* first. He got them to within ten miles of the river, but another sudden gale heaved the ship onto the rocks. The *Santiago* held together just long enough for them to jump to the beach, and then she was torn to pieces.

"Only one hand was lost," Bilbao went on. "Captain Serrano's slave, it was. He jumped too late and was swept away. Then the sea took all of their food. They were left without shelter, provisions, or tools. Well, after eight days of waiting for enough wreckage to drift ashore, they managed to build a raft. Somehow they managed to carry the thing over mountains where the snow was deep enough to bury them, all the way back to the Santa Cruz River. Garcia said they'd have starved there if the fish hadn't been so easy to catch. They decided their raft was only big enough for Garcia and Gascon, so just the two of them came all that way back to us. They found no water to drink along the way, only snow and ice, and they found no more than a few frozen roots and ferns to eat until they crossed the swamps and reached the sea. Even there they could only get a few barnacles. It took them eleven days to reach us."

Elcano asked, "Then the other men may still be alive? All thirty-five of them?"

"The way Garcia tells it, they were left in a bad way on that river. We can only hope they're still alive. Men must be sent to help them at once, but the captain-general says he won't risk another ship while the winter storms are still raging. That means a group of men will be going on foot."

"How many men?"

"Twenty-four is the number I heard," said Bilbao.

"Crossing seventy miles of frozen wasteland on foot, then trying to make it back again?" Elcano shook his head, "We could lose them all. May our Blessed Mother help them."

The provisions and men were quickly gathered together and the next morning, with a buffeting wind at their overloaded backs and a darkening sky overhead, the rescue party set out for Santa Cruz.

By the time the work on the ships had wound down to the final stages of sealing, polishing, and mending, Elcano had counted the passing of twenty long days since the rescuers' departure. July was nearing its halfway mark but winter still held a tight grip on the prospect of leaving San Julian safely.

On a day so foul that the prisoners could do little but huddle in the hold stitching canvas and twisting rope with cold-stiffened hands, Elcano was surprised to glance up and find Acurio standing at the bottom of the steps and motioning for him to approach.

When Elcano met him, Acurio eyes shone as he said, "They let me come to you at last."

Elcano reached up with the intention of clasping his arm, but let his hand fall when he noticed how closely two guards were watching them. "It is better than bread and wine to see you," he said.

"And you, sir," Acurio said, whispering the last word. "I'd have come sooner but things would have gone harder on you."

"I understand."

"But now," Acurio's voice fell and his gaze wavered, "they've let me come to tell you."

Elcano searched Acurio's face. "It's Juan."

"Yes, sir. He breathed his last just an hour ago."

Very slowly, Elcano nodded and lowered his head.

"I wanted you to know, sir, they've said I could arrange a funeral with songs and dances from our homeland. I'll see that he gets a burial his family would be proud of."

Elcano nodded again, and said through a tight throat, "Thank you, Boatswain Acurio."

"Ah, sir, please. Not so formal. Not with me. It's enough to break me, coming after this news."

Elcano met his eyes. "Very well, then. Thank you, Acurio, my faithful friend. I will not forget this kindness."

When the wind eased late in the day, a group of men went ashore to chip and hack a grave from the frozen earth. After rites were observed aboard the *Trinidad*, Acurio was among the first members of the funeral party to reach the beach. Joined by more than a dozen others, he lifted his voice in the words of a song that had been born ages earlier in the heart of the Basque country. Rolling and boldly lyrical, the words praised the valor of their fallen warrior. Their voices rose deep and clear, reverberating out and across the water. When Acurio and the others brought the song to an end, a txistu flute and Basque drum took up a new tune, one in which primal tones announced the coming of a ritual that had been practiced in similar forms since their people dwelt in the depths of caves.

Acurio stood to the side as nine men, all wearing red berets and six carrying swords, formed three parallel lines behind Elorriaga's canvas wrapped body. With eyes straight ahead, they began to dance, stepping uniformly in place. At a point in the music they all knew well, the three men in the center line bent down and lifted Elorriaga's body high over their heads. The six outside dancers raised their swords and crossed the steel tips of their blades over him. Holding their swords in place, the men continued to step and kick in intricate and uniform patterns. Acurio moved to the head of the group and fell into step with them. And while the heart-stirring music played on and the men moved their bodies in dance, the faces of those offering Elorriaga this final tribute of honor remained grim and proud.

Elcano, standing in his chains at the rail of the *Concepción*, listened to the music and watched the men at the edge of the beach dance the txankarreku. No one approached or spoke to him, but those who glanced his way saw far more than sorrow reflected upon his face. In his piercing gaze, the carriage of his head, and the set of his jaw they saw the same grimness and the same pride that was worn at that moment by the men holding his friend's body up to the sky.

# The Captain-General's Judgment

## 12

Late one evening, Father Valderrama boarded the *Concepción* with a bulky sack slung over his shoulder, landing among the prisoners with a look of satisfaction. Two other men from the *Trinidad* followed the priest up the ropes and dropped several more sacks beside him. Carvalho, Acurio, Chindarza, and the rest of the *Concepción's* original crew had been returned to their ship not long after Elorriaga's funeral, and they now looked on with great interest.

"Men," said Father Valderrama, "you've waited a long time for these." He opened the sacks to reveal fur boots, and amid the whooping, yelling, and shoving, he doled out the much-anticipated footwear.

"Keep 'em out of the water, lads," one prisoner warned. "They'll not last otherwise."

"Ah, but aren't they lovely!"

"These are too small! Who's got bigger ones?"

"Over here!"

Pulling off his own ragged boots that, holey as they were, had been a luxury in the months passed, Elcano replaced them with a pair made of guanaco fur. He couldn't help chuckling along with the rest of the men at the sheer pleasure of their comfort.

Smiling, Father Valderrama said, "I know you've noticed the bounty of meat lately. Our hunters have had a fine couple of weeks, and the tanning and sewing have also gone well."

A man called out cheerfully, "We've smelled the work of the tanners for weeks."

"Their pots smell even worse than this crew!"

"Yes," Father Valderrama laughed, "and finally you can share in their handiwork. With luck, we'll have cloaks for you soon."

The evening deepened but its rare mildness lightened their spirits even more. Elcano wrapped his ratty blanket more tightly around his shoulders, wiggled his toes inside his boots, and asked, "Have you heard when we're to sail, Father?"

"No, I've heard nothing yet, but the weather is still—."

A sudden reedy shout, then several others burst from the shore. Every man clamored to his feet, and stood listening and squinting toward the darkening coast.

More cries reached them. "Hail, the fleet! Loosen the boats and come ashore!"

"It's our men!" cried Acurio.

Grasping the rail and leaning out, Elcano could see the dark shapes hobbling toward the ships. God be praised, it *was* them! Some waved their arms in frantic greeting while others struggled forward under the weight of those they supported. Scanning, counting, Elcano burst out, "Fifty-nine! All of them! They're all alive!"

Cries of recognition came from each ship as eager oars pulled the launches from the ships and drove them toward the beach. Elcano spotted Magellan standing in the lead boat. Climbing to the beach, he limped from silhouette to silhouette until he found Serrano leaning heavily between two of his men. To Elcano's amazement, Magellan threw his arms around the captain and held him, baring his own relief and joy as he offered a heartfelt welcome.

Malnourished and completely spent of energy, the men of the *Santiago* and their deliverers were gathered into the boats one load at a time. Before long the shipwreck survivors were divided among the remaining four ships of the fleet, with the *Victoria* receiving a number slightly higher than her one-fourth share. Serrano and several of his weaker men were delivered to the *Concepción*, where they were carefully tended.

Despite being the oldest man of the fleet, Captain Serrano's wiry toughness revived within days. Whether it was initiated by his own request or because of the captain-general's wishes, Serrano replaced Magellan's brother-in-law as commander of the *Concepción*. Not a man aboard the *Concepción* showed the least sign of displeasure when Barbosa strode wordlessly from among them and headed toward his new captaincy aboard the *Victoria*.

Coca spat over the rail after the skiff had pulled away, and said to Elcano, "The devil may take that one, with my compliments."

The recovering crewmen of the *Santiago* were fascinated by the circulating stories of the Patagonians, of whom they had seen no sign, and their curiosity only grew as several stormy days passed without the appearance of a single native. Finally, after a week of waiting, four huge male Patagonians appeared on shore just after dawn.

Though colored with caution, the relationship between the fleet's men and the Patagonians had remained friendly thus far. When the weather had allowed it, small groups of natives interested in trading or simply inquisitive about their ways had occasionally grown bold enough to visit the ships, and the fleet's hunters had moved about on shore unmolested. Yet both sides remained wary.

Serrano called Elcano to the rail, pointed out the new arrivals, and asked in amazement. "Are they all that big?"

"The men, yes, sir."

"And they're cannibals?"

"Pilot Carvalho believes so, Captain. He would be able to give you more details."

"Yes, yes, but I'm interested in your insights, Elcano," he said, watching as the four on the beach beckoned for the seaman to bring them aboard the ships. "Do they seem intelligent?"

"Their ways are exceedingly primitive, sir, yet they learn quickly."

They watched a boat from the *Trinidad* land and then carry the Patagonian group and their bundles toward the flagship. Serrano's eyes trailed the skiff and continued to observe the activities aboard the *Trinidad*. "Ah," said Serrano, "it looks like we'll soon have more of those fine furs. My, my, is the captain-general always so generous in his trading?"

Elcano frowned. "Well, no, sir. I've never heard of him giving so much for so few furs."

"Mirrors and knives I understand, but look at that. He's handing them each a set of shackles."

Before they could speculate further, several of the *Trinidad's* crewmen bent down at the feet of the two youngest Patagonians and the sound of hammers striking iron rang out. An instant later, the pair of natives roared in outrage as they hopped about and yanked at the chains. When their startled older companions reached for their bows and arrows, crewmen lunged and wrestled them to the deck. One native was quickly brought down and tied. But the last Indian fought with such ferocity that at least nine seamen were needed to hold him down while he was bound. The Patagonians suddenly began bellowing out the word, "Setebos! Setebos!"

Serrano beckoned to Carvalho and asked him, "What are they saying, Pilot?"

"They're calling on their demon, a sort of god, to help them, Captain."

"They'll be heard all the way to the village," Serrano muttered.

The captive voices soon quieted, but for over half an hour the beach was watched for any sign of a rescue. The *Concepción's* men had just begun to resume their chores when a boat from the *Trinidad* came along side with a message for Captain Serrano.

"I'm to tell you, sir," said Albo, "that the captain-general means for Pilot Carvalho to lead a party ashore and bring back a woman belonging to one of our Patagonian captives, and perhaps a few other women as well."

"Women?"

"The captain-general intends to take some of these natives back to the king, sir, and he believes they'll go more willingly if their women are brought with them."

Serrano hid his own reaction to this plan, and obediently relinquished Carvalho from his command.

Behind a veil of regrouping clouds, the sun had not yet reached its zenith when Carvalho, ten armed men, and the two older Patagonians rowed ashore. They had just stepped out of the water when one of the natives managed to free his tied hands, break clear of the nearest seamen, and sprint for the trees. He disappeared into the brush so quickly that those in pursuit had little hope of overtaking him.

The other Patagonian twisted at his bonds and began to run, but he was tackled from behind before he could reach cover. To quiet the yelling, twisting captive, Carvalho stepped over him and smashed the butt of his musket down on his skull. The stunning effect of this blow lasted only an instant before it was replaced by a rage that erupted into an echoing howl.

With the escaped captive now free to warn his distant village of their coming, even if the cries of his tribesman did not, Carvalho hesitated only briefly before plunging ahead toward the vegetation with his men and their bleeding captive following close behind.

Once they were out of Elcano's sight, not a sound came to him from inland. And he tried to forget that poisoned arrows were nearly as silent as they were deadly.

While other seamen drifted away from the rail and only occasionally glanced back toward shore, Carvalho's young son remained beside Elcano, staring at the landscape. At last, Elcano signaled inconspicuously to Chindarza, who drew Juanito away and assigned him some unnecessary task.

The sun sank low and still the landing party failed to reappear. Just before complete darkness fell, the captain-general ordered the ships' muskets and cannons to be loaded.

After a short and fitful night's sleep, Elcano bolted awake at the sound of musket fire. When he reached the half deck, he heard Acurio say to Serrano, "It's the village, sir." The noises of battle were soon followed by the sight of great billows of smoke rising into the dull sky.

Serrano demanded in frustration, "What the devil is going on?"

His question remained unanswered until Carvalho and his party burst from the brush, raced across the scrubby dunes, and scrambled into the waiting skiffs.

"They're one man short," Serrano observed. When Carvalho's skiff neared them, Serrano called out to him, "What happened, Pilot?"

"We found the village last night, sir. The Patagonians attacked us this morning with poisoned arrows and they killed Diego Barrasa. Then they fled with our captive."

"So you set fire to the village?"

Carvalho's tone toughened. "Yes, sir. We set it ablaze while we buried Barrasa."

"Were many Patagonians killed?"

"Not many, sir. The devils kept dodging behind trees."

Shaking his head, Serrano said, "You'd better be off and report to the captain-general."

"Yes, sir," Carvalho said, and with visible reluctance directed his boat on toward the flagship.

"Acurio, keep a double watch posted," Serrano said with resignation.

Even the hunters did not dare to go ashore during the days that followed, and the decline of the food supply made the search for another harbor an unavoidable necessity. But the weather once again vented its foul temper upon them and did not lessen its raging for several days. When the winds at last grew weary of their onslaught, final preparations were made for their departure.

To reduce the possibility of trouble from the two Patagonians still held captive, one of them was transferred to the *San Antonio*. Stores were stowed and the ships readied until all that remained undone was the task of carrying out the sentence against Cartagena and Father Calmette.

Although Magellan allowed Coca and several other friends of the condemned men to escort them to a small island not far from shore, Elcano chose to remain aboard the *Concepción*. Instead, he watched closely, reflectively as the boat landed and unloaded the two men and four trunks. Coca embraced Cartagena and the priest, then embraced each of them again. He and the other free men turned away

162

and reboarded the launch as Father Calmette fell to his knees and lowered his head to his folded hands. Cartagena sat down on a trunk with his back to the fleet.

When Coca returned to the *Concepción*, he turned his tear-streaked face to Elcano and said, "Swords, tools, wine, and biscuit. That's all they've been given. Without a shelter or a boat, with the savages stirred up by Carvalho's raid, they won't last a day once we set sail."

Yet setting sail was postponed again by the weather. For nearly two more weeks, while Cartagena and Calmette dug and fashioned a primitive shelter, the fleet was forced to wait for a break in the consecutive storms. On August 23, the skies and wind finally began to calm. Rather than being ordered to help raise the sails, however, Elcano was surprised when Captain Serrano called him to the main deck and said, "The captain-general wants to see you." His glance faltered as he added, "A boat is waiting."

Elcano tensed instantly. "See me? For what purpose, Captain?"

Serrano's deeply wrinkled face could not hide its concern, "I don't know, but it would be unwise to keep him waiting."

As the oars of his skiff dipped and pulled across the choppy water in the direction of the *Trinidad*, Elcano turned his face to the island where the ex-captain and priest were hidden within their crude hut, and he wondered with building dread whether he was soon to be added to their company. After the hell he'd endured for the past twenty weeks, slaving in this frigid wasteland, was he now to be condemned to die here?

Elcano's thoughts, even more than his chains, made climbing the ship's ropes difficult. Once he reached the main deck he was taken to Magellan's cabin without delay. The captain-general glanced up from his writing as two guards ushered Elcano in and closed the door behind them. Setting down his quill, Magellan sat back in his chair and crossed his arms over his chest. When Elcano's eyes met those of Magellan, he was struck by the realization that the captain-general had changed much in the last months.

Magellan was thinner, as they all were, but he seemed to have lost more than his weight. His fiery manner and his ability to hide his inner self appeared to have dwindled. His gaze had grown less broodingly intense, and he now studied Elcano steadily, openly. He asked, "Have you guessed why I have sent for you?"

Hesitating for only a moment, Elcano chose to dispense with both pretense and formality. "I have."

One of the guards shoved him from behind and barked, "You're addressing the captain-general."

With an impatient wave, Magellan said, "You men may leave us." When they had obeyed, he continued. "So, you understand why you have been brought here, but I must ask you nevertheless, do you accept this willingly?"

"Willingly? Willingly!"

Surprised by this reaction, Magellan scowled at him. "What's the matter with you, man? Are you refusing?"

Suddenly less certain, Elcano said, "Perhaps it would be best if you simply state what your judgment is to be?"

"My judgment?" Magellan scowled even deeper. "What in the...? Elcano, I'm offering to restore you to your former rank."

"My, my rank?" Elcano tightened the muscles of his legs to keep them from buckling.

"Yes, your rank."

"I thought that you, I thought..."

"It seems that you were mistaken in what you thought. It is my wish that you be restored as shipmaster of the *Concepción*."

The images of torture during the trial abruptly stilled Elcano's tongue. His mind whirled with the memories of every misery, every indignity that Quesada, Father Calmette, Cartagena, the other prisoners, and he had suffered.

Watching closely, Magellan said, "Think carefully before you speak. Do not refuse what I offer." It was more a request than a command.

Forcing himself, Elcano asked, "Why?"

"Because your skills would increase the chances of our survival and our success, and because your men would readily die for you. That kind of loyalty can't be bought."

"Is your offer not an attempt to buy mine?"

"*True* loyalty can't be bought. I'm merely granting you a second chance to serve the mission of this fleet. By doing so, you will also facilitate your own ends."

Slowly, Elcano looked down at his chains and then at his fur boots worn parchment thin and cracked beneath the shackle rings. He doubted that the circles of calloused skin around his ankles and wrists would ever heal or that the ache within his bones would ever ease.

Magellan had followed his gaze and now called out, "Noya!" When the man appeared at the door the captain-general said, "Send the smith to me, and have him bring what tools he needs to remove these chains."

Elcano held his body still while the heavy hammer knocked first one locking bolt, then the others free of the shackles. When the chains that he had worn for nearly five months fell away, he raised cold eyes.

"Leave us," Magellan ordered, and the smith departed. "Sit down, Elcano."

Elcano pulled the empty chair in front of the desk and sank into it. Rubbing his left wrist, he asked, "Why do you trust me to lead the men?"

"I know you, Elcano, better than you imagine. Before I ever accepted you as one of my officers I made it a point to study your people, your family, and that taught me much about you. I also asked questions of experienced seamen in Seville. Through all that has happened, your character has varied little from what I first judged it to be." He ignored Elcano's look of disbelief, and went on, "Also, I knew Quesada. That is why I am convinced that you would not have acted against me on your own. Oh, you may have agreed with Quesada's sentiments, but what caused you to raise your hand in mutiny was the order of your captain."

At this, Elcano could not keep silent. "It was never meant to be a mutiny! Our intention was to *stop* a mutiny!"

"Perhaps that was *your* intention. I doubt it was Quesada's, and it certainly was not Cartagena's."

Elcano pushed on heedlessly. "We were not beyond our rights under the Laws of Rhodes and Oleron. Quesada, we all meant only to enforce the king's will, a will that was being disregarded to the endangerment and death of our men."

"Upon that claim rests the ultimate disagreement," Magellan said in a slightly lowered voice. "For I alone know whether I acted in the best interests of the king or whether I *unnecessarily* endangered the men. And I am in command."

To this, Elcano did not respond.

"I give you this one chance to speak freely."

"Very well then, you say that you trust me enough to restore my command, but how can I trust you? Men are dead, good men, and many more have suffered greatly. How can I believe that you have acted in our best interests, or will do so in the future?"

Rather than answer him directly, Magellan said, "Have you never reflected on the similarities between us?"

Elcano stared back at him defiantly.

"Like it or not, there are many parallels. As I told you, before accepting you in Seville, I learned a great deal. Let's see, you were born to Basque nobility and at the age of twenty you left your home to sail under Córdoba. Two years later you were appointed as master of a ship under Cisneros, under whom you fought the Moors in Oran. At the age of just twenty-three, you bought and captained your own ship, then willingly offered that ship and your services to King Ferdinand. You fought in the battles of Tripoli and Gelves, and probably other places. But when the long years of fighting were over, what rewards were you granted? What honors did your grateful king bestow?"

Tightly, Elcano answered, "You must know the answer to that as well."

"Yes, I know. You were given nothing, not even the salaries the Crown owed to the men who had fought under you. You waited, but the king ignored your requests for payment. In the end you borrowed money from Savoyard merchants to pay your men. You *continued* to wait for the late king's payment but the money never came. You were forced to sell your own ship to pay off the merchants. In doing so, you broke a law written in your absence that forbade the sale of Spanish ships to foreigners. Rather than returning with wealth and honor, you came back to Spain an impoverished criminal. Is this not all true?"

"You never spoke to me of this, even when you first questioned me for the voyage."

"As it turned out, there was no need. When I sought the necessary approval to hire you from the Casa de Contratacíon, they already knew of your past. They, most of them chosen by Ferdinand himself, were familiar with his methods. Yours was far from the first debt he had conveniently overlooked. That is why you were not arrested when you first returned to your country, and why they approved of your appointment to this expedition."

"I see."

"Only partially, but I will explain the rest. The shame and the rage you undoubtedly felt at the injustice of what had been brought upon you by a king, a king you had repeatedly risked your life to serve; that, I have felt myself."

"Manuel of Portugal."

"Yes. After years of military service, after being wounded three times in battles, I too was rewarded with dishonor. I fought at Chaul and Goa. This last wound," he said, slapping his bad knee, "I got at Azamor. Afterward I was granted a pittance by a king, a man who had served with me as a page when we were boys. When I asked for a new assignment, he laughed at me before the entire court." Magellan's face hardened as he relived that day, but he went on. "I then asked if I could offer my services to another ruler, and he said he didn't care in the least what I did with myself. As I left his court, he degraded me further by declaring me a useless 'club foot'. After that, I went to Spain. To my amazement, I was welcomed and shown respect. I was even knighted by King Carlos, who gave me the opportunity to regain my honor."

He stared at Elcano with complete sincerity. "You may trust me, Elcano, because I will not break the trust of my new king. He has given me another chance, just as he has given you. Accept my offer and do what you can to see that neither of us fails him."

Elcano did not answer at once. At last, he slowly shook his head and asked, "Why would one loyal to King Carlos bring about the deaths of his appointed captains?"

"His appointed captains," Magellan echoed with surprisingly little anger. He stood and walked to a trunk tucked beneath his bunk. Taking up a small key that he wore on a chain around his neck, he unlocked the chest, opened it, and pulled a folded letter from inside the leaves of a book. Handing the letter out to Elcano, he said, "I have shown this to no one but Captains Mesquita and Barbosa."

Elcano opened it and read the words of Magellan's father-in-law, warning of the plans Cartagena, Quesada, and Mendoza were hatching to bring about Magellan's death. When his arm lowered the letter to his lap, Elcano said, "It's not true."

"There is uncertainty in your voice."

"No, I am certain that they were not plotting against you from the beginning."

"I could not take that chance," Magellan said with finality. "I will not fail this king."

"Even if the letter were based on truth, the other men had no part in this plotting. If you knew we were just following orders—."

Magellan abruptly pushed to his feet. "An example had to be made! These men must fear me more than they fear whatever lies ahead of them! If my orders are not carried out, we face only disaster!"

"But the men—."

"When you lead men you can't afford the luxury of sensitivity! Sometimes that means watching them suffer, even watching them die for the good of the fleet! You have been a captain yourself! You know this!"

Elcano bent down, grabbed a length of chain, and rattled it in his hands as he shot to his feet. "Has this suffering been *good* for the fleet? You speak of shame. What of *this* shame? What greater shame can be inflicted upon a man?"

"Watch yourself, Elcano."

"I *will* speak freely. Your ways are too harsh, too singular. Yes, I have captained a ship, but I was raised to listen to the voices of others, *especially* as a leader. Had you listened to your officers many of our hardships might have been avoided!"

"Had I listened," Magellan shouted back, "I might well be dead, along with every man loyal to me, and you and your men would be facing execution if you ever returned to Spain!"

Like two duelists in a frozen stance, each man's eyes bored into the other's. When their breathing calmed a bit, Magellan said, "I ask you again, do you or do you not accept the offer to reassume your position as master of the *Concepción?*"

"You did not answer my question. What of the shame that these shackles have inflicted?" Elcano let the chain slip from his fingers and clatter to the deck. "Do you imagine that such a thing will be forgotten?"

"The memory of these last months will stay with you forever," Magellan acknowledged without hesitation. "But any dishonor will be expunged when you accept your former position within this fleet. To King Carlos and everyone else, my willingness to reinstate you will speak for itself. What happens from this day forward is up to you."

"And you."

Magellan leaned upon his desk and peered at him keenly. "I doubt I shall ever allow you to speak your mind so freely again. Now, I want an answer."

After one heartbeat, then two, Elcano said. "I accept your offer."

Magellan nodded and eased back in his seat. "Good. Then, Master Elcano, return to your ship and free your men."

"Free my men? All of them?"

"Of course, all of them."

Only half believing, Elcano offered a silent prayer of thanks. With difficulty, he said aloud, "For this decision, I am grateful."

"For your men or for yourself?"

"For both...sir." Slowly, Elcano asked, "Would you have released them if I had declined your offer?"

"I was confident that you would not decline. As I told you, we are much alike."

Elcano gave no reply.

"Go back to your ship, Master Elcano, and do not mention what we have discussed."

"Yes, Captain-general."

Magellan ordered the guards to call Espinosa to him, then said to the master-at-arms, "You will accompany Master Elcano back to the *Concepción*. He alone is to remove the shackles of every prisoner. Captain Serrano is then to restore the men to their previously assigned ships and duties."

"Yes, sir," said Espinosa, casting a glance of acknowledgement at Elcano.

"You may leave at once."

When Elcano reached the door, he turned back. Magellan had already picked up his quill and bent his head to his writing paper. Elcano said nothing more, but he bowed stiffly before leaving the cabin.

With the closing of the door, Magellan's eyes moved to the chains lying on the floor, and he sighed with relief and satisfaction.


Aboard the *Concepción* the bolts fell from the shackle rings as quickly as Elcano's hands could knock them loose. Chindarza and Juanito followed behind him with buckets of water to rinse the battered ankles and wrists of the men. A few of the bolder sailors, knowing that Elcano's restored rank would normally forbid them such liberties, clasped him on the arms in thankfulness. Tears flowed for sufferings too recent to be relinquished as suddenly as their chains, but they mingled with sobs of joy.

Before returning the newly freed men of the *San Antonio* to their ship, Captain Serrano offered each a swallow of wine from what precious little remained. The boat carrying them away from the *Concepción* had just pulled away when Acurio stepped up beside Elcano. "Sir," he said in a well pleased voice, "the captain asks if you'd care to wash up."

"My dear Acurio, not even a hot meal sounds as good as a warm bucket of water or two to wash this filth away."

"Bustamente is anxious to take his shears to your hair and beard, sir, just as soon as you're finished."

"Bless you, Acurio, and the barber, and the captain. Lead the way."

Acurio lingered outside Elcano's cabin and listened as moans of pleasure followed the first few splashes of water. When Chindarza joined him, the two shared a prolonged grin before moving off to see to their tasks.

At the end of his next watch, with clean skin, hair, and clothes, Elcano eased onto a dry bunk and fell immediately asleep. Several times during the night, however, he jerked awake when his movements failed to trigger the jingling of his chains. When morning dawned cold and calm, Elcano stood before the filling lateen sail on the *Concepción's* stern deck and reminded himself that he was once again her shipmaster.

As the ships eased away, Elcano could not keep from looking back toward the island where Father Calmette and Cartagena knelt and wept at the water's edge. Their pleas for mercy lifted and mingled with the light wind. Elcano's heart tightened as he turned away from them, turned away from the skulls of Mendoza and Quesada that gaped from their spikes, turned away from the torment that had been Port San Julian. With the last cries of the marooned men ringing in his ears, Elcano faced the opening that led to the sea.

The four ships that now comprised the fleet moved southward down the coast and began to encounter storms that seemed only to vary in their ferocity, but the vessels still managed to reach Santa Cruz within two days. Here, to the joy of all, were fish, sea wolves, sea geese, and other seabirds in abundance. Though precautions were taken in case of attack, no time was wasted before hunters and fishermen were busy at work, and those assigned the duties of drying and salting had difficulty keeping up with the haul. That night, and for the fifty-three nights that followed, there was food enough to fill every hungry belly.

Winters grip began to show signs of easing as October's first half waned, and preparations were made to leave their rich harbor.

Master Elcano, draped in his new sea wolfskin cloak and standing at the bottom of the steps leading up from the *Concepción's* hold, gazed with great satisfaction on the full barrels he'd just checked for the last time. When he felt his ship pull forward with the lifting of her anchor, he took the stairs three at a time to join Captain Serrano on the foredeck. Serrano greeted him with a nod, and they both stared ahead as the clouds lifted above them to let in the early light.

# Bay of 11,000 Virgins

## 13

"It's an opening all right, Master Elcano," Acurio said, pointing toward the sharply curving shoreline ahead. "The flagship is already heading in, sir."

After inching forward against headwinds for two days, the gusts had suddenly shifted the morning before, driving the fleet forward at a perilous speed and demanding a grueling effort from the men just to keep the ships under control. Elcano welcomed any bay that would allow a short layover to rest the crews. And every waterway was worth investigating.

As they sailed abreast of the opening, Acurio whistled in appreciation. "Why, it's huge, sir."

"Larger even than Santa Cruz, and it may be as deep as it is wide."

They sailed around the end of a long finger of land pointing to the south and entered the mouth of the vast bay.

"It must be twenty miles across," Acurio said in awe. "Do you suppose, sir...?"

Elcano was no less impressed by the size of the inlet, but he said warily, "I see no opening to the west, Acurio." His eyes scanned the three hills that rose over a hundred feet above the water, then he studied the waterway more closely. Over the ages it had cut broadly and deeply into the landscape all around, but there was no sign of its source. Through the overhanging mists, he caught glimpses of an unending file of snowcapped mountains marching westward.

Serrano had already ordered the sounding lines to be dropped when Elcano joined him on the half deck. Standing nearby, Carvalho was hastily sketching the outline of the bay onto a sheet of parchment. Elcano glanced at the sketch before asking the captain, "How deep are the lines running, sir?"

Serrano eyed him keenly, and said, "So deep that we haven't found the bottom yet."

They'd been in a promising body of water before, Elcano cautioned himself, in a river wider and deeper than was reasonable, but a river just the same. And yet, Elcano couldn't help thinking, never one *so* wide or *so* deep.

The tide swelled and swirled around the ships as they proceeded westward, their crews gawking at the shorelines ahead. They finally made their anchorage on the northern edge of the bay near the shallows of the shoreline. Almost at once, Magellan sent an order to Carvalho to take a boat ashore, climb a nearby hill, and come back with a report on the lay of the land as well as the course of the water.

His assignment was readily carried out and, after reporting to Magellan, Carvalho returned to the *Concepción*. "From where I stood I could see little to the west but mountains and snow," Carvalho admitted to Captain Serrano. "Even so, the captain-general has commanded that the *Concepción* and the *San Antonio* are to follow the waterway as far as it may lead, but to return within five days. The other two ships will remain here."

"When are we to leave?"

"At once, sir."

"Well, at least we can hope for calm waters in this sheltered place. Has he chosen a name for the bay yet?"

"Yes, Captain, after today's feast day, the Bay of the Eleven Thousand Virgins."

"Very well, Pilot. Update your charts. Master Elcano, take us out. I see that the *San Antonio* is already heading westward."

As the scouting ships eased along the northern shoreline, their men studied every hill and stream. Two hours later, with an abruptness that caught them unprepared, a storm broke upon the bay with its brutal winds and cold rain driving from the southeast. Elcano shouted and his men scurried to the lines in time to veer their ship away from the curving northwestern shore. Glancing far back toward the *Trinidad* and the *Victoria*, Elcano could see that they were heading out of the bay in an effort to avoid incurring the same fate as the *Santiago*.

The *Concepción* and the *San Antonio* made an initial effort to rejoin the other half of the fleet but they were too far inside the monstrous bay to overcome the battering headwinds. Giving up their attempt to reach the others, the ships struggled to pull farther from the shoreline and hold a position near the center of the bay.

Nearly blinded and frozen by the piercing rain, Serrano, Elcano, Carvalho, and their men held the *Concepción* behind the *San Antonio* all through the bruising night. When dawn finally appeared, they were startled to find themselves heading directly toward the rolling shallows off the southwestern bank. Exhausted men threw themselves against the tillers, and the two ships swayed and strained for every yard they gained against the current.

At last Elcano saw what he judged to be calmer waters near the western shore just ahead of them and he dared to take a hopeful breath just before the *San Antonio* suddenly rushed forward with renewed speed, swerved sharply, and disappeared before his eyes. There was no sound of crashing wood, no screaming from the men. She was just gone. Anxious seconds later he and Serrano spotted a narrow gap in the rocks, and they directed their ship toward it. He caught a glimpse of the water rushing on through a gorge banked by high walls of stone before the current seized the ship with unyielding force and thrust her forward.

For a terrifying moment Elcano thought that the *Concepción* would be swept against the northern bank. He clung to the half deck railing and held his breath, but she slipped cleanly through the break. The ship shot down a long southwestern stretch of narrows at a perilous speed until she finally plunged into another wide bay. There, with the *San Antonio* visible not far ahead, the crewmembers gathered their shaken courage and rode out the next stormy hours.

The winds finally subsided late in the morning and the two ships drew together to allow their captains to confer. Serrano and Mesquita quickly agreed that the *San Antonio* would investigate the bay's northern shore while the *Concepción* explored to the south.

Fascinated and unable to deny the stirrings of hope, Elcano watched the hilly southern shoreline give way to a land of glacial rumblings. Walls of vertically lined ice hugged the sides of crowded mountains that rose steeply from the waters edge. These glacial masses moved, and breathed, and growled like living things. In awe, Elcano stared into the crystal surfaces, discovering that the clear ice took on a bluish color where its fissures ran deep, ultimately darkening to a midnight blue. When daylight managed to penetrate the clouds for moments at a time, the sudden displays of light-scattering prisms seemed nothing less than magical.

Here and there the ice and snow had melted away, yielding some of the lower slopes to pine and beech forests carpeted with ferns. Elcano could feel the icy breath in the wind that blew down from the heights above, and he could hear it whistle among the tree branches, adding its rising soprano voice to the deep, reverberating bass of the moaning ice.

Methodically searching each inlet they encountered, the indistinct sun had nearly set when the *Concepción's* lookout called, "Captain, I've lost sight of the *San Antonio!*"

Serrano appeared below the main mast and, gazing aloft, asked, "What was her position when you saw her last?"

"She'd all but reached the northwestern curve of the bay, Captain. Her sails vanished as if she'd been swallowed by another stretch of narrows, sir."

"If she's headed to the west, I'm sure all is well, Alonso. Keep a steady eye out for her return." Serrano stepped away from the mast and muttered, "Why the devil would they leave the bay without so much as signaling us?" Turning to his officers he said, "We'll continue probing until we've charted each of these southern inlets. There seems to be a hundred of them, but we can't risk missing any passage. The *San Antonio* knows where we are. I just hope the winds stay calm long enough for her to make it back here before we have to return to the captain-general. If it means missing our rendezvous date, we can't wait for her."

A day and a half later, Elcano and Carvalho were sketching small additions to the latest charts when, glancing up to check their drawing against the shoreline ahead, they both saw the opening at the same time. "Captain," Elcano called out, and his voice was immediately joined by those of other seamen proclaiming the location of the gap. Before they had reached it, however, the sails of the *San Antonio* came swiftly into view.

Serrano strode up beside Elcano. "Look at her men." His voice rose with excitement as he added, "Why, they're celebrating. Holy Mother, you don't suppose—?"

Elcano could just hear the men calling out at the top of their lungs, "We've found it! The passage! The passage!"

Riotous cheers burst from Serrano and the others around him, but Elcano stood frozen at the rail. All he could think was, "He was right all along. It was here. It *is* here." After a moment or two he was able to smile and accept the hearty congratulations and festive antics of the others, but he was strangely unable to surrender himself to either relief or joy. Distracted and puzzled by his own reaction, Elcano waited as the *San Antonio* drew up next to them. With unbound exuberance Mesquita eagerly beckoned Serrano, Carvalho, and Elcano to board his ship and meet with him.

Once aboard the *San Antonio*, the *Concepción's* officers were nearly deafened by the continuing commotion of the sailors from both ships. An exultant Mesquita, along with Pilot Major Gomez, directed the officers to his cabin at once.

"Tell us everything," Serrano said eagerly as they gathered around Mesquita's table.

"We sailed through the mouth of these narrows, which are much wider than the first stretch, and found a bay so vast and long that we couldn't see its end."

"And it took you to the South Sea?"

"I didn't want to risk running into foul weather and being late to reunite with the rest of the fleet," said Mesquita, "so we turned back before actually reaching the end of the bay."

"You didn't even see the ocean?" Serrano demanded in surprise.

"No, but the ebb and flow of the tide is just as strong and regular as it is in the Bay of Eleven Thousand Virgins. We tested the water again and again. The water is the saltiest I've ever tasted and our lead lines could not find the seabed.. I have no doubt that this is the passage."

"You're absolutely certain?"

"As sure as if I had seen the South Sea with my own eyes. The evidence is too strong to leave any doubt. We've found it." Barking for one of his cabin boys, Mesquita ordered a round of wine, and they toasted and drank to their blessed find.

After his first swallow, Elcano asked, "May we see your maps, Pilot Major?"

Gomez happily rolled out his charts, and every officer bent his head over them.

As his eyes searched the maps, Elcano's uncertainty intensified. Before him lay evidence that they had found the westward passage. This was the great prize that so many had doubted even existed. Some had even died because of their disbelief. Staring at the map, he couldn't help questioning his own doubts, his own choices that had led up to this moment. Again, a voice seemed to echo, "*It was here all along.*" If Cartagena, Mendoza, and Quesada had known this, Elcano's troubled mind concluded, they would have lived to see it.

After re-boarding the *Concepción*, Elcano learned that his preoccupation hadn't passed the notice of Captain Serrano, who asked, "What is it, Master Elcano? Where is your elation at this day's news?"

"Forgive my reserve, Captain. I am, of course, very pleased."

Serrano gave him a searching look, then said, "On second thought, perhaps your reflection is understandable. Yes, quite understandable. Let's get underway."

Their ships left at once to retrace the miles they had covered. At the end of Elcano's next watch, he entered his cabin and happened to glance at his image in his small mirror. For the first time since his rank had been restored, he paused and truly looked at himself. Who was this haggard creature with the haunted eyes? He was surely not the same man he had been before his imprisonment in Port San Julian. His features had been thinned and lined, but the transformation went much deeper than this. As his eyes stared back at him, he acknowledged how acutely his very spirit had been scathed. The reckless anger he'd vented at Magellan the day of his release had died away. Now he was more quiet, more thoughtfully hesitant, than he had ever been, and he did not like either of these changes. He did not want to be scarred, perhaps beyond recovery.

As gratifying as it had been to leave the accursed port behind and to take up his duties as the *Concepción's* shipmaster once again, he could not seem to keep from looking back. Had he left a portion of his soul next to the bones of his former captain and Mendoza, or with the doomed Cartagena and Father Calmette? Should his own bones be sharing the ground where Juan Elorriaga now rested?

And after today's discovery, how was he to feel about all that had come to pass? No answers came to ease his mind. Slowly, he shook his head and turned away from the mirror.

When he emerged from his cabin, Elcano gradually allowed a share of his men's jubilance to seep into his questioning moodiness. Chindarza found him on the half deck whittling a piece of wood into the shape of a sea wolf.

After watching him for a few moments, Chindarza said, "Master Elorriaga would be so pleased to know we have found our way, wouldn't he, sir?"

Elcano gazed up at the lad, amazed at his keen and innocent perceptions, and suddenly realized how true his words were. "Then we must be joyful for his sake as well as our own, eh, Chindarza?"

That night, as they held their position near the eastern mouth to the first narrows, even the ice walls seemed to rumble with anticipation. The fair wind of next morning allowed them to pass back through the channel and to the Bay of Virgins with little difficulty.

Aboard the flagship, Magellan sat alone in his cabin with his head in his hands. Enrique and Cristóbal had each come to him to offer what comfort they could, but he'd sent them away. He had prayed for days, but it was time to face the truth. The *San Antonio* and the *Concepción* were lost forever.

The storm four nights earlier had ripped the foremast from the *Victoria*, smashed in the *Trinidad's* hatches and gun ports, and tossed several men irretrievably into the sea and to their deaths. All this, after they had been lucky enough to reach open water and hold the ships a safe distance from shore. What chance had the other two ships had of surviving, trapped in this bay?

There had been no sign of his missing ships, not so much as a broken plank. The wind and sea must have driven them onto the icy rocks and taken them to the very depths of this heartless bay. Magellan told himself that he must accept that Mesquita, Serrano, and the rest of his men were gone. And with them had died any hope of continuing the voyage. He dared not even probe the borders of this bay in search of their bodies to bury. To do so would put his last two ships at risk of being caught up in another storm, crushed, and pulled down into the icy deep.

Now that the repairs had nearly been completed, he must turn his thoughts to Spain. Tomorrow he must return, and he would return a failure. After the claims he'd made to the king and the decisions he'd made at Port San Julian, he might even be branded a traitor. As such, Magellan would be sentenced to the same punishment that he had ordered his men to carry out against Quesada. At this thought, he could feel the muscles of his neck tighten.

Very slowly, Magellan untied the rolled bundle of sheets that comprised his journal, read the last lines of his previous entry, and reached for his quill. He had written only two lines when Cristóbal banged on the door, threw it open, and announced, "There's a column of smoke rising in the west, Father!"

"Smoke?" Magellan said, standing and heading for the door. "From a signal fire?" Without waiting for an answer, he brushed past Cristóbal and hurriedly made his way to the port rail. He saw it at once, a white line of smoke ascending from the base of a western cliff. The line was drifting, no, trailing, as if it were coming from a moving fire. "Please, God," he muttered, "Please." Before Magellan's straining eyes, a set of sails emerged from what had appeared to be wall of solid rocks.

He clutched the rail and sucked in his breath as men scrambled and jostled to the side of the ship and up the lines. Simultaneous shouts rose from his crew and from the men of the *Victoria*. "It's the *San Antonio*! She's come through the storms! Another sail! The *Concepción*! They're alive! They're alive!"

Magellan cried out with unrestrained joy just before successive thundering roars erupted from the guns of the *San Antonio* and the *Concepción*. His blurry eyes caught sight of banners of crimson, silver, yellow, blue, gold, and green fluttering from every approaching mast and yardarm. He leaned far out and took in the view of the returning men as they wildly flourished their cloaks and scraps of canvas over their heads. In uniform rhythm, drums large and small began to beat out a heartening, heralding roll across the pitching water. When the ships were closer still, Magellan heard voices yelling out the impossible, "The passage! We've found the passage!"

Still clinging to the rail, Magellan uttered, "Could it be?"

The four ships came together in a concussion of jubilation and questions. Magellan ordered Mesquita, Serrano, and their pilots and shipmasters aboard the *Trinidad* immediately, and once they'd arrived astonished them all, especially Elcano, by throwing his arms around each man in turn.

Beaming broadly, Magellan ushered them, Barbosa, and the other senior officers into his cabin.

"Fine work. The finest of work!" said Magellan. "I can't tell you what it means to see you safely back. And you even bring news of the passage! Tell me what you've seen."

SOUTH AMERICA

Rio de Janeiro

Cape Santa Maria

Port San Julian

Cape of Virgins

After their accounts had been shared and their charts had been studied and speculated upon, Magellan rubbed his hands together, saying, "Well, at the very least, it looks promising. You men have earned a long rest and a good meal, but the wind is already shifting and we mustn't wait before investigating the passage all the way to its end. There'll be time for rest once we've reached the far sea. Captain Mesquita, lead us through those narrows and keep heading west. I'll take the position behind you. The

182

*Concepción* will follow the *Trinidad*, and the *Victoria* will
hold the last position. Now, back to your ships, gentlemen.
Let's be off at once!'"

When the officers of the *Concepción* returned to her
decks, Elcano was met by a smiling Acurio.

"The captain-general appeared excited to see us back,
sir."

"Yes, even me, it would seem. But there is to be no
reprieve from our duties until we've found the western end
of this channel. Let's hope it's a painless search."

With the altering of the wind, the clouds soon lifted to
allow Elcano a wider view of the landscape than had been
visible since their first arrival. He was watching the southern shore when the *San Antonio's* lookout shouted, "A village, Captain, a mile ahead to the west, northwest!"

Despite Magellan's impatience to move ahead, orders
were passed down the line of ships to halt long enough for a
landing party of ten men under Carvalho's command to go
ashore in search of food. Before long the men returned,
reporting that they had discovered only a mound of whale-
bones and extensive funeral grounds containing the
remains of hundreds of natives. Unwilling to delay further,
Magellan commanded the fleet to push on.

For the next three days Elcano trailed the *San Antonio's*
course, passing through the first narrows, the second bay,
the second narrows, and into the third gigantic bay that
bent out of sight toward the south. Once within this inlet,
Elcano noticed plumes of smoke rising from behind the cliffs
of the eastern shore and concluded that their sources could
only be campfires. The ships avoided this shoreline and did
not drop their anchors until they had reached a long,
tapered island lying just off the bay's western edge, thereby
leaving the wide expanse of water between the fleet and the
fire makers.

Magellan called his officers to his cabin that evening and
asked each of them to give an accounting of his ship's food
stores. The supplies of the *San Antonio* were the first to be
tallied since she transported the greatest share of their con-
sumables, including nearly all of what remained of their

garbanzos, currants, and figs. After each of the other ships had been accounted for, Magellan reviewed his reckoning of the amounts reported and concluded, "With careful management we should have food enough for three more months. Now, I do not doubt that this strait leads to the South Sea. The signs are plain enough. The only question I wish to discuss is whether to press on from here to our final destination. I'm interested in your willingness to sail all the way to the Moluccas, given that our food supply must continue to be carefully rationed."

Elcano tried to conceal his surprise that Magellan was actually asking for their opinions. He felt Magellan's gaze touch on him for just an instant, but it was long enough to exchange a common thought, a common goal. *We must stand together.*

Pilot Major Gomez was the first to reply. "Captain-general, while the supply of food may seem adequate, we don't know the length of this channel, let alone the breadth of the South Sea. To head into an ocean that no man has ever crossed while carrying minimal provisions would be to recklessly tempt fate. Weather may well forestall the fleet, as it has so many times thus far. I advise that we return to Spain, sir. The king will be most pleased to learn what we have discovered, and he will likely grant us the means for another expedition."

For a moment no one else spoke, but Magellan merely waited.

Mesquita ended the pause by saying, "I must disagree with my pilot. We can reprovision our meat as we make our way through this strait and up the western coast. We'll have enough to spare before we attempt to cross the open sea."

Serrano stated his own willingness to continue the voyage, as did Barbosa.

Again Magellan held himself silent, but no others voiced their thoughts. "Since the rest of you still hesitate, I will speak. While it is true that we have no charts of this strait or of much of the sea beyond it, men of science have estimated the size of our earth for ages. We must rely on their conclusions, which tell us that the South Sea is far smaller than the Atlantic. It should take us no more than a few weeks to reach the Spiceries. However, to allow for the possibility of weather delays, we will add to our stores for as long as we remain near land."

Heads began to nod in agreement, but Elcano saw Gomez frown deeply. Gomez was the pilot major of the fleet and he had been forced for many months to let Mesquita, a man both unqualified and brutal, to take credit for ruling the *San Antonio*. Gomez had piloted their way through the majority of the strait, had confirmed that it did indeed lead to the sea, but again Mesquita accepted the undeserved praise. Now, when the survival of his crew was at stake, he seemed determined to be heard.

"Captain-general, for the sake of our men—."

Magellan cut him off. "I have given each of you a chance to make your will known, but I have decided to move forward."

Gomez said, "But, Captain-general, if—."

Glaring, Magellan snapped, "Are we men of the sea or are we not! It is impossible to anticipate every danger that might befall us. But we will go on! If we run into storms, we will face them. If we meet enemies, we will fight them with all our strength. If we run short of food, by heaven, I will eat the leather straps from our own yardarms before I will be turned away from my commitment to the king." Easing back in his chair, he said in a slightly moderated tone, "God has guided us to this channel. He will lead us on to fortune, and safely home again."

Elcano saw resentment flash across Gomez's features. To be ordered to serve day after day under the heavy-handed and inept Mesquita and then to be rebuffed before the other officers seemed to have stripped away the mask of acceptance Gomez had maintained over the last few months. His mouth and eyes set in a silent declaration of smoldering dissent.

Magellan did not appear to notice the indignation his words had forged in Gomez. Addressing the captains without a pause, the captain-general said, "Each ship is to send a small hunting party ashore to kill whatever game they might before the light fades. The fleet will depart immediately after our evening meal. That is everything for now, gentlemen."

Because of the time of year and their extreme southerly location, daylight hours now stretched far longer than what Elcano or the other men were accustomed to. Each day was followed by little more than four hours of darkness. Judging from the birds and sea wolves visible from the ships, the elongated day might allow the hunters time to bring back enough food to keep the cooks, stewards, and tanners busy for a week. Following these thoughts, Elcano decided to ask his captain for permission to be among the hunters.

Upon returning to the *Concepción*, Serrano showed no hesitation in giving his approval. Elcano felt his excitement build as he grabbed his bow and quiver, quickly chose the members of his hunting party, and boarded the ship's launch along with them.

To feel the rocky shore beneath his feet, to stretch his long leg muscles as he ran and leaped after prey, to breathe deeply of the crisp air, to raise and sight an arrow, and to stand motionless until it found its mark; these were things he gloried in as he never had before. He tried not to think at all, tried not to remember, only to use his senses to their fullest. And the land seemed to offer its riches up to him and his men without hesitation.

When their boat was heavily loaded with pelts and meat, Elcano returned to the ship weary, blood splattered, and, in no small measure, renewed. He and his fellow hunters came aboard to the congratulations of their shipmates and the proud display of the fishermen's haul. The cabin boys of the *Trinidad* and the *Concepción*, including Chindarza, had added to their ship's prosperity by bringing armloads of wild rhubarb back to the decks. Their combined success had been as bountiful as Elcano had hoped, and the butchering and cleaning was immediately followed by cooking.

Hours after they had feasted on the fruits of their labors, Elcano and three other hunters stood together at the *Concepción's* bow, bragging shamelessly about the huge long-snouted sea wolf they had shot. In truth, it had been so huge that it had required the efforts of all four of them to drag it back to the beach. Elcano found himself laughing for the first time in what seemed like years. With the smile still on his face, he sighed and looked toward the shore they were gliding past, where here and there the red spots of isolated campfires blinked. He studied them for a moment before lifting his eyes to the stars, which were extraordinarily close and brilliant on this clear night. There was the bright group forming the corners of a crucifix that could not be seen from his homeland, or even from the Canary Islands. He had heard Magellan say the cross was a sign that God was watching over them. Tonight, Elcano let himself believe that it just might be true. Magellan had been disastrously wrong about the location of the passage, but not about its existence. No, he had been right about that.

"You men had best turn in," Elcano said pleasantly, and soon made his way to his own bunk.

The fleet sailed on until, at mid morning and during Elcano's next watch, they approached a rounded point of land that split the bay. The land broadened until it appeared to merge with other expanses farther on, obscuring the continuous prospect of the bay for the first time. Here also the eastern shore of the bay gave way to another extension of water that curved out of sight to the northwest. Faced with this three-way division in the watercourse, the ships obeyed the flagship's signal to draw together.

Elcano noticed that the countenances of several officers and many men reflected uncertainty and disappointment, but the captain-general seemed completely undeterred as he issued new orders.

"Since the inlet to the southeast heads away from our desired direction," he declared, "it will be disregarded. The *San Antonio* will head south by taking the eastern course of the strait. The rest of the fleet will take the western channel. In four days, Captain Mesquita, you must meet the rest of the fleet at the western base of those snow-topped peaks to the south. Any questions? Good, then let's proceed at once."

187

Separating, the ships glided off in their appointed directions.

That day and the next the *Concepción* continued to the south with her two partner ships, but on the third day the western shore, which had been gradually curving away, leveled off and abruptly cut to the northwest. Elcano stared as hungrily as the rest of his crew at this new stretch of water, turning away from the strait's fork that continued on to the south. At last he was directing his ship's anxious sails in a northwesterly direction. Their way was far from clear, however. This narrow reach of water was still bordered by land on both sides, and its breadth continued to taper rather than expand to reveal an unobstructed sea. On their port side, waterways that had been gnawing away at the rock and ice for many ages spilled over the glacial cliffs and crashed into the waters below. So the ships hugged the inner shore until they at last found an anchorage.

The time when they should have turned back to rendezvous with the *San Antonio* had already slipped by and Magellan seemed unwilling to relinquish the miles he'd gained even temporarily. Instead of ordering all three ships to retrace their course, he sent word to Captain Serrano that the *Concepción* was to head out at the break of day, meet the *San Antonio*, and lead her through this new passage to their present landing.

Serrano, Elcano, and Carvalho had no difficulty in backtracking down the now familiar route, but even making good time the *Concepción* arrived four days behind schedule. And when she arrived, the *San Antonio* was nowhere to be seen.

"Not a sign of her," Acurio said as Elcano continued to glance up one side of the strait and down the other. "Do you suppose she's still on the other side of this mountain, sir?"

"Possibly."

"Or maybe, when we didn't turn up, she came after us and took that southern fork."

"Yes, that's possible too."

After a pause, Acurio said, "Sir, you don't suppose Pilot Gomez, that is, there's been talk that he might try to..."

"Yes, I know, Acurio, but let's hope the *San Antonio* has only been delayed, as we were."

"She's got most of our food in her hold, sir."

Elcano looked directly at him. "That, she does. Heaven help us if we've lost her."

Captain Serrano commanded Elcano to take the *Concepción* a safe distance from the mountainside and have the gunners fire a salvo, but the only response they received was a roaring echo that sent great chunks of ice splashing into the water. When the noise had died away, they began combing the bay, zigzagging back and forth northward across the wide glassy surface and searching every indentation in the shoreline large enough to conceal an injured ship. By nightfall, they hadn't seen so much as a plank or a barrel, and Elcano found it more and more difficult to put the image of Gomez's angry, insulted face from his mind.

It was late afternoon of the following day when they reached the spot where the *San Antonio* had first left the fleet. Finding not a trace of her there either, they again turned to the south, intent on delivering this disturbing news to the captain-general. They had not yet arrived at the fork in the strait that bent to the northwest, however, when their lookout cried out that the *Trinidad* and the *Victoria* were sailing toward them. Elcano joined Serrano and Acurio on the stern deck as the *Concepción* pulled close to the flagship.

Magellan called, "What news, Captain Serrano?"

"No sign of the *San Antonio*, sir, and we've searched this side of the strait up to the point where the ships originally parted."

Elcano watched the concern on Magellan's face quickly change to confident resolution. "Captain, we now have three ships with which to search for her. The *San Antonio* could easily have lost her way in this labyrinth of rivers and islands. We will find her."

"As for us," Magellan released his smile as he continued, "we have brought news that I trust you will find much more welcome. I sent a handful of my men north from our anchorage in a longboat and they reached the open sea! They saw it with their own eyes! We've found our way to the South Sea!"

Elcano had known, or thought he had known that they were close, but at these words he closed his eyes and leaned his head back as the men around him whooped and yelled. For a second, he simply inhaled this confirmation. When he opened his eyes, he found himself staring into Acurio's glowing face.

"The South Sea, Master Elcano!" Acurio yelled, and when Elcano laughed out loud his boatswain shouted, "Hurrah!" and tossed his beret across the stern deck. They shook hands heartily, and congratulated Serrano while men dropped to their knees, or burst into tears, or danced and whirled. Chindarza raised his voice in a high, reverberating, "aiyeeyeeyeeheehee!"

This particular cry had resounded from the peaks of the Pyrenees, the mountains of his homeland, for ages out of mind, and hearing it now struck a chord deep within Elcano. To Chindarza's, Acurio's, and a dozen other voices, Elcano added his own, surprising and pleasing his men as it rose higher and higher until it bounced off the icy mountains and echoed back to them.

As Elcano took a breath, Acurio turned shining eyes on him and said, "All will be well now, sir. All will be well."

This man, thought Elcano, this man had risked his own freedom to send him food when he was a hungry prisoner, had stood by him in the face of storms and death and despair. Elcano's own eyes filled as he gently placed his hands on Acurio's shoulders. In a thick voice he said, "Yes, Acurio. All will be well."

Before Acurio could respond, Magellan shouted from the *Trinidad*, "Captain Serrano!" When the uproar subsided enough to be heard, he continued, "Since we have six hours of daylight remaining, we'll use them to pursue the *San Antonio*."

As the hour grew late and the ships again drew together without finding a hint as to the *San Antonio's* whereabouts, Elcano noticed that even Magellan's elation at finding the strait's western opening had begun to dim.

The next day proved no more rewarding, nor the next. Finally, after an entire fruitless week had passed, the captain-general assembled his officers in his cabin. "I've decided to send the *Victoria* back to the Bay of Virgins in the hope that the *San Antonio* may have returned there."

Although Elcano did not voice an objection, he felt that this assignment offered little promise, and he knew he was not alone. Why would the *San Antonio* make her way back to the Bay of Virgins rather than the rendezvous point, unless she meant to continue on toward Spain? But then, perhaps even the slightest chance was worth chasing.

Magellan handed his brother-in-law a large lidded jar, and said, "Captain Barbosa, this contains charts and instructions. If you do not locate the *San Antonio*, place a marker on a high hill and bury the jar. Its contents will allow Captain Mesquita to follow us."

Not one of the other officers chose to express his doubts about the wisdom of this assignment. Nonetheless, days later this belief was confirmed when the *Victoria* returned alone.

When the officers were recalled to Magellan's quarters, the fleet's astrologer, Andrés de San Martin, was also summoned.

"Tell us, San Martin," said Magellan, "did you read the stars last night, as I asked?"

"I did, Captain-general, and for many nights before that."

"And what have you learned from them?"

San Martin had not forgotten the torture he had endured at Port San Julian, and he now hesitated before finally saying, "The stars indicate that Pilot Gomez has overpowered Captain Mesquita and taken the *San Antonio*. They say also that Captain Mesquita has been wounded, but he will survive."

Magellan gave him a hard stare. "Is the *San Antonio* far from us now?"

There was another pause. "Sir, we will not catch up to her unless we sail at once for Spain. The *San Antonio* is already well away, across the Atlantic."

Suddenly forbidding, Magellan said, "If Gomez has done what you say, he will pay for this act with his life."

Magellan glowered at the floor as silence held them all.

At last, Barbosa cleared his throat and said, "Sir, with this new misfortune, we dare not proceed with our voyage. With the *San Antonio* goes much of our food."

"The loss of our largest ship leaves us in a desperate situation, Captain-general," said Serrano. "Without her, the chance of calamity befalling us is greatly increased."

"Three ships remain in our keeping," said Magellan, stubbornly. His voice strengthened as he went on, "Captain Serrano, after you left us to search for the *San Antonio,* we moved our anchorage farther to the northwest and found a river alive with sardines. There were also sea wolves and small ostriches, similar to those given to us by the Patagonians. We may have little else in the holds of our ships, gentlemen, but we have plenty of salt to preserve any meat we bring in."

Barbosa again pointed out, "Sir, the *San Antonio* carries most of our sea biscuit in her hold."

"We have enough for several weeks yet," Magellan countered.

With growing frustration, Barbosa persisted, "And the garbanzos and dried fruit, Captain-general?"

"We can survive without them. There will be plenty of fruit in the Spice Islands."

Seeing that further argument was useless, all dialogue from the officers abruptly ended.

"In the morning I will have another jar buried at the base of a cross my men will erect on this shore," Magellan said, casting a pointed glance at San Martin, "just in case the stars are wrong. We'll return to the River of Sardines and fill our holds. Then, we'll leave Patagonia and head out into open seas."

# Insatiable Ocean

## 14

The three ships were released from their anchorage and shoved forward by the current even before the sails had been completely unfurled. Elcano and Acurio were at the rail of the *Concepción's* foredeck, intent on keeping her from veering back toward the cliffs of the shoreline and from ramming any rocks or ice lying just below the waters' surface.

"It's a fine thing to be leaving this cheerless land and its talking ice, eh, Master Elcano?" said Acurio, studying the surface of the churning channel. "Now that we've a good supply of fish and meat, I'm well ready to be off." He lifted his beret to scratch the top of his shaggy scalp. "I suppose there's little hope that we'll ever lay eyes on the *San Antonio* again, sir."

"Not until we reach home, if then," said Elcano.

"Have you noticed how the captain-general's been watching for her every evening, sir? Some of the men are surprised he's ordered us forward today."

"We can't afford to wait any longer."

"No, sir, that's true." After a thoughtful pause, Acurio said, "Do you suppose Pilot Gomez killed Captain Mesquita, sir?"

Elcano's voice deepened a note or two. "Many men hated Mesquita enough to kill him, after the part he played at Port San Julian. And Gomez made it plain enough that he wanted to return to Spain. He said that it would be folly to go on. Who knows what he might have done?"

"Do *you* think it's folly, sir, us going on?"

With sudden severity, Elcano said, "I have learned that it is best not to voice my thoughts concerning this voyage."

"I, uh, of course, sir."

At once Elcano saw the pain he had just inflicted. Shaking his head, he said, "Forgive my harshness, Acurio. You are the last man I would have bear the brunt of my bitterness. My mood grows dark at times when I least expect it, even today when there is hope of us reaching our goal." He forced a small smile upon his lips. "I should have said that if it is folly that we go on, the *Concepción* will carry us into the face of danger as proudly as any ship upon the seas."

"That's the plain truth, sir. Our lady," Acurio said, trying to hide his hurt as he patted the ship's railing, "she's as ready to be away as I am myself."

"Imagine that in a few weeks her hold will be bursting with the sweet scent of spices."

"May our Lord have it so, sir."

"Look, she's pulling with the current even as she picks up speed, Acurio. Let's keep her well clear of the waterfalls. The highest ones show signs of a fierce backwash."

"I'll watch them, sir." Acurio hesitated, then said, "But, sir, I know what you've lived through, and I'm not likely to forget. A man ought to be allowed a moment or two of harshness after such treatment as you've endured."

With that, Acurio left him, barking orders to the men at the sail lines as he went.

For the next two days their ships carried them northwest, avoiding the vertical walls of rock and cascading falls to their starboard and a lacework of snowy mountains, inlets, and glacial sheers to their port. Slowly, the land's height began to diminish and the trees on the lower slopes became fewer. Elcano heard men mutter amongst themselves that they could hear the roar of surf far ahead, and from that point on he listened with greater attentiveness.

On an overcast morning Elcano, Serrano, Carvalho, Acurio, and Chindarza anxiously watched as the shoreline tapered away from their port side. The *Concepción* pitched as she rode out the collisions of the incoming rollers and the outgoing tide, but none of the four officers and none of their watchful crew seemed to feel her surging movements. Their eyes were straining toward what appeared to be the end of a spit of land. All of a sudden the men of the forerunning *Trinidad* let loose a riotous racket. The land to the west vanished, and there it was. The wide, open sea.

"Dear God," Elcano breathed.

Serrano, smiling from ear to ear, lifted his arms and shouted to be heard above the exaltations of his crew, "Men, today we've reached the South Sea! Mark your log books and your memories, and never forget this 28th day of November!"

As Elcano let his eyes drink in the sight, he knew that there was no need to record this date with a quill and parchment in order to remember it. The vastness of the unobstructed sea, the heavy smell of seaweed in the misty air, the feel of the *Concepción's* salt-eroded wood beneath his palms, the sounds of Serrano's words and the men's rejoicing, and the look of rapture on Acurio's face and marvel on Chindarza's when they turned to him. These would stay with him in poignant clarity for the remainder of his life. He would record the date, but for others who would come after

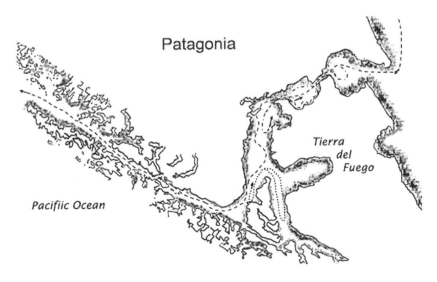

Patagonia

Tierra
del
Fuego

Pacifiic Ocean

him rather than for himself. Locking the moment safely away in his mind, he surrendered his attention to the needs of his swaying vessel.

For hours the full-hearted men of the fleet maneuvered their ships through the undulating sea and up the coastline before being rewarded with waters both calm and beautiful. The rhythmic growling of the surf quieted and the clouds fled as if they'd been abruptly called back to some forgotten haven in the southeast. The ships continued to sail upon tranquil waters and under a lenient sky until the vessels drew together at sunset.

The routines to be used during their ocean crossing had been established before leaving the River of Sardines, and the appropriate salutes were now offered. Afterward, Magellan addressed the men of his fleet with reflective satisfaction. "We must offer our Heavenly Father abundant thanks for delivering us at last to this ocean. Although it has been known as the South Sea for many years, I have decided to bestow a more fitting name upon it. It will henceforth be called the Pacific Sea. May this name hold true as we journey across its waters.

"Now," he continued, "I mean to follow the coast until we meet a wind blowing from the southeast, such as exists off the African coast. Until we head to the west, every waking man should keep watch on the shoreline for signs of natives. Rest well tonight, men!"

Rest did come easier, throughout that night and many that followed, but no humans were sighted as one week elapsed, and then two. There was little deviation in the gentle weather even after Magellan's prediction of a change in wind direction was confirmed. The fleet left the security of the nearby land without taking time to search for more provisions. After all, their holds contained many barrels of meat and, with conditions such as they'd been experiencing, the crossing would take little time and give them few challenges.

On a smooth sea before steady winds, Elcano observed Christmas services on his knees and with a bowed head, praying in deepest gratitude. Since the temperature had continued to grow blessedly warmer as they'd held to their northwesterly course, and since the furs they had been wearing were now rotting and stinking, he and the other men celebrated the birth of Christ by flinging their rank coverings overboard. Watching his shabby cloak float away, Elcano felt as if he'd just discarded a small share of the haunting winter. He turned and watched the hopeful faces around him, reading the unspoken declarations that the approaching year of 1521 would surely fulfill the brightest of their expectations. Raising his face to the sun, Elcano prayed that they were right.

That afternoon a bare-footed and sweaty Chindarza appeared on the half deck where, moments before, Elcano had resumed his carving on a four-inch wooden shape. For a moment Chindarza studied his shipmaster's activities without interrupting, but because most of the wood was hidden by Elcano's hands, he could not make out what its intended shape might be. Elcano had not let him see this latest carving yet, so with curious anticipation, Chindarza asked, "Another animal, sir?"

Elcano had already given his cabin boy a carved shark, a sea goose, a sea wolf, and a whale, but he was pleased that Chindarza always hoped for more. On many nights, Elcano noticed, Chindarza voluntarily sharpened his carving knife, undoubtedly to encourage the possibility of enlarging his wooden menagerie. It was enormously satisfying to bring the strange animals encountered on their voyage to life under his blade, especially when they brought joy to Chindarza. As with Acurio, Elcano felt deeply indebted to the young man for the many kindnesses he'd shown to a lowly prisoner.

Elcano paused and held out the object of his handiwork for Chindarza's inspection. "Do you recognize it?"

Chindarza smiled as he took it and turned it over in his hands. "Why, it's one of the long-necked Patagonian mules, sir."

"When it's finished it can keep the others company."

"Thank you, sir." Chindarza handed the figure back and then noticed Juanito motioning to him from the main deck. He waved Juanito up to join them, and said, "Master Elcano, Juanito wants you to teach him to read the astrolabe, like you taught me."

Elcano brushed away some shavings. "The astrolabe? Now, Chindarza, that is something Pilot Carvalho should teach him."

Juanito appeared at the top of the stairs, hurried over to them, and sat down beside Chindarza. Hesitantly, he said, "Father busy, sir, much busy."

"Is he busy right now?"

"Father sleep now, sir."

"Perhaps you should ask him when he wakes up, Juanito."

"Sir, you would be the best man for this job," said Chindarza, echoing words that Elcano had often spoken to him.

Elcano stilled his knife. "When were you given authority to make such decisions, Chindarza?"

"Forgive me, sir." Chindarza leaned in closer. "It's just that Pilot Carvalho beats him when he asks too many questions."

Having witnessed Carvalho's intolerance with the boy many times, Elcano accepted this with little surprise. Even now, Juanito's left shin bore a suspicious egg-shaped bruise.

Chindarza pushed on, "You *did* give me the responsibility to look after him, sir."

"Just be careful you don't overstep your rank, young man," Elcano warned with little severity. He shifted his gaze to Juanito, gave the matter a moment's consideration, and said, "So, you want to learn about navigation?"

"Sir?"

"About the astrolabe? About steering the ship?"

Juanito nodded vigorously.

"All right, then. You two wait here."

Elcano went to his cabin, left his nearly finished animal and knife on his desk, and collected several other items. When he returned, he began the lesson by holding out a round metal instrument with a pivoting arm anchored in its center and numerical markings around its seven-inch circumference.

"Now Juanito," he said, "with the help of the sun and the stars, the astrolabe can tell us how far we have sailed from the equator."

Juanito cocked his head. "Equator, sir?"

"Here," Elcano said, spreading out a map and pointing at the thin stripe that ran evenly across its center. "It's a horizontal line that circles the middle of the earth."

"Earth, yes."

"The astrolabe," he said, again holding up the instrument, "tells us that we are now near the latitude of 27° south of the equator. Show him on the map, Chindarza. Now, one degree of latitude is approximately equal to sixty-nine miles. Do you understand that number?" Elcano glanced at Chindarza questioningly.

While Juanito nodded, Chindarza confirmed, "He understands, sir. I've taught him to count higher than a hundred. He can count every plank in the ship."

"All right, then, we know the Spice Islands are near the equator since the Portuguese have journeyed fairly close to them by way of Africa. Captain-general Magellan has sailed much of that way himself. See?" He ran his finger around the map to indicate their route. "So, since we know the Spice Islands are not far from the equator, and the astrolabe tells us how far to the south of the equator we are now, it also tells us how far to the north we have yet to sail. Today we are..." he scribbled some figures on a corner of his paper, "about 1865 miles to the south of the Spiceries."

"But Chindarza say we must go west too, sir. How far west?"

Elcano smiled at the boy's quickness and at Chindarza's previous instruction of his small page. "That's correct. We must also continue to sail to the west. Just how far to the west we don't know exactly. As you can see, the Pacific Sea is not yet drawn on the map because no one has ever sailed across it before. We are the first. But very wise men have told us that it is about half the size of the Atlantic Sea, over here."

Juanito studied the chart and nodded.

"So," Elcano went on, "we have done our best to estimate how many miles we must sail to the west."

"How long we sail north and west?"

"The captain-general has said about two more weeks. Perhaps we'll be there by the end of January."

When a shadow spread across the map, all of them looked up to see Serrano peering over Elcano's shoulder.

Rising to his feet, Elcano said, "Yes, Captain?"

"Do these two young seamen show any promise as pilots, Master Elcano?"

"I believe so, sir. Much promise."

"His Majesty can always use good pilots and masters," Serrano smiled encouragingly at the boys. "Master Elcano, I need a word with you."

"Of course, sir." Carefully handing the astrolabe to Chindarza, he said, "As soon as you hear the call for the noon watch, show Juanito how to take a reading. You may use my quill and parchment to note your findings."

Lighting up like a lantern on a moonless night, Chindarza said, "Yes, sir," and took his first possession of the brass device as if it were made of glass.

Serrano went with Elcano to his cabin, gathering the ship's barber and acting physician, Bustamente, along the way. When they were alone, Serrano said with anxious directness, "We must address what's to be done about our provisions."

"With the Patagonian meat starting to spoil, sir," said Elcano, "we've already set extra men to fishing. As you know, they've had little luck, but the cabin boys are gaining skill at clubbing any flying fish that land on deck. We've recently noticed larger fish mingling with the schools of flying fish, and I can set a couple of harpooners at the rails when the times are right."

"Very Good. Now, what about the water?"

"It's becoming more rancid every day, sir," said Elcano. "Our caulkers have done their best to keep the barrels sealed, but this heat continues to swell the wood and unsettle the seams."

"Have the steward and the caulkers check them again, Master Elcano."

"Yes, sir."

"Bustamente, the captain-general sent me word that the Patagonian giant is very ill. He's grown so weak that he can no longer walk or speak. Do you think some of our own men may be suffering from the same ailment, some sort of plague?"

"It appears to be the heat that's killing the giant, sir. He seems to have trouble breathing this hot air."

"But what of our men?"

"Some are a little listless, sir, and some complain of soreness in their limbs, but nothing worse."

"Captain," said Elcano, "I've noticed dark circles under the eyes of some of our boys and younger men."

"Do what you can to help them, Bustamente. Keep a close watch on them, and keep me informed."

The day after the next, Elcano learned of the death of the young Patagonian that had been captured at Port San Julian. The crew of the *Trinidad* had baptized him and named him Paulo, and because he had become a Christian, Paulo was to be given a respectable burial.

As the ships came together, Elcano saw a cannon ball being tied to Paulo's feet. The weighted body was then wrapped tightly in a worn sheet of canvas. Eight men placed the bundled form upon a six-foot plank that was lifted up and slid half way across the *Trinidad's* main deck railing. There, the plank was held steady while Father Valderrama prayed for the redemption of Paulo's soul, and Antonio Pigafetta, a young supernumerary who had befriended the Patagonian, wept freely. Glancing to the side, Elcano noticed how the other Patagonian captive towered above the *San Antonio's* crew even with his great head bent low.

When the prayers ended, Magellan signaled to the men at the plank. Hands tilted the end of the board upward, and the body slid off, splashed into the sea, and quickly sank from view.

Elcano turned away to see Chindarza staring with troubled eyes at the spot where the body had entered the sea. "Chindarza?"

The youth faced him with a look of foreboding. "Some of our men are growing worse, sir."

"Most are still strong."

"The men who had sailed on the *Santiago* before she was lost seem to be more sick than the rest of us, sir."

"I've noticed that too."

"Will more of us die, sir?"

"That is up to God, Chindarza." Elcano's words were delivered with little hesitation. But he felt a stab of insight at the pain he would suffer if death claimed the particular young soul standing before him. In a quick and silent prayer Elcano asked, "Please, not Chindarza, Heavenly Father. If death comes to this ship, let him be spared."

Placing a hand on Chindarza's arm, Elcano said, "We men of the *Concepción* are a hearty lot, are we not? Come what may, we'll be the last to surrender to anything, be it weather, or hunger, or illness."

"Or even cannibals, sir." Chindarza said.

"Even them."

"Yes, sir, the very last."

But the sickness that had taken Paulo had already begun to dig its claws more deeply into the flesh and bones of the other men of the fleet. Every day more men, half-crippled by the pain from their swelling joints, groaned as they performed simple tasks. Their gums swelled, turning a sickly bluish hue, and their teeth loosened and began to fall out.

As the meat grew more putrid, it came back to wriggling life in the form of long white maggots, and the crew balked at eating the meat even after it had been boiled. Maggots soon spread to their small, precious stores of sea biscuit, devouring it even as they defiled it. A scum formed over the ever-yellowing water. The bravest among them chewed the tough meat as thoroughly as their sore mouths would allow, and held their noses when they took a drink. The more finicky eaters were attacked most unmercifully by the unnamed ailment. Their already thin bodies shrank like withering leaves, and were discolored by swellings that had taken on distinct red, yellow, and blue hues. Soon, by night and by day, the moans and cries of the stricken men filled the reeking air that hovered like an apparition above the ships.

The first day of the new year brought the death of the *Victoria's* Basque man-at-arms. Three days later her Castilian blacksmith was taken and one of her Castilian apprentice seamen, and then a seaman from Venice. Perhaps because of their physical trials after the sinking of the *Santiago*, her former crewmembers aboard the *Victoria* were most susceptible to the ravages of scurvy.

Like the maggots that spread from the food to clothing, sails, and ropes, the illness delved deeper into the weakened bodies of the fleet's crewmen. It collected its toll one life at a time, without regard to age or family or prospects, and it fed the lifeless bodies of the *Victoria's* crew to a seemingly insatiable sea.

Aboard the *Concepción* one sweltering afternoon, Elcano and the other gaunt and haggard officers sat crowded around the captain's table. With the other cabin boys and the captain's servant ill, Chindarza had assumed the duty of serving them, and he ladled a weak brownish-gray broth and chunks of meat into their bowls. A most uninviting aroma arose with the steam.

Carvalho took one glance at his biscuit and whirled around swinging at Chindarza, cuffing him so hard that he almost dropped the kettle. Elcano jumped up and threw out his arm to block Carvalho's raised fist, shouting, "Leave him be!"

Momentarily taken back by Elcano's interference, Carvalho jerked his finger toward his biscuit. "Look at that thing! It's crawling with maggots! Are we *officers* expected to eat such filth?"

Chindarza reached out for the biscuit and picked at the maggots. "I'm sorry, Pilot Carvalho. The rest of the biscuit, what we eat, sir, it's yellow with rat urine."

Serrano let out a spent sigh. "The last of the biscuit and the last of our quince preserves." He reached for the small clay pot in the center of the table and removed its lid. "Since the captain-general was good enough to share his precious preserves with us, let's take full advantage of them. Gentlemen, if the biscuits are no longer firm enough to hold this treat, let's use our spoons."

Elcano had grown skillful at sneaking small amounts of the preserves to Chindarza, so when the talk had again reached an active level, he quietly summoned the boy closer and pointed out that he was in need of a new spoon. Chindarza unobtrusively tucked Elcano's quince-filled spoon under his shirtsleeve, moved to the corner of the cabin where he rummaged in one of the captain's chest for a moment, and returned to place a clean spoon on the table at Elcano's elbow.

A little while later, Carvalho made an exaggerated show of holding his breath and taking a sip of his water. With a gag he banged the cup down upon the table. "Unspeakable! Excuse me, Captain, but how much longer can any of us survive under these conditions? We need rest and decent food, as do our sick men if they are to have any hope of regaining their health. More of them die every week. I tell you, sir, there's something poisonous in the very air over this sea."

"Compared to the *Victoria*, Pilot, we have been remarkably fortunate. For that, each of us should be grateful."

"It's true that we've had no deaths from among our own crew yet, sir, but for how much longer will this hold true? A third of our men are so weak they can't even pull a sail line." He shoved his bowl away and went on in a voice deepening with resentment. "Two and a half months in this cursed ocean, and in all that time we've sighted only two islands; one too small to yield even water, the other with no anchorage whatsoever. Our ships are rotting beneath us. We sweat and starve and die near the equator that was to bring us glory and riches. When will it end?"

Looking weary and even older than his advanced years, Serrano said, "I have noticed long ago that hard times bring out the worst in some men and the best in others, Pilot. Regardless of what befalls us, I expect all of my officers to keep themselves among the latter group." When Carvalho frowned but held his tongue, Serrano proceeded. "We are now six degrees south of the equator, just four or five days from reaching it. With the captain-general ordering not to shorten our sails at night, our advancement will be increased and our men will be spared labor at the lines."

Carvalho seemed unable to stop himself from saying, "Did you hear, Captain Serrano, that the captain-general threw his own maps overboard two weeks ago? Even *he* has realized that they are worthless. We've shown every map of this sea to be a fraud and every scientist that ever calculated its measurement to be a fool. If any of them had been right, we would have reached its eastern boundaries long before this."

"Captain," said Elcano, "as you know, the farther west we sail, the closer we come to the domain of the Portuguese. If the Moluccas lie too far to the west to be deemed a possession of the Spanish realm—"

Carvalho interrupted, "This whole expedition will have done nothing more than prove that King Carlos has no claim to the Spiceries."

"No," said Elcano slowly, trying to maintain a temper that Carvalho had first sparked when he struck Chindarza, "that will *not* be all that we will have done." Again to his captain, he said, "Forming agreements with the natives and establishing trading posts along the way will be all the more important in holding our claim to the new territories."

"So we simply wait for some cooperative natives to present themselves," Carvalho scoffed.

Ignoring this with an effort, Elcano turned to Chindarza, who stood back awaiting their orders, and asked, "How is young Jean Flamenco this evening?"

"Not well, sir. This morning we tried to get him to eat some biscuit crumbs but he lost another tooth and his gums bled fearfully. After that, he refused to take even water." Keeping his voice as steady as possible, he added, "He's little more than skin pulled tight over bones, sir."

Conversation died away, and after a hastily consumed dinner Elcano went to visit Jean. Adding his efforts to those of Chindarza and Bustamente did no good, however. The boy, moaning from the constant pain, refused to eat or drink. Bustamente finally motioned Elcano aside and said, "Sir, please, it's time to let him die with whatever peace God will grant him." Elcano nodded and, sitting down with Chindarza, remained by Jean's side until well after dark.

In the harsh brightness of early morning, the *Concepción* reluctantly surrendered the first of her crewmembers to the jaws of the waiting Pacific.

As the condition of the men continued to worsen, it seemed to Elcano that each passing day brought one of two things; a burial, or the probability of one on the morrow. Reproaching his own weakening limbs and occasional listlessness, he rallied himself enough to bolster the crew with the news that they had finally passed the equator. But those strong enough to stand searched the horizons in every direction and, finding nothing but boundless water and sky, resumed their tasks with faces even less hopeful.

The *Concepción* doggedly held her middle position behind the *Trinidad* as she took to a more northerly course, and Elcano soon guessed that the flagship's shift in direction indicated the captain-general's growing fear of blundering into Portuguese ships. The Portuguese might well have reached the Spice Islands by now, perhaps even a fleet carrying orders to destroy Magellan's vessels. With

Magellan's men in their present condition, such a task would be pitifully easy.

Elcano gazed out at the sea for hours upon hours, in search of a land with enough food and water to strengthen the dying men and decrepit ships. But the ocean stretched on and the days dragged by without mercy and seemingly without end.

One late February afternoon while Elcano was pouring over estimations of their longitudinal position, his attention was roused by Acurio's voice shouting, "Stand back men! Back off, I say!" Handing the chart to Carvalho and descending to the main deck, Elcano stood back as Acurio pushed two struggling men apart and demanded, "What's this about?"

A supernumerary, his belly swollen by malnutrition, asserted, "It's mine, I say! I offered the right price but this dog's out to cheat me!"

"That was the price *three days* ago," shot back a second man shielding something behind his bony ribcage. "You know well enough there's but a few left aboard!"

"It's all the money I have, you son of a whore!" Thrusting out a coin, he shouted, "Half a ducat, you said, and here it is!"

"Come now," said Acurio gruffly, "settle this at once."

With an uneasy glance at the silent Elcano standing just yards away, the man brought forth the prize he'd been hiding. "All right then, seeing as it's a scrawny one." His grimy hand extended a dead rat by its tail, and the rodent was greedily snatched up by the swollen shipmate. Money was hastily yielded and the victor slunk away, darting furtive glances at the hungry eyes that followed his movements.

When the men shuffled off to their various spaces and corners, Elcano said to Acurio, "So, a rat has come to be worth half a year's wages."

"It has, sir. In a few days there will be no rats to be had at any price."

Noting Acurio's hesitance to meet his gaze, Elcano said, "Well, Acurio?"

"Perhaps I'd best warn you, sir, about what's to be served at our own table tonight."

Elcano grimaced. "You'd best warn the captain and Pilot Carvalho before Chindarza tries to put it in on their plates."

"Yes, sir."

"Heaven help us, Acurio. In a day or two we'll have nothing to eat but maggoty crumbs."

"And in four days we'll not even have them, sir."

Knowing he could voice such thoughts to Acurio, Elcano said, "Do you remember what the captain-general said before we left the River of Sardines?"

Acurio's gaze lifted and followed Elcano's up the rigging. "Sir?"

"He said we would sail to the Spice Islands even if he had to eat the leather wrappings on our yardarms."

Acurio tried to swallow, but his throat had been dry for so long that it did not respond. "I remember, Master Elcano."

"I imagine leather will need quite a bit of soaking before it softens enough to chew."

"I imagine the same, sir."

"When it gets dark, send one of our healthiest men up the mast to cut a few strips down. We'll drag them in the water behind the ship. And, Acurio, if we don't sight land within two days, have Chindarza grind some sawdust fine enough to mix in with the last of our biscuit and water."

"Yes, sir. It will be something, at least. And after that?"

"After that, there will be nothing."

Acurio nodded, and lowered his raspy voice. "What a shame it would be, sir, to come all this great, great distance and never set foot on the Islands."

"We must hold tight to what remains of our hope, Acurio."

Nodding again, Acurio said in a wistful voice, "Do you ever think back to the meals at your mother's table, sir?"

"Don't torture your stomach with such thoughts, Acurio."

"No, sir. I won't."

"Don't torture your soul."

"I'll try not to, sir."

With the last of the rats and the biscuit went the last breath of more of the fleet's men, including the *Victoria's* Pilot Vasco Gomez Galego. Cocooned in a maggoty canvas shroud, Galego's body plunged with a deep-throated splash to join his shipmates in the largest of the earth's watery graveyards.

A few days after Galego's funeral Elcano found Captain Serrano writing in his cabin, where his waning strength now kept him confined much of the time. Elcano entered the room and leaned heavily against the door.

"Captain," he said in a hollow voice, "you ordered me to report the name of any man showing new signs of the disease."

"I did," Serrano said, setting down his quill. "Go on."

"It's, it's Chindarza, sir."

Serrano slowly slumped back in his chair.

Elcano's gaze remained fixed on a leg of Serrano's desk. "His gums are already turning blue, sir."

"Even Chindarza," Serrano muttered, "even Chindarza." In sudden anger, he let out an oath and rubbed his hands roughly across his gaunt face. "Nineteen men! Nineteen good men! And how many more will we lose to this pestilence? How many more will this sea demand in payment before we've sailed beyond its reaches, every single man of us?" Serrano raised glaring eyes to Elcano's and took in his unspoken anguish. "Master Elcano," he said, "sit down."

Elcano mutely sank into a chair.

"Is Chindarza in much pain?"

"He doesn't cry out, but his legs can only support him for a few minutes at a time. The illness is in the early stages, sir, but..."

"But we have nothing to feed him."

"The sawdust gruel of yesterday was the last, sir."

"We've already lost one out of every ten of our men. In a day or two, half of those remaining will likely be dead."

"Yes, sir."

"In four days hence, our ships will be manned by nothing but ghosts, your spirit and mine along with the rest."

"Even so, sir, to be powerless to heal a boy like Chindarza, to stand by while his body and mind wither with the passing of each hour, this is the worst of it."

For a moment their dry, red eyes searched each other for any answer, for any expectation other than hunger, pain, and ultimate death. Then Serrano said, "Are you afraid of death, Master Elcano?"

"Of death, sir?" Remembering, he said, "Captain Quesada once asked me the same thing. Perhaps I should be afraid. Most of my life has been spent at war or at sea. Heaven knows I am less than a righteous man. But no, Captain, I do not fear my own death."

"For that, I envy you. Even in my sleep now, I see the figure of the dark angel, waiting, and each night I pray he will not come for me before the rising of the sun. I fear that his image speaks of my damnation."

Elcano said earnestly. "Forgive me, sir, but to look helplessly on while those you've grown to love die in torment, how can hell be worse than this?"

Serrano sighed and let his chin fall. "I hope I never learn the answer to that question."

They sat quietly together for another few moments before Elcano feebly pushed himself up from the chair. "I'll go back to Chindarza now, sir. A space can be made for him in the shade. It's cooler there than in my cabin."

Without warning the door of the cabin burst open and Acurio stood panting and swaying in the doorway. "Sirs!" A sob escaped him and he fought for enough control to force out the words, "Navarro is hailing us from the *Trinidad*! He's saying there's land to northwest! Land!"

"Help me up!" barked Serrano. "Help me up!"

They had just cleared the cabin's threshold when all three of them started violently at the roar of the flagship's cannons. All eyes jerked to the northwest, toward which the *Trinidad* was already veering. Far ahead, just visible beneath a halo of delicate clouds, a swatch of deep teal lifted from the ocean's surface. The sobs and shouts of croaking voices swept from the flagship to the *Concepción* and on to the *Victoria*. Acurio burst into unrestrained weeping as Elcano and Serrano tried to hold back their tears.

Wiping at his eyes, Elcano stared at the land then pulled his gaze away and down to the main deck. Chindarza was staring up at him from where he sat upon the deck and wrapped his bony arms around the shaking shoulders of Juanito. A wobbly smile formed on Chindarza's discolored, cracked lips, and Elcano, unable to hear anything over the clamber of the men, saw him mouth the word "land". Then Chindarza buried his face in Juanito's shoulder and surrendered to his emotions.

Captain Serrano stood braced between Elcano and Acurio, holding tightly to them. "Dear Father above, let there be food and water. Wait, look, do you see it? There's a larger island to the southwest. The flagship's already altering her course. Stay with her, Master Elcano. Stay with her!"

A less necessary order could not have been given. Elcano, in spite of his withered muscles, was not about to let the *Concepción* lose the *Trinidad*. He urged on his straining men and added his own strength to theirs to give his ship her full set of sails, and before long she had pulled nearly adjacent to Magellan's ship.

"That's it," said Serrano, now seated on a chair in a corner of the half deck. "Fine work, fine work. Hold her here."

Elcano kept his sunken eyes locked on the approaching land. If this patch of earth yielded food and water, it would give him a chance to fight for Chindarza's life. For all their lives.

He thought of Magellan and, after a moment's searching of the *Trinidad*, he spotted the captain-general kneeling on her stern deck. His shaggy head was bent low over his clasped hands as he rocked back and forth.

For that single moment, Elcano forgave him everything. And for the moment that followed, Elcano even forgave himself.

211

The land drew his attention again, leading his thoughts back to the dangers as well as the deliverance it might hold. He cupped his hand and shouted down to the main deck, "Load the guns, Acurio! Load the guns and pray that we won't need them!"

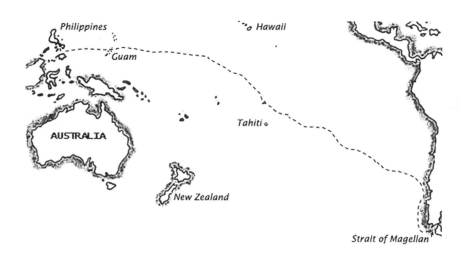

# The First Islands

## 15

For thirty torturous hours, while desperately ill men clung to life, the fleet searched and probed the coast of the island for any safe harbor. At last, to the nearly unbearable relief of every man aboard the three ships, a bay was sighted on its southwestern edge. With the *Trinidad* leading the way, they sailed toward a hill-rimmed bay.

Repeatedly checking the shrinking distance to shore, Elcano and Acurio approached Serrano's chair on the stern deck with the sluggishness of old age. "As you ordered, Captain," Elcano said, trying to give his reedy voice as much volume as possible, "I've placed the strongest men I could find at the masts. They've got their axes ready. We may not have men enough to haul the sails lower, but the canvas will come down quick enough when the lines are cut."

"Good, good. Hold our position behind the flagship and await my signal, Master Elcano," said Serrano.

Elcano nodded and glanced ashore. "Do you see them, Captain?" he said, pointing. "Boats. Dozens of boats."

"Praise God! Where there are boats there will be food and water."

As the fleet moved closer in, slender outrigger canoes with patterned lateen sails pushed from the beach and leaped from wave to wave as they sped towards the ships, reaching and circling the *Trinidad* even before her sails had been brought down. The men of the *Concepción* and the *Victoria* gaped at the scene as naked, longhaired natives swarmed the flagship without the slightest sign of fear.

"They're armed, sir," said Acurio. "I see clubs and spears."

"Look there," said Serrano. "The captain-general's crossbows are already getting into position on their stern deck."

Elcano felt the grip of apprehension as thirty islanders reached the *Trinidad's* deck and began pushing aside the wretchedly weakened sailors as if they were nothing but bothersome children. Grabbing axes and knives right out of the hands of hesitant and enfeebled crewmembers, along with ropes, canvas, and anything else lying unattached from the decks, the first of the natives quickly passed the stolen goods back to their canoes. Obviously reluctant to use weapons against the looters, Magellan and his men tried through increasingly urgent shouts and gestures to stop the plundering. But while the noise and mayhem mounted, a native spotted the rope that secured the skiff trailing in the water behind the ship, and untied it from its mooring.

"Not our boat!" Magellan shouted. "Stop them, men!"

Swords that had been held at bay suddenly flashed and bit into oval shields tufted with human hair, but the arms that wielded the blades were all but spent of their vigor and were deflected with relative ease. As the first natives jumped into the *Trinidad's* boat, a command of "fire!" was instantly followed by a hissing volley from the row of six crossbow archers stationed on the stern deck. Five islanders fell writhing to the deck, one tumbled off the side of the ship, and their companions stared at their fallen men in confusion. As the islanders began to move back, one warrior bent down, grabbed the shaft of an arrow protruding from his friend's body, and with a savage yank tried to wrest it free. An unearthly scream burst from the lips of the native before he fell suddenly still. Dark eyes darted from the archers, already reloaded and ready, to the closing ring of swords and knives, to the *Concepción* and the *Victoria* that had drawn to well within the firing range of their own crossbows.

With a burst of cries, the islanders broke through the line of swordsmen and vaulted over the rails, reaching their canoes and hastening them as well as the captured skiff back toward the beach. Swinging his gaze from the fleeing islanders back to the *Trinidad*, Elcano saw three of the wounded natives manage to gain their feet and try to reach the railings, but they were quickly cut down by sabers. Two others, the warrior on deck and the one that had fallen overboard, were already dead. The last of the six wounded was roughly shackled and handed over to the surgeon.

"Curse our luck!" spat Serrano at Elcano's side. "Now we'll have to fight for every scrap of food."

When Magellan's order to move the ships farther out to sea was delivered to the *Concepción*, men groaned and wept in despair, but they obeyed. Once the ships had been repositioned, Elcano went to Chindarza and sat down beside his lethargic body. Mustering an encouraging tone and working to hide his anguish, he patted Chindarza's bony hand and said, "The captain-general has promised that tomorrow we will have fresh water and plenty of food. You must hold on until the morning, son, just until morning."

Forty men were chosen, forty men barely strong enough to stand and hold a weapon, and they were crowded into two boats and ferried ashore at first light. Elcano sat silent and grave in the boat just behind Magellan's. In his mind rang the grisly words uttered by one of his starving men as he left the *Concepción*, "If they refuse to surrender any food, sir, bring us back their hearts and livers."

As they landed, Elcano saw natives positioned on a ridge rimming the beach. He, Espinosa, and Magellan had just enough time to warn their men before a shower of spears and stones rained down upon them. This action, made futile by the metal shields of the landing party, did little but fuel the feral fire in the eyes of their starving men. They pushed on with what speed they could force from their legs and exploded into the first village they met, cutting through a line of warriors with a barrage from Elcano's harquebus marksmen. A moment later Magellan's crossbows opened fire on a cluster of warriors, slaying seven with their first volley. When both combatants and civilians fled in every direction, Magellan yelled for the men to hold their fire and scavenge for food.

Needing no further encouragement, the men of the fleet scrambled to the nearest hut and fell ravenously upon the stores left behind by the villagers. Elcano and two of his men found two large jars of water and several baskets of fruit. Snatching up crude wooden cups, Elcano splashed water into them for his panting men and himself.

Elcano jerked his cup to his lips and gulped down the clean water until he began to choke and cough. Lowering the cup only long enough to gasp for air, he hastily raised it again. This time he slowed his swallowing enough to taste the fresh sweetness. He had almost forgotten that water could taste like this; pure and clean around the tongue. Hearing a moan of pleasure he looked up to see his companions take their first bite of fresh food in almost a hundred days. As he reached out for a long yellow fruit such as he'd never seen before, one of his men held up his half-eaten piece of the same kind, and asked, "What manner of fig is this, sir?"

Elcano pulled back the peel, took a bite, and grinned as he chewed, "The best kind I've ever tasted, Corfu. Call it what you will." After several more mouthfuls, he noticed his companions reaching for another piece, and cautioned, "Not too fast, men, or it won't stay down."

They heeded this warning and tried to eat more slowly but their shrunken stomachs began to cramp and revolt almost at once. Rubbing his own rumbling belly, Elcano stood up and said, "That's enough for now, men. Let's pile what we can onto these mats and haul them back to the boat."

They each left the hut towing a bulging mat, but they had made it only several yards before a sailor hurried over to speak with Elcano.

"The captain-general sent me to find you, Master Elcano," said the seaman. "He says you're to oversee the loading of the boats, sir. He means to keep most of the men with him until all the huts have been emptied and burned."

"Burned?"

"Yes, sir, to punish the natives for stealing the flagship's skiff."

Elcano knew that any thoughts he might have concerning such an action would not be heeded, yet he had to ask, "Has the skiff been found?"

"Yes, sir. We're to fill all three boats and get the first load of provisions back to the ships as soon as we can."

"Then go back to the captain-general and tell him I'm already on my way back to the beach."

Offering a quick bow, the man set off.

With the hilt of his sword as near as his belt, and his shield planted in the sand not far from his feet, Elcano remained on the beach for hours to help organize and load the plundered stores. But there were no further attacks. Even before black clouds of smoke began to spew from the village, fresh fish, fruit, and coconuts had been packed and rowed out to the depleted crews. The skiffs soon returned with barrels, and these were scoured of their slimy growth, refilled with untainted water, and sent back across the bay to the ships.

Although Elcano dearly wished that he had been aboard his ship to watch the faces of his men as they took their first tastes of the life-sustaining bounty being delivered to them, he satisfied himself with the mental picture of Acurio bending over Chindarza with a cup of water and a piece of sweet fruit. Surely, they would help strengthen the lad and rid him of his sickness.

It was late afternoon when Magellan stepped from the trees and came to Elcano with a group of men loaded down with bundles of coconuts. Magellan's son, Cristóbal, came to a halt at his father's right side, and Antonio Pigafetta, the Pope's young envoy, stood at the captain-general's left. Magellan's devoted slave, Enrique, placed himself behind his master and scanned the ridge above them with a watchful eye.

"That's the last of it, Master Elcano," Magellan said, signaling the men to stow the coconuts in the boats. His face, hands, and drooping clothes were sweaty and grimy. Excess skin sagged around his eyes and jowls, and yet there was triumph and a new hopefulness that enlightened the lines of his features. He cast Elcano a keen look and said, "The men will live now, Master Elcano. They will live."

"Yes, sir," said Elcano. "The food we've gathered should last us many days."

Magellan pulled in a huge breath and took in the view around him. "Beautiful, isn't it? It's a shame we can't stay here for a few days."

"A rest in such a place would do the men much good, sir."

"Pigafetta, what did that captive call this island?

"Guam, Captain-general."

"Ah, that was it. Guam. For now, we will use that name for our records. Inform your captain and pilot, Master Elcano."

"Of course, sir."

When Elcano was relieved of his shore duty and allowed to return to the *Concepción*, he was met with enthusiasm by Acurio. "I know it's early yet, sir, but there's improvement already. Just come and see for yourself."

Elcano found Chindarza still lying under the foredeck, but when he knelt down beside the boy, the eyes that opened to meet his own were clear and aware. Chindarza's thin lips curved into a smile and he whispered, "Sir."

Elcano took his hand and returned his smile. "Has Acurio given you enough water?" Acurio huffed good-naturedly, but Chindarza said, "More than enough, sir, and some fruit. I can swallow again."

Juanito, his eyes huge and his limbs like sticks, crept up and sat beside Chindarza. In each small hand he held a big crescent-shaped, yellow fig. Elcano grinned at him. "And you, Juanito? Is that stomach of yours full of those long figs?"

"No, sir, but Señor Acurio says wait. Says Juanito not eat too much all at one time."

"I see you have your next meal all ready," said Elcano pointing to his hands.

"These figs for Chindarza, sir," the child said proudly.

"Oh, I see."

"Chindarza's tooth fall out, sir. He eat only soft fruit for now."

At an inquiring glance from Elcano, Chindarza pulled back his lower lip to show a gap where his left canine had been. "I see," Elcano repeated. "Well, Juanito, Chindarza is obviously in good hands. I doubt he'll lose any more teeth." To Chindarza, he said, "You must rest now, son."

Before Elcano could rise, however, Chindarza said, "Sir, you said last night that I was to hold on until today, but I didn't know if I could. Then I thought of my mother, sir, and about how upset she'd be at you if I never came home. I'd hate for you to see her that angry, sir."

"An angry Basque mother is nothing to take lightly, I agree," said Elcano.

Suddenly hesitant, Chindarza pushed on with an effort, "But she's a fine woman, Master Elcano, and I got to thinking, since she's a widow and you're unmarried and all, sir, you might want to meet her someday." He raised earnest eyes to his shipmaster.

Hearing Acurio cough back a response behind him, Elcano squeezed Chindarza's shoulder and said in a gentle voice, "It would be an honor, Chindarza. And thank you for not dying, son, for my sake. Now, rest quietly."

The fleet soon withdrew even farther offshore and the rest of the day was dedicated to feasting. To the great surprise of the hands, a few bold islanders made the long approach to the ships and offered to trade for more food. Their offers were gladly accepted, and more provisions were soon lowered into the ships' filthy holds.

By the next morning, crewmembers were able to raise the fleet's sails and point the ships westward. As they left the harbor at Guam, however, scores of outriggers filled with derisive islanders flanked the ships, throwing verbal insults, stones, and feces at the men. Without responding, the commander of the *Trinidad* led them away, far out into a placid blue sea.

The location of a safe place to rest and heal the men was now their immediate goal, and the gravity of this need became painfully clear when the *Trinidad* slowed her pace near noon and all three ships gathered together for another funeral. The water and fruit of Guam had not been delivered soon enough to loosen scurvy's grip from the body of the fleet's master gunner, the amiable Englishman called Andrew of Bristol. Magellan did not linger after Andrew's respectful but brief funeral ceremony, lest the disease claim even more victims.

But no island that might serve as a haven appeared until a full week had passed, eleven hundred more nautical miles had been traveled, and the small body of one of Magellan's cabin boys, Gutierrez de Bustillo, had been committed to the ocean's depths. Then, just before sunset, not one but a whole string of islands revealed itself, an archipelago that stretched on and on to the south.

Drawing near but unable to locate a bay, they threaded their way between the islands. At one point, they startled a group of men in canoes that fled in fear before the ships. At long last, they eased their crafts into a perfect half moon bay along the southeastern shore of a small island.

From the *Concepción*, Elcano and Carvalho peered keenly at the tree line. "No boats," said Elcano, "no smoke."

"The captain-general must like the look of it too," said Carvalho. "His boat is already being lowered."

The first landing party returned with the news that two streams of fresh water had been found, but for safety's sake the men were to remain on board the ships until the sun rose the next day and the island had been thoroughly scouted.

After this precaution had been taken, canvas awnings were set up on the beach to shade the sick from the brutality of the rising sun. Then every man was brought ashore with the exception of those assigned to skeleton crews ordered to remain on the ships.

Elcano saw to it that Chindarza joined the *Concepción's* first boatload of ill men. Once ashore he was placed near the ailing crewmembers of the *Victoria*, including Antonio de Coca, who remained despondent and silent under the shade of the canopy.

Although Chindarza's coloring had improved and some of the swelling had subsided, he could still only walk a few steps unaided, and Elcano worried about the slow pace of his recovery. Once all of the sick had been settled upon blankets atop the soft sand, Elcano returned to Chindarza and squatted down beside him. He couldn't help smiling when he saw the peaceful joy on the boy's face. "You look contented, Chindarza."

"I was just thinking, sir," he said, scooping up a handful of warm sand and letting it drift slowly through his thin fingers. "This is the first sand I've touched since we left the River of Sardines." He lifted another handful and rubbed the grains between his fingertips and thumb, reveling in its coarse texture. "It seems like years, sir, like many years."

"I'm sure it does."

"What is today, sir?"

"March 16th, no, 17th."

"And we left Patagonia near the end of November, sir?"

"That's right, Chindarza."

"It's not even been four months," he said in wonder.

"No, not quite. But I've learned that a man can experience the pains and pleasures of an entire lifetime in the span of four months."

Chindarza closed his eyes and sighed as he continued to finger the sand. "It's good to be on land again, sir."

"Take a little more water, Chindarza, then get some sleep. The sand will give you a soft bed for a change."

When Elcano got to his feet, he saw Magellan at the far side of the awnings, sitting cross-legged in the shade with a huge bowl in his lap. Quietly, Elcano approached him and watched as Magellan worked a large pestle to mash a mixture of what looked like boiled roots and fruit.

"May I help you, Captain-general?"

"What?" Magellan glanced up from his task. "Oh, no, no, Master Elcano, this I wish to do myself."

A few moments later, Magellan rose, spooned the mash into a smaller bowl, and began feeding it to the weakest of his men. Elcano watched this gentle solicitude in concealed amazement, watched until he was forced to reevaluate his judgment of the captain-general's character. But there was a limit to Elcano's acceptance of this side of the man who had sentenced his captain to death and him to chains and

hardship. Even considering the possibility that he might
have acted similarly if their situations had been reversed,
forgiveness for the past refused to take hold. To steel his
mind against softening his opinions too much, Elcano
reminded himself that it was Magellan's refusal to follow
the king's orders that had led to all of their trouble.

"Captain-general," said one of the sick men, "is it true
that you came from the east and sailed among these islands
once before?"

"No, not so far as this."

"Are we near the Spice Islands, sir?"

"They lie somewhere to the south, but we will try to build
treaties with the rulers of any islands we reach along the
way."

"Will you tell us about the Moluccas, sir?"

"Well, Captain Serrano's brother, my good friend,
Francisco Serrano, has lived on the Moluccan Island of
Ternate for years. He's written me many letters about the
glories of his island, as well as all the Moluccas."

"Are the women beautiful, sir?"

Magellan laughed. "He claims they are. Although he
married a woman from Java."

"Is that an island in these parts, sir?"

"Yes, yes, it lies even farther to the south, but enough
questions. You must eat and rest so you will get well soon.
Just remember, nothing awaits you now but cloves, riches,
and the women of these islands."

For a full day they remained undisturbed as they
breathed in the flower-scented air and listened to the
singing of birds, appreciating these delights almost as much
as the food and water. The peace was short-lived, however,
for the following day an outrigger bearing nine men cautiously approached their beach. Magellan ordered his men
to hold their fire before he and Pigafetta approached them
alone.

As the natives landed, showing only signs of welcome
and openness, and armed with no more than the curved
knives at their waists, Elcano stood beside three archers
and studied them warily. With skin nearly as light as

Elcano's, the newcomers were tall and strongly built, making the malnourished Magellan and Pigafetta look puny by comparison. Their long black hair was held back from their faces by bands of cloth tied around their foreheads. Four of the men wore only loin coverings, which appeared to be made from some variation of tree bark. The most impressive looking men among the group of islanders wore headbands of dyed silk and cotton skirts richly embroidered with shiny silken threads. But their clothing held Elcano's interest less than the markings on their skin, for the islanders' shoulders, chests, and thighs were intricately tattooed in black patterns of crosshatched arcs, tubes, and diamonds. These shapes touched from tip to tip to form parallel lines that flowed over the course of their entire bodies. Their earlobes had been pierced and then stretched by the weight of heavy gold bobs or loops, some hanging low enough to touch the tops of their shoulders. Gold bands adorned arms, wrists, and ankles. Necklaces of gold rings or beads the size of cherries shone brightly around their necks. Overall, Elcano concluded, they presented a striking picture.

With Pigafetta using hand gestures, he soon had the newcomers trading all of the food they carried in their outrigger for cloth, combs, and other Spanish goods. Greatly pleased by the generosity of the strangers, the natives departed with their prizes, but not before offering up the name of the island, Homonhon.

After four more recuperative days had passed, during which Elcano was gladdened to note Chindarza's undeniable improvement, the same nine islanders returned with a much larger supply of oranges, chickens, coconuts, rice, fish, bananas, and, to the elation of the seamen, jugs of palm wine. Before departing with their bounty of trade goods, the natives told Magellan through signs that much more food could be traded for at any of the larger islands nearby.

It took several more days of rest before most of the men had recovered from the worst of their maladies. Most, but not all. Ochote de Erandio, a young seaman known aboard the *Victoria* for his fish stories and his flute playing, was quietly buried. Elcano began to fear that the former shipmaster of the *Santiago*, Baldassare Palla Genovés, was near death, but when the fleet headed away from the island's shores the next morning, Genovés sailed with them.

On the evening of their departure, Magellan collected his officers in his lantern-lit quarters and said to them, "Gentlemen, several of you have made calculations as to our present westerly position. Tell me what you have concluded."

After a brief discussion, Magellan spoke persuasively. "The consensus seems to be that Homonhon Island lies 189° to the west of what has been considered by some, even by many, to be the Tordesillas Treaty line of demarcation, nine degrees into Portuguese territory. However, this line begins at the most *eastern* point of the Cape Verde Islands. Since the treaty is not specific on the crucial detail of where in the Cape Verdes it does begin, a strong argument can be made that the starting point should lie at the *western* coast of the most westward island of San Antonio. Even with this ambiguity, since it is unlikely that the Portuguese will fail to challenge our claims, we must move quickly to solidify trade agreements with the islands' leaders."

When no one offered a comment or a question, Magellan went on. "As you've undoubtedly heard, our men have found grains of gold in the streams on the island we have just left. The native chieftains that traded with us wore a small fortune in gold. Now, from the beginning our main aim has been to barter for spices, and it will remain so, but if gold is *readily* available we must not overlook it."

To this, men nodded and muttered their agreement.

"Although our long ocean crossing has sorely depleted our numbers, enough of us remain to establish small trading posts on several islands and still sail fully loaded ships safely back to Spain. Although we do not know the exact location of the Spice Islands, I believe they lie not far to our south. We, therefore, are close to achieving what we set out to do. Pray, gentlemen, that the natives will be cooperative and that the Portuguese will keep their distance."

Elcano and his fellow officers of the *Concepción* left the meeting and warmly accepted Serrano's invitation to raise a generous cup of palm wine in toast to their excellent futures.

The fair weather that had befriended the fleet throughout the past months turned unexpectedly stormy once they had sailed out of the shelter of Homonhon's harbor. This tempest proved to be little more than bothersome, however, compared to what they had faced while delving the Patagonian strait, and it soon began to ease. The storm, gentle and short-lived though it was, seemed to steal what little had remained of Antonio de Coca's health, and the ships were signaled to gather around the *Victoria* for yet another burial, this time to be conducted upon a swelling, protesting sea.

No drums rolled to honor this man whose once proud rank had never been restored, and the hush that hung over many of the waiting men was tainted with discomfort as well as regret. Prayers were said as the men stood in the continuous drizzle. When the board bearing Coca's swathed body was tilted and the wet bundle slid grudgingly from the rain-soaked wood, Elcano stared after it with eyes incapable of conjuring a tear. He focused on the sea and tried to sort out his sentiments for the man he had served with through so many miseries.

Coca had shared his imprisonment in Patagonia, and that experience had formed common emotions between them, some of which were as regrettable as they were undeniable. And yet the two men had avoided each other much of the time since then. Seeming unable to recover from the loss of his freedom and the marooning of Cartagena, Coca had shown resentment toward Elcano's attempts to put both events behind him. Now Coca was gone like so many others, delivered to the depths of a sea that, to Elcano, grew more ravenous with each body she claimed.

As the other men shuffled away, Elcano remained long enough to pray that Coca had finally found a permanent escape from the trials he'd endured, a quiet, peaceful escape. Consigning Coca's spirit into God's hands, Elcano made the sign of the cross and turned back to his duties.

As the fleet resumed its course, the last of the heavy clouds moved off to the east and the ocean's swells subsided. Before long the *Trinidad's* lookout called out and Elcano looked up to see the red glow of an island campfire not far ahead. The fleet was directed toward it and no sails were lowered until they had entered the protection of a fine sandy harbor.

At the sight of a canoe being paddled determinedly toward them, the thievery and battle at Guam leaped freshly to Elcano's mind. He obtained Serrano's approval and then had Acurio distribute armaments with the strict order to hold all firing until commanded to do otherwise. Just as the canoe reached the *Trinidad*, the *Concepción* and the *Victoria* took up defensive positions at the flanks of their flagship.

Elcano stood tense and alert as he listened to every word of the strange language being shouted up at Magellan. Expecting Pigafetta to move forward and communicate through signs, Elcano was surprised to see Enrique step to his master's side and mutter something to him. For a moment Magellan looked stunned, and then he enthusiastically nudged Enrique forward. Enrique stepped to the rail, but hesitated until Magellan said, "Go on, go on." To the amazement of all, Enrique offered a greeting that was immediately answered by the men in the canoe.

Serrano, leaning against the railing beside Elcano, said, "Enrique knows their tongue! He's actually talking to them!"

Words were passed with increasing rapidity until Enrique was pausing only long enough to translate to Magellan and receive his reply. After the first few verbal exchanges had been made, Magellan lifted his voice loud enough to be heard by all. "They say we have a mighty vessel, and they ask where we come from!" The force of the responding cheer momentarily startled the islanders but Enrique quickly reassured them that no harm was intended. The dialogue picked up again and, with Magellan passing along Enrique's messages, Elcano soon learned that they had landed at the island of Limasawa, and that it was ruled by Rajah Colambu.

Although the words continued to flow freely, no amount of encouragement could convince the Limasawans to bring their canoe closer to the ship. Accepting their reluctance, Magellan ordered a plank to be lowered into the water and loaded with gifts of berets, cloth, and mirrors. Then the board was gently pushed to the men in the outrigger.

"Tell them that the gifts are for their ruler," Magellan instructed Enrique.

Once this had been communicated, the island men accepted the gifts and turned their craft toward shore. As they sped away, the men of the *Trinidad* slapped Enrique on the back and head in good-natured congratulations.

"The world and its mysteries," Elcano said to Serrano as their gazes followed the landing of the canoe. "I remember hearing that the captain-general had bought Enrique in the city of Malacca. Isn't that right, sir?"

"I heard it was in Sumatra, about thirteen years ago. It could be either one. If our estimations are correct, both places are still well to the southwest of us. I suppose it's possible that a previous master taught him to speak the language of these islands, but it's more likely that he was stolen from here when he was very young and auctioned off elsewhere. Either way, it really matters little how he came to know their tongue. What matters is that this stroke of luck will help our bargaining efforts immensely!"

"But if Enrique *is* from these islands, sir," said Elcano thoughtfully, "then he would be the first man to have traveled all the way around the earth."

"What a strange idea," muttered Serrano. "But there's no way of knowing where he started from, not unless he somehow recognized the island of his birth. Enrique's been away from this part of the world for at least ten years, and I very much doubt that he'll meet up with any relatives.

After a slight pause, Serrano went on, "You know, the captain-general had me witness the signing of his will before we left Seville. It specifies that, upon his death, Enrique is to be granted his freedom and a small sum of money." He gave a short chuckle. "I thought that extraordinarily generous at the time. Today, I think it quite appropriate."

The day brought more sadness along with its hope. Death overtook Juan Rodríguez de Mafra, the former pilot of the *San Antonio* who had transferred to the *Concepción* before the fleet had departed from Port San Julian. With this casualty, Elcano wondered anew about the fate of the *San Antonio*, and whether Mafra might have lived if he had not transferred ships.

Not two hours after Mafra's funeral, Rajah Colambu, resplendently seated upon a platform of woven palm mats mounted on a canoe twice the size of those seen earlier, visited the fleet to exchange words with his strange visitors. Although he declined Magellan's invitation to come aboard the *Trinidad*, he allowed a handful of his men to tour the flagship. Afterward, seeming satisfied that the Europeans posed no immediate threat, Colambu offered Magellan a basket of ginger and a bar of gold. These, the captain-general politely declined. Instead he asked if Enrique might go ashore in the morning to negotiate trading arrangements, and Colambu graciously consented to this request.

The next afternoon Serrano sent Elcano and Carvalho to the flagship in order to update their charts as well as the calculated location with Magellan, his pilot, and his shipmaster. Shuffling parchments in the captain-general's hot quarters, they were interrupted by one of Magellan's cabin boys.

"Excuse me, sir," he said to his commander, "but Enrique has returned with the island king."

Magellan and the officers hurriedly left the cabin and descended to the main deck to meet Rajah Colambu. He stood beside Enrique and in front of several of his men, and Elcano appraised the rajah covertly but thoroughly. His head was large and round, and his entire body was heavily tattooed and accented with jewelry of polished gold. Everything about his manner implied a bold yet controlled power. And yet, when Magellan approached Colambu and bowed, the rajah opened his arms and embraced him as warmly as if they had long been friends.

This time his offered gifts were baskets of fish and three porcelain jars of rice, which Magellan readily accepted. In return the captain-general presented him with a fine hat, a robe, and brocaded cloth, all of which Colambu seemed to greatly appreciate. Magellan then showed his visitor the details of his ship and served him as fine a meal as their stores could provide. At last, Magellan turned to Enrique and said, "Tell Rajah Colambu that I wish the two of us to form a lasting bond."

Enrique hesitated, "Master, the rajah may misunderstand. He may think you wish to perform the ritual of casi casi with him."

"That's exactly what I do wish," Magellan spoke evenly. "You explained the rite to me clearly, Enrique, but I am quite willing. Tell him."

The apprehension on Enrique's face could not be entirely concealed as he turned to Colambu and delivered the message.

The rajah's eyes shifted quickly to Magellan's, reassessing him. After a moment he spoke to Enrique.

"The rajah asks what manner of bond you desire to form, Master."

"Tell him I want to be as close to him as a brother."

Words were again exchanged, then Enrique, after the slightest of pauses, said, "He says he would be honored to perform casi casi with you, Master."

Elcano had never heard of the rite the captain-general had just initiated, but he joined the other officers as they seated themselves cross-legged in a half circle facing Colambu and his men. Magellan's son, Cristóbal, watched uneasily as a page helped remove Magellan's doublet and shirt, revealing loose skin over a broad, pale chest covered with curly gray hair.

Enrique, who had left the group momentarily, reappeared holding a silver chalice and looking resigned to his role. Respectfully motioning his master and the rajah to the center of the circle, Enrique placed a goblet between them then stepped back. The two leaders seated themselves, facing each other with their backs straight and their features calm.

Leaning close to Elcano, Carvalho whispered, "What the devil is he doing?"

Elcano did not answer, his attention being captured by the sight of the rajah drawing a curved, gold-hilted knife from its sheath that hung from his cotton belt. Colambu set the knife before Magellan and watched him keenly as the captain-general lifted the blade. With unflinching control, Magellan inserted the tip of the knife into his skin three inches beneath his right breast and drew it across his ribcage before easing it out again. As Magellan's blood flowed from the incision, Enrique quickly took up the goblet and pressed it to the skin just below the wound, catching much of the spilling blood. When the bleeding lessened slightly, Enrique placed the goblet and the knife before the rajah. Showing no more emotion than Magellan had, Colambu picked up the blade and steadily sliced the skin of his own chest. Again Enrique placed the cup so that it captured the stream of blood. As the red fluid leaked downward to stain the bellies of the participants, Enrique held the chalice up, poured in a small measure of wine, and then swirled it several times to mix its contents. He offered the cup to his master, and Magellan raised it in a solemn toast toward the rajah. Lifting it to his lips, the captain-general drank an even half of the concoction. He then lowered the goblet from his reddened lips and handed it to Colambu, who nodded with approval before emptying it completely.

Both leaders rose to their feet, and Magellan heartily clasped Colambu's hands. "Now, my brother," he said through Enrique, "you will see that I can be of great help to you and your people. I can even help defend you against any who might wish you harm."

To demonstrate his ability to carry out this claim, Magellan had the cannons made ready, and Colambu was brought to the rail to observe their power. But when the guns erupted, the smoke and roar so terrified the rajah and his islanders that they would have leaped from the ship if Magellan's men had not moved quickly to stop them. After hurriedly assuring the startled men that the guns would be used only against those who opposed Colambu, the men of Limasawa calmed and consented to remain aboard. To entertain his guests further, Magellan gave a full display of Spanish armor and armaments. Before the muskets were demonstrated, however, he forewarned Colambu of the noise they would produce.

It was growing late in the day by the time the rajah's entourage at last left the flagship, and Elcano and Carvalho returned to the *Concepción* not long afterward.

"So," said Acurio once he had drawn Elcano away from the other men, "in this part of the world they've taken to blood drinking. And the captain-general has joined them. What will come next?"

"That, my dear Acurio, I wouldn't dare to guess."

The next few days, however, brought nothing more startling than the sighting of women by affection-starved seamen, which Elcano and the other officers were ordered to keep strictly confined to the ships. But as Easter approached and Magellan passed down the word that the majority of the men would be allowed to go ashore to celebrate Easter mass on the beach, many thoughts turned to pleasures that were less than pious in nature. This news, along with a fairly dependable flow of fresh fruit and water from the island, did much to enliven the health of the ill men.

To signal the commencement of the Easter religious ceremony, the flagship's cannons boomed to great effect. Adding to an impressive show of formality, Magellan initiated Colambu, the rajah's brother, Siani, and their people, in the ways of Christianity by encouraging them to pray. Colambu accepted the invitation warmly, and seemed sincerely moved by the earnestness of those participating in the rite.

After the service had ended, the Limasawans helped to erect an eight-foot wooden cross upon the highest hill overlooking the harbor.

Although access to the women of the island had been strictly withheld from the men, Easter feasting was heartily enjoyed. Colambu made their meal even more joyous by declaring that in just a few days the island's rice would be ready for harvest, and that it would then be fairly traded to the Europeans. In addition, Colambu and Siani agreed to lead the ships safely through the surrounding shoals to the island of Cebu, where a more abundant supply of food and goods could be found. Elcano cheered this good news along with his men, but after eating his fill, he returned to the *Concepción* earlier than most.

First, he checked on Chindarza, whose health had improved so much during the past week that he was growing restless to be up and about. Then Elcano went to each of the other ailing men, offering a kind word or two, until he at last climbed alone to the stern deck and let his gaze slowly rise to the crescent moon.

As he stood beneath the soft lunar glow, the many memories of the past year, memories he'd been holding at bay all day, awakened with unmerciful clarity. Exactly a year earlier, in a very different place and under very different circumstances, he had become a participant in a rebellion that had claimed the life of Juan de Elorriaga. It had also taken Quesada, Mendoza, and, surely, Cartagena and Father Calmette. Elcano and the others that had followed these four men had been imprisoned, and they had suffered until most of them had wished for death. When they at last had found the icy passage that united the two great oceans of the world, the *San Antonio's* crew had either perished or abandoned the rest of the fleet to their fate. While they'd made their way across the monstrous Pacific with too few provisions, fate had demanded the souls of twenty men. More crewmembers had died since they had reached the islands, and several others still teetered near death. All this hardship in a single year.

Yet, his mind whispered, he and the other survivors had been the first to cross the previously unimagined breadth of the Pacific Ocean. They had been the first to uncover the great mystery of the world's dimensions, adding seven thousand miles to its known circumference. And now they were nearing their goal. They were obtaining adequate food and water, and were beginning to form trade agreements with local authorities. For a moment, Elcano felt his breast flare with the hope of returning to Spain with honor and, perhaps, enough wealth to purchase another ship. Yes, perhaps these things were still attainable. Perhaps, even at the age of thirty-four, there would still be time to start a family of his own, a family with fine sons that would grow to be like Chindarza.

As if summoned by Elcano's thoughts, Chindarza stepped quietly up to the rail and, after a moment, said, "It's a fine, calm night, isn't it, sir?"

"It is indeed."

"Are you thinking about home, sir?"

Elcano's face broke into a gentle smile. "So now you can even read my thoughts."

"It's just that I've been thinking about it too, sir."

"And what about home have you been dwelling on? If you were Acurio, I would guess it to be your mother's cooking."

"No, not her cooking, Master Elcano." Chindarza lowered his gaze a little and said, "Did you know, sir, after my father died, Acurio wanted to court my mother?"

"Why, no. He never mentioned that."

"She said no, though, sir, not because he was a sailor, but because he was three years younger than she was. My father was a man of the sea. I think she might like to marry another seaman, one that was a little older, that is." He shot Elcano a glance to gauge his reaction to this.

The smile on Elcano's face broadened ever so slightly. "I suppose she's beautiful."

"My father always said she was, sir."

"What's her name?"

"Maria Teresa, sir."

"A lovely name. Well, it sounds like I would be most unwise to pass up a chance to meet Maria Teresa de Chindarza when we return home. She may even find me tolerable if I bring her back a rich son."

Much pleased, Chindarza said, "Master Elcano, when we land, the first thing I'm going to do is buy some clothes."

"Oh?"

"Yes, sir. Before I left Bermeo, my mother told me she would know I had made my mark as a sailor if I came back to her wearing fine new clothes."

"Made your mark, eh? In that case, Chindarza, we must make certain that you show up in the finest clothes she has ever seen."

# Humabon's Land

## 16

Shifting uneasily as he awaited Serrano's signal, Elcano cast a glance at the crowded bay they were swiftly approaching. When Serrano gave a short wave in his direction Elcano immediately yelled out, "Fire!" Cannons from all three ships leaped in their frames as they erupted with great puffs of smoke and jarring percussions, momentarily deafening the crews and terrifying the inhabitants of the capital city of Cebu. Silently questioning the wisdom of entering a harbor with guns blasting to impress and intimidate their potential hosts, especially ones who could build such a prosperous looking city, Elcano ordered the lowering of the *Concepción's* anchor and the furling of her sails.

A boat was moved from the deck of the flagship to the water, and soon Magellan's son, Cristóbal, Enrique, and a contingent of other rowers pulled toward the harbor. When they reached the shore, a crowd of milling Cebuans, some of whom appeared to be members of a royal guard, immediately surrounded the landing party and led them up a road that climbed behind a row of houses, completely hiding them from Elcano's sight.

Rather than a collection of scattered and primitive huts, organized rows of prosperous homes that had been built upon stilts marched up and away from the waters edge. Even from the outer harbor, Elcano could see enough to be very impressed by this strange city.

To Captain Serrano, who now came to stand at his side, Elcano said, "This Rajah Humabon must be a man of influence, sir."

"It certainly appears so."

"Do you think he'll agree to trade with us, sir?"

"I have faith that he will. Cristóbal will undoubtedly inform him that the captain-general is a representative of the king of Spain, a man even more powerful than the king of Portugal. Even people this far from India will have heard of the battles of Dabul and Goa. The captain-general took part in both, you know. Although he is not the sort of man to have willingly joined in the killing of innocents, the stories of the butchery that took place are notorious."

"I have heard of those battles, sir, but not of any details, nothing of the captain-general's role in them."

"He was wounded during the early fighting at Dabul, but he still saw or heard about much that happened afterward. He once told me that after Almeida captured the Egyptian ships, he ordered their Venetian gunners to be tortured. Then he had the gunners strapped to their own cannons and blown to pieces. When Almeida landed, he ordered every man, woman, and child to be cut to pieces. In Goa the number tortured and slaughtered by Albuquerque's armies was even higher. Having seen the savagery for himself, the captain-general believes the people of Cebu will be anxious to avoid its recurrence."

Elcano looked toward the harbor and said, "The outriggers that accompanied us from Limasawa are reaching shore, sir. Let's hope that Colambu and his representatives will help our cause."

Whether through duress or diplomacy, after the mighty Humabon had taken the time to consider his choices, he sent the fleet's shore party back to the ships with word that his nephew, the crown prince, would meet Magellan aboard his ship to formalize a trading treaty. When the appointed time came, Serrano, Carvalho, and Elcano were called to the flagship to witness the solidification of the arrangements.

Under a blazing afternoon sun and with the air filled with the beating of gongs, the huge royal canoe arrived. The rajah's nephew, elaborately decorated with gold jewelry but dressed only in a length of embroidered silk that wrapped around his waist and hung to his knees, emerged from under a canopy of red and yellow silk and climbed with his dignitaries to the *Trinidad's* main deck.

After the initial bowing and other cordialities had been observed, the prince was seated in a chair covered in red velvet between Colambu and a counselor that, to Elcano's surprise, was a Moor. The rest of the prince's men found their places upon palm mats that had been arranged to form an arc. Magellan's velvet chair was positioned across the deck from the prince, and from it emanated the leather backed chairs of his captains then the cushions of his other officers, which completed the ring of men.

Elcano found himself the last European on his half of the circle, with Pilot Carvalho shifting restlessly on his left and a curious young Cebuan eyeing him up and down on his right. A strange yet pleasant scent rose from this warrior of Cebu, and its spicy nature helped to mask the smell of sweat that slicked Elcano's skin as well as that of the nervous bodies around him. Holding himself erect and attentive, Elcano concentrated on Magellan's words in spite of the distracting aroma and open stare of his neighbor.

With Enrique acting as Magellan's interpreter and the Moor speaking for Humabon's nephew, the formalities began. The first question to be addressed was whether the prince had authority to act as Humabon's agent in transacting so important and so binding an agreement. After assurances were received, Magellan laid out his wishes for an exclusive trade agreement on behalf of King Carlos. The prince replied with gravity that his uncle, the Rajah Humabon, wanted the same thing, and wished nothing more than to commit himself to such a compact.

Dressed in heavy formal clothing, Magellan listened carefully, his hands lightly resting on the arms of his chair. He turned to Enrique and asked softly, "Are you certain he understands what he is committing to?"

"Yes, Master. He understands."

Magellan closed his eyes for a moment, then, before his officers, men, and guests, he left his chair and knelt upon the planks of the deck. Bowing his head and clasping his hands tightly before his face, he prayed fervently, "May this alliance for which we have labored so long be pleasing to you, Almighty Father." Elcano and the men of the fleet were already scrambling to their knees, and were soon followed by the confused but willing Cebuans, but Magellan did not pause for them. "May you bless your servants, oh Lord, in our continued efforts to bring glory to your holy name and to faithfully serve our earthly king. Accept our humble thanks for your mercy in delivering us to this hour, Dear Father. Amen." Stiffly, Magellan tried to rise to his feet but Enrique and Cristóbal immediately came to his assistance. With eyes awash with compassion, the captain-general beamed upon those gathered around him as they too came to their feet.

This impassioned prayer of thanks so impressed the Cebuans that the discussions about trade were replaced by a tide of questions about social and religious customs. Delighted, Magellan explained the basic tenets of Christianity, highlighting the worldly benefit of King Carlos' protection during the lifetime of all believers as well as the reward of heaven when a Christian's life came to an end.

Through the interpreters, the young prince said, "Long ago the Moors brought the words of Allah to our shores and to the shores of the other islands. Many of our people now follow the teachings of Islam, but your words intrigue me greatly. Would it be possible for you to leave several men with us to instruct us in the ways of your God?"

Father Valderrama looked plainly relieved when Magellan answered, "Unfortunately I am unable to spare even one man from my fleet. However, our priest would be happy to perform the rite of baptism while we remain here. It is through baptism that a person becomes a Christian, but no one should be baptized out of fear or for personal gain. This choice is to be made only if there is a true desire to follow the ways that God's son taught us."

After another round of questions, during which all of the sacraments were touched upon, Magellan said, "One more thing must be made clear; once a man has been baptized, he is forbidden to have sex with a woman that has not also chosen to become a Christian."

At the irony of this announcement, coming after the activities of the fleet's personnel at Rio de Janeiro, Carvalho let out a soft sputtering cough, which he quickly suppressed. He quieted and leaned close to Elcano's ear, saying, "Is he implying that we won't be committing as great a sin if we sleep with their women *after* they've been baptized?"

Elcano scowled at him then tried to remain attentive as Magellan delivered more of the teachings of the Church to the captivated Cebuans. But under the growing weight and heat of his sweaty velvet tunic, Elcano began to wonder when the conversation would revert to the king's business.

Carvalho proved that his thoughts were running along the same lines when he whispered, "Was this meeting called to finalize a trade alliance or to convert these savages?"

Again, Elcano ignored him.

Finally, Magellan said, "I will hold no ill will against those that choose to keep to their old ways, but any man of Cebu who becomes Christian will be held higher in the esteem of the great King Carlos and his people. As a sign of this, I will bestow a suit of armor, such as you will soon be shown, upon those choosing to be baptized."

Even the loyal Serrano stared in amazement at the captain-general when this offer was announced.

Carvalho hissed to an equally surprised Elcano, "Our armor in exchange for their souls?"

Nothing in the king's orders had encouraged the conversion of natives, and Elcano could only wonder along with the rest of Magellan's men at the purpose of such a proposal.

The captain-general now led the prince and his company on a tour throughout the ship, then ordered the performance of a mock battle between armored swordsmen. When the sun was lowering in the western sky and its intensity was just beginning to subside, Magellan handed the Cebuan prince and his interpreter a written copy of the treaty.

The prince bowed deeply and said, "Most powerful emissary of Spain, we wish to convey our assurances that Rajah Humabon will happily sign this accord. We wish for many years of peace and prosperity between our people." His Muslim interpreter faltered for an instant before relaying the prince's final words. "Moreover, we believe that Rajah Humabon may desire to be baptized, as do those standing before you now."

Magellan's face filled with emotion. He opened his arms and embraced the prince, and then Colambu, and then each of the royal guardsmen in turn. This spontaneous action triggered a hugging exchange in which the sweet smelling Cebuan enfolded Elcano in a sudden embrace that nearly lifted him off the deck. As quickly as courtesy allowed, Elcano freed himself but he was immediately clutched by the next of the royal attendants, and then the next.

Before the prince's departure, gifts for Humabon were brought from the hold and loaded into the outriggers just as rice, goats, chickens, and pigs were bestowed upon Magellan. Once the canoes had pulled well away from the *Trinidad*, Magellan turned to his men. "We've served both our earthly and our heavenly master's today. Tonight, we feast and enjoy our blessings."

This news was heartily cheered and attended to without delay. But the festivities ended sadly when the *Victoria's* boatswain delivered news of the death of one of their supernumeraries, Martin de Barrena.

In the early hours before dawn, another body, that of Juan de Aroche, who had served as sergeant-at-arms on the ill-fated *Santiago*, was securely wrapped and placed beside the enshrouded form of his shipmate, Barrena. Magellan sent a landing party ashore with a request for Humabon to allow them to bury their dead within his realm.

Humabon agreed, and Elcano met him for the first time near the center of town upon land already prepared to receive the remains of the two seamen. With the majority of the townspeople and a good portion of the fleet's personnel looking on, the initial greetings between the rajah, Magellan, and the other officers of the fleet were warm but brief. Somewhat to Elcano's surprise, Humabon was a short, rotund man with perceptive, intelligent eyes but far less physical beauty than the majority of his people. What redeemed his body from being wholly unimpressive was the intricacy of his tattooing. The black curves and triangle-filled parallel stripes ran continuously from his ankles to his wrists, rolled from one edge of his round chest to the other, and did not halt until they had crossed each of his broad cheeks. He wore a heavy gold chain around his neck, golden bands around his arms and ankles, and wide hoop earrings that were embedded with precious stones and pearls. His only articles of clothing were an embroidered silk wrap worn around his waist and a gold threaded band that held back his thick, waist-length hair. From his belt, the jewels that had been inlaid in the gold hilt of his curved knife caught the reflection of the sun whenever he moved. The rajah's manner was unassuming as he took his place beside Magellan at the commencement of the funeral mass.

For Elcano, it was deeply satisfying to see that the two fallen members of the fleet were being given burial services with a great deal more ceremony than had been possible for the many men that had been delivered into a watery tomb. He noticed that Humabon, too, seemed impressed with the pageantry and solemnity of the occasion. Scanning the Cebuan townspeople, Elcano saw that many heads were bowed, as if they shared in the universal nature of grief and commiserated with the loss of their visitors.

After the final "Amen", Magellan and his officers were led to the rajah's grand house where an extravagant feast awaited them. Through the interpreters, the two leaders

241

exchanged many compliments and promises before their conversations turned to more serious matters, such as trade and religion, and Elcano watched the exercise of Magellan's diplomatic skills with growing appreciation. Between bites of food both plentiful and exotically delicious, he listened until the captain-general had convinced Humabon to allow him to construct a trading post on the islands that very day. Magellan, obviously delighted, turned to him and said, "Master Elcano, you are to begin directing the construction at once. Enrique will help you translate your wishes to the men Rajah Humabon will provide."

Elcano left Magellan, his host, and the fine food reluctantly but also with the intention of carrying out this order with swift efficiency.

In spite of the language and national incongruities of the two sides, Elcano and his mixed crew experienced remarkably few mishaps, and a sturdy hut was erected before nightfall. When all was in order, Elcano thanked his Cebuan workers with praise and small gifts from the stock of trade goods already arriving from the ships.

Turning next to his crew of sailors, and noticing how sweaty and grimy they were, he ordered all but their armed guards to head straight into the waters of the bay. The Cebuans looked on, most of them grinning, as Elcano shed his doublet, belt, and boots, and dove in after his men.

The embrace of the water felt nothing less than heavenly. He came up briefly, took a huge breath, and swam as deep as the air in his lungs would allow, reveling in the caress of the cool water against his skin. Surfacing again, a loud sigh escaped his lips. With gentle strokes he swam parallel to the beach, taking his time as a good share of the filth was rinsed from his body and clothing. With his men carousing and splashing nearby and the sun sinking into a showy splash of reds and golds, he resolved to leave the rest of the stocking of the trading post until tomorrow. Right now, there was only the sea.

When dawn broke the process of transferring a portion of the ships' stores to the island commenced with eager hands and high spirits. Today, Magellan brought Antonio Pigafetta and Father Valderrama ashore with him, and these three stopped only briefly at the trading post to discuss its progress with Elcano before leaving to meet with the rajah.

Elcano had allowed Chindarza to come to the post for the first time but he remained watchful, making certain that the youth did nothing to slow his recovery. They and several other seamen were organizing the trade goods onto shelves when a stocky Cebuan and Pigafetta approached the large hut.

Pigafetta, who had evolved into something of a translator and a clerk, said to Elcano, "Sir, this man is one of Rajah Humabon's nephews, and he wishes to trade an article of gold for some of our goods." Pigafetta nodded politely to the islander, who handed Elcano an object completely foreign to him.

Turning it first one way and then the other as Chindarza looked on, Elcano carefully examined the golden article. It was about an inch and a half in length, as thick as a goose's quill, and capped on each end with a three-dimensional star of gold. "It's a pretty thing," said Elcano. "Some kind of jewelry?"

"Very much so, Master Elcano, but of a nature I had never heard of before reaching Cebu. It is called a palang, sir, but perhaps it would be best explained by asking the rajah's nephew to show you how it is worn." Pigafetta turned and signaled encouragingly to the Cebuan. Without the slightest hesitation the man lifted his loincloth and proudly displayed his genitals.

Chindarza let out a short gasp.

Elcano's eyes shot wide open as he grimaced agonizingly and blurted out, "Heaven save us." Their reactions drew a smile from Pigafetta and a companionable laugh from the Cebuan, who then let loose a string of words the meaning of which even Pigafetta could not catch.

The pained look remained on Elcano's face as he took a more thorough if still sympathetic look at the metal spurs protruding from the front and back of the native's penis. Shaking his head, he asked with bewilderment, "How could a man allow such a thing to be done?"

"Every Cebuan male has his member pierced when he reaches puberty, sir. To the ends of the bolts, many attach star shaped spurs, such as these, but some prefer smooth balls or even small cross bolts. I've made something of a study of these mutilations, and each palang is slightly different."

"But the thing goes all the way through. How does the man urinate? How does he father a child?"

"I wondered about those things myself, sir, but notice this hole that's been drilled through the palang. When the tube is positioned properly, that hole allows the passage of body fluids."

"In the name of all that's holy, why would they hold to such a barbaric practice?"

"They believe that it gives their women more pleasure, sir."

"More pleasure!" Elcano worked to lower his voice as he eyed the undaunted Cebuan with renewed scrutiny. "It's a wonder their women let them sleep with them at all. Every encounter must be excruciating." His eyes trailed with reluctance back to the golden rod resting in his palm.

"Master Elcano, don't you think His Majesty would find the palang interesting, since it so clearly illustrates the cultural practices of these people?"

"*Cultural* practices?"

"Sex is an important part of any culture, is it not, sir?"

"And you've been doing a thorough study of the topic? For the king's sake?"

"Well, sir, my observations started during my earlier visit to the quarters of the crown prince. He generously entertained us with four beautiful girls, sir. They danced and played music on a drum and some brass cymbals."

"Go on."

"During the course of this...diversion, sir, I became aware, that is, I learned that the Cebuans begin preparing their female children for future sexual acts by the age of six."

"Prepare them?"

"Yes, sir, by stretching their private parts, to eventually receive a man's organ."

"From the age of *six?*"

"The prince said it takes many years, sir, to convert the female region so that the act is pleasurable."

"Pleasurable," Elcano scoffed.

"When I questioned Enrique about this practice, he said that the idea first came from the study of rhinoceroses, which the Cebuans' ancestors hunted. Evidently the male rhinoceros has a natural palang on its member. I was also told that the men of other islands have adopted a similar custom that entails embedding small bells, pearls, or glass beads under the foreskin."

"And I suppose they claim that this is for the sake of their women too?"

"For their women, yes, sir."

"Pigafetta, it's been a constant battle keeping the men working diligently, what with nearly naked women all around. Now I'm beginning to understand why the women seem so interested in us." He gave a last quick glance at the tool in his hand. "Thank God we were born in lands where such customs are unimaginable. Rhinoceroses indeed!"

Passing the palang to Chindarza, and noticing with what fascination the youth accepted it, Elcano asked, "What does this gentleman want in trade for the thing?"

After a deal had been struck and Pigafetta and the Cebuan had departed, Chindarza asked, "There's been a rumor, sir, that if the island women agree to become Christians the captain-general will allow our men to, um, mingle with them."

With quick and final authority Elcano said, "You're still too weak to think of fraternizing with these uncivilized women. Do you want to lose what strength you've just regained?" He turned and busied himself at the far corner of the shelter, giving Chindarza no further opportunity for speculative discussion.

Magellan reached the post soon afterward. Spreading his hands wide and beaming with satisfaction, the captain-general said, "Humabon wishes to be baptized as soon as possible, and I believe that many of his subjects will follow his example."

Chindarza's face lit up and Elcano aimed a scowl at him to erase his hopeful smile.

"Master Elcano," Magellan went on, "gather up the same team of men that built this shelter and set them to work on a platform in the town square. Pigafetta is right over there. He can help with the Cebuans. Make the platform several feet high and broad enough to hold an altar and a good number of chairs. The rajah's baptism must be conducted with the utmost grandeur. We want to encourage as many of his people as possible to accept God's blessings."

"Yes, Captain-general." For Chindarza's ears, he added, "I'll keep our men so busy they won't have any energy to waste on unhealthy daydreaming."

"Fine," Magellan replied. "I'll leave you to your tasks."

In a day and a half the palm tree surrounded center of the village had been transformed for the extraordinary occasion. Fluttering banners, woven garlands, and sprays of flowers scattered colors across the new platform and altar. When it was time for Father Valderrama and his assistants to lead the procession up the steps, Elcano allowed himself a touch of pride at the beauty of their surrounding.

The opening prayer of the mass began at ten in the morning, and during the next six hours Elcano witnessed not only the baptism of Rajah Humabon but also those of twenty-two hundred other Cebuans. A seemingly endless line of men, women, and children obediently bowed their heads before the cross and Father Valderrama, and accepted the mysterious words and water with awed humility.

This long, solemn rite was followed by feasting and music that lasted well into the night, and the men of the fleet were allowed to go ashore in small groups to join in the merriment. Chindarza arrived in the early evening and, being both young and handsome, soon gained the attention of several Cebuan girls. Easily sizing up the situation, Elcano stayed close by Chindarza's side. To the young seaman's discernible disappointment, Elcano kept him well within the torchlight of the main festivities throughout the evening. When their time ashore came to an end, the two of them had no choice but to listen to Acurio's tales of rapture all the way back to the ship.

Magellan's loosening of the restrictions concerning contact with the island women soon led to trouble. To Elcano's disgust, Carvalho had risked inciting Humabon's anger against them all by making a clandestine raid on the rajah's own harem. Once Serrano had informed Magellan of this, Carvalho was restricted to the ship for the remainder of their stay. But Carvalho was not the last of the officers to infuriate the captain-general. Just as he had done in Rio de Janeiro, Captain Duarte Barbosa became enamored with a particular woman, left his ship one evening, and did not return the next morning. Magellan was so outraged at such irresponsible behavior that he had his brother-in-law brought back to his ship and relieved him of his command of the *Victoria*, replacing him with his own son, Cristóbal.

The fleet's reaction to this appointment was mixed. Cristóbal had left Spain as a supernumerary, was in his early twenties, and was inexperienced at leading men. Yet Barbosa had been respected by very few. Elcano thought that more capable men were clearly available, but Magellan had once again made it clear that he valued personal loyalty above competence. And he was in command. Magellan had taught his crews well when it came to keeping their opinions to themselves. Grumbling was held to a minimum.

After these flagrant transgressions by members of the fleet and the continual cavorting between seamen on shore leave and the island women, Elcano began to perceive a less friendly attitude developing among the men of Cebu. How must such antics look to them after being told by Magellan that Christians were forbidden to have sex outside of marriage? Elcano's attempts to keep Chindarza from interacting with the women had kept his own activities curtailed. Thoughts of customs related to the palang also had a restraining effect on his urges. Still, the beauty of the Cebuan females was not easily ignored, nor the temptation easily denied.

Working with four other men to stow a load of Cebuan gold in his ship's hold, Elcano placed the last bar in the heavy chest, shut the lid, and set the sturdy lock.

Rubbing his sweaty face with his shirt sleeve, Acurio said, "Amazing, isn't it, sir, how these islanders gladly trade a pound of gold for a pound of Spanish iron?"

"And the Cebuans believe they're getting the better of the bargain. Now, let's all get out of this sweltering pit."

They climbed to the deck and Elcano went to the rail to pull in deep, slow breaths of clean air.

Acurio asked him, "Are you meaning to go ashore, sir? Your watch is nearly over."

"I haven't decided yet, Acurio." He leaned heavily against the railing and said, "The heat's terrible today."

Acurio looked at him more closely. "Why, sir, you're face is as red as a cherry." He reached over and touched Elcano's arm below his rolled up sleeve. "And you're burning up, Master Elcano. You ought to go to your cabin and lie down, sir."

"No, Acurio, not my cabin," Elcano said in a voice quickly losing its strength. "I want to stay out in the breeze."

"Then you'll need a chair, sir." Acurio sent the nearest hand for the chair from his cabin. When it came, he eased Elcano into the seat and handed him a fresh cup of water, muttering all the while, "Looking after the boy, looking after the rest of us, and here you've gone and let yourself get sick with a fever."

"Stop fussing, Acurio."

"I'll just go and fetch Bustamente to take a look at you, sir."

"I said stop fussing. I'll be fine in a minute. It was just the heat and the foul air of the hold."

"Pardon my saying so, sir, but I don't like the look of you at the moment. It's more than the hold that's to blame. I say it's a fever that's got to you."

"Don't you dare concern Chindarza with your imaginings. When he and Juanito return with the captain, you're not to say a word."

Carvalho, who had been roused from his resting place in the shade of the foredeck by their discussion, walked up to them. "I must agree with Acurio. You look like you've been roasted over coals."

Elcano found that he had less and less patience with Carvalho with the passing of time, and he was about to give him a gruff reply when the three of them were interrupted by the arrival of Pigafetta. He greeted them politely then said, "The captain-general has sent me to inform the officers of each ship to arm ten of their men. There's to be an attack on the village of Bulaya."

"What!" barked Carvalho.

"What is the reason for the attack?" Elcano demanded.

Hesitantly, Pigafetta resumed, "Remember, after the baptism, sirs, the captain-general sent messengers out to warn all of the chieftains that if they did not submit to Rajah Humabon's authority they would be killed and their possessions confiscated. Well, the chief of Bulaya has refused to acknowledge the rajah's superiority or to pay the demanded tribute, so the captain-general means to carry out his punishment."

Even Carvalho let his objections remain unspoken while in the presence of Magellan's agent.

Elcano said, "Captain Serrano is ashore. Has he been informed?"

"Yes, sir. He's with the captain-general now."

Elcano wanted to ask what Serrano thought of this invasion into the affairs of these people, but he dared not. Instead he asked, "Ten men, you say?"

"Yes, sir, only two boats are being sent. Now, please excuse me so that I may deliver this message to the *Victoria*." Pigafetta, seeming to notice Elcano's appearance for the first time, paused long enough to ask, "Excuse me, sir, but are you well?"

"He's burning with fever," snapped Carvalho. Before Elcano could stop him, the volatile pilot added. "Tell our captain of his illness at once."

Within minutes Elcano's stomach began to cramp and his bowls to loosen. Reluctantly, and insisting to Acurio that this was nothing serious, he agreed to retire to his cabin until his body had flushed itself of whatever was twisting his guts and scorching him from the inside out.

Although he was dealing with a far less cooperative patient than Elcano had previously treated, it was Chindarza who now took on the roll of caretaker. Quickly learning that Elcano would not rest easy unless he was given constant news of the developments with the islanders, Chindarza told him of the successful raid on Bulaya and of all the livestock that had been confiscated.

Elcano's condition remained unchanged under Chindarza's care, but the following evening Captain Serrano entered the open door of the cabin and said, "Leave us, Chindarza. I must speak with Master Elcano." As Chindarza departed, Elcano leaned forward at the edge of his cot and moved to get to his feet.

"No, no. Stay where you are," Serrano protested. "You couldn't stand for five seconds. Besides, what I have to say is best heard sitting down." When Elcano once again leaned his back against the wall of his bunk, Serrano settled into a chair and went on. "I'll get right to the point. The captain-general has ordered us to prepare for another battle."

"I don't understand, sir?"

In a downcast voice that led Elcano to believe Serrano had made an effort to convince Magellan to act more prudently, his captain said, "Lapulapu, the chief of Mactan, has refused to pay the tribute. The captain-general intends to punish him as he did the people of Bulaya."

"Using our men, sir? Our ships?" When Serrano nodded, Elcano asked, "How powerful a chief is this man, Captain?"

"I've been told his warriors use poisoned arrows and spears, and he commands many men." Serrano slumped deeper into his chair and crossed his arms across his chest. "I have seldom voiced disagreement, but today I tried to point out to the captain-general that we barely have enough men to insure the safety of our ships, especially since the warriors of Bulaya may choose to seek revenge. He countered this by saying he'll take only sixty men, and not even fighting men. He's determined to use mostly supernumeraries and servants, to show how even a small group of untrained Spaniards can defeat an army of natives. When he told Humabon of his intentions, even the rajah tried to dissuade him, but it did no good. The captain-general insists on impressing him with our invincibility. He even made Humabon swear to keep his warriors out of the battle. They are to come with us but only to observe him and his men in action."

"Will he speak with the officers, sir, to ask for our thoughts?"

"Yes, tonight. He has agreed to meet with us aboard the *Trinidad*. But before you ask, no, you may not come. You are much too ill. Even if you were healthy, I fear it would make no difference. He seems unwilling to change his mind."

Knowing that if Serrano was unable to dissuade Magellan, he had little chance of success, Elcano lowered his red eyes. "I hope you can convince him, sir."

After the meeting with Magellan that evening, Serrano returned to the *Concepción* and stopped by Elcano's cabin to say, "My fears have been confirmed. Under the protests of every officer, me loudest of all, the captain-general stood firm. Tomorrow we sail to the northern end of Mactan. We have been instructed to do no more than Humabon and his men, to watch while the captain-general storms the village with his supernumeraries."

"I will be much better by tomorrow, sir."

Serrano said in a level tone, "My next order will be as little to your liking as the captain-general's order was to me. You, Master Elcano, are to remain at the trading post and be cared for along with two other sick men."

Elcano tried to sit a little straighter. "But, Captain, I'm well enough. My place is with the ship, the men."

"You're feverish, and as feeble as a drunkard. You will remain ashore." When Elcano opened his mouth to speak again, Serrano cut him off, "Do you wish me to endanger this undertaking by placing an ill officer over the men?"

After a lengthy pause in which Elcano silently cursed the weakness of his own body, he found and held Serrano's gaze. "No, Captain. I would never purposely endanger this crew."

"I know."

Still struggling with acceptance, Elcano added, "May God watch over you all."

# The Fallen

## 17

Elcano, weak and clumsy as a newly born colt, was taken to the trading post just as the light of dawn was touching the beach. Chindarza saw to it that he was settled onto a cot with a cup of water close at hand, then crouched down next to him, hesitant to leave.

"Damn this heat," Elcano grumbled, although the temperature outside his body was still mild."

"Yes, sir," said Chindarza

"Damn this trading post."

"Yes, sir."

"Damn being left here like a useless chest of trinkets!"

"Yes, sir."

"And damn my blasted temper!"

Chindarza, evidently thinking it best not to agree with this last statement, looked at the sand around his feet.

Elcano exhaled loudly and kept his feverish eyes open long enough to study Chindarza. When he spoke again his voice was softer, mellowed by reflection. "You've grown at least four inches in the last year and a half. How you've managed to do that on so little food is a wonder."

Chindarza lifted his gaze to Elcano. "You must get well, sir."

"And you must get back to the ship, but first listen to me. You have not been chosen to fight today, but in warfare additional men are often called into battle." Elcano already felt his wavering strength begin to ebb, draining the power from his voice, but he was determined to finish. "I've seen your passions get the better of you at times, as they do with most young men. But today, if you find yourself on the bat-

tlefield, you must not waste your courage on reckless brava-
do. You must think clearly and act prudently."

"I will, sir."

"You are anxious to join your shipmates in this battle. I
can see it in your eyes. I suppose that's only natural at your
age, but I will not be there to see that, to make certain..."

"I will be careful, sir. If I draw my sword, I will imagine
you fighting by my side."

"You and Acurio must come back and tell me all that
takes place today."

"Yes, sir, of course."

Elcano reached out and took hold of Chindarza's wrist,
gripping it for a moment until the two other ailing crewmen
were carried into the trading post and placed on cots a few
feet away.

"You must be off now, Chindarza."

But Chindarza hesitated a little longer. "I, I had a dream
last night, sir. In it, you were forced to sail away and leave
me behind. Why do you suppose I would have such a dream
when it is I who must leave you behind?"

"Dreams are mysterious things, Chindarza. You must
not dwell on them. Now go, and fare well."

Elcano watched him through the doorway until he was
out of sight and the sun's light spilled into the hut's wide
eastern window. Closing his eyes and saying a silent prayer
for Chindarza's safety, he felt the sun's heat build. The
greater heat of his own body began to swirl and boil as the
ache in his head pounded with every heartbeat. At last, a
sleep more relentless than his resistance overtook him.

For hours he tossed and mumbled in a slumbering haze
of sweat, pain, and anxiety. Then, from far away, as if the
sounds came from the depths of an underground cave, he
heard the wails and weeping of many Cebuans. His feverish mind hushed the cries, muffling them to no more than
distant whispers. But they rose again, louder and more persistent. His fevered brain and body refused to let the sounds
touch him even when they suddenly mixed with the voices
of his own kind, even when someone nearby cried out in
anguish, "It can't be!" Nothing reached his consciousness

until strong hands lifted him and he heard Acurio's voice hiss harshly, "Gently, I said! You men, take the other two. The rest of you, attend to the stores."

Elcano tried to speak but his throbbing head revolted and only a moan escaped his dry lips.

"There now, sir," said Acurio. "We'll have you aboard in no time."

Forcing himself to take a deep breath, Elcano tried to open his eyes but failed. Ultimately, he managed to utter only, "Chindarza."

"He's well, Master Elcano. He's preparing your cabin. You just sleep easy, sir."

He felt water touch his feet and buttocks before he was lifted into the skiff. Men propped him up between them, but his head fell limply to his chest where it swayed with the movements of the boat. With a great effort he stirred, whispering, "The crew, Acurio, the *Concepción*."

"Sleep now, sir," Acurio said, and Elcano's body betrayed his will by obeying.


Slowly and gradually surfacing from a deep stupor, Elcano moved his hand and then licked his chapped lips. Chindarza's voice came from close by his side, saying, "Here, sir, have a drink."

Feeling as though every drop of moisture had been wrung from his body, Elcano gulped the liquid greedily, willing to suffer the terrible cramping that he expected to follow. He eased back on his cot and kept his eyes squinted open. Juanito lay curled in the corner, sleeping soundly. To Chindarza, Elcano said in a rough whisper, "Did you get pulled into the fighting?"

"No, sir."

"Then all went well?"

"Have another drink, sir."

Elcano accepted the cup again. "You did not answer me, Chindarza. What has happened?"

"Pardon me, sir, but Señor Acurio asked me to find him straight away when you awoke. May I, sir?" Hardly waiting for a nod, he disappeared out the doorway, but he was soon back with Acurio in tow.

Acurio looked Elcano over, and in a tone that spoke of hours spent at his bedside, he said, "So, you've come back to us, sir. Last night, well, that was the worst of it and I'd not soon spend another night like it. You've slept for nineteen hours since we brought you aboard, sir, twelve of them like a dead man."

"Tell me about the skirmish with the natives, Acurio. Were any men lost?"

Acurio's eyes drifted to Chindarza's. "Yes, sir. Some."

Elcano's heart chilled at the tone of Acurio's voice as much as at his words. "How many?"

"Eight, sir, and twice that were wounded."

"How many from among our men?"

"From the *Concepción*, sir, Juan de la Torre, and from the *Victoria*, Rodrigo Nieto."

"And the flagship, Acurio?"

Again Acurio glanced at Chindarza, whose gaze fell to the deck. "Sir, along with four of his men and his own son, the captain-general was cut down. He's dead, sir. Captain-general Magellan, he's dead and gone."

Elcano whispered, "Magellan? Dead?"

"He is, sir, killed by the natives on Mactan."

The details of every struggle, every disagreement, every emotion that had ever passed between Magellan and Elcano flashed through his pounding head. The tortures, and terrors, and deaths of Port San Julian clutched at his mind. Other memories, too, crept in, memories of Magellan hiring him in Seville, Magellan reinstating him to his rank, Magellan claiming that the two of them were much alike, and Magellan feeding his sick men on a small island in the Pacific Sea. Elcano pictured him enduring every hardship borne by his men during their icy passage and their great ocean crossing.

And now the captain-general was dead. Although even this news could not erase Elcano's lingering bitterness towards Magellan, he recognized with brutal clarity the tragedy that had just befallen the fleet.

Once his thoughts had refocused, he sighed, "Please, both of you sit down. Tell me all that you saw."

Acurio began in a voice deepened with sorrow, "Well, sir, the ships anchored at the north end of the island about three hours before sunrise. The captain-general sent one of Rajah Humabon's men ashore to see if Lapulapu might change his mind about paying the tribute. But the devil kept delaying and delaying with his answer until the tide was running out. We had to pull the ships so far from shore to keep them from grounding that our cannons were out of range of the beach. Our officers tried one last time to talk the captain-general out of going ashore, and even the rajah warned him that dawn would be a bad time to attack, but the captain-general said he wasn't about to break his word to Humabon. He had some of our smaller guns set up in the skiffs and he ordered all the men going with him put on heavy armor. Only their legs were left bare, since they now had to wade so far to reach the shore.

"When they landed, sir, they headed for the village. Pigafetta, who was with the captain-general, told us that when they got there the place looked to be deserted. They set torches to the houses, and all at once Lapulapu and his men loosed their arrows and spears from the cover of the trees. Our men were outnumbered nearly thirty to one, and they held their own for quite awhile but more and more of the natives kept pouring out of the jungle. By the time our men were beginning to run low of shot and darts, those islanders were swarming around them, so the captain general ordered a retreat back to the beach. Some of our men took off running, leaving the captain-general and the others in the rear to keep fighting as they went.

"We saw them break from the trees and head for our boats, but the skiffs were too far out and, weighed down in that armor like they were, our men had a terrible struggle crossing the reef. Before they were knee-deep in the water, our men were being hit in the legs by poisoned arrows. I saw Captain Cristóbal Ravelo fall, sir, and the captain-general stopped and stood over his son, refusing to take another step back.

"He fought like a tiger, sir, swinging his sword and throwing any spear he could lay his hands on, and all the while he kept yelling for the men to get to the boats and looking back over his shoulder to see that they were safely on their way. We thought he'd get away at last, sir, but he stayed on, never leaving Cristóbal's body. His fighting was cut short when a spear knocked the helmet from his head and another spear grazed his face. Even hurt, he managed to run the savage that wounded him clean through. The captain-general was trying to free his lance from the man's chest when a hoard of demons closed in around him. Pigafetta and Enrique were still fighting not far from the captain-general's side when a warrior slashed him across the thigh with one of our own swords. He went down, sir, and the savages leaped on him like a pack of wolves. Master Elcano, it was terrible, and we could do nothing but watch as they stabbed and hacked at him. They butchered him to pieces."

For moments the small cabin was held by a ghostly silence. Then Elcano asked softly, "No one came to his aid?"

"Well, sir, he had forbidden any of us from joining in the battle. Even so, some of Humabon's canoes went against the captain-general's order and headed as close in as they could to help. But our men in the launches, seeing that the captain-general was being overpowered and thinking to protect him, fired a volley. Their shots hit two of Humabon's canoes, killing four of his warriors."

"God help us."

"That was the last of the firing, sir. We were too far out for our guns to help at all, and the captain-general's men had our boats. By the time the first of them reached the ships, it was all over."

"And now he's gone," said Elcano, "along with other good men."

"Yes, sir. All but seven of our men made it back to the ships, but the poison on the arrows that had struck Pedro Gomez killed him a short while later. The rest of the wounded, Enrique and Pigafetta and several others, they're still badly swollen, sir."

"Has a funeral been held?"

"No, sir. Captain Serrano asked the rajah to claim the bodies of our fallen men, but Lapulapu just laughed at his messengers."

Elcano shook his head, drew his hand across his face, and stared at the wall. He hadn't noticed that Juanito had stirred, but the boy now sat on the floor beside Chindarza's chair, his eyes open and attentive. Elcano inquired of Acurio, "What has been done about the command of the fleet?"

Shifting in his chair, Acurio said, "It's been hard enough telling you about the battle, sir. Well, I guess it'll get no easier by putting it off. Duarte Barbosa has been chosen to captain the *Trinidad*. What's more, a supernumerary, Luis de Goes, has been given command of the *Victoria*."

"They gave Barbosa command of the flagship after Magellan took the *Victoria* away from him? And Goes? Heaven help us all." Elcano took another drink of water and stared at the empty cup in his hand. "And who is to be the new captain-general?"

"Captain Serrano and Barbosa, I mean Captain Barbosa, they're to share that title. Captain Serrano and Pilot Carvalho are aboard the flagship right now, sir."

"Magellan gone, and Barbosa and a supernumerary made captains. And the captain-general was going to prove our invincibility." He gave a short, harsh laugh. "Life seems bent on proving that its ironies are endless."

In a sudden burst of frustration Elcano flung his cup across the room, but the weakness of the toss only served as testimony to his present state of helplessness.

Juanito picked up the cup and handed it to Chindarza, who set it upon Elcano's tiny desk.

Elcano pulled in a breath. "Chindarza, get me some water and, Juanito, find me some fresh clothes. I've got to get to the flagship."

Before Elcano could scoot to the edge of his bunk Acurio shot up from his chair and took a step closer. "Hold on, Master Elcano. Begging your pardon, sir, but you're not well enough to go anywhere."

Elcano looked at him with mild surprise. "Has your rank been elevated to one higher than mine in the last two days, Acurio?"

"No, sir, it hasn't," Acurio's voice suddenly broke with unexpected emotion, "but I'll not stand by and see you leave that bed where you were fighting for your life just hours ago. I'll not stand by, I say, and watch you drive yourself to your death, not if I can stop it."

Now Chindarza stood up and braced himself before Elcano's bunk. "I'll not let you go either, sir. We need you. More than ever."

Elcano stared at the pair of them until his aching eyes forced his eyelids closed. Making an effort to sound as gruff as possible, he said, "Such insubordination! Acurio, you encourage the boy in his rebelliousness." A tight silence held them all until Elcano said at last, "I trust you two have no objections to asking Captain Serrano to come to my cabin when he reboards?"

With measurable relief, Acurio said, "We'd be pleased to do that, sir."

"And you won't object to me cleaning up a little?"

"As to that, Master Elcano," said Acurio, "you'll hear not a word of complaint from us."


It was two more days before Acurio reluctantly agreed that Elcano was strong enough to accompany Carvalho and Captain Serrano to the flagship for one of the many meetings being held between the new leaders of the expedition.

As they came aboard the *Trinidad*, Barbosa's voice could be heard coming from the foredeck. "Why, you lazy worm, we need those guides to get us past the shallows. You'll do as I say!" Barbosa's angry glare was so fixed on Enrique that he didn't seem to notice the approach of the visiting officers.

"My leg is still badly swollen, Captain," said Enrique, leaning on his good leg and holding onto the rail for balance.

"That wound is no more than a scratch. You'll go ashore again today, do you hear me?"

"Sir," said Enrique with his eyes downcast, "the rajah is displeased that the trading post has been abandoned. He's also afraid that the other island leaders may attack him if we leave here too soon. If I ask him for guides he may feel betrayed. He, like many of us, is still grieving over the death of my master."

"*I* am your master now, and I will not accept disobedience from a slave."

At this Enrique's head shot up. "Captain Barbosa, I am no man's slave. Not any more, sir. The captain-general told me himself that I would be set free upon his death."

"You impudent savage," Barbosa snarled. "You *are* my slave until I hand you over to the captain-general's wife in Seville. I doubt my sister will be as soft hearted with her slaves as her late husband was. I'll not hear another word about your being set free. You will comply with my wishes or you will be whipped, chained, and tossed into the hold, where you will rot until you learn to obey. Do you understand me?"

Serrano said, "Enrique, Captain Barbosa and I are now in command of this fleet. It will go much easier on you if you obey our orders."

"Sirs," said Elcano, "perhaps —."

Barbosa cut off his words. "Captain Serrano, if you and your officers will wait for me in my cabin, I will meet with you there shortly."

Elcano tried again, "Captain Barbosa, it was the captain-general's intention that—."

Between clenched teeth, Barbosa ground out, "I said, in my cabin."

Serrano and Carvalho turned away, but when Elcano did not move, Serrano said quietly, "Master Elcano, after you."

With an effort Elcano edged away to join his captain. As they made their way toward the stairs to the half deck, they heard Barbosa snap, "No more of your nonsense. Get into that boat or I'll have the whip brought out." Addressing

Espinosa, he said, "Master-at-arms, see that the boat gets off safely. Once it's away meet me in my cabin."

When these five officers and Master Polcevera had gathered in what had previously been Magellan's quarters, Serrano spoke up at once. "Captain, if Enrique's right about Humabon's uneasiness, we must be cautious. The rajah may not understand our intention to depart just days after the captain-general's death."

"It matters little whether he understands," replied Barbosa. "Despite the disaster on Mactan, Humabon isn't foolish enough to interfere with our plans. He wants our alliance too badly. I've promised that we will send a much larger fleet to take revenge against Lapulapu and to establish a permanent trading post."

"What of the growing unrest among the Cebuan men? They are showing little tolerance when our hands go ashore."

"We can sail as early as tomorrow. The sooner they provide us with guides, the sooner we'll leave their women alone."

They spoke for some time of a possible route to the Spice Islands, of eliminating any more delays and distractions, and of the best timing for returning to Spain. Still not entirely well, Elcano grew lightheaded and found it more and more difficult to keep his focus trained upon the charts and the discussion.

Serrano turned to ask him a question and said, "Master Elcano, you're as pale as a new sail! Captain Barbosa, if there is nothing else that needs discussing today, we will return to the *Concepción*."

"Anything else can wait until morning."

As Serrano and Carvalho rose and helped Elcano to do the same, someone knocked at the door. Barbosa opened it to find Enrique standing there alone.

"Excuse me, sirs" he said with deference, then addressed Barbosa directly. "Humabon is saddened to hear of our departure, Master, but he has agreed to give us the guides you requested."

"You see, gentlemen, heathen or no, this Humabon is clever," said Barbosa. "He wants what Spain can provide him. Enrique, did he show any sign of the anger you had feared?"

Enrique lowered his head a bit, "No, Master, only great sorrow. He even bid me to tell you that his craftsmen have been making a gift to take back to our king. He says it is nearly finished."

"Ah, what sort of gift?"

"I do not know its exact nature, Master. The rajah said only that he selected the jewels himself, so perhaps it is a curved knife much like his own. He wishes to present it to you and Captain Serrano at a parting feast, to which our crews and the entire village have been invited."

"Are you certain he was not upset at our departure, Enrique?" Serrano asked. "We can ill afford any more trouble with these people."

Barbosa asked with impatience, "Do you fear even Rajah Humabon, Captain Serrano?"

Serrano's face reddened as his eyes narrowed. "I merely advise caution, a thing we have practiced too little recently."

"Each man will bear light arms. Will that serve to quiet your nerves?"

After a pause, Serrano said tightly, "Very well."

"Fine. Then tomorrow we'll complete our final provisioning, present ourselves at the feast, and then set sail. Agreed?"

Serrano gave a reluctant nod.

"Good, then I'll send word to the *Victoria* at once."

"Until tomorrow, then. Come, Pilot Carvalho, let's get Master Elcano back to our ship."

As they left the *Trinidad*, Serrano muttered, "I must admit that I'll be glad to put the memories of this place far behind us."

By late afternoon of the next day, the ships had been restocked and selected officers and crewmembers had begun preparing to go ashore for the last celebration before bidding the Cebuans farewell. Although Elcano would have enjoyed going with them, drinking large quantities of palm wine was considered complementary to a Cebuan host, and in his present state of recuperation he would not have lasted long among the revelers. As the launch carrying Serrano, Carvalho, and several others drew away from the ships, Elcano was content enough to stand at the rail beside Acurio and Chindarza and merely observe.

Showing them much honor, Humabon met the three captains at the beach and greeted them warmly as he awaited the arrival of the rest of his guests. When all had landed, Humabon's company escorted them into the city to the accompaniment of clanging gongs and beating drums.

Acurio said with a good-natured huff, "No dancing women or palm wine for the likes of us tonight, eh Chindarza?"

Elcano offered, "I can do little about the dancing women, but I've managed to put aside a small jug of palm wine, enough for three cups at least. Keep a close watch on shore until our men return. Tonight, after we're well underway, meet me in my cabin and we'll raise a toast to our departure."

Elcano climbed to the half deck and rested a moment before taking the steps to the stern deck. Once there, he scanned the beach where two of their boats rocked gently with the tide. The sounds of the feasting drifted to him on the breeze. He crossed to the northeast corner of the deck, braced his straightened arms against the rail, and let his eyes take in the profusion of colors that had been cast across the sky by the setting sun. "Well, my lady," he said to his ship, "it's a fine evening. With Humabon's guide to see us through the shoals, we'll soon find a quiet place where we can see to your repairs."

"Master Elcano," said Acurio from the main deck, "two of our boats are returning."

Elcano turned his gaze toward shore and spotted Carvalho and Espinoza, each alone in a boat, rowing hastily back to their ships. Elcano hurried down to the main deck and, when Carvalho was within hailing distance, leaned far out and called, "Any trouble, Pilot?"

When his boat was closer, Carvalho replied, "It is most likely nothing, but we didn't like the moods of some of the natives. We've come back to get heavier arms and more men to discourage any aggression."

Elcano turned to Acurio and said, "Get the gunners to their posts."

Acurio faced their apprehensive men on deck and let loose a string of commands that got the gunners hustling below.

Facing Carvalho as he landed on the main deck beside him, Elcano said, "How many more men do you need, Pilot?"

Before a response could be given, musket fire and screams erupted from the village. The shooting ended almost at once but shrill cries of terror rose and merged with gut-deep wails of pain and outraged bellows of betrayal.

"Where are our men, Pilot?" Elcano demanded. "Can we cover their retreat?"

When Carvalho ordered, "Pull closer to shore!" loud enough for the crews of all three ships to hear, it suddenly struck Elcano that the *Concepción's* pilot was now the highest-ranking officer aboard the ships. When Elcano, Espinosa on the *Trinidad*, and Rodas aboard the *Victoria* turned to their men and repeated the command, feet leaped into position, hands grabbed at lines, and the ships began to move.

When they were within range, Carvalho called out, "Open fire on the center of town!"

Elcano hesitated only long enough to dart a glance toward shore. The screaming, and any hope, was already dying away. To Acurio still poised at the hatch, he shouted, "Fire!"

Trees, dirt, and smoke exploded into the air. Pillars of flames began to rise. As the guns were being reloaded, Elcano shouted, "Hold, Acurio! Pilot, Captain Serrano's on the beach! Look to the beach!"

The other two ships also held their fire as all eyes locked on the warriors dragging Serrano to the water's edge. The group came to an abrupt halt and Humabon, looming over his captive, lifted his curved sword. At this sight, the men of the fleet let out a roar of fear and outrage.

Elcano raised his voice above the rest and yelled, "Silence, men!"

Taking a gasping breath, Serrano shouted out, "Hold your fire on the ships!"

Carvalho raised his hand and this order was immediately passed to all of the fleet's gunners.

Serrano was roughly forced to his knees and his hands were tied before him. Elcano could see that blood was spreading through his captain's white hair.

Carvalho called, "Captain, what has become of our men?"

"They've been slain!"

Another outcry burst from the crews, and again they had to be shouted down.

"Enrique alone was spared," Serrano declared "He betrayed us, men! He promised Humabon our ships and our stores if we were taken!"

"There are *no* other survivors, sir?" Carvalho demanded.

"Father Valderrama may have been taken alive, but the others died with knives at their throats."

Humabon shoved Serrano impatiently.

"They want ransom," Serrano told his men, "in exchange for my life."

"What ransom will they accept, sir?"

Elcano suddenly cried, "Pilot, the canoes!"

In the deepening dusk, the Cebuans had crept to their many outriggers, and several of these were already being shoved into the water.

Carvalho yelled to Serrano, "Tell them to call back their boats or we'll start firing!"

Fumbling to communicate with his hands tied, Serrano made himself understood and Humabon ordered his men to return to shore. Now, the fleet's crews watched the canoes with sharper vigilance.

Serrano spoke up again, saying, "They want guns, Pilot. They want you to send them two of our cannons."

At first Carvalho made no response. When he broke his silence, he said, "Sir, if our boats are brought ashore and captured, the fleet will be greatly endangered. Please tell them, sir, that we will make the exchange by sending cannons in a launch half way to shore. One of their canoes must meet it with you aboard."

With gestures, Carvalho conveyed this plan. Humabon spat out a response that relayed his answer even before Serrano could address Carvalho. "He refuses, Pilot. He says our boat must come ashore."

Carvalho stood still and silent at the rail.

Serrano suddenly struggled to rise but was pushed down again and held in place by many hands. In a strong voice he called out, "Pilot Carvalho, it is better that I die than that the fleet be taken!"

"Yes, Captain."

"Leave now, Pilot! Set sail before the canoes are let loose!"

Sensing that the negotiations were failing, more and more Cebuans began inching toward their canoes.

Carvalho saw them and acted decisively. "I'm sorry, Captain Serrano."

Serrano shouted, "Hurry!"

In a voice that now thundered above the growing clamor on the ships and the shore, Carvalho roared, "Weigh anchors! Full sails!"

A hundred canoes suddenly shot into the water and drove toward them.

Elcano's heart hammered for one terrible, jarring beat before he tore his eyes from Serrano and lifted his voice to repeat Carvalho's orders. Shocked men jumped to the *Concepción's* ropes, but the canoes were fast approaching. "Cut the anchor line!" Elcano commanded. An axe was grabbed and savagely swung at the rope cable. The ship lurched and turned, her sails already filling. The *Trinidad* was just ahead of her, the *Victoria's* crew still struggling with their anchor. Amid the taunting cries of the Cebuans, the crackling of the spreading fire, and the anguished sobbing of many of the sailors, the three ships pivoted from their moorage to face the southward sea.

And above the sound of carnage, rage, and despair, Serrano's voice carried to them from behind. "Remember me to my family in Seville! Pray for—!" His words were sharply silenced.

Elcano leaned back heavily against the main mast, feeling the eyes of his devastated crew casting frightened glances his way. Holding very still, he refused to look back at the beach. But he saw Chindarza turn around toward shore, then lift his gaze. In a voice made old by sudden tragedy, Chindarza said, "They're tearing down the cross on the hill, sir."

# Carvalho's Choices

## 18

As the ships sailed on through a dark, comfortless sea, Elcano did his best to hide his own anguish from the men shuffling heavily about the decks or crouching in dark corners to let their tears fall. He silently prayed for the souls of their lost captain and the others, but, to his shame, felt unsure that his prayers were being heard. Nevertheless, he entered Serrano's cabin, quarters Carvalho had not yet taken over, to find Serrano's small wooden cross and nail it to the outside of the door.

All night and on through the next day the ships continued until their weary sails at last were lowered before the white sands of a large, hill-covered island. After a scouting party had gone ashore, Carvalho called Master Elcano, the *Victoria's* Master Rodas, the *Trinidad's* Master Polcevera, Pilots Albo and Espinosa, and the boatswains to the captain's quarters of the flagship.

The men eyed one another uncertainly before Carvalho said, "After the tragedy of last night, the fleet is mine to command. I will take this cabin as my own."

Espinosa nodded but the others gave no reaction.

"We must discuss what our next actions will be," said Carvalho.

Elcano spoke up, "Without Father Valderrama there can be no funeral mass, but those killed on Cebu must be honored, their souls must be prayed for."

"Yes, this we should do," said Carvalho.

Elcano went on, "Our stores are very low and our ships are leaking badly, especially the *Concepción*. She has been so long without adequate attention that her hull is being eaten away by shipworms. We need to find a place to restock and make repairs without delay."

Carvalho cleared his throat, "We have less than one hundred and twenty men remaining, too few to manage all three ships. I have decided that the *Concepción* is to be burned."

"Burned!" Elcano cried.

"She must not be allowed to fall into the hands of our enemies."

"But she can be repaired! *All* of the ships must be repaired!"

"I am captain-general," shouted Carvalho. "And you, Master Elcano, should have learned by now not to question the orders of your commander."

Before Elcano could move or speak out, Espinosa lightly took hold of his arm.

Seeing this, Carvalho said, "Our master-at-arms understands the rules of the sea. Heed his caution. Remember that you have been quite ill, Master Elcano. It would be most unfortunate if you were to suffer any excessive strain and jeopardize your health."

Elcano held his body rigid and locked his jaws.

This restraint seemed to please Carvalho, who went on smoothly, "What have the rest of you to say?" He paused briefly, but no other suggestions were made. "Nothing? Very well then, we will hold a brief funeral service over which I will preside. Immediately afterward, the *Concepción's* decks will be stripped, her hold emptied, and her goods divided between the flagship and the *Victoria*. While this is being done I will take a vote among the men to determine who will serve as the next captain of the *Victoria*.

At this, Master Polcevera spoke up with controlled courtesy. "Sir, I mention with respect that Master Elcano and I are next in line to hold such an office, and Master Elcano has prior experience captaining a ship."

"True, but Master Elcano has been unwell, and you would be of great service to me aboard the flagship. Still, we will let the men decide."

Carvalho ordered the funeral service to be organized at once. A four-foot cross was planted at the beach's tree line, and the men on the decks of the ships turned to face this symbol of their faith.

Carvalho stood on the *Trinidad's* stern deck and led the men in prayers. Then, from a list scribbled on the sheet of parchment in his hands, he read twenty-six names one by one. Elcano lowered his head and closed his eyes, and the image of one man after the other rose clearly in his mind. With the reading of each new name, more men wiped at their eyes and noses.

"Captain Juan Rodriguez Serrano,
Captain Duarte Barbosa,
Captain Luis de Goes,
Pilot Andrés de San Martin,
Notary Sancho de Heredía,
Notary León de Ezpeleta,
Father Pedro de Valderrama,
Pedro García,
Guillermo Tanegui,
Francisco Martin,
Simón de la Rochela,
Cristóbal Rodriguez,
Antonio Rodriguez,
Juan Sigura,
Francisco Picora,
Francisco Martin,
Antón de Goa,
Rodrigo de Hurrira,
Francisco de Madrid,
Pedro Herrero,
Juan de Silva,
Francisco de la Mesquita,
Hernando de Aguilar,
Francisco Paxe,
Nuño Gonçalves, and
Peti Juan Negro"

When Pigafetta lifted his high-pitched voice and led the men in the singing of a psalm, Elcano's throat tightened before he could complete even the first verse. In the quiet that followed, Carvalho said a final "Our Father". Then their new captain-general turned away from the cross on the beach and, it seemed to Elcano, from the souls and memories of the dead.

"Now, men," Carvalho said, "there is much to do. We can honor our slain by fulfilling the tasks that were previously assigned to them. Go about your duties."

It was torturous for Elcano to oversee the stripping of his beloved ship, and yet he would let no one else see to it. Feeling as if he were preparing her for execution, he ordered every brace, covering, and valuable removed. Finally, there was nothing left but her naked, sea-scarred body that he must destroy before its time. To abandon her once proud form when she could be healed, when she could be saved to serve them well again, deepened the wounds of his already mournful spirit.

When the last boatload had been taken to the *Victoria* and Elcano stood alone aboard his ship, she was towed farther out to sea by the *Trinidad*. A half mile offshore the flagship positioned herself upwind from the *Concepción*, drew in her sails, and waited.

Telling himself there was nothing to be gained by hesitating, Elcano took up a jar of oil that had been left behind, removed its lid, and suspended it from his outstretched arm. And yet his hand was unwilling to spill the jar's contents. He drew his arm back in, held the jar against his body, and slowly turned in a full circle, allowing his eyes to sweep the *Concepción's* decks one last time. When his feet once again pointed to the foredeck, he said softly, "Thank you, my lady, for carrying us so far."

This time, his arm was less steady when he straightened it, and it trembled as the oil poured out and splashed upon the wood at his feet, its wetness shining the worn surface of the deck. Elcano moved quickly to the wall of the half deck and lifted a lit lamp from its bracket. With a soft moan he heaved it to the center of the spill, watched the flame catch and spread, took a breath, and another, and finally swung his legs over the railing and dropped into the waiting skiff. With each stroke of the oars the black billows of smoke rose higher and the clamp on his heart squeezed tighter.

Carvalho was waiting for him when he reached the *Trinidad*. Wasting no words on compassion, he said, "Master Elcano, I have tallied the men's votes. Master-at-arms Espinosa has been elected to serve as captain of the *Victoria*. Albo will be her pilot. You will maintain your current rank and assist them in any way they see fit."

Elcano stared past Carvalho, past the men watching from the decks, and walked to the farthest corner of the ship, keeping his back to the burning *Concepción*.

When the *Victoria* came abreast of the *Trinidad*, Albo accompanied Elcano, Acurio, Chindarza, and other crewmembers of the *Concepción* to their new ship. Elcano tried not to look or listen as the *Concepción's* stern castle sank beneath the surface with a hissing expulsion of smoke and steam.


Elcano was not immune to the grief that hung over the fleet like a wraith, breeding gloom and anger as Carvalho led them on a wandering southern course that gave no evidence of bringing them closer to their goal. But Elcano managed to develop an efficient if somewhat stiff relationship with Espinosa and Albo, and all three officers of the *Victoria* prayed for a chance to stock and repair the ships. They coasted past an island that showed signs of providing safe harbor, but upon its beaches small black men armed with blowguns and spears emerged from the forests to taunt them, and the fleet sailed on.

Helplessly, Elcano watched their food supply shrink, and he and his shipmates felt the too familiar pains of hunger. At last they reached a long thin stretch of land from which rose a mighty peak, and in a small bay on its western shore the fleet came to rest.

They quickly learned from a landing party directed by Pigafetta that the natives called this western region of their peninsula Quipit, and their leader, Rajah Calanao. Negotiations began at once with Calanao and, against strong objections by Polcevera and Espinosa, and silent cursing by Elcano, Carvalho agreed to relinquish possession of the skiff from the *Concepción* in exchange for a small amount of perishable food.

When Carvalho explained his desire to trade for spices, Calanao readily provided sailing directions to the city of Brunei on the legendary island of Borneo. There, the rajah declared, the great Moorish sultan had an abundance of spices and would provide them with whatever they might need. Before the fleet departed, the rajah gave them another valuable piece of information; beware of every ship that approaches. All of the seas south of China were traveled by pirates willing to kill for the value of a ship and its cargo.

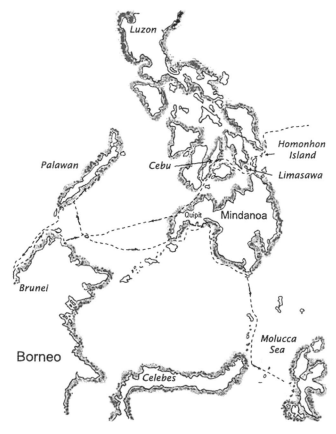

Even with this warning fresh in Elcano's mind, as the crews of the *Trinidad* and the *Victoria* set out for Borneo he felt a reignited hope, for now they finally had a specific destination. They diverted from their new course only long enough to restock their emergency food stores on the island of Palawan. With the holds partially refilled, the ships were making preparations to leave the harbor when the sails of a strange ship appeared, heading directly toward them.

Espinosa, Albo, and Elcano came together on the *Victoria's* foredeck to study the approaching ship.

Espinosa asked, "Is she Portuguese, Pilot?"

Albo squinted ahead. "My eyes are not what they once were, Captain, but she appears to be an Eastern junk."

"Yes, sir," Elcano agreed.

All three of them turned sharply around when Polcevera shouted from the flagship, "Prepare for battle!"

Espinosa stared at each of his other officers, let out a curse, and called back to the *Trinidad*, "Is Captain-general Carvalho commanding us to take that ship?"

Carvalho appeared at the *Trinidad's* rail. "That's exactly what I'm commanding. Prepare for battle at once."

Espinosa muttered another oath before hastily issuing the required orders. Elcano hesitated, then pulled his questioning gaze from his captain and obeyed.

As the junk came within range, the flagship's guns let loose a warning shot that slowed the junk enough to allow both ships to come along side. Out-gunned and out-manned, the junk's Muslim captain and crew surrendered without a struggle. With the crew of the *Victoria* under orders to stand by, Elcano watched Carvalho and two dozen armed men scour the junk for valuables, returning to the *Trinidad* with food and three captives; two pilots and a seaman. The junk was allowed to proceed and the European ships left the harbor under full sails.

Even with the aid of the Muslim pilots, it took over two weeks for the vessels to creep through the labyrinth of reefs and rocks along the western shore of Borneo to reach the harbor of Brunei. Sailing to within sight of their destination early in the day, with all its promise beckoning, they were forced to await a favorable shifting of the wind to approach. It came at last in the afternoon and, keeping the ships a cautious distance from the inner port, the seamen of the fleet gaped and muttered as they drew closer to the wondrous city.

"Would you look at that, Acurio," said Elcano, gawking like all the rest.

What could only be a palace, with its pointed towers and glinting gold trimmings, rose up from behind the city's waterfront structures. The entire city appeared to be built upon piers. Houses, shops, bridges, and walkways stood close together on tall stilts like so many giant storks, balanced above the sea and the fresh water tributaries that flowed into it.

Acurio shifted excitedly as he said to Elcano and Espinosa, "How many houses would you say there are, sirs?"

"Twenty-five thousand at least," said Elcano as Espinosa shrugged distractedly. "And it looks like there's a canoe for every house. According to Pigafetta, those sail-fitted canoes are called proas."

Acurio observed, "There must be twenty junks at the docks."

In his low, gruff voice, Espinosa said, "Whatever they're called, the boats are thick as bugs on a pond."

"Captain," said Elcano, "our guide has served us faithfully. I suggest we ask the captain-general to set him and his two companions free."

Espinosa cast a thoughtful glance at the Muslim standing at Acurio's side, staring stoically at Brunei. "That's a reasonable suggestion, Master Elcano. They've been treated well. If we pay them for their services they might even give a decent report of us to the people here. Signal the captain-general."

In minutes a skiff carrying the *Trinidad's* Moorish guide and seaman nudged the *Victoria* just long enough for its third passenger to sling a bag of goods over his shoulder, nod to the officers, and climb aboard before it pulled away toward the main pier.

The boat had gone less than fifty yards when Espinosa exclaimed, "They've spotted us. Good Lord, look at them come!" The skiff's rowers had seen the proas too. They lifted their oars uneasily from the water, glanced back toward Carvalho, and held their position.

Even before the two ships had first nosed into the Brunei bay, their crews had prepared for the possibility of defensive military action. Elcano quickly directed Acurio, "Get the men to their stations." Acurio immediately took his place near the hatch and ordered his gunners to move to the cannons and stand ready.

Most of the other hands took their stations on the main deck, where spears, crossbows, muskets, swords, and shields were placed within reach but out of sight of the approaching proas. Muscles tightened and breathing quickened as the small lateen sailed crafts began to circle the skiff carrying the newly freed Muslim captives.

Espinosa said, "Stay close by, Master Elcano. You've picked up more of their heathenish language from Pigafetta than I. With him on the flagship, you're the closest thing to an interpreter we have at hand. Let's just hope we're given the chance to exchange a few civil words before we have to let loose our guns."

While the lead proas blocked the advancement of the *Trinidad's* skiff, most of the others proceeded to ring the two ships. Pigafetta waved his arms over his head and hailed them. A few short phrases were relayed between him and one of the Bruneians. To the surprise of all, the native spokesman then shouted to his men and the entire fleet of proas departed, accompanying the skiff to the pier, and then allowing its crew to return with it to the flagship.

A collective sigh of relief was expelled as the armaments were collected and stowed away. After relocking the armory doors, Elcano rejoined Espinosa, who said, "Well, so far so good."

Listening to every sound and scanning the harbor for every movement, Elcano spent a vigilant yet quiet night. At dawn he stood on the main deck, his eyes wide with awe as he watched the approach of a magnificent ship.

Half the size of the *Trinidad*, its prow and stern bore dragonheads plated with gold, which shone and glimmered in the early light. A blue and white banner adorned with brilliant peacock feathers fluttered from a staff at the ship's bow. In the center of her deck stood eight elderly Bruneians, each beautifully draped in a different color of shimmering silk. With utmost ceremony and cordiality, these emissaries drew near the *Trinidad*, wished their visitors welcome, and presented them with gifts of food and wine.

Pigafetta returned their sentiments and presented them with token gifts. When these had been accepted, he relayed Carvalho's request to allow them to come ashore to obtain water and wood. With grave politeness the island emissaries replied that they would be honored to carry this request to Sultan Siripada, and then they departed.

One day of waiting stretched into six, and Elcano became convinced that the sultan was bent on teaching them the virtue of patience before granting their request to come ashore. Nerves and belts tightened with the passing of each day. But when the sultan's response finally came, Elcano had to admit that it came in style. This time, three exceptional ships came out to meet them, each more richly decorated than the one before. Musicians aboard the vessels played a modulating cadence on drums and cymbals that grew in volume and tempo as they approached.

After formal greetings were offered, gifts were again exchanged, but these were of much greater value than the first offerings. Pigafetta and Carvalho conversed with them for a few minutes, and a seaman was sent to the *Victoria* to relay what had been concluded.

"Captain Espinosa," he hailed, "the captain-general orders you to choose two men to accompany you to the flagship. You are then to pick up Señor Pigafetta and three others before making your way ashore to begin trading for what we need, sir."

Espinosa turned back toward his crew and found sixty pairs of anxious eyes staring at him. He cleared his throat and said, "Master Elcano, you will come with me. Pilot Albo, you will look after the ship in our absence."

Elcano could see that Acurio had somehow managed to hide most of his disappointment, but Chindarza's face was almost painful to behold in its hopefulness. When Espinosa said, "Master Elcano, you may choose our last man," Chindarza appeared to stop breathing altogether. Elcano hid his smile as he asked, "Chindarza would you be willing to face the dangers of so mighty a city?"

Chindarza blinked. "I would, sir. I surely would."

This settled, they set out for the *Trinidad* where Pigafetta and two Greek sailors, Mateo Gorfo and Juan Griego, joined them in the launch. To his great delight, little Juanito was allowed to become the seventh of their group.


Everyone aboard the skiff stared unabashedly at the strange houses and people they rowed past. In minutes they had reached the pier only to find that the sultan's emissaries had arrived before them and stood on the dock waiting.

Other than a velvet covered chair, the gifts from Carvalho of cloth, robes, and iron were already being placed in huge porcelain jars and lifted to the shoulders of twelve muscular bearers. Following the musicians, the bearers, and several officials, Espinosa's group made its way down the pier and into the bustling city.

As they turned the first corner and their view of the adjacent street began to open, Chindarza, who was walking a few paces ahead of Elcano, suddenly stopped short and gasped. A second later Juanito let out a shriek of horror and clung to Chindarza's arm as a grinning Pigafetta clapped his hands in surprised pleasure. Hurrying forward, Elcano came to a faltering halt and whispered, "Saints above," as Espinosa, stood speechless and wide-eyed beside him.

Seeming well pleased by these reactions, their guides led them forward, some more willingly than others. Moving protectively in front of Chindarza and Juanito, Elcano stepped closer until he stood beside two huge kneeling elephants.

The nearly identical mammoths bore four-foot upward curving tusks capped with pointed cones of etched gold. Upon the blanketed back of each beast towered a howdah railed in polished wood and canopied in blue silk. Allowing Elcano little time to study the amazing animals, one of their guides patted an elephant's bent leg and gestured at the tall fenced seats, urging Juanito, Chindarza, Elcano, and Espinosa toward one, and Pigafetta along with the two sailors toward the other.

Gathering his nerve, Juanito leaped onto the elephant's leg and scrambled to the back corner of the howdah. After the others had mounted, Juanito's bravery momentarily failed him when the monstrous animal straightened first its front legs, then its back two as it lurched to its feet. Throwing his arms around Chindarza, Juanito cried, "Too big, too big!" Elcano did his best to reassure Juanito as he too grabbed for something to keep from losing his seat.

Once the elephants started walking, the riders gradually grew accustomed to the swaying gait of their mounts, and their heartbeats regained some semblance of normalcy. Before long they were taking advantage of their lofty perches to survey Brunei and its occupants. The closely grouped houses were well made of wood and bamboo and were arranged in an organized manner. With musicians marching ahead to herald their coming, the Europeans were greeted by many people who paused in doorways, in fields, and at the river's edge to bow at their passing.

At last they came to a halt in front of a large ornate house and, to Elcano's surprise, were welcomed into the home of the city's rajah by the noble governor himself. The rajah explained that they would be escorted to the sultan's palace in the morning. In the meantime, he wished to offer them every comfort. He motioned to one of his head men and then withdrew.

The number of servants that jumped to the task of seeing to the visitors' wellbeing seemed countless, and Elcano watched in wonder as they brought cushions, poured wine, and presented an incredible array of refreshments without a single word being spoken. At the urging of a servant Elcano sat down on a cushion next to Espinosa's, picked up a small rice cake, and put it in his mouth. The rich, spicy flavor spread over his tongue, and he almost moaned out loud. He reached for another bite, and another, delighting in each exotic taste of the unnamed dishes. Pausing briefly, he grinned as he watched his two young charges chewing with as much relish as he.

When they had eaten and drunk their fill, the head servant respectfully asked if they cared to bathe. Both Elcano and Pigafetta sensed that declining this offer would insult their host, and, to Juanito's horror and Chindarza's indignation, Espinosa accepted with thanks.

They were led into a courtyard where an enormous wooden trough was already being filled with steaming water.

"Isn't it hot enough without them boiling us in water?" Espinosa grumbled.

"It must be their custom, Captain," said Pigafetta. "We dare not refuse now."

When a male servant approached Juanito and offered to help him undress, the boy insisted, "Chindarza will help me!"

Chindarza and the rest of them, however, submitted with varying degrees of grace to being disrobed in the open air by strangers. When they all stood naked on one side of the wooden pool, their bodies thin and ghostly except for their darkened faces and lower arms, Elcano unexpectedly began to sputter. Perhaps it was the wine, or the elephant ride, or the pure pleasure of having a full belly, but his normal restraint continued to slip and he began to chuckle. "Forgive me, Captain Espinosa," he tried, but Espinosa was already breaking into a laugh.

"By heavens," howled Espinosa, "we look no better than scrawny chickens!"

With an effort Elcano mastered his mirth as he was gently motioned forward. He lowered himself gingerly into the hot water, as did the others. When the steaming water reached the top of Espinosa's legs, his laughter was abruptly replaced by a sharp intake of breath and a string of curses. Within moments the water began soaking not only the filth and salt from Elcano's skin, but also the fatigue and tension from his shoulders. He let out a long, deep sigh and closed his eyes.

After the bath, feeling refreshed and relaxed, Elcano and the others were dressed in silk robes and led back to the dining room. Each of them was given a gold spoon with which to eat another meal, this one consisting of no less than thirty-two courses. With the implausible array of meat, fish, poultry, fruit, rice, and rice wine before them, they did not hesitate to, once again, eat and drink with relish. At last, fully sated, they were taken to a large room where seven cotton-stuffed and silk-covered mattresses had been placed upon the floor.

His companions fell fast asleep before the moon had even risen but Elcano lay awake a while longer, wonderfully aware that he was lying upon the first fresh mattress he had used in twenty-two months. Privately reveling in the softness of his trundle and the rich silk against his skin, he listened to the quiet sounds of a city settling in for the night. He alone was still awake when Chindarza stirred in his sleep and muttered softly, "Elephants."

What Elcano guessed to be Chindarza's dream came true the following day when they were carried to the sultan's palace by the same magnificent tusked animals that had borne them the day before. Taking a broad road, they came to the outskirts of the palace and passed through a gate at the base of a towering wall. Elcano glanced up and saw the mouths of sixty cannons gaping threateningly above their heads. After dismounting, he ushered Juanito and Chindarza before him as they climbed a series of carved ladders to gain entrance to the sprawling stronghold. Once inside the palace, they were led to a great hall filled with sarong-clad noblemen.

Their group was approached by an important looking gentleman who spoke to them respectfully and patiently until he was certain that he had been understood. Elcano, still not Pigafetta's equal as an interpreter, willingly allowed him to turn to Espinosa, and say, "This is the chief of protocol, sir. He insists that none of us speak directly to the sultan. If something must be communicated, it must be done through him and several other of the sultan's most trusted men."

Espinosa nodded his understanding, and the attention of every man was drawn to the end of the hall where a platform of ornately carved wood rose several feet above the main floor. A huge brocaded drape at the rear of the platform was pulled back to reveal a window, behind which the sultan sat playing with several very young boys while being attended to by many beautiful women.

Elcano forced his focus from the women to the sultan. Of middle age, corpulent, outwardly serene, and robed in a sarong of deep blue silk, the sultan did not seem to notice them at first.

"Please," the chief of protocol said with urgency to Pigafetta, "you must *kowtow* at once! Do exactly as I do."

Pigafetta immediately conveyed this message to his companions, and all seven of them attempted the rather awkward and somewhat embarrassing exercise of clasping their hands over their heads, raising first one foot, and then the other, and finally blowing kisses toward the sultan. Once this observance of court etiquette had been adequately if ungracefully fulfilled, the visitors were invited to sit crosslegged upon cushions on the floor.

Only after another high ranking servant spoke into a tube running through the wall to a servant on the other side, who in turn spoke reverently to the sultan, did the ruler of Brunei glance their way. More servants came forward and displayed the gifts that the Spanish delegation had brought. The content of each of the twelve porcelain jars was revealed and Sultan Siripada again gave his visitors a brief, unreadable glance. Almost imperceptibly, he nodded, and servants at once approached Espinosa and presented him, on behalf of his king, six measures of silk that had been embroidered with gold thread. As Espinosa bowed in thanks, the separate lengths of silk were folded and placed in six porcelain jars. After another slight nod from the sultan, the curtain to his window was lowered. Servants stepped forward to accompany the guests out of the hall.

"That's it?" whispered Espinosa to Pigafetta.

"Yes, sir. We must leave now."

As short and seemingly meaningless as the meeting had been, when they returned to the rajah's house they learned that the sultan had already sent word giving them permission to remain with the rajah in order to formulate a formal trade agreement. To Elcano's further surprise, the rajah requested that Juanito be allowed to linger in his house and play with his children while the men went about their business. Juanito agreed. When Chindarza was ordered to help Pigafetta take the gifts to the ships, he requested to be allowed to return to shore afterward, but Espinosa chose to leave this up to Pilot Albo. In the end it was Juanito, Espinosa, Elcano, and the two Greek sailors who stayed behind.

For three weeks Elcano and Espinosa familiarized themselves with the city's wealth as well as its wants, investigating and organizing the best methods, routes, and articles of trade. Between Elcano's clumsy but improving skill with the Malay language and their fortunate hiring of a Portuguese interpreter, they managed to communicate reasonably well with the locals. Their efforts began to show much promise, and the details of their maturing negotiations continued to clarify with each passing day.

One especially hot afternoon, accompanied as usual by four of the rajah's personal guards and the interpreter, Elcano and Espinosa made their way to the waterfront in order to meet with a trader newly arrived from Java. After completing their dealings with the trader, they meant to rendezvous with their two sailors, who had been assigned to take possession of a load of rice being delivered from the eastern end of the city.

During their days together, Elcano had noticed many times that Espinosa, lacking the formal training or bearing of a captain of noble blood, often lapsed into a familiarity of conversation that would have been frowned upon in Castilian society. With Elcano, however, this familiarity had gradually worked to earn his grudging acceptance and even a sort of companionability.

Glancing over his shoulder at their guards, Espinosa said softly, "They may mean well, but I'd give a high price to have them busy elsewhere. They're like shadows that a man can't be rid of.

At the sudden burst of cannon fire coming from the bay, they jerked to a standstill. A second later they were racing down the road and around several corners to gain a clear view of the harbor. When it opened before them, they came to another abrupt halt. Disbelieving, Elcano said, "He's firing on the sultan's boats! Carvalho is *firing* on them!" As he spoke, several proas exploded in a shower of bodies, wood, and water. Two hundred proas began to close in around the ships and three junks appeared to be blocking any attempted retreat by the Spanish ships.

As Elcano stared at the scene, the *Trinidad* opened fire on one of the junks, blasting her rudder to splinters. Moments later, members of the flagship's crew leaped to the junk's deck, swinging swords and firing crossbows as they boarded.

Scanning the piers, Elcano spotted their two Greek crewmembers at the end of a dock, standing in stunned rigidity beside a tall pile of bagged rice as they gaped at the ensuing battle. Before he could call out to them, his and Espinosa's own guards drew around them, preventing them from moving any nearer to the bay.

"What's happened?" Espinosa growled in frustration as he shuffled and shifted within the ring of the rajah's men.

Hearing the sound of running feet behind them, Elcano pivoted around to see twenty of the sultan's elite armed guards rushing toward them. With hands on their sword hilts these warriors quickly surrounded them, and the rajah's men backed away. Facing the pier again, Elcano watched helplessly as the two sailors were seized by men that had been helping them load rice just moments before. Nudged backward by one of the guards, Elcano and

Espinosa were forced to turn around and march up the road all the way to the palace. There, they were separated.

Elcano was taken to a heavily guarded yet well-appointed chamber, where the door was locked behind him. He stood in the middle of the room, his back straight and his arms stiff at his sides. At the sound of every explosion from their ships' guns, he clenched his teeth tighter. He seemed to hear the voice of each cannon, roaring, "Doom! Doom!"

Before many hours had passed, he and Espinosa were brought to the sultan's hall. They kowtowed to the man sitting on the other side of the window and waited for a response.

The sultan's previously serene face was now dark and ominous. Through the interpreter, he demanded, "Why have your ships attacked my seamen after you have been shown such kindness here?"

"Please tell his Highness," said Espinosa to the interpreter, his tone respectful and honest, "I do not know."

The sultan's hard brown eyes studied the two men speculatively. "Your ships have left our harbor. It would seem that you are of little value to your countrymen."

Elcano fought to keep the image of Serrano, surrounded by enemies as the fleet left him behind, from his mind. Neither he nor Espinosa said a word.

The sultan lowered his eyelids half way, saying, "I will now decide what value, if any, you may be to me."

At an unseen signal, the curtain was lowered again and their short interview ended. Elcano and Espinosa were taken back to their separate quarters, where they would remain until the sultan chose to reveal his judgment.

# The Victoria's Captain

## 19

Though the sound came to him from far out in the harbor, Elcano recognized the roar of cannons even in his sleep. He jumped to his feet so quickly that he stood swaying for a moment as he fought to clear his mind. Those were Spanish guns. Carvalho had come back. But for his men or for some other purpose?

For three interminable hours after the firing had ceased, he was left to question and fear what had happened and what was to come. Then his door was unlocked and shoved open, and he was ushered with great haste into the sultan's hall where Espinosa appeared a moment later.

When the drape was raised, the sultan's countenance was grim as Elcano and Espinosa performed their kowtows. The interpreter had already joined the chief of protocol standing at the tube and ready to communicate with the room on the other side of the wall. The sultan wasted no words.

"You will return to your ships at once and tell your captain-general that he must stop waging war upon us. The proa fleet he attacked yesterday was leaving this harbor to fight my heathen enemies, *not* your people. What's more, the junks anchored near your ships were captained by this man," he said, pointing to a downcast official to their left whom Elcano had not noticed before. "He is my naval commander and the son of the rajah of Luzon. His three vessels had just returned from a battle on the island of Laut. He intended no harm to your ships."

Pausing only to be certain that they understood him, the sultan continued. "After his junk was seized by your ships, this captain, three noblewomen, and twelve other men were taken captive. My captain paid a ransom in jewels for his release, but the others are still being held as prisoners by your captain-general. In addition to this indignity, many men have been killed by your guns."

He motioned to some servants who immediately lifted a heavy wooden trunk from beside the naval commander and carried it to Elcano and Espinosa. "Take this chest to your captain-general. Inside it are trophies taken during the Laut war. Tell him this is proof that what I have said is true. Tell him he must release my people at once."

When the rajah leaned back and a servant reached up to draw the drape closed, Elcano took a small step forward, "Please, Honorable Chief of Protocol." The entire room froze. "Please, ask the great sultan if our two sailors and the son of our captain-general may accompany us to our ships."

The sultan stared at Elcano, his emotions completely masked. In a chillingly gentle voice, he said, "Return my people to me."

Twenty minutes later Espinosa and Elcano lifted the trunk onto the main deck of the *Trinidad* and Espinosa succinctly relayed the sultan's messages to Carvalho.

"Meant us no harm?" Carvalho snorted. "Two hundred proas and three junks meant us no harm?"

"He said the junks were returning from a battle on another island. In the trunk is proof of this, or so he claimed."

"Have you looked inside?"

"No, sir."

"Open it now."

Espinosa bent down and unfastened the latch. As the lid was raised a stench rose with it. Espinosa held his breath and lifted one of six oilskin-wrapped bundles from inside. Carefully peeling back the layers of cloth, he drew out a human head by its long black hair.

Grave murmurs circled the ship.

Carvalho gave the head a critical study. "It's no European, but this proves nothing." He motioned Espinosa to return the thing to the chest, to which he immediately complied.

"Sir," said Elcano evenly, "the sultan wants the hostages freed. He won't release Juanito, Gorfo, or Griego until the women and his seamen are brought ashore."

Anger, disgust, and fear appeared on the faces of some of the crew. Seeing this, Elcano asked, "Sir, are the captives still here?"

"The men are in the hold, the women, in my cabin," Carvalho said.

"Then we can return them at once, sir?"

"Come with me," Carvalho said, and strode away with determined steps.

Elcano and Espinosa entered the captain's chamber and stared at its contents in growing disbelief. Upon Carvalho's desk glittered gold curved swords with jeweled handles and many articles of gold jewelry. But upon his bunk sat three women, all exceptionally beautiful but tussled and shaken in appearance. Under the gaze of the three men, the women huddled together and tried to hide faces behind their hands. Elcano saw a darkening bruise on the jaw of the youngest woman.

"I will not return them," Carvalho said with defiance. "They are no longer...returnable."

One of the women began to weep but was quickly hushed by the other two.

Elcano felt his blood rising. In spite of Carvalho's superior rank, in spite of the punishment he'd survived at Port San Julian, and in spite of the penalty he might suffer now, Elcano spat out, "You mean they are no longer virgins? *You raped them?* Against the laws of the church, against the orders of your king, and when four of your men and your own son were held hostage by their people, you *raped* three of their noblewomen!"

"Remember yourself, Elcano," Carvalho warned sternly, dispensing with the formality of titles. "Remember who you are addressing."

When Elcano, his eyes flashing, opened his mouth again, Espinosa grabbed his arm, gave it one sharp jerk, and silenced him by raising his own voice. "The sultan's men are awaiting our answer, Captain-general. What do we tell them?"

After a brief, uncertain pause, Carvalho said, "Tell them we'll return their people once my son and our two men are safely aboard this ship."

"I fear the sultan will never agree to that, sir," said Espinosa.

Carvalho's eyes raked the women. "We have no other choice. Tell them. And give them back their stinking chest of heads. Now leave me, both of you."

Elcano shook off Espinosa's grip. "Tell me, Captain-general, how do you suppose our king will react when he learns that you captured your own personal harem to emulate the ways of your Moorish hosts?"

The anger that flared in Carvalho's face was shaded with uneasiness. Still, he growled, "I warn you, if you challenge me or my decisions again, be prepared to feel the bite of steel around your ankles and wrists, or worse."

Elcano glanced again at the cringing women, but Espinosa said, "Let's go, Master Elcano. The *Victoria* is waiting."

Two edgy days and nights passed with men working double watches and cannons kept ready, but not a single proa or junk approached the ships. Finally Carvalho commanded Elcano, and no one else, to row toward the docks and ask about the sultan's intentions. Elcano obeyed. The Bruneians at the docks responded to his question and even allowed him to return to the ships, but the answer he brought back was apparent in his countenance even before he spoke.

When Elcano straddled the railing and stepped onto the *Trinidad's* main deck, Carvalho demanded, "Well?"

Elcano took a moment, forcing himself to control his words. "I was told, sir, that our two men have seen the light of Islam and that they now refuse to leave the city."

"Impossible! What of my son?"

"They said, sir, that Juanito is dead."

Carvalho surveyed him with measured suspicion. "They're lying."

"I hope they are, sir."

Carvalho rubbed his bearded chin. "Perhaps they would accept their women back after all."

"These people are not like the natives of Rio de Janeiro or Cebu, sir. After they learn what...what's happened to the women, they will probably kill them, and Juanito, too, if he still lives."

Turning to Pigafetta, Carvalho asked, "You have observed some of their customs. Do you agree with this prediction?"

Pigafetta lowered his eyes. "I do, sir."

Giving it brief consideration, Carvalho suddenly pounded his right fist into his left palm, and muttered, "Then we'll offer him what ransom we can." His gaze swept over his men and fell upon Gonzalo Hernández and Domingo de Barruti. "You two, come with me and load what I tell you into the boat. You're taking it ashore."

Once a heavy chest was placed aboard, Barruti and Hernández rowed slowly away from the flagship. They were soon met by many proas and accompanied to the pier, where they were pulled from the boat and led out of view.

Forty-eight hours passed without a word or a sign from them or anyone else ashore. Carvalho finally ordered eight of the male captives to be transferred to the *Victoria* and commanded the fleet to weigh anchors.

With heavy hearts the men obeyed, sailing from Brunei in leaking ships with nearly empty holds, carrying fifteen captives, and leaving behind four of their crewmen and one small half-Tupi boy.

As they drew away, Elcano and Chindarza stared back at the receding houses and piers. Softly, Chindarza said, "Do you remember, sir, how little I wanted to look after him at first?"

"You accepted your role more quickly than many would have. And you soon became like a brother to him."

"Do you think he's still alive, sir?"

"Yes, Chindarza." Elcano had hesitated for only an instant, but it was long enough for Chindarza to know his true speculation.

Taking a moment, trying to accept the pain of Juanito's death, Chindarza finally said in a faltering voice, "He wasn't any trouble, sir. Truly he wasn't. He..."

"Chindarza, go and mourn Juanito in whatever solitude you can find. Since he will be given no funeral, his small soul will need your prayers."

Swallowing hard, Chindarza said, "My watch has just begun, sir. During this whole voyage, I have never failed to do my duties, not unless I was too sick to stand."

Realizing his mistake, Elcano said, "That's true. I was wrong to suggest it. Well then, my cabin is in need of cleaning, Chindarza. Attend to that at once, and take your time to do a thorough job."

"Yes, sir," Chindarza said, already moving away. "And thank you, sir."


Sailing along the northeast coast of Borneo without an experienced Malay pilot soon proved a treacherous endeavor. Despite their many attempts to avoid the reefs and shoals, the *Victoria* grounded. It seemed that she had just been freed when the *Trinidad* ran aground, requiring four hours of backbreaking work to loosen her. Both ships were in pitiful condition when they limped into the protected harbor of a small island and dropped their anchors.

They named the island Nuestra Señora de Agosto, and here the men worked through the last half of August and much of September, scraping, patching, and sealing their ships. It was during these many hours, while Elcano's hands and mind worked to make the *Victoria* whole again, that he gradually began to form a bond with this new ship, as he once had done with the *Concepción*. Almost grudgingly at first, he allowed his loyalties to transfer and solidify.

Working daily beside the male captives from Brunei, for the most part sailors themselves, Elcano was pleased when they proved to be both skillful and diligent workers.

Pigafetta gladly accepted the assignment of teaching the Bruneians to speak the Spanish tongue. By investing an hour each evening in this venture, it was not long before the two groups had constructed a fumbling means of communicating that helped to ease the tensions between them.

As September waned, Espinosa called Elcano away from the pitch caldron and drew him away from the beach. "Let's walk in the jungle awhile." Once they were out of the men's hearing, Espinosa said, "The ships will be ready to sail in a few days."

"Yes, sir, in five or six days, perhaps. The men have worked diligently."

"Not all of the men."

Elcano knew he referred to Carvalho, who had spent most of his time since their arrival drinking and using his women. "No, not all."

Letting out a slow sigh, Espinosa said, "We've lost Bautista and Godin since we landed here. I'm tired of burying good men. I'm tired of wandering aimlessly in this God foresaken sea. If we are to have any chance of finding the Spiceries and reaching home again, something must change. What must happen can no longer be ignored. Carvalho must be relieved of command."

Elcano stopped abruptly and turned to him, but Espinosa went on in a slow, persuasive voice. "You should have been given command of the *Victoria*, not I. Every time you address me as your superior officer, I feel the injustice of it. You are the one that should take the role of captain-general of what remains of this fleet."

Elcano's voice was intense and his words clipped. "When I last obeyed an order to help sway the leadership of this expedition, you were the one who saw that my sentence was carried out, sir."

"You know very well that I was under orders to do so. You also know how greatly events have changed our situation since then. We have no choice but to act. Carvalho's incompetence and corruption affect every man of us. It will lead to our destruction if we let it."

"He is the captain-general, sir."

"In name only, man! He's no leader."

"I will not help you to overthrow him, sir."

Espinosa cursed as he ran a huge hand through his unruly hair. "Listen, what if we can convince him to step down without a fight, what then?"

"Do you think he would *voluntarily* relinquish this command, sir?"

"We may be able to persuade him to do so."

"Without torture?"

Espinosa's chin jerked up and his lips tightened. "I thought we had grown to know each other well enough that such a question would be unnecessary. I have never had a taste for torture, but I, too, have done things that I am less than proud of while under orders."

Loosening a bit at this truth, Elcano said, "You're right, Captain. I was foolish to ask."

Espinosa grunted in agreement.

"But what of Master Polcevera, sir? His rank is equal to mine, and he has been carrying out most of the duties as captain of the *Victoria* for weeks."

"I've already spoken to him. He's agreed that you are better qualified. Polcevera is willing to put the welfare of the fleet before his own pride. He said if you agree to lead us the rest of the way, he will willingly follow your command."

Elcano turned back toward the beach. "After all that has happened, how can you ask me to do this?"

"I ask you because I must."

Out past the thickly crowded ferns and tall swaying trees, Elcano could see the *Trinidad* floating in the water and the *Victoria* still careened on her port side. "Did you know, Captain Espinosa, that Magellan commissioned me to buy our ships?"

"Yes, I remember hearing that you bought them from an old friend."

Elcano nodded, and his voice grew mellow with reminiscence. "Yes, his name is Domingo Laca. He lives in Lequeitio, a town not far from my village of Guetaria. The men of his family have been whalers for generations. Domingo and I met years ago when one of his many cousins married one of mine. After I wrote to him about our voyage, he found the ships and offered them to me at a good price."

Espinosa shifted restlessly, his expression asking what any of this had to do with the matter at hand.

But Elcano went on. "He warned me more than once that the ships would need a great deal of care because they had seen much previous use. I wonder, what would Domingo say if he knew of the abuse they have suffered since he delivered them up to me?"

Espinosa had tried to be patient and allow Elcano his time to reflect, but he needed an answer. Gently, he asked, "Juan Sebastian, will you take command of this fleet?"

Elcano turned his gaze to the man that, above staggering obstacles, had become his friend. "This much I will agree to do; if Carvalho volunteers to step down, and you will captain the *Trinidad*, then I will captain the *Victoria*. I will do this because she was built just outside of Guetaria. Weak though that tie might be, it binds me to her, and binds me to my home. If the *Victoria* perishes, I wish to perish with her. Master Polcevera will act wisely as captain-general. He is a good man."

"You are a far better pilot than any of the rest of us. Will you take the lead, sail before the flagship?"

"Yes, but I have very little skill sailing in these unknown waters."

"We will find local pilots, take them by force if necessary. It is the way of these seas, and it is the only choice left to us."

Espinosa held out his hand. Elcano sighed resignedly and took it.

"The day has finally come when I can call you *Captain* Elcano."

"Not unless Carvalho steps down. I insist on that."

"Yes, yes, I understand. Let's find Polcevera."

In the end, it was remarkably simple. At the evening meal, Espinosa gathered the men around a half-drunken Carvalho and took a unanimous vote to change the command.

Carvalho surveyed the ring of men before his gaze settled upon Espinosa. "I will step down on one condition; the women remain with me."

"Agreed," said Espinosa.

"Then go ahead! Take this doomed fleet with my blessing. It's plain to any sane man that God has cursed the lot of us." Standing with an effort, picking up his musket and sword, and ushering his women before him, he lumbered into the trees.

Polcevera stepped forward and said, "I will command as captain-general aboard the *Trinidad*, Captain Espinosa will transfer to her decks, and Pancaldo will serve as her pilot. Master Elcano will captain the *Victoria*, and all other officers will maintain their current ranks. Is this new command agreeable to you men?"

Voices raised in shouts of approval.

"My first action as captain-general is to name Captain Elcano as treasurer of the fleet." He cast a quick glance at Elcano, who, suspecting that Espinosa had intentionally failed to mention this detail, nodded with grace.

"Now," said Polcevera, "let's all have our meal."

The men took off in the direction of the cooking pot and, with lighter spirits, jostled each other for position in front of it.

Acurio followed Chindarza as he carried a bowl of fish soup to Elcano, who stood back a short distance from the milling men. Chindarza handed over the bowl and said, "Your soup, Captain Elcano."

Under his breath, Acurio uttered, "It's about time, Captain, that's all I've got to say. Maybe this lot has more sense than I've been giving them credit for."

Elcano smiled. "You two get back and see to your own food before these wolves eat it all."

"Yes, sir," they said. But Acurio had one last thing to add before leaving him. "Captain, have you noted what day it happens to be?"

Elcano thought for a moment. "Why, it's September 21."

"That's right, Captain. Two years to the very day since we first set sail. Now, sir, I know you would never have wished for things to take the turns they have, but I'm pleased that you'll be commanding a ship again at last."

Elcano shook his head. Two years. He had thought he would be home by now. He had imagined they would all be home by now. How differently things had turned out. Briefly, his mind traced their many travels, their many losses. And then his eyes returned to the two men before him. Softly, gratefully, he said, "Off with you now."

When the ships' renovations had been improvised with local materials to the best of the men's ingenuity, Carvalho and his women were taken aboard the *Trinidad* where the former captain-general made no attempt to interfere with the new command. Elcano directed the *Victoria* out of the harbor with Polcevera's last words gnawing at his mind. "We must hail any ship that might provide either food or information as to the location of the Molucca Islands. We can't risk squandering more time, watching our ships rot, and waiting for the Portuguese to find us. Neither can we risk landing on another hostile island and losing any more men."

They sailed to the north and came across a junk heading toward Palawan. Approaching her from both sides, they signaled her crew to lower her sails. When this demand was refused, the *Victoria* closed in on one side as the *Trinidad* hemmed in the junk on the other. Without a shot being fired they forced her to slow, then Espinosa boarded her with armed men and took one of Palawan's rajahs, Tuan Maamud, and his brother captive.

Maamud was brought aboard the *Trinidad*, where Pigafetta introduced him to Captain-general Polcevera, Captain Espinosa, and Captain Elcano, who had just boarded.

"Sir" Polcevera addressed the rajah, "We wish you no harm, but we are in desperate need of food supplies and information. If you provide us with both, we will set you free."

As these words were being translated to Maamud, his surprise became plain. He gave his response, and Pigafetta turned to Polcevera. "He asks what kinds and quantities of food you request, sir."

The three senior officers conferred for a moment before Polcevera said, "Tell him that we need four hundred measures of rice, twenty pigs, twenty goats, and one hundred fifty chickens within a week's time."

The rajah bowed and said that these terms were agreeable to him. His brother, his crew, and his junk were released to see to the task of gathering his ransom. Maamud made himself quite at home as the fleet drew closer to Palawan. Although he willingly gave directions as to where he believed the Molucca Islands might lie, these guidelines were very general in nature since, he admitted, he had never visited them before.

On the sixth day of the rajah's captivity, his brother met the two ships and began transferring every item that had been demanded into their possession. When Elcano had carefully noted that all had been delivered, much to the amazed relief of Maamud's brother, he ordered their own selected trade goods to be loaded onto the junk. When Maamud himself was thanked and respectfully returned to his lateen-sailed ship, he exchanged a few words with his brother, turned back to Polcevera, and called out to him.

"Wait, sir," said Pigafetta. He listened to more of Maamud's words, then said with a chuckle, "Captain-general, Maamud says that we have overpaid him."

"You can't be serious."

"But I am, sir. He wants to send us some things that he claims we might enjoy even though we did not ask for them."

"Very well, have him send half of whatever it is to us and half to the *Victoria*. And thank him."

Without delay, each ship was given generous quantities of palm wine, sugar cane, coconuts, and bananas. As the junk pulled away from the ships, the rajah raised his hand in friendly farewell.

Once he was back aboard the *Victoria*, Acurio said, "Have you ever seen a more agreeable man, sir? Him giving us this wine and such, after us taking him. It's almost enough to make a seaman consider a life of piracy."

Now that the ships were much better provisioned and carrying general directions to the Spiceries, Polcevera had Elcano alter their course to the east, southeast. Crossing north of Borneo's coast, they encountered another junk, one with men aboard, that agreed to anchor at a small island and barter. Here, along with more consumable goods, Elcano managed to obtain seventeen pounds of cinnamon.

Later that afternoon, after sending half of his find to the flagship, Elcano gathered the officers and men of the *Victoria* around his small keg of spice, and let them each have a turn examining it and breathing in its rich, sweet scent.

"Just think," said Acurio, "this small amount is worth enough to pay half the cost of a fine ship, and they say these natives just peel it off their trees."

"I never smelled anything so fine in my life," said Chindarza.

"Nor I," said Elcano. "Nor I."

Even after obtaining this proof that cinnamon groves grew nearby, the crews did not forget that they were bound for the Moluccas where cloves, an even more valuable spice, grew in abundance. The traders that had provided the cinnamon could give no first-hand knowledge of how to reach the Spiceries, so the fleet continued its search with anxious uncertainty. The ships veered again to the northeast and held this course until they found themselves resting on a windless stretch of sea where the water was as calm as a garden pond. The sails hung limp and their forward progress came to a halt. Just ahead of them, however, and held within the same calms, rode a large proa manned by eighteen men.

Elcano followed Polcevera's command to remain with his ship while Espinosa led two boatloads of armed men toward the Eastern craft. All seemed peaceful when the boats pulled near the vessel. Pigafetta called out a greeting and it was returned. But before another word could be exchanged, the ring of clashing steel jarred the still air. Who was first to pull his sword, Elcano did not see, but now the boats and the proa rocked and bucked as the sailors within them slashed viciously at one another. With swords and scimitars flashing in the sunlight and crossbows jerking in the arms of the archers, Elcano could do nothing but stare across the water and dig his fingernails into the *Victoria's* rail.

Acurio was in the midst of the combatants, and Elcano saw him strike a blow against the shield of a Malay sailor that knocked the native backward into the proa. As Acurio's opponent regained his feet, a crossbow arrow struck him in the chest, passing completely through his body and toppling him off the far side of the proa.

Better armed and better trained than the islanders, Elcano saw six other natives fall before they began dropping their swords and holding up their empty hands. Bloody and decisive, the battle was over in moments. The islanders' armaments were gathered up, the hands of the passengers were bound with ropes, and the proa was towed back to the *Trinidad*.

Although the captured proa held little food beyond the needs of its own men, it carried a rich bounty in the form of strong hands. Along with one three-year-old boy, eleven men were taken aboard. Of these, several identified themselves as chieftains, and one claimed to be the brother of the rajah of Mindanao. It was he that agreed to show them the route to the Moluccas. The day following the battle, five of the captive men were sent over to the *Victoria*, their proa was set adrift, and, when the wind rose again, the fleet proceeded with every sail straining.

Elcano questioned each of the new arrivals as to their prior positions on land and aboard their proa. After this knowledge had been gained and Elcano had drawn his first conclusions as to the character of each man, he addressed them all in broken Malay and sign language. "Will you pledge to serve this ship without endangering the lives of those aboard?"

The captives exchanged glances of wonder, then nodded their heads.

"Acurio, cut their bonds and assign each man to someone that will teach him our language and our ways of sailing."

One by one Acurio summoned forward five members of the crew, leaving the youngest of the adult captives to be matched with a man of the *Victoria*. Calling Chindarza's name, Acurio said, "Since you seem to be of a like age, this one is yours to teach. Instruct him well, my boy."

Showing neither eagerness nor disappointment, Chindarza said, "Yes, sir."

He and the islander studied each other openly as Chindarza took him around the ship, pointing and naming as they went.

Elcano looked on, seeing more anger than fear in the eyes of the bronze-skinned youth and seeing not the least intimidation in Chindarza's returning stare. He'll have his hands full, Elcano thought, then realized that this would most likely be true for both of them.

As the captured crew members adjusted to their loss of freedom, the fleet followed the route indicated by their new guide by paralleling the southern coast of Mindanao and shifting with it when it bent to the southeast. Within days they found themselves skirting a lush section of shoreline that tempted them to land and restock their fresh food stores. The Mindanaoans, however, once they understood these intentions, pleaded with the officers to steer clear of the coast. Casting fearful glances toward the beach, they claimed that the natives of this area were cannibals that lived only off of the hearts of their captives.

Before long, these dreaded man-eaters began to show themselves, looking every bit as wild as they had been described. Powerfully built and shaggy headed, the warriors carried huge spears, and arrows as long as a man's leg. Not wishing to test the claims of the Mindanaoans in the face of such evidence, the fleet sailed on without slowing.

Upon reaching the southern-most edge of Mindanao, a storm broke upon the ships with a fury that equaled even the tempests of Patagonia. Sail lines were snapped free as the wind drove like rams into the ships' prows, compelling the seas to rise and crash, and tossing men to the decks. For seven hours Elcano and his men directed the ship, wrestled the tiller, and fought to keep from being swept overboard. Alms were promised, pilgrimages pledged, and sins of the past were sorely regretted as the storm cruelly tossed them about.

Then, at the very height of the wailing of the wind and the crashing of thunder, when the rain lashed out with its greatest force and the sea crested to a towering height, a torch of light burst into a brilliant blue flame at the top of each mast.

At the sight of it, seamen cried out in thanks and homage.

Unthinking, Acurio grabbed Elcano's sleeve and shouted, "The fires of St. Elmo, St. Nicholas, and St. Clara!"

Master Rodas yelled out, "Steady on, men! We're safe now! We're not alone!"

In exhausted relief, Elcano bent his head over the half deck's forward railing and muttered, "Ride it out, my *Victoria*. Ride it out."

The saints' flames burned brightly atop the masts for another two hours, remaining with them until the ocean, air, and sky relinquished their powers and acquiesced to the will of heaven.

Elcano stood on the battered stern deck as his men raised the *Victoria's* sails and she moved ahead, leading the *Trinidad* on, undeterred now by the final distant grumblings of the storm. At last he brought the ships into a safe anchorage at one of two small islands off the southern shores of Mindanao, and there they remained throughout the night.

The following dawn spread with gentle clarity to the shore, as if no storm had ever dared to touch that land. Espinosa, Pigafetta, and a handful of others left the ship to discover what the island might offer. Soon they came across an old man with two younger companions who agreed to serve as the fleet's pilots as they continued on to the Moluccas. The next day, however, when only one of the younger men returned as promised, the remaining two voiced an inclination to abandon the ships unless their companion showed up. Espinosa, claiming an agreement was an agreement and promising that they would be well paid, had the younger man taken to the *Victoria*, while he kept possession of the old man. Polcevera then gave the order to set sail.

As they pulled away from their anchorage, Elcano saw canoes filled with angry natives shoving into the water and sailing after them. Their shouted insults and threats rang in his ears even after the ships had left them far behind.

Climbing the steps to the foredeck, Elcano found Pilot Albo looking gravely serious as usual, and Master Rodas trying to bat his brown curls away from his face. He nodded to the officers and came to stand between them and their Mindanaoan pilot, Banayat. This man had proven himself to be most knowledgeable about the waters through which they had sailed for the past few days. The Celebes Sea, he called it.

"Captain," said Rodas, "Banayat claims that Sangi Island is just ahead. On the other side of it lies the Molucca Sea."

Elcano gazed southward for a moment and imagined what the Spice Islands would look like. Addressing their native pilot, he said. "You have done well, Banayat. The watch will change in a few moments. You may go to your meal."

Banayat bowed and left them, and when the officers were alone, Elcano said, "Do you still trust his directions?"

"Yes, Captain, I do," said Albo.

"I do as well, Captain," Rodas added.

"So do I. What's your opinion as to how the rest of our Mindanaoan hands are adapting?"

Rodas thought for a moment then chuckled softly, "That young one, Baccay, every now and then he gives Chindarza a look that would shrivel a melon. He's the son of a chief, they say. He's very proud. As for the others, sir, I think some are wondering when we intend to cut their throats. It's their way. Once captives are no longer useful, they simply do away with them. They fear their fate will be the same when we reach the Moluccas."

"Do your best to reassure them that we have no intention of slitting their throats, gentlemen, and watch them closely."

Rodas asked, "Do you know what *is* to become of them, sir?"

"That is primarily up to the captain-general. As we've seen, predicting what will become of any of us is not an easy task. We'll wait and see what the Spiceries have in store for us. According to Banayat, we'll pass a string of small islands almost due south before we veer to the southeast. Then we will be close. Sometimes I think I can smell cloves on the wind." He breathed in deeply as if to test this theory and let himself smile, wanting to believe. "If Banayat is accurate, we'll be there in just a few days."

Grinning, Rodas said, "Just a few days, sir."

The men purchased food and water at Sangi Island and pushed on at full speed. They had traveled no more than ten miles, however, when the winds suddenly died and the current began dragging them backward. So powerful was this sternward draught that, despite the continued efforts of the crews, the ships drifted back dangerously close to shore. As Elcano and his men strove to keep the *Victoria* from running aground, he heard shouts coming from the flagship.

Turning toward them, Elcano saw seamen pointing excitedly toward the water, and he spotted two of the Mindanaoans swimming away from the ship. No, it was three. Clinging to the neck of the rajah's brother was his tiny son. Before the *Trinidad*'s crew could lower the skiff into the water, the two swimmers had covered half the distance to shore. They were within a hundred feet of the beach by the time the rowers were in position and the oars touched the water.

Just then, Elcano saw the child lose his hold from around his father's neck and go under. The father paused, fruitlessly searched the churning waves around him, and dove below the water's surface. He came up closer to land but there was still no trace of his son. He looked back once more as he scrambled onto the beach and, with his companion beseeching him to hurry, turned and stumbled for the cover of the trees.

The *Trinidad's* boat reached the spot where the boy had disappeared and the men scanned the swelling depths, but the ocean yielded no hint of him. At last Polcevera ordered them back to the ship and they took up their oars once again.

# The Realm of Almanzor

## 20

The sky of the aging afternoon was just beginning to bloom with quiet golds and pinks as Elcano focused hard on what lay ahead. He could have sworn that the very air was tingling. After fighting so hard and for so long to maintain his grip on hope, he could scarcely trust his eyes as they beheld the distant islands.

Chindarza stood beside him, as speechless as his captain. When words finally formed in his mind, all he could say was, "They *are* real, sir, and we've found them."

Elcano echoed, "We've found them. Breathe it in, Chindarza."

There was no mistaking it now. The essences of cinnamon and cloves perfumed the air, enticing them ever closer to the volcanic peaks of the emerald blanketed islands.

When Rodas, carrying parchment, quill, and ink, came up to them, Elcano waited until his shipmaster had checked the progress of their approach before asking, "You've seen that the gunpowder is still secure, Master Rodas?"

"Yes, sir. Not even our master gunner can gain access to it without the permission of the officer on watch." Slowly, Rodas shook his head. "It's strange, sir, the flagship losing two gunners in just two days, and both by mishandling gun powder. Sánchez and Bautista were fine gunners too. It wasn't like either of them to be so careless."

"From all accounts their deaths were accidental," said Elcano. Noting Rodas' glance toward the captives sitting apart from the other men of the next watch, he said, "We must not suspect malice when misfortune is to blame. Don't forget that it was Banayat who warned us not to land where we had intended to yesterday. If he hadn't, we might well have been attacked by the hostiles we saw soon afterward."

"Yes, sir," agreed Rodas, "but it still gives me comfort to know that the gun powder is securely locked up."

Seeing Acurio come up beside Chindarza, Elcano nodded toward the islands and said, "Have you ever seen anything more fine, Acurio?"

"Not a thing in this world, Captain. Not one blessed thing."

The rest of the ship's personnel were moving to the rails for a better view, and Elcano spoke to all within the range of his voice. "The island to the north is Ternate, where Captain Serrano's brother has lived for years. The other island is Tidore. The small one to the south is Mare and the farther ones are Motir and Makian."

"Captain Elcano," the barber, Bustamente, asked, "isn't Francisco Serrano trading for the Portuguese?"

"Possibly, if he's still alive. One of the Mindanaoans claimed to have been a guest in Serrano's house recently. If that's true, Serrano is obviously still living and most likely still serving as vizier for Ternate's rajah. But Magellan once told me that Serrano has no great love for the king of Portugal. He might be persuaded to change his loyalties to Spain. We'll anchor first at Tidore, where we hope neither treaty nor trading post has yet been established."

Someone called out, "Are the natives friendly there, Captain?"

Elcano now raised his voice to be heard by all. "Let me make this clear, men. The captain-general, Captain Espinosa, and I are all in agreement about this. Only those chosen to perform specific duties will be allowed to go ashore. We've learned through hard experience that the risk of death is too great to allow anyone ashore for mere pleasure." When he heard the first grumbles, he spoke with the power of his determination. "Of the five ships that began this mission twenty-seven months ago, these last two have crossed many thousands of miles to reach these islands. Only a hundred and seven of us remain. We've suffered hunger, sickness, betrayal, and death. When we reach the shores of Tidore, we will use every precaution to see that not one more man is lost. Not one more man! With God's blessing and with our holds full of spices, *all* of us must stand together when we sail back to Spain!"

The men of the *Victoria* let out a cheer loud enough to turn the heads of the crew aboard the *Trinidad*. As if connected by some melding of spirits, they began to cheer as well. The cries grew louder as their vessels glided ever closer to the rising green slopes of the island, an island that had filled their minds and sustained their souls through more adversity than they had expected to bear throughout ten lifetimes.

When they came to rest at last in the calm blue waters of a bay as beautiful as they had imagined, every cannon in the fleet fired with a thunderous roar. As the smell of gunpowder mixed with the tang of spices, and natives began gathering along the shore and waving in welcome, Elcano, Espinosa, and every other man of the fleet knelt down and bowed his head as Polcevera led them in a prayer of thanks.

Almost at once the people of Tidore began to approach the ships in proas, bringing small amounts of cloves with them. But strict orders had already been issued on both ships to trade only for food until official trade agreements for spices could be established. The question of how to bring about their first meeting with a high official was answered quickly. As the sun's light diminished and lantern flames kindled to life, a finely clothed messenger in an ornate proa rowed close to the ships, delivering the news that the master of Tidore, Rajah Almanzor himself, would come to their ships early in the morning.

That night, Elcano slept with his cabin door wide open to welcome in the clove scented breeze.


Almanzor, arriving on the beach not long after the appearance of the sun's first rays, made Elcano's waking worth while. The rajah's gold accented and silk canopied proa pushed off from shore and had rowed only half way across the bay before it was met by the fleet's skiffs and accompanied to the ships. When they had drawn near Pigafetta acted as their interpreter and Polcevera offered formal greetings to Almanzor and his company on behalf of King Carlos.

Unlike the Muslim rulers whom they had encountered on the other prosperous islands, Almanzor was well proportioned rather than corpulent. He appeared to be at least fifty-five years of age, and his deep chestnut skin was magnificently adorned with gold and silk. Taller than his guards, Almanzor rose from the raised cushion in the middle of his proa, and in a resplendent voice translated by Pigafetta, he said, "Most honored guests, long have I awaited your coming. I foresaw this day in a dream years ago. From that prophesy, I learned that we would become great allies. You have only to name what you wish from me and, if it is within my power to grant it, it will be yours."

Astounded by these words, Polcevera managed to say to Pigafetta, "Thank Rajah Almanzor for his kindness, and ask him if he will join us aboard the flagship so we might discuss this great alliance."

His offer was accepted without hesitation, and within minutes Almanzor was seating himself in a chair draped in velvet on the *Trinidad's* main deck. Captain-general Polcevera bowed as he introduced himself, and then turned to present his captains, and Pigafetta. He then brought forth carefully selected gifts and bestowed them upon the rajah.

After thanking his hosts, Almanzor said, "Please tell me how I might show my high regard for you and your king."

"The king of Spain," said Polcevera through Pigafetta, "has sent us across two great oceans so that we might trade for cloves, Your Majesty."

Surprising them afresh, Almanzor said, "I know of your great king and of his powerful people. It would give me great pleasure to trade the harvest of my island for the goods of his nation. I hope that this will be the first of my actions to bind us together in good will."

At these generous words, suspicion sprouted in Elcano's mind. He realized that he was not alone in his doubts when

309

Polcevera asked smoothly. "Rajah Almanzor, how did you happen to learn of our king and country?"

"As you must know, the Portuguese have visited this land for the last ten years. We learned of Spain from them."

This explanation chilled the hearts of every crewmember but most of them concealed their reactions. Polcevera's expression was mild when he asked, "Your Highness, do you mean to say that you have traded with the Portuguese for years?"

Almanzor nodded and said, "Yes, but only because I was given little other choice. My first encounter with the Portuguese happened just after a man named Francisco Serrano arrived at the neighboring island of Ternate. This Serrano formed a friendship with Boleyse, the rajah of Ternate." Almanzor's features subtly darkened as he continued. "Before Serrano came, Boleyse and I left one another alone. But then I was told I must bow to Boleyse's wishes, that I must offer the fruits of my island to none but the Portuguese. I was given no opportunity to refuse these demands. To show my acceptance of this distasteful agreement, I was even forced to surrender one of my own daughters in marriage to Boleyse." Almanzor sat back in his chair and folded his hands in his lap. "Honorable Captains, I hold no love for the Portuguese. "

Casually, Polcevera asked, "Your Majesty, have the Portuguese established a permanent trading post on your island?"

"No, that, I have not permitted them to do."

"I understand. And does Francisco Serrano still reside on Ternate?"

Almanzor's calm tone did not change as he replied, "He came to me eight months ago to pick up a supply of cloves. I invited him to a feast that he enjoyed very little. His food had been poisoned. He died four days later."

The tight hush that followed ended when Polcevera said, "What was Rajah Boleyse's reaction to this...event, Your Majesty?"

"Whatever his reaction might have been, it did not last long. One of Boleyse's daughters, the wife of the rajah of

Bacan, poisoned her father ten days after Serrano's death. But, good captains, that unpleasantness is in the past. We must look to the future now. My daughter bore Boleyse a son, Colanoghapi, and although he is the youngest of Ternate's princes, I hope that he will one day rule as the rajah of Ternate, so that peace will reign between our two islands."

Almanzor now cast a benevolent glance over them all. "Today we have a new beginning." He rose from his chair with grace and approached Polcevera, Elcano, and Espinosa. "I will have my workers begin gathering the finest of our cloves for your inspection. You and all of your men are invited to come ashore whenever you wish. You will be welcomed by me and my people just as if you were entering your own homes."

"We are grateful for such generosity, Your Majesty," said Polcevera with a bow.

After Almanzor's party had left the ship, Polcevera motioned the two captains into his cabin. Once inside with the door closed, Espinosa said, "It seems to be an unhealthy practice to accept a dinner invitation in this part of the world."

"It certainly does," said Polcevera. "Captain Elcano, as the fleet's treasurer you will be doing most of the negotiating here. Take every precaution while ashore. I suggest you eat as little as possible."

"Of course, sir."

In the days that followed, the men remained aboard the ships but graciously received many visitors, including Checchily de Roix, one of the princes of Ternate. Even a Portuguese trader named Pedro de Lorosa and his servant, Manuel, were among those asking permission to come aboard the Spanish ships. When Lorosa showed up first at the *Victoria*, Elcano accompanied him and his servant to the flagship to meet with Polcevera and Espinosa in the captain-general's quarters.

Lorosa, his oval head shaved as bald as an egg and his eyes hinting of mischief, accepted the seat offered by Polcevera and motioned for his servant to stand by the door.

He gave the officers a cursory gaze then let out a burst of laughter. "Come, gentlemen, come! I have never seen such cautious faces. You have nothing to fear from me. I may be Portuguese by birth but, after living for sixteen years in this corner of the world, I am my own man, and I have learned much that could be of service to you."

"At the moment," said Polcevera, "it would be most helpful if you could tell us any news from Europe."

"Of course, you have gone a great while without word from home. Well, it will interest you to know that King Carlos was officially named Holy Roman Emperor last October. That's made things friendlier between him and the pope, but Carlos has had nothing but trouble from the Castilian nobles."

"Holy Roman Emperor at the age of twenty-one," Polcevera mused.

"Now, if you don't mind telling me," said Lorosa, "other than the acquisition of cloves, what are your goals while you are here?"

More diplomatic sparring and polite questions were exchanged before the four began to share limited confidences. After the basic elements of their mission had been explained, Lorosa asked, "Are these two ships all that remain of your original fleet?"

Elcano eyed him warily. "We've said nothing of other ships."

"Ah, but I recognized the names of your vessels. What have become of the other three, and of Magellan?"

Before Lorosa could move, Elcano and Espinosa had drawn their swords and pointed them at the throats of the trader and his servant. To the surprise of all, Lorosa began to shake his head and chuckle softly. "I told you, good gentlemen, you need not fear me. If I were a spy, I would be a very poor one to reveal knowledge that I intended to use against you. Put down your swords, please. You've given my poor Manuel a dreadful scare."

The tips of the swords were withdrawn only a few inches, and Elcano demanded, "Tell us all you know and how you know it."

Lorosa stared with mild displeasure at the swords until they were lowered a little farther. "Not quite a year ago, a few months before Serrano was killed, a Portuguese ship landed at Ternate to purchase cloves. I met with the captain to learn the news from my homeland. Your fleet was news indeed. It seems that King Manuel was bent on seeing you destroyed even before you left Seville. He sent two full squadrons of warships to cut you off; one to Africa's Cape and one to Cape Santa Maria south of Brazil. Did you have any trouble avoiding them?"

"We've seen no Portuguese ships," said Polcevera.

"None at all? Then you have been most fortunate."

"We have had our share of misfortune," Elcano said.

"Perhaps, but God must have been watching over you, especially in recent days. You see, when the ships returned to the king without success, he was furious. Diego Lopes de Sequeira, the commander of his naval forces throughout India and these islands, was ordered to blow your Spanish ships out of these waters if you ever arrived. Just a few days ago Sequeira sent a caravel and two armed junks to Bacan, a large island to the south. They were to collect cloves there but only after combing the area in search of you. And they might well have spotted you if the men from the two junks had been better behaved while ashore. Some of the native women were badly abused. Bacan's rajah responded by seizing seven Portuguese seamen, removing their heads, and commandeered their junks. The caravel managed to flee the harbor before she could be taken. I have no doubt that her captain has returned to Malacca to report the incident to Sequeira. This unexpected turn of fortune may have prevented you from being discovered here."

Elcano and Espinosa gently slid their swords into their scabbards, and Polcevera said, "This helps explain our warm reception by Almanzor."

Lorosa nodded. "Many of the leaders here hate the Portuguese, but they deal with them out of fear or to enhance their own power. Almanzor hates them more than most. Did you know that three Portuguese, former employees of Serrano, were recently murdered at the spring where your men have been collecting water?" To relieve the suddenly troubled faces of the officers around him, he said, "It is unlikely that Almanzor would allow such an attack against your people. You see, your arrival offers him, as well as the other rulers, an alternative, a balance. And Spain has the advantage of not having slain many thousands of people all along the coasts of Africa, India, and these islands in order to gain dominance."

The minds of the three officers leaped back to the battles at Guam, Mactan, and Brunei, but they did not speak of these. Instead, Polcevera said, "Sequeira will undoubtedly send more ships to teach the rajah of Bacan a lesson. When would you guess they might arrive?"

"It's hard to say," replied Lorosa. "Sequeira has his warships occupied right now, fighting the Turks in the Red Sea. That may take weeks or months. On the other hand, his ships could show up within a matter of days."

Espinosa let out a curse. "Then we have no time to lose."

"You are right to be concerned, Captain, but if the cloves were important enough to risk what you have already lost, I advise that you take the time necessary to gain the friendship of Almanzor and the other rajahs. I know these people. You would be wise not to rush them too much. Most of them understand the danger you are in, and they'll be watching to see how you respond to it."

After a pause, Polcevera said, "This information, as I'm sure you know, is of great value to us. What do you ask in return?"

Lorosa smiled, "Whatever you feel is appropriate, Captain-general."

"Would you consider remaining with us, Señor Lorosa?" Elcano asked. "Your knowledge of these islands, their rulers, and their crops would be most helpful."

Espinosa leaned forward in his chair as Polcevera added his voice of persuasion. "You would be well paid for such help, sir."

Tenting his fingers and pressing his fingertips to his lips, Lorosa contemplated a moment before asking, "How long are you proposing that I remain in your service?"

Polcevera's gaze touched briefly on each of his captains to be certain they agreed. After each of them had nodded, the captain-general said, "All the way back to Spain. The king himself will be most grateful."

"You know," Lorosa said thoughtfully, "Serrano once told me that when Magellan finally reached Ternate, and he never doubted that he *would* arrive some day, he planned to transfer his allegiance to Spain. Serrano trusted me enough to share such a secret. He knew I would understand because I also knew that, long ago, Serrano was tortured unjustly by a Portuguese official. He never forgot the wrong done to him. At some point he began to hope that Spain would be more just. Perhaps I have come to hope the same thing."

Lorosa pulled in a deep breath, nodded gently, and slapped his hands upon his knees, saying, "I agree to join you, gentlemen." After accepting the felicitations of the offi cers, Lorosa inquired, "Given the brevity of our acquaintance and the delicacy of our dealings, am I right to presume that you wish me to relocate my possessions, my wife, and myself to one of your ships."

"That is most understanding of you, Señor Lorosa," said Polcevera. "We will do our best to make you welcome aboard the *Trinidad*."

"And do you wish to send some of your men to assist me in wrapping up my business and my household affairs?"

"If you don't mind."

Lorosa smiled knowingly. "Even if I do mind. But, of course, Captain-general. I am at your service now. Therefore, I offer you one more piece of advice. Almanzor is a devout Muslim and it would be wise to respect his beliefs."

"We are here to trade, not to convert," said Elcano, and he was not corrected.

The fleet's senior officers saw to it that Lorosa and his wife were given a small but comfortable cabin aboard the flagship.

In the days that followed, Elcano met often with Almanzor, and each encounter worked to lessen his wariness of the rajah. Almanzor gave every sign that he intended to deal with them fairly, even to the point of providing a choice location upon which a trading post could be built. Using Lorosa's insights while keeping him in the background, Elcano was able to formulate a trade agreement that seemed as pleasing to Almanzor as it was to him, Polcevera, and Espinosa.

On the very day that the trading post was erected, Elcano decided it might also be time to bring the matter of their hostages to the foreground. After discussing them with Almanzor, Elcano returned at once to the *Trinidad*.

Finding Polcevera and Espinosa, he accompanied them to the half deck and informed them of his meeting with the island leader. "When I told him about our captives, Almanzor was delighted."

"Delighted?" said Espinosa in amazement.

"Yes. He asked if we would consider transferring them into his care."

"What does he intend to do with them?" Polcevera wanted to know.

Elcano shook his head, still having a hard time believing. "He said he wants to send them throughout his lands, accompanied by some of his own men, so that they can teach his people about the power and goodness of the king of Spain."

"Well, I'll be," Espinosa muttered.

"The captive men have been well treated," Polcevera thought aloud, "especially by the standards of this region, but the three women won't forget how Carvalho has abused them."

"That's true, sir," said Elcano, "They will say little good of us, but the women will prefer staying here rather than being transported all the way to Spain."

"All right, Captain Elcano, you may free the women and the Mindanaoans, but not the men we took in Brunei. They were seized in battle, and some of our own men were taken hostage in return. They've conformed amazingly well to our ways and we would be dangerously short-handed without them. We must retain all of them."

"Then may I take the others ashore at once, sir?"

"Patience, Captain. You may tell them and Carvalho of our intentions now, but tomorrow will be soon enough to take the captives ashore."

"Thank you, sir. I'll speak to them at once."

Carvalho offered less resistance than Elcano had anticipated. Whether it was because of the palm wine that he consumed too freely or the variety of diseases that he had contracted, Carvalho's health was declining noticeably. When Elcano informed him that the women were to be freed, Carvalho said, "Take them. They're getting to be more trouble than they're worth."

The women and the men taken near Mindanao were ushered to the half deck and Elcano delivered his news. The disbelief on the faces of the captives quickly gave way to postulating chatter. The three women locked their hands together, both fearful and hopeful of how this new land and new ruler might change their lives. After getting permission from Polcevera, Elcano ordered the women transferred to a separate cabin, where they were allowed to wash themselves and their clothing.

A few minutes later Elcano repeated his announcement aboard the *Victoria* to the other Mindanaoans. To the Brunei captives, he carried word of Polcevera's decision that they were to return with the fleet to Spain. The hopefulness of those being freed stood in stark contrast to the grimness of the men less fortunate.

The following morning Elcano presented the male and female captives to Rajah Almanzor as free people. They were kindly greeted and led away to be washed, clothed, and fed, and Elcano withdrew from the audience hall with a slightly lighter heart to see to his other duties.

The sturdy new trading post, already under the operation of five men Elcano had selected for their trustworthiness, bustled with activity. All was going so smoothly, Elcano learned, that the first large bundles of cloves were ready to be delivered to the ships. To the great delight of the crews, that evening the holds of both ships began to fill with pungent sweetness.

At Elcano's dinner table, he withdrew a small handful of the dried buds from his pocket, gave a few to each of his officers, and slipped a couple to Chindarza, who was serving them. The men studied them with animated fascination before taking a taste.

"Well!" Acurio exclaimed, "it's got a taste strong enough to bite you back, does it not?"

The rest of them chuckled and proceeded to spend a good share of the evening congratulating themselves on their fine efforts and discussing the many possible foods that might be enhanced by adding the flavor of that glorious spice.

The next days brought more cloves, and still more. And just as Lorosa had predicted, Almanzor was not the only rajah anxious to deal with them.

One morning Acurio spotted the approach of a regal proa and Elcano wasted no time in heading over to the flagship to meet the new arrival, who turned out to be Rajah Halmahera.

The ancient ruler of Gilolo, a larger island lying to the east, required the aide of five of his men to reach the rail, roll over it, and lumber to the center of the *Trinidad's* main deck. There, he stood gasping for breath, his many rings of fat drooping loosely around his huge body. Introductions were made, then, with little preamble, Halmahera declared in a deeply nasal voice, "My land is larger than the holdings of Almanzor. As you clearly can see, I am a bigger man than he. But my greatness goes beyond my size and my kingdom."

Fascinated, Elcano listened without a thought of interrupting this confident orator.

Placing his hands on his massive hips, Halmahera went on. "Almanzor has the same number of wives in his harem as I. Yet with two hundred wives Almanzor has managed to father only *twenty-six* offspring, while I, Halmahera, have fathered over *six hundred*! Now, does it not seem reasonable that any trade offered to Almanzor must surely be offered to such a man as myself?"

Elcano conferred only briefly with Polcevera and Espinosa before the treaty with the rajah of Gilolo was drawn up and signed.

To the great joy of the fleet, additional treaties with the rajah of Makian, the princes of Ternate, and the rajah of Bacan soon followed.

While the harvesting, drying, trading, and loading of cloves were underway, the fleet's personnel were kept busy making new sails for their homeward journey. When the sails were finally completed, they were each carefully fitted to the ships' yardarms. Elcano made certain that he was aboard and watching as the huge sheets of canvas unfurled for the first time, revealing the newly painted crimson crosses of Santiago. Elcano felt his chest expand as he read the words that had been written under the main sail's cross; "This is the sign of our good fortune." For, indeed, good fortune at last seemed to deem them worthy company.

Standing beside his captain and looking up at the sails, Acurio said, "They'll take us home in fine fashion, sir."

"Yes, with God's blessings."

Thoughtfully, Acurio asked, "Isn't it something, sir, that we'll be sailing on westward 'til we've rounded the whole of the world? When we left home we thought we'd be recrossing the Pacific to get back, little knowing how vast a sea it truly is."

"In this season the monsoon winds point west. Despite the Portuguese, that way holds our best hope. But yes, to complete the full circle, a thing no fleet has done before, such a deed will surely sweeten our welcome home."

Acurio breathed deeply and grinned. "And we'll have the sweetness of these cloves scenting our decks every mile of the way."

The days preceding their planned departure gradually dwindled, and Almanzor invited all the officers to a parting feast set for the eve of their leave-taking. Although the rajah had done nothing to foster distrust between him and the officers, they were not about to forget the slaughter at Cebu or the local custom of poisoning honored guests. Polcevera and his captains, therefore, politely reversed the offer and requested that they be allowed to host a farewell dinner aboard the flagship. This proposal Almanzor happily accepted.

Under the glow of a generous moon, the night overflowed with food, wine, and an abundance of gratitude and promises. Elcano was mildly surprised when, after the meal had been cleared away, Almanzor asked that his Holy Koran be brought forth. Placing both hands upon its cover, Rajah Almanzor raised his earnest voice and swore his lifelong faithfulness to King Carlos of Spain. In return, Polcevera bestowed upon the rajah several harquebuses, small cannons, and the shot and powder they would require.

Clearly moved, Almanzor took these prizes onto his proas and wished them all a blessed sleep. "Though my heart will be heavy to see you leave my land," he said, "I will be on the shore tomorrow to wish you all a safe journey."

At the end of their watch, Elcano found Chindarza on the foredeck, and said to him, "You seemed unusually quiet this evening."

"I'm well, sir. I've just been thinking about leaving here, about the long voyage we have ahead of us."

"We have a few more islands to visit before we face the open seas."

"Yes, sir, I know," he hesitated, "it's just that I remember the last crossing so clearly. The hunger and the deaths."

"Ah, my boy, I remember them too. We can only pray that our return will ask less of us. For tonight, let's both try to think of *being* home rather than what it will cost us to get there."

Chindarza gave him a pensive smile. "I'll try, sir."

"You have yet to introduce me to that pretty mother of yours, you know."

"I'll picture that, sir, your meeting her." He chuckled softly, "If she hears of our coming, she'll fuss for days beforehand."

Elcano grinned back at him, then bid him goodnight and went to his own rest.

When dawn broke upon the shore, Almanzor was there as promised. With him were gathered a large number of his family and subjects. The officers met him on the beach to exchange final embraces and thanks. Then they drew away and reboarded their laden ships.

All stood ready. When Polcevera shouted, "Lead us out, Captain Elcano!" a rousing cheer rose from both crews.

Elcano waved to Master Rodas, and Rodas in turn signaled to Acurio, who bellowed, "Weigh the anchor! Full sails! Away, men, away!"

Almanzor joined his people as they shouted their farewells and good wishes.

The *Victoria*, riding low because of her heavy cargo, floated like a pregnant goose to the mouth of the harbor. Elcano turned back one last time, and the smile on his face froze with uncertainty and then slid away. There was trouble aboard the *Trinidad*.

Calling out, "Hold the ship!" he stared back with growing concern.

The flagship's crew was frantically trying to loosen her anchor line but the wind had already caught her sails. The *Trinidad* tilted dangerously far to her starboard side before a seaman with an axe ran to the anchor line and cut the leaning ship loose. At this sudden freedom, she listed to the other side and then swayed back and forth before finally resettling. But just as her men began to take up their stations again to reposition the sails for departure, shouts of alarm drifted up from the hold and spread to the decks and across the water to Elcano.

"She's filling, Captain-general! Man the pumps!"

Rodas appeared at Elcano's shoulder in time to hear him say, "Turn the *Victoria* about, Master Rodas."

By the time the *Victoria* drew near the flagship, her crestfallen crewmen were already unloading their precious cargo. Espinosa came to the rail and called out to Elcano, "She's leaking badly."

Elcano immediately dispatched some of his men to help lighten the load of the injured *Trinidad*, and these hands were soon joined by countless willing islanders.

The next few exasperating hours were spent in an urgent hunt to find the source of the leak. Almanzor even sent divers into the sea, but no hole or crack could be discovered that might explain the source of the water still gushing into the hold. Constant operation of the pumps was needed to keep the water level from rising.

The sun had swung into the western sky before Polcevera, Espinosa, and Elcano came together on the beach, all of them sweaty and exhausted from physical labor and crushing disappointment. Elcano loosened the ties of his shirt and opened it wide to expose his chest to any friendly breeze. "Well, Captain-general," he voiced what they all knew, "it's clear her hull's been badly breached. It will take weeks, maybe even months to repair her."

Polcevera ran his hand across the back of his neck and shot off a string of curses.

Elcano sighed heavily. "Almanzor says the monsoon winds will change before long. If we're to rely on them to take us west, we have no time for delay."

Staring out at the tide, watching it roll gently ashore and then diminish to a line of tiny bubbles before receding again, Polcevera said nothing.

"Sir," Espinosa voiced, "we have choices that must be faced. First, whether both ships should wait until the *Trinidad* is seaworthy, or whether the *Victoria* should head back alone. Since the Portuguese are hounding these waters in search of us, I suggest that the *Victoria* depart at once. That increases the chance of at least one of our ships reaching Spain. As for the *Trinidad*, by the time she can sail again, the winds will have shifted to the east. So we can remain here and wait months for them to shift back, during which time the Portuguese may find us, or at the first opportunity we can sail her back the way we came."

"The way we came?" Elcano asked. "You mean across the Pacific?"

"Not all the way down to Patagonia," Espinosa clarified. "We can sail north until we catch the winds that will drive us east, cross the Pacific until we reach the northwestern coast, and then follow it down as far as the isthmus of Panama. Avila's new settlement should be well established by now. They may even have horses. We can cart our cargo overland to the Atlantic and hire another ship to carry us home."

At last Polcevera spoke up. "I've thought of that possibility, Captain Espinosa, along with a hundred others. But none of us has ever sailed before those northwesterlies."

"None of *us* has ever sailed before the monsoons blowing from the east either, sir, not even Captain Elcano. The fleet's Portuguese officers, the ones that knew that route, they've perished. Carvalho is the last Portuguese who should have been able to help with navigation, and he's not far from death. I doubt he will last the month."

"Well," Polcevera said, mustering a rueful smile at Espinosa, "unlike the first crossing, at least we now have some idea of the actual *size* of the Pacific Sea."

Elcano said, "Sir, if we separate and either ship encounters trouble, there will be no one to give the other aide, no one even to carry word of our fates back to loved ones."

Polcevera hunched down and picked up a handful of sand, then stood and watched it slip slowly from his palm. "I think we should discuss this with the men. They should know what choices lay before us."

"Yes, they should know," Elcano said, and Espinosa gave a nod.

"The two of you tell your crews. Do your best to hide how high the odds loom against us. Report their reactions to me in the morning and we will come to a final decision."

That evening Elcano addressed his crew and then remained with them long after a consensus had been reached, talking of things large and small to hearten them in light of their decision. He spent the rest of the night pacing the half deck and tossing in his sleep, dreaming that he had been set adrift in the middle of a wild, endless sea in a boat without a rudder, charts, or oars.

The day broke to find him, Polcevera, and Espinosa near the trading post, where Elcano disclosed that his crew had agreed with Espinosa's plan to separate the ships. He was not surprised to learn that the men of the *Trinidad* had felt similarly.

"Then it's settled," said Polcevera. "I did a lot of thinking last night, gentlemen, and I've decided that the two guides offered by Almanzor and the eleven Bruneians should sail with you, Captain Elcano. No," he said, holding up a hand, "I'll listen to neither argument nor complaint. That is an order. I told you before, we need those men. By having them sail with you, more of the trained men will remain here to work on the *Trinidad*. Also, Pigafetta has requested to sail aboard your ship and I've given him my permission. He can help the Brunei men improve their Spanish and he may be useful as a translator when you stop to take on more food supplies."

"Yes, Captain-general."

"Choose six of your men to remain with us to equalize the crews."

"Yes, sir. If you don't object, Captain-general, I'd like to lighten the *Victoria's* load by removing about sixty quintals of cloves. It would ease some of the pressure on her seams."

Polcevera hesitated. "That's undoubtedly prudent, Master Elcano, but unload no more than is absolutely necessary. You may store the excess cloves in the trading post. Is there anything else?"

"I wish we had been able to trade for salt while we were here, sir. I hope Almanzor is right in his belief that it can be purchased on Timor."

"Yes, we too must find a supply of salt. Without it, the meat and fish we acquire won't last long. When do you intend to sail, Captain?"

"As hard as it will be to leave, sir, there is nothing to be gained by waiting. I thought to set sail tomorrow. We could be ready as early as this evening, but I'd like to give the men remaining here a chance to write letters. We'll do our best to deliver them before you reach home."

"Excellent idea, Captain Elcano. I'd like to add my own letter to your package."

"Mine too," said Espinosa.

"One more thing, gentlemen," Polcevera said, "Tomorrow, when the *Victoria* sets sail, we will no longer be in need of a captain-general. I will then relinquish my position and assume the office of pilot aboard the *Trinidad*." Espinosa opened his mouth to object only to be silenced by Polcevera just as Elcano had been. "You've shown yourself to be a fine leader, Captain Espinosa, and I have full confidence in your abilities. Much to my own surprise, I've discovered over the last few weeks that I have little taste for command. I believe the prospects of our ship's safe return and of our venture's successful completion will be increased under your steerage."

Standing tall and clearing his throat, Polcevera gave each captain a quick, poignant glance. "For your many services and for your loyalty to me, gentlemen, I thank you both sincerely." Allowing not a word in response, he turned and strode away.

Elcano and Espinosa stood silently watching until Polcevera disappeared into the trees. Then Elcano said, "Well, Gonzalo?"

"Who'd have believed that, out of all the men that started out on this expedition, I'd be captaining the flagship on her voyage home?"

"Even so, she'll be in capable hands."

"Ten thousand miles at the least."

"Through unknown waters most of the way."

"God help us."

"I think he will, Gonzalo. Remember that the *Trinidad* will have fifty-four good men serving under you."

"You will be sailing the *Victoria* through waters guarded by Portuguese wanting nothing more than to kill every man aboard her. And if you're lucky enough to make it to Africa's southern point, you'll face the most treacherous cape in the world."

"I'll do my best to keep out of the Portuguese sailing routes. As for the cape, there, I will ask for extra help from

God. You, my friend, must stay watchful for treachery even before you leave Tidore. So far, Almanzor has shown himself to be trustworthy, but be wary of his chiefs and the rajahs from the other islands."

Espinosa nodded. "Most of the natives to the south are cannibals, if what I hear is true." A scowl grew more pronounced on Espinosa's face until he burst out with, "Damn it all, Juan Sebastian! Curse the luck that forces us from each other's side! Come what may, it would be easier if we faced it together."

"There's no doubt of that, but we've seen first-hand how seldom providence asks what our preferences might be."

"I will hold the thought that in a few months we will meet again in Seville," said Espinosa. "There, we will tell each other a story for every day we've spent apart. Every one."

With the utterance of these words, a strange premonition came over Elcano, a feeling telling him there would never be a reunion with Espinosa in Seville. Was it his own death he sensed, or that of his friend? His eyes searched those of Espinosa. Shaking off the unsettling notion with an effort, he smiled and said, "They will be stories worth hearing."

"Damn it all, Juan Sebastian." Espinosa repeated, his voice falling. "I shall miss you."

"And I shall miss you."

Espinosa pulled his gaze away. His breathing grew rougher and his voice wavered as he said, "Go now. You have much to do before dawn."

When Elcano threw his arms around him, Espinosa gave him a quick but vice-like hug in return. Releasing his hold, Elcano stepped back and said with determination, "We will see each other again, Gonzalo, in this world or the next." Nodding once to reinforce his words, Elcano turned away and walked toward the skiff.

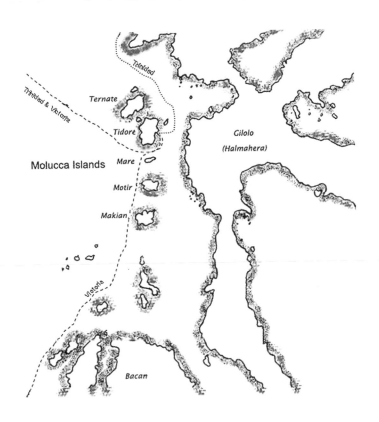

Trinidad

Trinidad & Victoria

Ternate

Tidore

Molucca Islands    Mare

Motir

Makian

Victoria

Gilolo
(Halmahera)

Bacan

# The Valediction

## 21

After reflecting carefully on its likely affect upon his crew and upon himself, Elcano had finally decided not to go ashore with the others. To bid what may well be an ultimate farewell to these men, men that were fiercely bound to him through unimagined trials and death, was a thing he feared he could not do, not if he meant to maintain an encouraging countenance before his sailors. He had deemed it better to remain aboard the *Victoria* and offer strength to those aboard.

But the hours had crawled by with grueling sluggishness and Elcano now noted, for the fourth time, that the sun had already passed its zenith and that the winds were still favorable. It was time to be off and end the prolonged torment of this parting. Standing a little stiffly at the corner of the half deck, absently tightening and loosening the rolled chart in his hands, he watched as the last crewmembers boarded the *Victoria* and the skiff was raised to the main deck.

When Chindarza climbed up the steps to him with pain filled eyes and a canvas sack stuffed with letters over his shoulder, Elcano's hard-won mask of calm nearly yielded. He had borne the weight of tears of most of the forty-seven Europeans and one or two of the thirteen islanders, but Chindarza's sadness tightened Elcano's chest and forced him to push his pent-up emotions back into submission.

Somehow he held his voice steady as he asked, "You've said your goodbyes, Chindarza?"

"I have, sir. It's hard to leave them."

"Yes, son, very hard."

"They'll be all right though, won't they, sir?"

"We must believe that they will."

"Captain Espinosa sent you a message, sir. He said, 'Tell that Captain of yours that my prayers will go with him.'"

Elcano turned and looked ashore. Espinosa was there, standing in the shade of the trees beside Polcevera. After a moment, as if sensing Elcano's gaze, Espinosa lifted his head and waved his outstretched arm. Elcano returned the gesture, thinking, *May God be with you too, my friend.*

Chindarza pulled in a breath and said, "We'll manage, won't we, sir."

"That we will, Chindarza."

"We're heading toward home, Captain Elcano."

"Yes, we are, and we'd better get started, hadn't we? Get those letters stowed in my cabin, Chindarza, then see that nothing in storage shifts out of place as we set sail."

"At once, sir."

Acurio, who had been overseeing the securing of the ship's launch, turned to him and called out, "All's ready, Captain."

Elcano gave the signal to Master Rodas, who passed it along to Acurio, who barked the orders, "Man aloft and men to the lines! Up anchor! Sails full away!"

Even as the *Victoria's* men moved to obey and their ship began to stir, their eyes shifted back to the shore. Elcano watched with them as the *Trinidad's* two skiffs slid into the water and unfurled their small sails to grasp at the breeze. Their prows lifted and the boats heaved forward. As they neared, Elcano could not pull his eyes away from the men in the oncoming boats. Some waved arms and some their shirts. Some called out good wishes and blessings, and some sobbed unashamedly under the glaring sun.

Espinosa was at the head of the lead boat. He drew close astern, cupped his hands, and yelled, "Farewell, until Seville! Farewell!"

Elcano stretched out over the stern castle, his face betraying his internal struggle to keep from weeping. His throat tightened with such force that it would allow little air and not a single word to pass through. Mutely, he continued to wave as a fresh wind filled the *Victoria's* sails and shoved her farther and farther from the small boats. At last, Elcano lowered his arm, allowed himself one final look at the diminishing faces, and then forced his mind and body to come around, to face his saddened men, to face the south sea and whatever it might bring.

After a moment or two, Elcano joined the two pilots that Almanzor had provided to direct them as far as the island of Timor, and together they bent over his chart to study and discuss their next landfalls.


Four days after leaving their companions at Tidore, Christmas dawned hot, calm, and lonely. Without a priest aboard, no mass could be conducted, but Elcano led the men in special prayers and songs to mark their third Christmas away from home. But this Christmas, the men repeatedly reminded one another throughout the day, they were sailing back to family and loved ones with the scent of cloves and cinnamon filling the air to attest to their accomplishments. And to these they raised a toast with cups holding the small measure of palm wine that their captain had allotted.

In the first few days of the year 1522, the *Victoria* approached a string of islands that stretched from east to west before the much larger island of Timor and, according to the native guides, ran nearly to Sumatra. While the ship was still several miles out to sea, however, the clear sky that had been calm for so long suddenly gathered itself into a dark and swirling fury. As if bent on vengeance, the wind, the rain, and the sea conspired for days to jar and batter the solitary ship while her crewmembers gritted their teeth and strained their muscles to hold her to her course. Heavily laden as she was, the stress from the continuous storm caused small fissures to open in the *Victoria's* hull, allowing water at first to seep and later to pour into her hold. Elcano ordered his men to the pumps and added his own prayers to those of his men, pleading for divine help to remain afloat. When they finally brought their leaking ship to a safe anchorage off the island of Ombai, Elcano inspected the hull carefully and concluded that it would take over two weeks to reseal it properly.

Dusk was still two hours away, and Elcano sent Acurio and an armed landing party ashore to see what food the island might offer. When the boat reappeared, Elcano could see by Acurio's expression that his news would not be good.

"There's little food to be had, Captain," Acurio reported. "What this island has plenty of is natives. We encountered three of them while they were fishing. Pigafetta and Almanzor's guide talked to them a bit and found out that they eat fish only when there's nothing better to be had. What's better, according to them, is human flesh, Captain. After hearing this, we didn't tarry long enough for the rest of their clan to show up."

Elcano cast a glance ashore. "The men are worn out. We can't afford to set guards night and day and still hope to finish the repairs quickly. Acurio, are you willing to go ashore again and barter with the natives."

"Barter with them, Captain?"

"Yes, take the same men, plenty of arms, and a few of our trade goods. Have Pigafetta tell them that the gifts are for their leader, as a sign that we want to form a friendship with him. If they insist on giving us anything in return, accept it."

"You know I'm willing, sir. But you've never seen the likes of these creatures. To think of them as friends is enough to give a grown man nightmares."

"Better friends than foes, Acurio."

"True enough, Captain. I'll be off at once."


Acurio was back before the sun had set, informing Elcano that his gifts had worked as well with the cannibal leader as they might have with a far more civilized man. "The heathen pledged to let us be, Captain, and I believe he means to keep his word." Acurio held up two strings of fish for Elcano's inspection. "He sent you these, sir, and I was mighty glad that it wasn't man flesh he was offering us."

"I couldn't agree more. Well done, Acurio."

Though the locals persisted in visiting the ship daily, Elcano and his crew found these appearances more fascinating than hindering. At their first appearance, Elcano understood Acurio's comment about them inspiring nightmares. Every brown-skinned adult male wore his hair piled high upon his head and held in place by a crude collection of long-toothed combs. Their beards were divided into many strands and then twisted and fitted into long bamboo tubes. The natives' adornments, combined with an invariably fierce countenance, created such an astounding effect that they drew startled gasps or curses every time a native appeared unexpectedly.

Despite these frequent distractions, the men worked with diligence, and Elcano was pleased when the repairs were completed in good time. Before the end of January, the *Victoria* left Ombai, crossed the strait to the south, and resettled her anchor off the shores of Timor.

As the men made final landing preparations, Elcano and Pilot Albo scanned the sandy harbor, noting the single junk and many proas resting there. The natives, many of which were clearly visible as they moved about their small village at the water's edge, looked much like those they had seen at other less than prosperous islands. They wore no clothing other than a two-inch wide loincloth made from tree bark, and they wore their hair long and bound only with a thin strip of cloth. A young woman near the water's edge drew Elcano's attention and he pointed her out to Albo. "Look at her, Pilot," he said with a sinking voice.

"Leprosy, Captain?"

"It may be. And look over there, that woman's face and chest have the marks of the same disease."

Elcano called Bustamente over to join them. The barber studied the women for a moment before offering, "Sir, I've seen similar disfigurements on those suffering from the pox of St. Job."

Albo asked, "The whore's pox?" He stared back at the islanders. "Yes, it's possible."

"And this is our last chance to stock up on food for the crossing," Elcano muttered in frustration. "Well, whether it's leprosy or the pox, we can't take a chance of the men catching it."

An unhappy murmur was already spreading throughout the crew when Elcano stood before them and announced, "As you all know, we must still purchase provisions to see us back to Spain. Because of the disease here, very few of you will be allowed to go ashore." When voices began to rise in protest, Acurio shouted them down so that Elcano could continue. "Our two guides from Almanzor, as we agreed, will part from us here. That will leave only fifty-eight men to get us across the Indian Ocean, around the Cape of Good Hope, up the long coast of Africa, and back to San Lúcar. We can't afford to lose any men to whatever sickness has infested this island." Noting the furtive glances between a few of the men, he added, "If any man is even considering going ashore without permission, think again. To do so would put our entire crew in danger. Other than those specifically chosen by me to acquire food, all must remain aboard the *Victoria* during our stay here."

While most of the crewmembers began to accept this dictate with varying degrees of grace, an apprenticed seaman named Martín de Ayamonte called out, "It will be months before we reach home, Captain. Surely one night ashore is not too much to ask."

Elcano's brows lowered, "Did you not hear me, Ayamonte? One night ashore could mean the death of this expedition."

Astounding most of the men, Ayamonte strengthened his voice and challenged the captain again. "But, sir, we are not even certain what manner of disease it is. It may not be fatal."

Fastening a stare on Ayamonte that would have quelled a less determined man, Elcano said, "So that there will be no mistaking the gravity of my order, hear me now. Any man who leaves this ship and endangers this crew for no better purpose than to slake his lust or appease his curiosity will be subject to execution. Have I made myself clear?" When even Ayamonte held his tongue, Elcano said, "All right then. Back to work, men."

Acurio, noticing a couple of men gathering and grumbling around Ayamonte, strode toward the group and barked out, "You heard the captain. Get your minds off the island women and get back to work."

They dispersed, but Elcano caught sight of the glare Ayamonte aimed at his boatswain before turning away.

Elcano left the half deck to find the two guides from Tidore and asked them to remain in their company just long enough to help in the acquisition of provisions. When they consented, Elcano called Pigafetta to join them. "We need your skill with languages to negotiate for our food."

"I agree, Captain."

"Almanzor's guides will assist you. Take every precaution with your safety and be back well before nightfall."

"I'll do my best, sir."

Pigafetta followed his instructions to the letter, then presented himself at Elcano's cabin just as he and his officers were finishing their evening meal. Addressing Elcano, he said, "There are signs of the pox everywhere, sir, but I avoided contact with all but the village chief. He's willing to trade with us for rice and meat, but the price he's demanding is not only ten times what is reasonable, it's far more than we can pay with the trade goods we have aboard. The old devil seems to know how badly we need the supplies."

"Did you explain that we are unable to pay his price?"

"Yes, sir. He did not believe me."

"Are you certain he can't be persuaded to change his mind?"

"Unfortunately, I am, sir."

Elcano sighed and rubbed his forehead, considering. "Then we must find another village and hope its ruler is more reasonable. Tomorrow we'll sail down the coast and pray for better luck."

"There's one more thing, Captain," Pigafetta said. "There is no salt to be found here, not at any price. Even if we are able to purchase the meat, how will we cure it, sir?"

"We must keep searching for the salt."

Their luck did not improve during the next day or the next. But Pigafetta at last returned to the ships with a barrel-chested chieftain from a village a short distance to the west of their original landing. Elcano welcomed the head-man cordially and took up where Pigafetta's efforts had ended. The island chief confirmed that salt was to be found nowhere in the region. He then said that he could easily pro-vide the other goods Elcano requested but named a price that would have been unheard of on any of the surrounding islands.

Finally, after several fruitless hours of attempted per-suasion, Elcano motioned Master Rodas and Acurio to come closer. "Master Rodas," he said, "please make our guest com-fortable in your cabin. He will remain with us until we can come to some agreement as to a reasonable value for the goods we need."

The chief, suddenly surrounded by unwavering faces, understood his position at once. Obtaining Elcano's permis-sion to do so, the native chieftain went to the rail and called down to the men in his proa, instructing them to provide their visitors all that they requested.

While they awaited the delivery of the victuals, Elcano and his officers repeatedly considered the matter of the lack of salt. Their problem soon became known among the men and one of the Brunei seamen, whom they had named Manuel, stepped forward.

"Captain," he said in heavily accented but adequate Spanish, "my people use pepper."

"They cure meat with pepper?"

Manuel nodded.

"How long does the meat last under this method?"

"Long time, sir."

Bustamente spoke up. "Sir, I noticed some of the women on Tidore curing meat with pepper. It must be a common practice."

"Black pepper, like what we took on at Brunei?"

"Yes, sir."

"Strange. The last time we bought salt was also in Brunei. Manuel, do you know where we can buy salt, other than in Brunei?"

"No, only Brunei."

"But pepper will make the meat last a long time?"

Again Manuel nodded.

"Can you show our men how to cure with pepper?"

"I show," Manuel agreed.

Late the following evening, loads of rice, vegetables, fruit, and the meat of ten pigs, six water buffaloes, and ten goats were delivered to the *Victoria*. When the local chief was released from Rodas' cabin, he was presented with two silken robes, two dozen knives, several decorative swords, and a quantity of other goods that seemed to satisfy his greedy heart. The chief waited aboard until they had been delivered over the side of the ship to his waiting proa. Giving Elcano a parting perusal, he bowed his head and uttered something under his breath before joining his men and returning to shore.

Pigafetta grinned and tried to contain a chuckle.

Elcano looked at him with suspicion, saying, "His last remark was less than favorable, I presume?"

"On the contrary, sir, as closely as I can translate it, he said he wished he had a man like you among his advisers."

Eyeing Pigafetta with even more mistrust, Elcano said, "Is that *exactly* what he said?"

"No, sir, he made a rather bold speculation as to the size of your male organs."

Elcano lifted an eyebrow and they both burst out laughing. "My reputation has preceded me even this far from home."

"Indeed, sir."

Noticing the glances they were drawing, Elcano straightened his expression and said, "Well, Pigafetta, now that the meat is aboard we'd better put the islander's method of curing it to the test."

Within the hour, the crewmembers were better acquainted with the practice of peppering meat than they had expected was possible, but they worked on and on until the sun hung low in the sky.

Hours after the last barrel of cured meat had been stowed, Chindarza's fingers were still tingling from the pepper as he settled into a quiet spot in front of the rear capstan. He started to doze but before sleep had fully overtaken him, Ayamonte's hissing voice drifted to him.

"I tell you it *was* his decision. He was the one that had some of the cloves unloaded back in Tidore. What was left behind means that much less reward for the likes of us. And after all we've suffered."

Chindarza's eyes were open wide now, his ears straining for every word. A voice he didn't immediately recognize said, "But he had to lighten the ship for our own safety. Have you forgotten that the *Trinidad* is still back there being repaired because she was too heavily loaded?"

"Nobody asked you to speak, Galego," said Ayamonte. "We all know you'd lick the captain's boots, given the chance. The rest of you, I say Elcano's got no right to shorten our share of the profits, any more than he has to keep us from going ashore."

"No right?" said Juan de Zubileta, one of Chindarza's fellow cabin boys. "He's the captain."

"Shut your mouth, you young whelp," Ayamonte snarled.

Quietly gathering himself into a crouch, Chindarza inched closer to the men huddled beneath the foredeck.

Ayamonte continued impatiently, "Listen, you lot. It's time we did a bit of our own thinking. Never did men deserve shore leave more than this crew, and I for one am going ashore. I'll be back well before dawn, before I'm ever missed. Now who's coming with me?"

"I'll come," said a cabin boy named Bartolomé de Saldaña.

Before anyone else could answer, Chindarza rose up in front of Ayamonte and said, "You all heard the captain's warning. It's death to any man foolish enough to—"

Chindarza didn't see the knife being drawn as Ayamonte got to his feet, but he saw it now, clutched in Ayamonte's right hand as he shifted slightly from side to side with a sneer on his face.

"Foolish is it? And I suppose you mean to tell him of our plans."

"Have you lost your mind, Ayamonte?" said Galego urgently. "Put the knife down!"

Men from other areas of the ship began to stir and move toward Ayamonte's group. Chindarza lifted his foot to step back but Ayamonte grabbed his arm, yanked him close, and held his knife to his chest. "Oh, no you don't. You'll not move an inch 'til we're gone."

"Gone where?" someone demanded.

"What's going on?" another sailor growled. "Let him go, Ayamonte."

"You're not leaving this ship," said Galego, but Ayamonte was already sidling toward the rail with the knife still held against Chindarza's ribs.

"Come on, Saldaña," Ayamonte said. "It's time to be off."

Acurio burst from his cabin four steps ahead of Elcano, but both men froze at the top of the steps when they saw Ayamonte jerk the knife to Chindarza's throat.

Elcano's eyes pinned Ayamonte, and in a voice that chilled those who heard it, he commanded, "Put it down."

In a sudden eruption of motion, Ayamonte shoved Chindarza so hard that he toppled to his knees, and Galego and Zubileta lunged. Elcano and Acurio were leaping down the steps as a cry of pain burst from Zubileta.

Shoving seamen out of his path, Elcano could see several men struggling at the rail. He heard a sudden groan then two loud splashes before he reached the site of the trouble, but the fight was already over. A quick glance revealed Zubileta and Chindarza standing near the rail on either side of Galego. The men stood back to give Elcano a clear view of the water, but it was too dark to see any movement on its black surface. Only his ears told him that the swimmers were moving quickly toward the beach. He yelled out, "Ayamonte, get back to the ship!"

"Saldaña is with him, sir," said Galego, just as Pilot Albo and Master Rodas appeared among the men.

Elcano lifted his voice. "Saldaña, I order you to turn around! You'll find nothing but death on that island!"

But there was no response and no change in the rhythm of the swimmers' strokes.

"Should we man the boat, Captain?" asked Albo.

"They'll have reached shore before we can get near them." Letting out a frustrated oath, Elcano said, "The villagers will cut them to pieces for coming ashore at this hour."

"The bloody fools," muttered Rodas.

Without warning, Chindarza crumpled to the deck.

Elcano dropped to his side, turning and lifting him in his arms, searching for a wound. "Bring a lantern! Bustamente!" he shouted, but his left hand was already wet with blood.

Four lanterns were thrust toward Chindarza while Bustamente pushed through the crowding men and Elcano quickly untied and opened Chindarza's shirt. Elcano's lungs squeezed tight. So much blood. Bustamente knelt down beside him and wiped at Chindarza's chest with a large cloth, sopping up blood, searching for the wound. "There!" he said. Before Bustamente covered the gash with a cloth Elcano caught a glimpse of it. He offered a quick, silent prayer of thanks. The wound did not seem to be as serious as he had feared. Chindarza was bleeding heavily, but his heart and lungs appeared not to have been punctured. If the deep slice below his collar bone remained free of contamination, Chindarza would surely live.

Elcano lifted his gaze to find Zubileta watching over them with worried eyes. "Are you hurt, son?"

"Just a slight cut, sir," Zubileta said, moving his hand away from his forearm to reveal his bloody sleeve.

"As soon as he's finished with Chindarza, let Bustamente see to it."

Zubileta obediently settled down near Chindarza as Acurio knelt down between them to place a bucket of water within Bustamente's reach. Just above a whisper, Acurio said, "You'll be needing this."

With Bustamente's first stitch, Chindarza jerked back to consciousness and let out a howl of protest loud enough to reassure every man on the ship of his chances for survival. Even so, many of them stayed close by as Bustamente worked. While Acurio held a lantern overhead, Elcano remained at Chindarza's shoulder, assisting Bustamente by repeatedly wiping away the blood from the wound. When the wound was nearly closed, Elcano realized that not a sound or sight had come from shore to reveal the activities of the pair that had fled the ship.

After both cabin boys had been treated and given a cup of palm wine to help them sleep, Elcano had his men move Chindarza to a cot in his cabin. Pilot Albo found his captain an hour later, sitting in a chair he'd moved to just outside of his cabin door and gazing up at the sky.

"How's Chindarza, sir?"

"Sleeping quietly, Pilot."

"Do you still intend to sail in the morning, sir?"

"I do. The boys will heal just as quickly away from this diseased port, and it would be senseless to send more men after the two we've lost."

"That's true, sir. If they're not slain, they'll face the sickness of this island."

"Two men gone and two boys wounded, Pilot. First storms, then no salt, and now this."

"Perhaps these will be the last of our troubles, sir."

"We must hope so. Bring a chair, Pilot. Let's study these stars while we can."


Over the next few days the men of the *Victoria* sailed westward down the coast of Timor, buying every bit of available food and searching unsuccessfully for even a small amount of salt. When they reached the western tip of the island and veered to the south, the Indian Ocean suddenly opened before them and beckoned.

As Elcano directed his ship into this strange sea that was all too familiar to those who hunted them, every man was alert and watchful.

Reluctantly, Elcano ordered the ship's banners to be taken down. "If we are spotted by the Portuguese," he told his men, "anonymity may buy us a minute or two. Even that much time may mean the difference."

# Homebound Winds

## 22

"**N**ow, lad, where's your patience?" Acurio asked Chindarza, sitting on his cot in the captain's cabin with a heavy bible spread open on his lap. "It's been nearly a *week*, sir, and Bustamente says my wound is healing cleanly. Zubileta's been back at his tasks for days now."

"I know, but Zubileta's wound was a mere scratch compared to yours. Do you suppose the captain is likely to take chances when it comes to you? If you haven't realized it by now, you've come to be like a son to him, a son he may never have for himself."

"Even if I *was* his son I'd want to get back to work, sir."

"I haven't the least doubt of that. You're much like him, you know?"

"You think so, sir?"

"Well, at least as far as your stubbornness and impatience." The look Chindarza tossed him made Acurio laugh out loud. "Give it a while longer, my boy. I dare say you'll have work aplenty when the captain sends you back to it." Pointing to the bible, he said, "Just you take advantage of the time you have and read that holy book. It just might do you some good."

"The Greek is coming very slowly, sir. I don't want the captain to know just *how* slowly, so I sometimes ask Pilot Albo and Master Rodas to help me with the words."

"You're a lucky lad to have an educated captain, as well as two officers that happen to come from the isle of Rhodes."

The door swung open and Elcano stood there eyeing Chindarza thoroughly. "How's the shoulder feeling?"

Chindarza flexed his arm. "Quite well enough to be tested, sir."

"In a day or two, perhaps. We don't want that wound to open again. And I'll hear no arguments about it."

Chindarza flashed Acurio a dejected glance.

Not bothering to hide his smile, Acurio headed for the door. "I'd best go check on the working men, sir."

To Chindarza's relief, he was allowed to resume some of his duties the next day. When Acurio called him from the cabin, handed him a brush and a bucket, pointed to the forecastle, and said, "Use your left hand mostly," Chindarza actually thanked him. His workloads were increased slightly with each watch until he had retaken his full weight of responsibilities.

Chindarza was often allowed to assist Elcano with the navigation of the *Victoria* as he held her to a route running well south of Java and Sumatra, and out of what he guessed to be the sea-lanes traveled most often by the Portuguese. Elcano kept double lookouts aloft to watch for any sign of an unfriendly sail, but day after day passed with none being sighted.

For well over a month they sailed on before favorable winds and under hospitable skies. Walking about the ship, listening to men joke and describe the plans they meant to implement once they reached Spain, Elcano dared to hope that their voyage home would continue to be blessedly uneventful. He began to fantasize about Teresa, Chindarza's mother, forming a mental image of her appearance and her nature. He even began to nurture thoughts of building a family with her. At night, he often dreamed of her. Sharing his musings with no one, they became all the more real and promising in his mind.

By mid-March, his hopes for an undemanding crossing were threatened when the breeze became more brisk and began to shift. Soon the wind that had been driving the *Victoria* had half circled the ship and was beating at her prow with overwhelming force. Now Elcano and his men had to fight for every mile they gained.

The farther to the south they journeyed, the harsher the cold became on the breath of the wind. After so many months in the equatorial heat and with so little opportunity to replace or enhance their light clothing, the frigid blasts of wind and sprays of water bit like fangs into the exposed flesh of the sailors. Although rough canvas from the sail cloth was once again fashioned into rough cloaks to help buffer the worst of the cold, it became torturous to carry out duties when icy waves spewed over the sides of the *Victoria*.

With the passing of the first day of May, Elcano took heart in the possibility that they had finally worked their way far enough to the south to be able to clear Africa's cape by now heading west. He and Albo had tried for two days to take a reading of the sun in order to determine their latitude, but thick black clouds had blanketed the sky, mocking their many efforts. Frustrated by the uncertainty of their position but unwilling to subject his men to the bitter cold any longer than necessary, Elcano abandoned his efforts to confirm their location and directed the *Victoria* northwestward.

Late one morning as Elcano and Rodas stood over the compass box in front of the tiller, discussing the latest small adjustments to their heading, Acurio appeared before them with a look of dread on his face. "It's not good news, sirs. The *Victoria's* leaking badly."

"Show me," Elcano said, and they immediately made their way to the hatch.

Descending into the hold, where the combined scents of the cloves and bilge water bit at his nostrils, Elcano saw the tiny trickles spilling from several places on each side of his ship's hull. He waded through cold, shin-deep water and around the crates and barrels to reach the largest of the starboard leaks. Running his hand slowly over the seam and feeling the looseness of the decomposing caulking, he drew his arm away and stared at his wet fingers. "Damn," he said quietly.

"Yes, sir," Acurio agreed.

With slow resignation Elcano lifted his hand again. This time he patted the *Victoria's* hull and muttered low and unintelligible words, as if he were comforting a faithful but wounded horse.

Knowing that this weakening of his ship would slow their progress even more, and that their provisions were being drained with the passage of each day they wrestled against the contrary winds, Elcano had no choice. "Organize the men to work the pumps, Acurio. If the seepage doesn't worsen before we round the horn, a few hours a day should be enough to keep her steady. Now, we'd best get out of this water while we can still feel our legs."

Although the elements seemed to be withholding the worst of their fury, neither the weather nor the rolling sea allowed for the building of a fire, and Elcano was powerless to provide his officers or crew with even the comfort of a hot meal.

Rice could only be soaked in cold water, which did little more than make it chewable. The pepper-cured meat, though it had lasted much longer than it would have without its spicy pickling, had begun to rot in the kegs. To keep what was left of the untainted meat from going to waste, Elcano had recently allowed the men to eat their fill. Better that, than throwing it overboard in a day or two. The last of the spoiling fruit had disappeared weeks ago. What remained of the carefully rationed vegetables would not last much longer. And when those were gone, the men of the struggling *Victoria* would have only rice and water to sustain them.

Three days after the leaks had been reported, Acurio appeared in Elcano's cabin as he was unrolling one of the charts given to him by Polcevera. He looked up and into the troubled face of his boatswain. "What's happened, Acurio?"

"Captain," Acurio said, "I hate to be bringing you more bad news, but it's seaman Iruna. He's sick, sir."

Elcano heard the despair that Acurio was trying to keep from his voice. "How sick, Acurio?"

"Not so bad as yet, sir, but it…it appears to be the same illness that took so many during our crossing of the Pacific Sea."

Elcano released the chart in his hands. "Curse that plague! It hits us when our men are already drained from work and weather. Is Iruna the only one with signs of it?"

"Well, sir, one or two of the Bruneians have been complaining that their teeth hurt when they try to eat."

"What does Bustamente say?"

Acurio took in the dark rings of fatigue under Elcano's eyes, the weary sag to his shoulders. "He says we need to get the men some rest as soon as possible, sir."

"Rest," Elcano echoed, as if the word held a meaning that his mind had almost forgotten. He placed his roughened hands limply on his desk and stared at them. After a moment, he lifted his gaze and said, "See that the sick men get some rest, Acurio, give whatever time we can allot them without dangerously weakening the others. We've still not been able to take a reliable reading of our position, but we should be within a few days of land. Encourage the men to hold on to their faith until then."

"That I'll do, sir."

Rest, however, became a difficult commodity to dole out as more men fell ill with each passing day. When at last a small dark patch of land revealed itself from beneath a hazy cloudbank far ahead, rather than jubilation the sight brought dawning disillusionment. As they drew nearer, more of the barren hills of the African shoreline became visible, confirming that this was no island. But this land that should have appeared to their starboard side lay to their port. They had yet to clear the cape.

Elcano leaned against the *Victoria's* forecastle beside Albo, and in a toneless voice said, "Not far enough to the west."

"Perhaps the clouds will lift tonight, sir, and we can get a reading. The cape surely can't be far."

"We'll still have to face its fury."

"Yes, sir."

Elcano forced himself to rally his dashed hopes and address the situation at hand. Lifting his gaze and scanning up and down the coast as they headed nearer, he called to his lookout, "Keep a sharp watch for sails, Huelva!" Then he looked back over his shoulder, and ordered, "Master Rodas, organize a shore party to search for food and water. See that the men are well armed."

The *Victoria* anchored in a small cheerless bay, and the boat was immediately lowered and loaded. Before it pushed off, Elcano instructed Rodas, "Climb the highest of those hills and read the lay of the coast. God willing, we're not far from the tip of the horn."

Whether by God's will or fate's, Rodas returned several hours later and met Elcano on the main deck with the news that he could see no end to the stretch of the coastline running to the southwest. "What's more, Captain, there's not a sign of man, beast, or edible plant anywhere near this place. All we could gather was a little water."

Grim faced, Elcano said, "Pilot Albo and I managed to take a reading of the sun during its brief showing an hour ago. Your observations coincide with our calculations. We're still six hundred miles from the cape."

Most of the crew had gathered around to hear Rodas' report, and they now began to murmur among themselves. "Sir," a seaman spoke up, "some of the men are sick, the *Victoria's* leaking badly, and we've had little rest in weeks. I say we head for Mozambique." Several other voices echoed this suggestion.

Elcano stretched to his full height, held his head high, and in a tightening voice said, "Mozambique is a Portuguese stronghold."

"The Portuguese may imprison us, sir, but at least—"

Elcano's voice cut him short, "Do you think the Portuguese would show us mercy? They'd more likely torture then behead the lot of us than give us food and a cell. And what of our sworn duty to the king? We now safeguard his cargo, a cargo worth a fortune. Do you propose to surrender it as well as our lives to Portugal? Think back on how far we've come, men, how much we've endured. We *must* finish this mission! Hear me now, every last man. I would far rather die in my attempt to reach Spain than willingly surrender myself, my crew, and this ship to the Portuguese!"

Before Acurio, Chindarza, or anyone else could respond, Bustamente sang out, "We're with you, sir!" Many other voices were quick to join in this pledge, emboldening even the weakest and adding shouts of "To Spain!" and "Home or death!" This refrain rose until all voices of dissent sputtered and stilled.

Elcano ran his gaze over the men shouting and raising their fists before him, and he felt as if his swelling heart would fill his entire chest. He lifted his arms to quiet the men, and said simply, "We'll meet what comes together, men, be it death or glory."

As the crew began to disperse, Elcano noticed the strength of the breeze slowly building.

He kept the *Victoria* at anchor throughout the rest of that day and night, but by early morning the winds had become gales that forced the captain to direct her out to sea to avoid being driven ashore. The sea responded to the rising wind by lifting and rolling into increasingly higher swells. And to the wailing of wind and the crashing of waves, the sky now added its thunderous music.

The *Victoria* rode the hills and valleys of the writhing sea as her men hunched their shoulders against the freezing rain. Hours passed, and then days, and still they grappled against the relentlessness of the storm as they carved their way to the southwest.

On the fourth day of the tempest, Bustamente found Elcano with Acurio directing eight men that were working the lines of the tiller. Reaching for a hold as the ship swayed, Bustamente forced himself to deliver the words, "We've lost a man, Captain. Iruna, he just died."

Elcano gripped the overhang to keep from being tossed about and took a moment to consider Bustamente's news. At last, he said, "May God have mercy on his soul."

"Yes, sir," said Bustamente. "I know it's soon, Captain, and we can't give him much of a service at the moment, but his body, it should be removed, sir. The hold is the only refuge the men have from this storm and many of them are sick."

"Sir," Acurio put in, "we've not much left in the way of old canvas. It's been used up to make our cloaks."

"Find enough to provide Iruna with a hood, at least," said Elcano, "and bind his clothes tightly. When you're ready for me to lead the men in prayers, Bustamente, send someone for me. That much, at least, we must give him."

Short though it was, Lorenzo de Iruna's funeral brought back the memories of many other bodies that had been commended to a different sea but because of the same cruel disease, a disease they did not know how to defeat, or to even ease. And Iruna's was not the last body to be lifted over the *Victoria's* rail by men in danger of slipping into the heaving waters along with it. The body of one of the natives from Brunei, a young man they had renamed Jorge, was the next to splash into the icy waves and disappear. And soon afterward, Bernard Maury followed.

At a brutally ponderous pace, the *Victoria's* officers and crew continued to gain against the sea. They had just crawled beyond the southern most point of Africa and to within seventy-five miles of clearing the huge cape when the storm burst upon the ship with unprecedented force.

Tightly gripping the stair rail, Elcano was descending the last step to reach Chindarza and his group at the tiller, when the first roaring blast of wind hit him head on. He flung himself sideways across the icy main deck at the same time seaman Arratía, who had been emerging from the hatch, was thrown back against it. Both men heard a sudden grinding of wood and metal, and darted their gazes toward the foredeck in time to see the top of the foremast explode.

"Look out!" Elcano yelled. He threw himself behind the base of the main mast an instant before the fore masthead crashed against it, fractured in half and flew up into the air. With his pulse racing and his ears ringing Elcano glanced out to see if Arratía had been crushed by the masthead, but there was no sign of him at all. Before Elcano could gain his feet, the sound of snapping ropes and crackling wood forced his gaze back toward the front of the ship just as the wind ripped the yardarm from the lower section of the foremast and flung it over the port railing as if it were no more than a stick of kindling.

Fumbling to his knees only to discover that one of them had been badly bruised, Elcano managed to stand. He looked toward the hatch again and was relieved to see Arratía lifting his head above its opening. Glancing over his shoulder, he saw Chindarza and Acurio working their way toward him.

"Was anyone hurt?" he asked as Acurio reached out and demanded, "Are you all right, sir?"

The three of them retreated to the cover of the half deck. When the wind lessened slightly, Elcano decided that repairs to the foremast must at least be attempted. But as the storm raged on, they were unable even to replace the lower yardarm, and they were forced to sail the damaged and leaking *Victoria* forward by sheer muscle and will.

With the foremast useless, even more men were needed to maneuver what sails they dared to raise to drive the ship on. For two days and nights, with no sleep for any man with strength enough to work, they fought the storm's onslaught. At last Elcano climbed with faltering steps to the foredeck and clung to the base of the ruined mast to search for what he knew must be close. There in the misty distance, a sharp point of land curved toward him. A mile farther and they would clear the cape.

As the sleet beat against his drenched clothes and skin, Elcano silently pleaded, "Blessed Mother, help us now! Ask your son to have mercy on this ship!" He blinked toward shore. So close. So close. Cupping a hand to his mouth, he shouted with the wind, "We're almost clear, men! Hold her steady!"

As the current grabbed at the *Victoria's* keel, thrusting her forward and turning her slightly to the north, the wind shifted slightly and suddenly surrendered a measure of its power. The ship swept past the cape's point and then its curving outer coast until land no longer impeded her progress. The shoreline broke to the north and the wind, capitulating even more, lowered its howl to a soft, muttering moan.

Weak cries of deliverance burst from the men of the *Victoria*. Wet, calloused hands reached out and clasped those of the next man. Soaked bodies clutched at one another as tears spilled and mingled with the rain.

Chindarza climbed to the foredeck where, against every law of sea etiquette, Elcano reached out and pulled him to his chest, holding him tightly and saying not a word. A moment later the ship's movements drew them apart, and they descended to the main deck to join the rest of the crew. The storm continued to relent with each mile they sailed.

Knowing they needed to find a harbor that would offer a protected place to repair their ship, Elcano ordered the men to sail on throughout the day. Seventy miles from the cape, they brought the decimated *Victoria* into the quieter waters of a sizeable bay. Cautiously scouting its inner edges for any sign of a Portuguese presence and finding no human of any kind, Elcano finally allowed the men to lower the anchor inside a secluded inlet. After the crewmembers had tied off their lines and eaten a bowl of hot gruel, all but a small group assigned as lookouts were allowed to find the driest space available and fall into a deadened sleep.

One step at a time Elcano pulled himself up the stairs toward his cabin. Before he entered it, however, he scanned the rocky shore once more, noting in the fading light the multitude and variety of birds. As he watched, he could just make out through the thinning clouds a warm, half moon and the very first of the evening stars. He heard footsteps behind him that he recognized as Chindarza's and, turning, he offered a weary smile.

"Aren't you going to sleep, sir?"

"My body is ready, but my mind resists."

"What are you thinking about, sir?"

Elcano leaned his back against his door and gave a short, sad laugh. "Actually, I was wondering if my mother might have a cure for our men. She's a healer in our village. She always had a cure for whatever ailment showed up at our door. Bustamente's doing all he can, but this disease ignores our efforts. Men are still dying."

"Now that we've passed the cape, sir, we'll get the rest we need. That should help."

"Yes, it should, but Ortega may be too far gone already. Is he still refusing to eat?"

"He is, sir, even the gruel we brought him this evening."

"Tomorrow I'll have the healthiest of our men do some fishing and hunting. We'll all welcome something in our bellies besides rice and water."

"I'm healthy, sir. I'd like to go." Chindarza said, before releasing a huge yawn.

"All right, but it's time we both got some sleep. Your cot and my bunk will feel like feather beds tonight."

As had been feared, the next day began with news of Juan de Ortega's death. "At least," Elcano told Acurio, who had just been the bearer of these tidings," we can see to it that Ortega is given the benefit of a funeral service and a grave ashore."

After the last prayer of farewell had been said, and the body had been lowered and then covered with dirt, they marked Ortega's grave with a simple wooden cross.

To help bring their minds back to the matters of the living, Elcano had Rodas and Acurio organize the men into details to gather what food, water, and wood the harbor might yield. Others were set to work pumping the ship and preparing her seeping seams to be caulked. With the less than hearty state of the men, the hunters brought only three birds back to the ship by late afternoon. The fishermen had a little better luck with the nets, however, and late that afternoon the crew feasted on as much hot fish stew as they could eat.

At his table, Elcano and his officers eyed Chindarza approvingly as he ladled out their soup. Suggesting that his cabin boy join them, which Chindarza agreed to only after the request had become a direct order, Elcano and the others set to the task of slurping up every mouthful. The bowls were soon filled for a second time.

"Another week in this bay," said Rodas, lifting his brimming spoon, "And we'll have food enough to see us on our way."

"If only we had the salt to keep it well," said Albo.

"Yes, but we still have a little pepper left," said Elcano. "That will help. Now, for tonight, let's enjoy our supper, Pilot. We have earned it."

When Chindarza let out a loud belch, even Albo grinned.

That single meal seemed to add vigor to the efforts of the men the following day, and by mid morning they had brought in more fish than they had caught the entire preceding day. The sun appeared, forcing the memory of its warmth upon the chilly landscape and sending light down the hatchway and into the hold. There, Elcano stood with his hands on his hips, scrutinizing the work of the ship's carpenter, Richard Normand.

"She's nearly dry enough, Captain. In a few hours we can start the caulking. I just wish we had more than a bucketful of pitch left, sir. It won't go far."

"One thing at a time, Normand. The men have done a fine job pumping her dry. She'll soon..." He hushed at the sound of running feet above their heads. Striding quickly to the stairs, he was half-way up them when he nearly collided with Acurio. "It's a Portuguese trading nao, Captain! One of our men just spotted her entering the bay."

"Has she seen us yet?"

"Not yet, sir. She's barely cleared the mouth."

"Get the men aboard, Acurio," Elcano said as he took the rest of the stairs three at a time.

Acurio was on his heels until they reached the main deck, and then he hurried to the stern to call the men back to the ship. Chindarza, who was fishing from shore, lifted his head at Acurio's holler. Without waiting to be asked, Chindarza thrust his length of net into the hands of the man standing next to him, called for Zubileta to come with him, and raced off to collect the rest of the crew. The hunters had been instructed not to wander far from the ship, and Chindarza caught up with them within minutes.

Onboard the *Victoria*, which had been anchored behind a point where she was not immediately visible from the mouth of the bay, men were already in position at the anchor and sail lines. Elcano stood at the forecastle with Rodas and Albo, his eyes fixed on the Portuguese ship just drifting into view. "See that Acurio stays with the gunners, Master Rodas, and that he keeps the portals closed until I give the word." Rodas hurriedly left his side to convey these orders while Elcano said to Albo, "Look at her, Pilot. She's more heavily armed and in far better condition than the *Victoria*. Our best defense may lie in looking too shabby to bother with."

Glancing over his shoulder, Elcano saw that the fishermen had just finished boarding, the skiff was pulling away to return to shore, and the hunters had nearly reached the waterline. Facing the Portuguese ship again, he watched as she slowed and her remaining sails were lowered between them and the mouth of the bay. "She's blocking our way."

Albo said tensely, "They're lowering their skiff, Captain."

Elcano turned and strode to the top of the steps, staring at their launch already heading back toward the ship, willing it to move faster. The men were straining at the oars, their faces fearful. Silently, Elcano urged them, "Hurry, men!" Calling to the deck below, he said, "Master Rodas, we've not a moment to lose."

"Noted, Captain."

By the time the last of the *Victoria's* hunters was grabbed and hauled onto the deck, the Portuguese skiff had pulled to within seventy yards of her port bow. The hunters dropped the carcasses of four birds, leaped over the spilling nets of fish, and hastened to reach their shipmates at the lines. Holding the launch's lead line high over the head's of several braced seamen, Chindarza scrambled to the corner of the stern castle to tie down the skiff.

Observing that the gunports facing them had still not been drawn open, and praying that quick action would trap the Portuguese captain in indecision, Elcano signaled to his officers. At Rodas' shout, first the anchor line and then the sail lines were jerked into motion. Men gritted their teeth and pulled for all they were worth.

Elcano could see the faces of the men in the Portuguese launch now. Curious, suspicious faces. "Full ahead," he said and heard Rodas' immediate echo. Leaving the foredeck with measured strides, Elcano forced himself to move slowly all the way down the stairs, across the main deck, and up the steps to the half deck. Once there, he faced forward again. The *Victoria* was picking up speed and as she approached the skiff, a young Portuguese officer stood up and waved his arms for them to halt. He shouted out in his native tongue, "Lower your sails!" But Elcano and his ship slid past the boat as if its occupants had been neither seen nor heard.

The ship lay before them, holding her position squarely in the center of the bay before its mouth. She was new and magnificent, Elcano acknowledged, even as he sensed that she was concealing her superior power like a huge, watchful predator. He saw that her gun ports were still closed, and he guessed that her captain was playing the same waiting game as he. At this thought, a grim smile crossed his mouth, and narrowed his dark eyes.

As the *Victoria* decreased the expanse of waters between them, the Portuguese ship raised only enough sail to glide toward them on an intercepting course. Elcano did not slow his ship, nor did he move from his position on the half deck. He merely said, "Eyes ahead and steady on, men."

Elcano saw that the other ship had underestimated the *Victoria's* increasing speed, had been a moment too slow in raising her sails. She was not moving fast enough to cut them off. Keeping his chin up and his face aimed ahead, Elcano kept his eyes trained on the Portuguese gunports. If the foreign ship held its present speed, the *Victoria* would cross in front of her. But there were still her guns.

The Portuguese captain suddenly yelled across the diminishing space between them, "Declare yourselves! Where are your colors?"

Elcano gave no answer. His hands, clasped together behind his back, tightened imperceptively with every second that passed.

"Declare yourselves, you pack of pirates!" At this warning, the Portuguese gunports were heaved open and the snouts of polished cannons were thrust into view.

Albo tensed and locked his gaze on Elcano, anticipating the order to open the *Victoria's* cannon ports. But Elcano, almost imperceptibly, shook his head.

"I am Captain Pedro Cuaresma, in the service of His Majesty King Manuel of Portugal. Identify your ship at once!"

Elcano pivoted slowly toward the ship fast approaching their port side. Cuaresma's men were moving to and from their armaments storerooms, but Elcano gave no sign of noticing this. His eyes met those of the Portuguese commander. In a heartbeat he took in the immaculate dress, the thick chest, and the impatient expression of his adversary, and then he saw that his own sunken cheeks and tattered clothing had momentarily shocked his adversary.

"Captain Cuaresma," Elcano addressed him in Portuguese and in a friendly manner, "It is always an honor to meet a relative at sea."

"Relative? I am no relative of yours, and slow that disreputable ship or—"

"But of course we are related, Captain," Elcano went on as he continued to gauge the distance between the *Victoria* and the ship bearing down on them. "And we are anything but pirates. Misfortune has tried us, as you can see, but we have been venturing on business of great interest to King Manuel. I suggest that you choose not to interfere with us."

"Then declare your business and your identities at once. And this is the last time I'll order you to lower your sails!"

"Very well, Captain." Elcano unhurriedly turned toward Rodas, a man who by now could read his expressions and tones as well as his words. "Master Rodas, do as the good captain requests. Lower our sails."

"Yes, Captain," Master Rodas replied, just as deliberately. He turned and barked out the appropriate orders while his two hands, held low and out of sight of the Portuguese seamen, gave signals that negated each one. His men responded by making convincing movements that produced no movement whatever in their sails.

Thirty seconds, Elcano thought, and nodded as if well satisfied with his men. He faced Cuaresma again and noticed that the sails of the Portuguese ship were slackening. She was already slowing. "Now, Captain," he shouted, "I was sent on a highly sensitive undertaking by a relative of King Manuel himself. Since we are but servants of our masters, we too are related in a sense."

"Exactly what manner of undertaking, and what is your name?" These words had just been called out when Cuaresma saw a fresh gust of wind tighten the *Victoria's* sails and thrust her forward. The *Victoria* sped past Cuaresma's vessel, slipping to within thirty yards of her prow. Cuaresma had no clear shot at them and no momentum to come about quickly. He watched them slip by, holding back from ordering his gunners to fire.

Just before the *Victoria* had reached the mouth, seeing that the Portuguese ship showed no intention of pursuing them, Elcano called back, "We are no pirates, Captain Cuaresma! I am Captain Juan Sebastian de Elcano, in the service of your monarch's brother-in-law, King Carlos of Spain and Emperor of the Holy Roman Empire!"

Elcano thought he could see amused disbelief on Cuaresma's face. The Portuguese captain gave Elcano a mock salute and shouted, "You'll never reach Europe in that ship, Pirate Elcano! Neither you, your crew, nor that floating wreck is worth the cost of our gun powder!"

The *Victoria* pushed into the open sea where Cuaresma's ship was soon lost from sight.

# A Grievous Toll

## 23

The crew's relief at having escaped the Portuguese ship was soon overcome by the fear that Captain Cuaresma's prediction of their never reaching Spain would prove true. Unable to properly caulk the *Victoria* at sea, the men could do no more than slow her leaking. What food had been brought aboard at their interrupted landing seemed to lessen the symptoms of several of the sick men, but only temporarily. And even though they were discouragingly short on both nourishment and rest, Elcano had no option but to ration the food and order the healthier men back to the pumps.

For ten days he directed the *Victoria* before the trade winds and held her to a northwesterly course. Then, as the heat intensified with every day that they drew nearer to the equatorial sun, more men began to die.

Midway through on afternoon watch, Manuel, the Brunei native who had become a spokesman for his fellow islanders, climbed with Master Rodas to the half deck to find Elcano writing in his journal. Elcano looked up at their approach.

In his mid twenties, copper-skinned, and bearing broad, stoic features, Manual had lost much of his muscular depth over the last ten months. Since he had gone without adequate nutrition for a shorter period of time than his European shipmates, however, his thinness appeared almost robust in comparison. Although his body had diminished, his quiet dignity seemed only to have increased since his capture.

"Captain, Manuel just told me that one of his men has died," said Rodas.

Elcano closed his journal and said, "Paulo?"

Manuel nodded. "I ask Captain for favor."

"Yes, Manuel, what favor?"

"One of my men die days ago, near great cape, sir. No funeral for him. Now one more man die. I ask for funeral for two men. We must sing their spirits to next world, to heaven, sir."

"In the Christian custom or as you do in your country?"

"In my country, we kill water buffalo to bear dead friends to heaven. Priestess sing songs. Here, no buffalo, no priestess. We must sing. If not, the dead will not find ancestors, not protect families left behind."

Considering for a moment all that these men had endured and weighing it against the possibility of showing any disrespect to his own faith, Elcano concluded, "We will honor your dead, Manuel, in both your ways and ours. Make what preparations you wish. The service will be held in an hour."

When all was ready, the funeral ceremony was indeed a combination of rites. Traditional Brunei funeral chants accompanied by drums were followed by Christian psalms and prayers. Manuel spoke words in his native tongue that described the bravery and diligence of his friends, and he asked that their ancestors guide them to the afterworld. After Paulo's body was at last consigned to the sea and the men began to disassemble, Manuel's gaze met Elcano's, offering solemn gratitude.

Acknowledging Manuel's thanks with a nod of his head, Elcano scanned the rest of his men, several of whom were too ill to stand. *So thin*, he thought. *So weak. And there is no remedy with which to fight this cursed plague.*

With a weariness that clung to his mind as well as his body, he climbed to the stern deck. Before long, Acurio wandered up to the rail where Elcano leaned upon his elbows, his face lifted to the breeze. After a space of thoughtful silence, Acurio said, "Do you wonder much, Captain, about where the *Trinidad* might be now?"

Elcano admitted, "I like to imagine that they've reached Panama. In my mind, Espinosa is leading a long train of mules over the mountains." He laughed softly. "I always suppose he's convinced Polcevera to let a few women trail along with him."

"I'd like to think that too, sir. I surely would."

For the next few minutes, they let the sea and sky enhance every color and texture of their daydreams. But when darker clouds began forming in the distance and heading in their direction, the two officers left the railing to prepare their ship for a new assault. The storm did not keep them waiting long.

Attacking in earnest less than twenty minutes later, the squall elevated the wind velocity and the waves until the weakened *Victoria* was being mercilessly tossed about. Although it was not the most violent storm they had yet faced, the drained men were forced to call upon any small reserve of strength just to keep their ship afloat. Elcano and his officers renounced all deference to rank and shocked their most exhausted men by shouldering them aside at the end of a shift and taking their places at the tiller. As they labored on with little reprieve, some men grew so frail that they could barely find the strength to stumble down into the hold to seek what little sanctuary its sloshing depths might yield.

After days of constant battle against the storm the ship's precious supply of fish had completely disappeared, leaving only a few small barrels of rice. Elcano watched with tormented eyes as men continued to die, and by the time the storm finally eased, scurvy and exhaustion had taken a malevolent toll. Eleven men had been stolen from the *Victoria's* decks and delivered by mournful, weakened hands into the body of a violent sea.

As the sea finally grew calm under a clearing sky, men sprawled about the decks too spent to move. Elcano fell into his bunk and awoke seven hours later, disoriented and angry that Chindarza had not wakened him sooner. But one look at Chindarza's gaunt, tired face silenced any rebuke he might have thrown his way. Instead, he said only, "Get some more sleep, Chindarza, and don't stir until I send for you."

Before sunset that evening, Elcano called his officers and crew together on the main deck and said without preamble, "We must decide whether to risk another landing, and if so, which one. We have two choices; the Guinea coast or the Cape Verde Islands."

"But aren't those islands held by the Portuguese, Captain Elcano?" someone asked tentatively.

"They are. They serve as a major Portuguese port. I told you before that I would never willingly surrender this ship to the Portuguese and I meant it. If we choose to land at the Cape Verdes, we will try to avoid capture by deceiving them as to who we are and where we've been. It may work. If so, there will be plenty of provisions available there. Even so, that landing will pose the greater risk."

"What about Guinea, sir?" someone else asked. "Don't the Portuguese patrol that coast?"

"They do, but not consistently. There is a smaller chance of us being taken if we choose to land there."

"What about food, sir?"

"I don't know what we might find, if anything. Whatever food there will be, we'll have to hunt for it ourselves. And we might have to deal with unfriendly natives. Still, we might *not* have to deal with the Portuguese."

"Which place is closer, Captain?" asked Zubileta.

"Barring another storm, we could reach Guinea in five days. Our present course will take us very near there. The islands lie about two weeks farther on."

"But, Captain, will our provisions not allow us to head straight for Spain?"

"We have only enough rice for three and a half more weeks, and water for not much longer. What provisions and rest we may gain by landing could save the lives of some of our sick men." He watched their faces as they took in this information, and saw them recognize the weight of their choices. "Let me hear the votes of the officers first," Elcano said.

"I say we try for the Guinea coast, Captain,' said Albo. "If we aren't successful there, we can still consider the Cape Verdes."

"That sounds like a good plan, sir," said Rodas.

Acurio gave a sharp bob of his head. "I'll be agreeing with that too, sir."

"Let's hear from the rest of you men," said Elcano. "Who's for the Guinea coast?"

All but a few voices called out their concurrence.

"And the islands?"

Only three or four made this choice.

"Then it's Guinea. As we near the coast, keep a sharp watch, men." As his gaze touched upon each face before him, he was struck by a sudden surge of pride in these dauntless, shabby men. He stood taller and added strength to his voice. "We've cast our net, men. Let's see what it yields."

There was no trace of animal life save for the men of Acurio's hunting party, slowly rowing the *Victoria's* launch toward a long stretch of palm strewn beach. Elcano, watching their progress from the ship, had given them no more than two days to hunt before they must return. The landing party had not even disappeared from his view before Bustamente approached him wearing an expression that had become crushingly familiar.

"Captain, we've just lost Gascon," he said. "Trigueros and Valpuesta look as though they'll not last much longer."

Looking back toward shore for a moment, Elcano lowered his head, and shut his eyes.

"Captain?"

"I heard you, Bustamente. Go back to them. Pray that Acurio returns with a full boat."

Men had already been assigned to cast their nets over the *Victoria's* side, but when the nets were pulled back in they held only enough fish to flavor a thin soup. All day, all night, and well into the following afternoon they pumped and caulked and waited and prayed. By the time Acurio again appeared on shore, downcast and quiet, the ship held three fewer men.

The boat rowed closer until Elcano could see into its bottom. Except for the barrels that had been rowed ashore, it was empty. Acurio climbed aboard and reported to Elcano with a disheartened face. "We found nothing but a bit of water, sir, and that was miles inland. To gather enough to fill these few kegs we had to wait at the spring for hours."

Knowing they dared not linger, consuming what little stores they had on a fruitless chase, Elcano ordered the anchor raised. Sluggishly, the *Victoria* yielded to her men and her sails, and again headed northwestward into open waters.

Stormy weather trailed in her wake like a pack of wolves after wounded prey, breaking upon the *Victoria* with ruthless persistence and gnawing at her bow as she tried to move forward. Several days later, Elcano buried another of his men.

Alone in his cabin that evening, he entered the name of Martín Magellan on a special page at the back of his journal, noting the date of June 26, 1522. He stared at the entry, remembering.

Martín had signed on as a supernumerary, no more than a passenger, but he had ended up serving the *Concepción* and then the *Victoria* in countless ways, far beyond what he could have imagined at his outset. Elcano pictured Martin on the day of the fleet's departure from San Lúcar, almost childlike in his enthusiasm to accompany his cousin, the great captain-general, on his glorious voyage. Glorious. Elcano held the word in his mind. Slowly, he scanned the column of names on the page before him. On the *Victoria's* return voyage fourteen Europeans and seven men from Brunei had already been lost. He thought of Magellan and the many, many others who had died, perhaps Espinosa and the crew of the *Trinidad* were now among the rest. What glory, what reward had been or ever would be bestowed upon them?

He closed his book, blew out the lamp, and sat in sad reflection until sleep overtook him in his chair. When Chindarza found him there a half-hour later, he helped

Elcano to his bunk and drew a patched cover over his haggard frame.

With the first easing of the latest tempest, Elcano again called his crew together on the main deck. They stood before him under the heat of a resurging sun. Shirtless and bony, they stared back, their faces bleak.

"Men, each of us must voice whether or not to land at the Cape Verde Islands. They lay but a week ahead. You all know the risks of capture. If you vote to land, we will tell the authorities that we were separated from a fleet of four ships sailing from the West Indies. We'll say that we were driven off course when we lost our fore mast in a storm. Given that our fore mast is indeed ruined, this tale has a chance of being believed."

Heads began to nod and voices to murmur.

Elcano went on, "Even if this story fools them initially, we have nothing with which to purchase food except the cloves in our hold. If the authorities find out about our cargo, they'll know we've been to the Spice Islands and they'll waste no time in seizing us. If that happens, we can expect no mercy. The landing party must get safely past the questioning at the port, then find a trader who's willing to keep silent until we sail. Now, if the majority of the crew votes for a landing, Martín Méndez and Gunner Argot have agreed to lead the shore party. Gauge the risks, men. It's land in a Portuguese nest or head for home with only a few days supply of food."

The officers voted, and then the remainder of the crew. To a man, they voiced their willingness to risk a landing. Satisfied, resolute, Elcano dismissed them to their rest.

As the days evaporated under the sun's heat, hope and fear built with equal strength in Elcano's mind. *Plan,* he told himself. *Plan to the smallest detail.* He, Albo, Rodas, Acurio, Méndez, and Argot rehearsed a myriad of answers to the questions that might be posed by the Portuguese. They carefully measured and packaged the cloves with which they would barter. They drafted a list of supplies, prioritizing them by those most desperately needed.

On the morning that the islands were finally spotted in the distance, Elcano collected the leaders of the shore party and went over the details of the plan for the final time. After all had been discussed, Elcano said, "Our prayers will be with your every word and step, men."

The wind bore them ever nearer the harbor on Santiago Island, and Elcano had the sails lowered until their speed diminished to a limping scuttle. With tattered sails, torn mast and yard, and a beggarly looking crew, the *Victoria* drifted to a halt within the subdued waters of a watchful bay. Her anchor had barely settled into the white sand at the outer reaches of the harbor before the launch was swung over her side and lowered into the water. Eleven of thirteen men embraced and bid their shipmates farewell. Argot and Méndez, however, bore expressions of determination as they loaded their rowers into the boat.

A moment before pushing off, Argot smiled up at Elcano and said, "We'll see you before sunset, Captain."

The skiff pushed off and Acurio, keeping his gaze on its progress, said, "Well, sir, that leaves just twenty-two of us aboard, and half of them sick. That boat will be a welcome sight when its heading back this way."

Elcano glanced down at the main deck's railing where Chindarza too stared after the boat. "He wanted to go with them."

"Ah, sir, the lad's of an age where danger's a thing to wish for, and he's more curious than most. That's all it is."

"It's more than that, Acurio. He's bent on proving himself, although how he can imagine he still has anything to prove is a wonder. He's done a man's job for nearly three years."

"Even longer than that, sir. When his father and uncle were taken by the same pox, his aunt and two small cousins moved in with him and his mother. He was but twelve at the time, but he became the man of the house. His mother, God bless her, she lightened his burdens as much as she could, but the times asked a lot of the lad. And now, just look at him standing there. Near fit to be tied. I'd best go and give him something else to occupy his mind, sir." With that, Acurio left Elcano to keep watch alone.

Despite Acurio's list of chores Chindarza was back at the railing a few hours later. So it was he who gave the first excited whoop that brought Elcano and the rest of the men rushing back to the rail. Just appearing from the tree line were the members of the landing party, and each man carried a bulging cloth bag or a brimming basket. Argot waved toward the ship, which caused the crew to let loose a responding roar. Elcano pounded heartily on Chindarza's shoulder and shouted, "They did it, my boy!"

Minutes later the launch was bumping the *Victoria's* side and handing bags of rice and coconuts as well as baskets of mangoes up to eager hands.

When Argot and Méndez climbed aboard Elcano gave them each a jarring hug. "Well done! Well done, men! Sit down to some fruit and tell me everything." Turning to Bustamente, he said, "See that our sick men are given something right away."

Each man aboard was hurriedly presented with a mango, and he received it more eagerly than if the fruit had been made of gold. Knives were grabbed from belts and stabbed into peels, and Elcano's short blade did not hesitate before carving free a section of the juicy pulp for himself. Sinking his teeth into the luscious fruit, tasting the sweet explosion on his flavor-starved tongue, Elcano moaned right along with his men. With his mouth filled with a second bite, he said to Méndez, "Was there no trouble at all?"

"None, Captain," Méndez replied as he chewed. "I still can't believe what an easy time we had. The soldiers at the pier didn't doubt us for a minute. Once we made our way to a pub and asked a few questions, we found a trader named Lopes who swore to keep our confidence."

Argot cut in. "He's so eager to get his hands on our cloves, Captain, he gave us these supplies on blind faith."

A chorus of laughter rose from the men crowded around them.

Elcano asked, "And you trust this Lopes to keep quiet?"

"I did as you instructed, sir. I told him we'd pay one-half today and the other half when we had all of the goods aboard," said Méndez.

"He showed little concern for king and country, sir," said Argot. "But after he's got his last payment, then it will be a matter of loyalties."

Questioning them further about Lopes, the meeting place, and the agreed upon price, Elcano finally asked, "Are you two ready to deliver his first payment?"

"Eager to, sir," said Argot. "The way this bunch is gobbling down this load, we'd best be off for more."

"Just one more thing before we go, sir," said Méndez. "It's odd, so odd that I don't know quite what to make of it, Captain, with so many of us keeping track like we've done. But the officials ashore, sir, they swore that today is Thursday rather than Wednesday. They claimed we must have lost a day in our reckoning."

"Lost a day?" Elcano frowned. "It's hard to believe that we've miscalculated."

Pigafetta, who had been listening closely, spoke up. "Captain, do you suppose, since we've been sailing constantly to the west, that we might have gone *backwards* in time by one full day?"

Elcano gave this a moment's thought. "It's possible, I suppose. Yes, quite possible, but I am not a man of science. We'll leave it for the likes of them to argue. As for me, I'll be content to see the cloves lowered to the launch."

The payment was soon loaded, transported past the inattentive port officials, and delivered to the trader without incident.

At the appointed time the following day, the skiff went quietly ashore to pick up a full boatload of the supplies Lopez had promised. When this bounty made its way safely back to the ship, Elcano met it with welcoming arms.

"There'll be another load tomorrow, sir," said Argot with a pleased grin.

"Were you able to get the pitch?"

"Not yet, sir. Our trader says it's not something he usually trades in, but he should be able to include some with our next haul."

"We need that pitch, Argot. Our men are too spent to work the pumps the rest of the way home."

"Yes, sir. I'll see that our next load includes a good supply."

"Are things still quiet ashore? Does Lopes seem calm?"

"Everything is as quiet and calm as this evening breeze, sir. We should have no trouble tomorrow."

In fact, all went smoothly with the next shipment excepting the trader's inability to find the pitch they needed. Obtaining his absolute assurance that he would have some the next day, arrangements were made for one more boatload of supplies. While that evening's sun sank at the edge of the horizon, Argot and Méndez joined the officers for a celebration dinner of goat and rice soup, mashed coconuts, and bananas. Elcano ate his fill and then rubbed his aching stomach in appreciation.

"Captain?"

"Yes, Argot."

"A couple of the men have asked if they might be allowed to go ashore tomorrow."

"After a meal like that, you have my permission to make whatever changes you feel are necessary. And now," said Elcano, rising and moving away from the table, "our good shore party has brought us a special offering. I've been saving it for last. We have just enough for a single toast." Pulling a bottle of Portuguese wine from the cupboard beneath his bunk, he uncorked it and poured a good couple of swallows into each of their cups. Raising his own, he said, "To home shores!"

"To home shores, sir," they all chimed, and lifted the rich wine to appreciative lips.

During the night, the soft breezes gathered themselves into winds so high that Elcano took the precaution of moving the *Victoria* farther out in the harbor. And when the sun reappeared, he decided to hold their position in anticipation of their departure the following day.

As the boat was being loaded, Chindarza hurried to Elcano and said anxiously, "Sir, Gunner Argot said that I may join the shore party." Without slowing his spew of words, Chindarza lowered his voice and went on. "I know you didn't want me going ashore before, sir, but the others have already made three trips, three safe trips."

Swallowing his first instinct to refuse, Elcano studied the pleading eyes before him. After all the young man had suffered, after all he had done, how could he be denied this request? "All right, Chindarza. Just—."

Before Elcano could even tell him to be careful, Chindarza was racing toward the rail and calling back, "Thank you, sir." Scrambling down to the skiff, he waited impatiently for the last man to land in the boat before shoving off, grabbing an oar, and thrusting it into the water.

The wait for the skiff's return felt even longer than before, and Elcano moved about the ship talking with his men to distract his apprehensive mind. Several of those that had been gravely ill were showing definite signs that the fresh food and the easing of their duties were loosening the effects of the disease. Sores were fading, throats were opening, swollen gums were shrinking, pain in joints was lessening, and sleep was becoming more restful. Even their general listlessness was giving way to flickers of anticipation. It would take weeks if not months for them to regain their full health, but Elcano clung to and rejoiced in these promising indications.

He brought a chair from his cabin to the half deck, sharpened his knife on his whetstone, and began to whittle on a small chunk of wood. This simple pleasure he had denied himself for months but with their newly restored supply of wood, he now succumbed to this small indulgence. Working slowly, taking as much pleasure in the process as the outcome, the hull of a small *Victoria* began to take shape. He was just holding it up to inspect the balance of its dimensions when one of his men shouted, "The boat, Captain Elcano!" Still holding his knife and the carving, he strode quickly to the rail. As they neared, Chindarza's expression told Elcano that all had gone well, and Elcano smiled back as if it had never occurred to him to worry.

Once aboard the ship, Méndez reported to his captain, saying, "We've brought plenty of rice but only a small barrel of pitch, sir. Lopes can't get more until this afternoon. I told him we'd come back at two hours before sunset."

Elcano said, "Give what we have to Acurio then. He'll see that it's used wisely."

When the others had left him and Chindarza alone, Elcano asked, "And what is your opinion of this Lopes? Did the man seem trustworthy?"

"I had no chance to speak with him, sir, but from what I heard, yes, he seemed so. But, there is something else." Chindarza hesitated.

"What is it?"

"It's Burgos, sir. He's Portuguese."

"He is. What's bothering you, Chindarza?"

"Well, sir, Burgos seemed very friendly with the men helping us load the rice. None of us could understand much of what he said to them. Perhaps it was nothing, sir. Still..."

Elcano looked around until his gaze fell upon Burgos. "I'll speak to Méndez about him."

After receiving strict assurances from both Méndez and Argot that none of the men would be allowed to fraternize with Lopes' men, Elcano watched the skiff ease away. Chindarza sat in the midst of the rowers, his expression easy as the breeze tossed his long hair into his face.

The sun lowered and Elcano scanned the harbor, telling himself that all was surely well. When the light began to fade, he began to pace. When it disappeared altogether and the boat still did not return, he brought his chair to the rail and positioned himself like a sentinel. He spoke little and then not at all. Only Acurio, who occasionally stood beside him in silence, knew the depth of his anguish.

As dawn's light spread over the decks of the ship, the men awoke to find him still there, watching. Whether he had slept at all, none could say. But when he stood and ordered the *Victoria* to be brought closer into the harbor, men scurried to obey.

Their ship had not yet reached her shallower anchorage when Elcano spotted a Portuguese longboat sailing toward them. They approached to within hailing distance and an officer aboard the launch called out in Spanish, "Captain of the *Victoria*, you are ordered by the commander of this port to surrender your men and your ship!"

The *Victoria's* crew stood unmoving and Elcano made no immediate reply.

The officer went on, "You and your men will be transported to Portugal on a ship due any day from India. There, you and your shore party will be tried for your crimes."

In a voice of undaunted authority rather than acquiescence, Elcano said, "You dared to seize our shore party?"

"They are safe for now."

"By laying hands on his seamen you have interfered with the orders of the Holy Roman Emperor. You will release my men at once, do you hear?"

The staunch expression of the officer faltered slightly under the strength of this command, but he forced out, "I have been ordered to take you and—."

"Unless it is your wish that the entire Spanish armada be sent against these islands, take your order back to your commander and tell him to release my men!"

The officer glanced uneasily at his oarsmen before replying, "I will take your request back to my superiors at once, sir."

Only minutes after the longboat had landed, Acurio voiced what Elcano could already see. "They're manning all four of their caravels, sir."

Albo turned to Elcano with expectant eyes, but his captain gave no order. "Sir, we must sail at once."

Elcano smashed his fist against the top of the rail and whispered the word, "No."

"If we don't leave them, sir, we'll be imprisoned with them," said Albo, the urgency in his voice building. "There will be no hope of their rescue if we, too, are taken."

Rodas, his eyes growing fearful, spoke up. "Captain, we must leave now if we hope to outrun their fleet."

Elcano could see the last of the Portuguese seamen climbing aboard their ships.

"Captain," Acurio said, "Pilot Albo is right. Our only hope of freeing them is lost if we fail to reach Spain." Under his breath Acurio pleaded, "You must leave him to save him, sir!"

Elcano turned tortured eyes on Acurio, forcing himself to accept what he already knew to be true. After a heartbeat, then two, he whirled around and roared as if the words were torn from his lungs, "Weigh anchors! Full sails!"

Men bounded and tripped over one another as they raced to snatch up the lines and heave with every ounce of their strength. The capstan lifted the anchor but there were too few seamen to work the main sail. In a moment Elcano and his officers were beside their men, grunting and pulling until every sail had spread to its full length. The patched canvas sheets with the stained red crosses caught the wind and swelled, driving the *Victoria* forward.

Quickly tying off his line, Elcano climbed and rushed to the back rail of the stern deck. The crews of the caravels were still scrambling to release their furled sails. Only one ship had lifted her anchor. The *Victoria* had a chance of escaping them.

Albo shouted to him from below, "The course, Captain?"

"Due south!" They would hold that course until they were well out of sight, then they would head to the west. Few would expect them to take the long way around.

Men continued to work the sails and position the tiller while Elcano stared back toward shore. They were pulling away from the caravels. And from his men. From Chindarza.

His gaze dragged toward the town, looking from building to building. And even as he searched, he tried to push from his mind the image of Chindarza sitting on the floor of a fetid cell, being taunted by a guard, one delivering the news that he had just been abandoned by his captain.

His breathing grew more sharp and ragged. Not even Acurio, watching with pain-filled eyes from the foredeck, disturbed him in his misery.

# The Request

## 24

Neither dark, nor light, nor the turnings of the half-hour glass now distinguished one watch from the next. The men of the *Victoria* toiled until they limped or reeled from their posts in exhaustion. To do less would have meant the misdirection or the sinking of their ship, but the relentless demands upon their already depleted bodies cannibalized what little flesh still clung to their bones. Straining even longer and harder than his men, Elcano drove himself on in a kind of madness. He slept little and would have forgotten to eat altogether if Acurio had not stepped in.

Reading the situation, Acurio took matters into his own hands. Twice a day he hovered over Elcano like a priest over a sinner, refusing to leave him in peace until his bowl and cup were empty, and he was almost as insistent with the other officers. Acurio cajoled and bossed the rest of the haggard crew into eating before he allowed them to fall into short stints of dreamless sleep. The scrawnier the men grew, the more persistent Acurio became in his caretaking.

Despite Acurio's efforts, however, three weeks after leaving Santiago, he came to Elcano at the tiller, drew him aside, and said, "Captain, Étienne Villon has just breathed his last."

Running his hand across his sweat-slicked forehead, then placing it heavily on Acurio's shoulder, Elcano said the most hopeful thing that came to mind. "Perhaps he will be the last."

Villon's funeral service was a weak affair, little more than two sad prayers shouted above the shrieking wind and the lifting of the end of a board to deliver his body into the roiling sea. That was all the men could offer before returning to their efforts to keep the *Victoria* above water.

Two days earlier they had spotted the towering mountain that dominated Pico Island. Elcano knew that Pico was one of the Azores held by the Portuguese and that no safe harbor would be found there. Reluctantly, he directed them past all of the islands, holding to a northwest heading in search of the westerly winds that would blow them toward Spain. Instead of finding the predictable air flows, they encountered building headwinds and a contrary current that grew in strength until the *Victoria* was being driven backwards. The ruthlessness of the wind persisted as one unyielding day followed another, and Elcano swore and prayed and cried out in fury as they futilely fought to advance against the elements.

Three and a half spirit grinding weeks after Villon's death, the Azores were still in sight.

Elcano was at the tiller ropes again when the howling of the wind stilled so suddenly that he and the men beside him froze. No longer trusting his own senses, he glanced at the other seamen for confirmation that they could hear the change as well. A moment later he felt the sea loosen its grasp on the tiller. Giving a distracted order to his men to hold the ship steady, Elcano released his line and emerged from under the half deck to stare at the sails and then the sea. He barely dared to breathe as his eyes darted back to the limp sails. Albo and Acurio stared down at him from the half deck railing, looking as if they were afraid to speak. The hatch to the hold opened and men climbed weakly to the deck, gazing upward in dazed wonder and hope.

The *Victoria* slowed until she was almost motionless. Very gently, a new breeze from the west puffed against her sails. The canvas ruffled once, then stilled. With the next breath, the wind, growing in both power and consistency, filled the flagging sails. As if she'd just been freed from heavy shackles, the *Victoria* pulled ahead through the calming waters, carrying them to the east, carrying them toward home.

Elcano clung to the edge of the capstan, and whispered in a cracking voice, "That's it. That's it. Full ahead now. You know the way."

With pitifully weak voices his men cheered their ship and the benevolent wind, and in their cries was the remnant of hope that even their grueling trials had not smothered. Elcano watched them, listened to them, and prayed that God would help him deliver these men through this last stretch of ocean.

That night, though their labors had been only marginally lightened, Acurio had no trouble getting the men to eat.

Over the next six days, the men of the *Victoria* did not waiver in their determination or their direction. They were nearing home. With every hour that passed, they were nearing home. Somehow they found reserves of strength to pump, and pull, and encourage.

It was on the fourth day of September, as Elcano was just emerging from the hold, when Pilot Albo shouted, "Land ahead, Captain! Cape St. Vincent!"

As quickly as his wobbly legs would carry him, Elcano hurried to Albo's side on the foredeck. Clear and bold, the cape rose before them. Elcano clasped Albo's arm and fought for control as he whispered, "By God, Pilot, I never thought I'd be so thankful to see Portugal."

He turned toward midship, cleared his throat, and called out to his men, "Two more days, men! Two days to San Lúcar!"

The eastward current glided the *Victoria* forward and the breeze murmured with the gentleness of a lullaby. That night when Elcano took his turn at the tiller, he and the men spoke of homecomings.

"Nearly three years, sir," said Acurio, "that's how long it's been since I've sunk my teeth into fresh bread. That and a glass of good wine will please me well."

"I'm going to eat and sleep for a full month, Captain," declared a seaman.

"What will your wife think of that?" demanded another.

"She's more than welcome to join me in bed!"

374

After the rejoining laughter had quieted, Bustamente asked, "What do you suppose our share of the cloves will come to, sir? Do you think King Carlos will take into account all that we've gone through, when the final counting is made?"

Elcano said, "I can only ask him, but that will come after I have asked him to bring our men home."

"He will find a way to free them, sir," Acurio assured. "Even old King Manuel wouldn't dare to hold part of *this* crew. After all, haven't we brought back cloves and treaties from the Spiceries? Haven't we found the passage to the Pacific Sea and circled the entire world, which was a *bit* larger than we'd been led to believe?"

"That we have, Acurio," said Elcano, his hopes holding fast to Acurio's confidence.


With the *Victoria* leaking worse than ever, there was no letting up on the demands of the pumps. The scrawny legs and arms of the men worked endlessly throughout the next day, and then the next. But as they continued to move closer to a homeland that had grown more beloved than any of them could have imagined, not one of them willingly faltered.

Holding a chart between them, Elcano and Albo sighted the mouth of the Guadalquivir River only seconds before the rest of their men. Elcano stood quite still and whispered, simply and humbly, "There it is."

A moment later the men erupted with wild acclamations. Those below left their pumps and scurried from the hold to gape, and yell, and clasp one another's bony shoulders.

Elcano shouted out, "On to San Lúcar, men!"

Before they turned toward the fresh waters of the river, men were sent in search of the banners that had been stowed away for so many months. Patches of cloth bearing proud lions and castles in red, gold, blue, and white, were hoisted to the top of the *Victoria's* two remaining masts. At the sight, the men raised their voices in cries of welcome and exaltation. Elcano, staring at the banners as his vision blurred and his chest tightened, felt as though something that had been stolen long ago had just been restored.

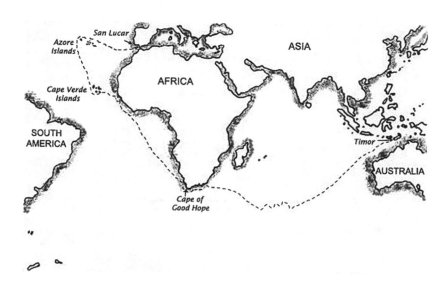

Remaining at the *Victoria's* prow as she pushed into the river and made her way toward San Lúcar, Elcano saw people ashore gawk and point at their passing. As his ship drew nearer to the port, he called out orders for Master Rodas to lower the main sail and prepare to secure the ship, but this was done as a matter of form rather than necessity. His men were already at the lines.

They had reached the outer edge of the harbor when Elcano saw a longboat sailing out to meet them. An officer stood up in the center of the boat and shouted, "I am Pilot Pedro Sordo. Please declare your ship."

Elcano, skinny, ragged, and grimy, lifted his voice and called back, "I am Juan Sebastian de Elcano, Captain of the *Victoria.*"

"The *Victoria*, sir? Have you come from the West Indies, Captain Elcano?"

"No, Pilot, we have come from the *East* Indies!"

Sordo and his men scanned the shabby crew and decrepit ship in open-mouthed amazement. "Not the *Victoria* that sailed with Magellan's fleet, sir!"

"The very same. My good men are weak and hungry, Pilot, and we've lost our launch. I would appreciate your assistance."

"I, of course, I am at your service, Captain. If you will follow our boat, sir, I will lead you across the sandbar."

This offer was gratefully accepted, and as the *Victoria* slowly glided to her berth, Elcano scanned the port city. Had it really only been three years since he'd left? It seemed impossible that his mind and heart could have been filled with so much wonder and pain in so short a time. Now, at last, he was back, but with so few others. Too few others.

With the lowering of the anchor, he turned around and took in the poignant expressions of his men. At least half of them wept quietly at the railing, some needing to be supported by others just to stand. Albo bent his head in prayer. Rodas stared ashore. Acurio busily checked the tightness of the tie lines as he wiped his eyes, and then threw a quick glance up at Elcano.

The Brunei sailors were exclaiming in their own language and pointing at the city before them. Of the eleven that had sailed with him from Tidore, only these three remained aboard. Manuel, though also alive, was with Chindarza in the hands of the Portuguese.

Elcano let his attention drift down to his bare feet, his tattered clothes, and his almost skeletal hands. With Bustamente too busy at the pumps to bother with so frivolous an activity as barbering, Elcano's dirty hair and shaggy beard were no more presentable than those of his crew. For a moment he considered taking the time to clean up a little before going ashore, but he disregarded the idea as trivial. Besides, he had no other clothes to wear.

Pilot Sordo, fulfilling his promise of service, had a skiff sent to them immediately. As soon as it arrived at the *Victoria's* side, Elcano and Albo were welcomed aboard and rowed to the dock. Sordo, his sailors, and several men from town were there to meet them, and welcoming hands reached down to help them climb from the boat.

For a moment, the two scrawny officers stood wobbling on the unyielding pier, uneasily trying to remember how to

walk on a motionless surface. While a cascade of congratulations and questions descended upon them, a couple of
kegs were rolled close and upended to serve as chairs. For
several minutes they did their best to respond politely, but
finally Elcano lifted his hands and said, "Please, men, allow
me a question or two. Have you any tidings of the *San
Antonio?*"

"Why, the *San Antonio* returned at least a year and a
half ago, Captain," said Sordo.

So, she had not been sunk after all. His eyes met Albo's
as they shared the realization that she had deserted them.
Elcano asked Sordo, "Did she return with a full crew?"

"That, I don't know, sir. I only heard that the crew over-
threw their traitorous Portuguese captain somewhere
south of the Rio de la Plata. They sailed back here with him
locked in the hold. Now, what was the captain's name?"

Elcano offered, "Mesquita?"

"That was it, sir! The scoundrel was brought back in
irons and he's been in prison ever since they arrived in
Seville."

"Who commanded the ship on her return voyage?"

"I remember hearing two names, sir, Guerra and..."

"Gomez?"

"Yes, sir, Gomez."

While Elcano and Albo tried to absorb the answers to a
mystery that had plagued them for so long, questions
flowed from the townspeople in increasing numbers.

"Wait, please," said Elcano, "I have one more question.
What have you heard of Captain Espinosa? He sailed on the
*Trinidad* from the Spice Islands to Panama."

"To Panama?" said Sordo. "I'm sorry, Captain, but I have
heard nothing of him or his ship."

Again Elcano and Albo traded a look before surrendering
a brief time to answer the eager queries of those around
them. At last Elcano insisted, "Please, our men are completely spent and our ship is leaking badly. We are in need
of fresh food and water, as well as men to work our pumps.
There is no time for repairs, since I must not delay our sail-

ing for Seville, but we need to keep the *Victoria* afloat for at least a few more days."

Several offers were immediately given.

"We also need a doctor—."

"A doctor?" asked a townsman. "What manner of illness is aboard your ship?"

"Only the seaman's curse, and it seems to be easing. No one ashore need fear us. Mostly, our men are in dire need of rest and good food, but a doctor's care might speed the recovery of the weakest among us. I also need to hire a messenger who can deliver a letter to the king."

He was told that a reliable messenger would leave for Valladolid early the next morning. A man was sent in search of a physician and more pledges for assistance were volunteered.

With great relief, Elcano said, "I am most grateful, and we now must return to our men."

Reluctant to part with such enthralling visitors, the harbor men nevertheless helped them into the skiff and rowed them across the water.

Once back aboard the ship, Elcano gave his crew the news of the *San Antonio*. The decks were still abuzz with this revelation when men from shore arrived to manipulate the pumps. By late afternoon boatloads of water and fresh food were lifted to the decks and divided by appreciative hands.

Elcano commandeered one keg of water for himself and had it delivered to his cabin. This, he saved for later.

On Elcano's order the officers sat down on the main deck beside the men to partake of their dinner together. All heads bowed in prayer, after which Zubileta filled each bowl with a hearty portion of chicken and leek soup provided by a nearby tavern. To the delight of every man, and to Acurio in particular, many loaves of fresh bread had been included in the town's offering, and Elcano had these doled out in equal shares as well. Their cups were generously filled with good Spanish wine.

At Acurio's first bite of bread, he closed his eyes and moaned so long and so low that several men chuckled in agreement as they ate. "This is near to heaven, this is," Acurio muttered before tearing off another mouthful.

"Not nearly so close as this," said Bustamente lifting his cup of wine.

"All right," said Acurio "it's close to a draw then. And just think, we'll be eating like this tomorrow, and the next day, and the next."

As the men chewed, their heads bobbed in grateful acknowledgement.

Not long after the food and wine had disappeared, men began to curl up in their places and fall into the soundest sleep they had known in what felt like ages. Elcano, who had anticipated this, had drunk only half his share of wine. Seeing both Albo and Rodas trying to keep their eyes open, he stood up and said to them, "Go and get some sleep. When I can no longer keep watch, I'll wake you." They stood up and moved toward their bunks, muttering their thanks as they went.

Stepping over slumbering bodies, Elcano made his way to his cabin and opened the water barrel. He carefully drew out a full pitcher and set it on his table. Then, feeling like a pampered king, he stripped off his clothes, dipped his hands deep into the barrel, and splashed water onto his face. Taking a deep breath, he plunged his head into its depths, staying under long enough to run his fingers several times through his hair and beard. He came up sputtering, and then repeated the dunking several times before taking up a rag and attending to the rest of his body.

When he finally emerged from his cabin wearing damp clothes, Acurio was standing at the rail not far from his door. Elcano joined him and took a drink from the cup he'd brought with him.

Acurio gave him a quick perusal. "I've all but forgot what clean feels like, sir."

"I'm not thoroughly clean, Acurio, but even that rinsing was long in coming."

The evening breeze brushed lightly against Elcano, and he breathed in the smells of the harbor, scents of their homecoming. He gazed out at the darkening horizon.

As if the importance of this day was too great to be expressed in mere words, he and Acurio spoke instead of smaller things; the dinner, the generosity of the townspeople, the beauty of the young girl standing at the door of the harbor's bakery. But all the while, Elcano's thoughts kept returning to Chindarza and the other men he'd left behind. He guessed that Acurio's mind held the same thoughts, and he was greatly comforted by his quiet, understanding company.

When the last of the sun's light had left the sky, the captain ordered Acurio to his rest and woke the officers of the next watch. Returning to his cabin and crawling into his bunk, he breathed a prayer of thanks, and finally surrendered his mind and body to the stillness of the evening.

After taking a watch halfway through the night, Elcano awoke early to find bright sunshine spilling over San Lúcar. He left his cabin only long enough to check on the welfare of his ship and crew before coming back to spread several fresh sheets of parchment out on his desk. He picked up his quill and paused to gather his thoughts. Although his mind felt almost as sluggish as his body, he had silently rehearsed his words so many times that they soon began to flow and his quill to move.

Beginning with, "To Your Most Exalted Majesty," he went on to write that he and seventeen others that had originally sailed with Magellan had just arrived at San Lúcar. With brevity he described their passage through the strait, the deaths of Magellan and many others, and of the destruction of the *Concepción*. He revealed that they had reached the Moluccas and had formed treaties of trade with leaders there, that they had purchased two full shiploads of cloves, but that one of the two ships had been forced to remain behind for repairs while the *Victoria* had sailed back to Spain.

His quill wavered for a moment before it scratched out the tragedy of their return trip and the deaths of twenty-two of their men. Then, with renewed purpose, he explained the need for his landing on the Cape Verde Islands, and of the capture of Chindarza and the others. At last, he wrote, "I

381

ask Your Majesty now to claim these thirteen men who have served you so well and for so long. They have been of great value in proving the earth to be a sphere, having sailed entirely around it from the west to the east. In recognition of the hard work, hunger and thirst, cold and heat that these men have borne in your service, I ask that Your Majesty graciously ensure their release, preserve their liberty, and award them their share of the reward which is due them."

Laying the quill aside and reading over his words, Elcano was dissatisfied. Wishing it was written more clearly, that his words were more persuasive, he nevertheless knew that he must not delay long before locating the messenger. He closed the letter, signed it, and called to Albo.

"Please read this, Pilot."

After Albo had done so, he said, "It's a fine letter, Captain."

Accepting it from Albo's outstretched hand, Elcano said, "May it be good enough to free our men."

With the use of the boat that had been loaned to them, Elcano took the sealed letter ashore and, after making inquiries, surrendered it to the care of the messenger.

Returning to the pier, he was met by a member of the Casa de Contratacíon, the council that oversaw the king's interests in foreign lands. Word of the *Victoria's* arrival had reached the excited councilman the night before, and when he graciously offered to provide fifteen men to tow the *Victoria* upriver to Seville, Elcano immediately accepted thankfully. They would leave at first light of the following day.

News of their coming traveled before them as if borne on the wings of birds. By the time the *Victoria* was hauled into Seville's harbor, crowds had gathered along both shores of the Guadalquivir River. Just as his ship came to rest, Elcano ordered the firing of her guns. To the mighty voice of the cannons, the hoards ashore roared in response. He watched from the half deck as people jumped up and down in their excited efforts to get a better look. Many waved, crying out blessings.

Beside him, Acurio said, "Now that's a grand sight, is it not, Captain?"

"A very grand sight."

"There will likely be much made of us, eh Captain?"

"By some, I suppose, but we have many questions to answer before we're free to enjoy our return fully."

"When do you suppose we'll be allowed to leave for home, sir?"

"We're dealing with a king now, Acurio, and kings have their own notions of time and favors. Still, I hope we will all be home soon."

As numerous boats pushed off from shore and headed their way, Acurio said, "Just look at them come, sir. We'll not be lonely for quite some time."

Though the visitors and invitations were many, Elcano and his crew remained onboard throughout the day. He knew better than to relinquish possession of the ship until he had received word from the king to do so and until the cargo had been officially inspected and taken ashore. But when the king's personal guards arrived that evening to assure the safety of the *Victoria's* valuable goods, Elcano decided that he and his men could take a few hours in the morning to fulfill a promise, one that should not be delayed even for a king's permission.

At dawn, Elcano and his seventeen fellow Christian crewmen left their vessel in the care of their three Brunean shipmates and the king's guards to gather at the end of the main pier. With their feet bare and their bodies covered in nothing but long, stained, and lacerated shirts, each of them took a candle from the chest that Elcano had ordered brought from town. The wicks were lit, and Elcano slowly led his procession of wraithlike men down the length of the pier and onto the narrow streets of Seville. Three of them leaned heavily on their fellows. One was carried on a litter by four of the others.

Townsfolk gathered along their path, making the sign of the cross and offering a silent prayer as they passed. One old woman in a long gray apron tossed yellow flowers into the street in front of Elcano. He nodded his gratitude and walked slowly on, the rough stones of the street scuffing the bottoms of his feet with each step.

At last they reached the church of Santa Maria de la Victoria, the same church in which they and the flags of their ships had been blessed so many months ago, and here they knelt down on boney knees before the stone figure of Mary and her infant son. From his shirt Elcano drew one of the ship's frayed and faded banners, and he carefully laid it at the foot of the statue.

Gazing up at the marble image of the woman, staring into her kind eyes, Elcano gradually became aware of the growing sensation that she was looking back at him, seeing not just his body but his deepest self, seeing every thought and action he had ever experienced. Rather than condemning him for his failings and weaknesses, she seemed to be offering him the peace and healing his soul so desperately craved. A swelling of grief, regret, humility, and gratitude, rose in him, building until it touched the forgiveness in the lady's eyes and spilled over the boundaries of his restraint. And Elcano bent his head and wept along with his men.

As tears fell, he prayed for the safe return of Chindarza, and then Espinosa and the rest, and he prayed for the souls of those who would never return, especially Elorriaga. At last, Elcano rose and led his men across the Triana Bridge that spanned the waters of the Guadalquivir. They continued on, entering Seville's great cathedral and making their way to the chapel of Santa Maria del Antigua. Here, their prayers were repeated. Only after this, after having settled their heavenly obligations, did they return to their ship with quieter and lighter hearts.

Elcano rarely left the ship during the next five days, but one of the few exceptions occurred that same afternoon when he paid a visit to Juana Elorriaga. He knew she would have learned of her husband's death not long after the return of the *San Antonio*, but he went just the same. When he entered her home, she approached him with searching eyes, then gently wrapped her arms around him and laid her head on his shoulder, saying, "You were his friend, Juan Sebastian. I know you loved him. Let yourself be at peace."

When he parted from her an hour later, he returned to the ship to find two of the king's messengers waiting for him. They bowed to him respectfully and one of them said, "Captain Elcano, His Majesty sends his congratulations on your distinguished accomplishment. He is most anxious to meet with you, and commissions you to select two knowledgeable members of your crew and proceed with them to Valladolid at once." Nodding toward Elcano's cabin, he continued, "We were ordered to present you with three chests that have been placed in your quarters, sir. They contain clothing and funds to cover your traveling expenses. His Majesty also commanded me to surrender this letter into no one's hands but your own."

Elcano accepted the letter and stared at its seal. "Are you to wait for a reply?"

"No, Captain. His Majesty instructed us that no reply is necessary since he will see you soon."

"Very well then. I thank you for this service."

Motioning Acurio to follow him to his cabin, Elcano gave the beautiful chests no more than a glance before sitting down and breaking open the seal. Quickly, he scanned the letter. With his voice unsteady, he read one sentence aloud, "Measures have already been taken to free your thirteen men presently held by the Portuguese." He handed the letter to Acurio, bent his arms upon his desk and lowered his forehead to rest upon them. After a moment or two, he stood and went to his window.

"Well, sir," said Acurio, sniffing loudly, "let's hope whatever measures he's taken with the Portuguese are hard to ignore."

# A Worthy Visitor

## 25

Large flakes of snow danced from the sky over San Lúcar and Elcano gave his attention to the unusual event from the closed doorway of an inn where he'd just taken a room. He pulled his cloak more tightly around his shoulders, pushed away from the door, and wandered down toward the docks. Before he had reached the main pier, however, a boy of no more than eight years raced up and greeted him with, "No sign of her yet, sir."

"It may be another day or another week, Diego."

"Well, I'll keep watching, Captain."

"Good lad."

Crossing a slushy stretch of sand, Elcano climbed the dock's ramp and made his way down the row of slippery boards. Once he'd reached the end of the pier he turned to face the south and let his eyes linger downriver, willing the ship to appear. But there was just him, the river, the snow, and the boats rocking nearby.

Remembering, he looked down, but newly fallen snow had covered the surface of the wood. He squatted down and wiped the snow away. Most of the letters were completely gone, but his fingers moved slowly over the scarred wood, calling the words that he had carved so long ago back to life. "For Honor. For Home." *One has been restored*, he thought, *the other—*.

"Why, Captain Elcano! Is it really you?"

Elcano turned to find Pedro Sordo quickly approaching.

"Good day, Pilot. Yes, it's me."

Sordo's smile broadened as he came closer. "I just heard of your arrival, Captain. How long has it been, five months? You look as though they've been good to you, sir."

"I've been fortunate in many ways."

"Is it true, sir, that you've been to Valladolid to see the king?"

Elcano nodded. "Yes, I've seen him."

"How I'd love to hear every one of your stories, Captain."

"Do you have time for a drink, Pilot?"

"Of course, sir." Elcano turned and led Sordo back toward the inn as the pilot continued. "May I ask what brings you to San Lúcar, Captain Elcano? Is there some service I may offer?"

"I'll tell you everything once we get inside," Elcano said. The muffled sounds of their steps retreating down the dock stilled when they reached the beach, and they soon entered the warmth of the inn's dining room.

Elcano and Sordo had just settled down by the inn's huge fireplace with cups of wine in their hands when the door burst open and Diego shouted, "She's here, Captain! It's the *Santa Cruz*! She's here!"

Slamming down his cup and jumping to his feet, Elcano muttered an apology as he grabbed up his cloak and trotted toward the door. Sordo, recovering from his surprise, was soon on his heels.

The doubts, hopes, and dreads that had been looming for the past few days now rose with such sudden authority that Elcano's feet faltered at the sight of the Spanish ship just gliding to a standstill in the waters offshore. *Is he well? Has he suffered greatly? Will he forgive me for abandoning him? Will he speak to me? Will any of them?*

He was there to meet the skiff when it reached the dock. After identifying himself and learning that all thirteen of his men were indeed aboard, he asked, "Are they sound or ill?"

"Sound, sir," said the shipmaster of the *Santa Cruz*, "they have been adequately fed while in our care, but they still need time to recover fully."

"None of them is ill?"

"Not from disease, sir. A few were beaten by their Portuguese jailers." He turned his head and spat into the water to show his opinion of the latter.

"Are they coming ashore?"

"Yes, sir. My captain has promised that they'd set foot on Spanish soil again this very day. He's even allowing them a full night in town. I'm to secure rooms for them. Our rudder mount needs mending and that will take at least two days."

"Will you tell them I'll be at the Crossbow?"

"Of course, sir. Why, I'll see about finding rooms for them there, too."

Less than an hour later, the door of the Crossbow was thrown open once again, and there stood Chindarza. Elcano jumped to his feet but couldn't take a step. It was Chindarza. Thin, dirty, and shaggy, but blessedly whole, Chindarza. An instant after this assessment was made Chindarza spotted him in the corner by the fire.

"Captain!" Chindarza rushed toward him, bumping a barmaid and knocking over a stool on his way. Elcano collided with him in the center of the room and locked his arms around him. "I knew," Chindarza mumbled through his tears. "I knew you'd see us home."

After several moments Elcano released him, but only to hold him at arm's length and take a closer look at him. He bore a new inch-long scar at the corner of his mouth, but when Elcano would have asked about it, about everything, Chindarza said, "I'm well, sir. Truly."

Before Elcano could speak, Méndez, Argot, and the rest of his men were suddenly crowding around him, shouting questions, and clapping him heartily and most unprofessionally on the back.

"How good of you to come, Captain," said Méndez. "You're a healing sight for these homesick eyes. You surely are."

"I was half afraid you'd want to string me up," Elcano admitted.

"Now, sir," said Argot, sounding offended, "we'd be a sorry lot indeed it we didn't know you're sailing for home is the only reason we're alive today. And today, by God, we're on Spanish land ourselves," he said, stamping his foot twice on the floorboards. "We're on good Spanish land." His voice faltered and his head lowered to hide the trembling of his lips.

"Sit down, men," said Elcano. "You're all in need of fattening." Scanning their faces, Elcano added, "I don't see Burgos."

"Well, sir, Burgos stayed aboard the ship," said Méndez. "You see, it was him that told the Portuguese that we were part of Magellan's fleet and that our ship was loaded with spices."

"I see. Well, all of you, sit down and eat."

They gathered at the tables and Elcano bought them as much food and wine as they could hold. He sat beside Chindarza, who listened more than spoke, evidently preferring to wait for a private conversation.

The men were almost as hungry for news as they were for the meat and bread, and Elcano did his best to tell them all he knew. He informed them first of the *San Antonio's* return and of Mesquita's recent release from jail.

"What of the *Trinidad*, Captain?" Argot asked.

Elcano shook his head. "All that's come to us is rumors by way of Portugal. We have no real word."

"What are the rumors then, sir?"

"Oh, what one might expect really; that the Portuguese have sent an entire fleet from India after her, that she's been blown from the water with all hands lost, that she's been captured and her entire crew executed, that she was found drifting with every man aboard dead from starvation from trying to cross the Pacific Sea. There's no end to the claims, and I doubt any one of them is true. What *is* true," he said with a satisfied smile, "is that our cloves were sold for enough money to cover the costs of the entire expedition."

"Glory be," whistled Argot.

"And the king has agreed to grant our crew a share in the proceeds."

A wave of questions and exclamations met this announcement, and Elcano tried to keep up with them. At last, he said, "Now I want to hear how you managed to keep yourselves able-bodied during the last five months."

While the men told of their time in captivity, of their voyage to Portugal and then homeward, the wine gradually took affect and several heads began to droop. As the candles in the dining room were being lit, all the men but Chindarza bid Elcano good night and helped each other up the stairs toward their rooms.

Chindarza had just managed to keep his eyes open and when he and Elcano were finally alone at their table, he said, "And how have you been, sir. You've said little about yourself."

"I'm well, son, doubly so now that you're safe."

"You've had audiences with the king, the emperor himself?"

"Yes, quite a few. I have been working with many others to formalize our claims to the Moluccas. But I have little hope that King Manuel will acknowledge any of our rights. He's bloody furious over the entire affair."

This brought a satisfied smile to Chindarza's face.

"Just last week, though, in recognition for my services," Elcano said, "the emperor absolved me of the old charge against me, for selling my ship to foreigners."

"Oh, sir. That must have given your mind great comfort."

"Yes, Chindarza, it did. But now, would you like to tell me of your imprisonment?"

"I was beaten at first, sir, but not for long." Chindarza pushed the sleeve of his jacket up to reveal a ring of scarred flesh around his wrist. With grim pride, he said, "We share the same scars now, sir. It's another link between us."

Moved deeply, Elcano gently wrapped his hand around the reddened wrist, wishing with all his heart that he could erase the scars and, even more, the memories that went with them.

390

Chindarza tried to ease his mind by saying, "Sir, I'd dearly like to hear about the rest of our crew. How are they?"

Elcano allowed himself a soft smile. "Most of them are home now and very happy to be."

When a quietness settled over Elcano, Chindarza said, "Have you been home, sir?"

"The king has not granted me such freedom yet, but I have written many letters to my family. They are thriving."

"And Acurio, sir, is he still in Seville?"

Elcano laid his hands flat on the table. "I just remembered that I have something in my room to show you. Have you had enough to eat?"

"Another bite would be the end of me, sir."

"Then let's go upstairs."

Elcano carried a candle up the steps and into his room. The stained canvas bag on the floor caught Chindarza's eye and, recognizing it at once, he let out a whoop of pleasure. He picked it up, tugged it open, and reached inside. Pulling out the wooden figure of a sea wolf and fingering it longingly, Chindarza said, "Sir, you saved them for me."

"Yes." For a few moments Elcano just watched the expressions play across Chindarza's face as he drew out and examined each animal. Then, walking to the other side of his bed and bringing out a round-topped wooden chest, he slid it closer to Chindarza. Elcano opened the lid and laid one item after another on the bed's covers. Before the chest was empty, a new woolen jacket, leather jerkin and belt, satin doublet, three tunics, four shirts, three pairs of breeches, two pairs of hose and a pair of buckled shoes had been neatly arrayed.

Chindarza let his eyes trail over them, and smiled broadly at Elcano. "They're truly grand, sir. It does me good to see you coming into what you deserve."

"They're not mine, Chindarza. I bought them for you."

Chindarza's tone faded. "Such clothes for me, sir?"

"For when you go home to your mother."

"Oh, sir. This is so good of you, but, my mother," his voice faltered, "I don't even know if she's still alive. I've been gone so long."

"Come and sit down, son," said Elcano, drawing Chindarza toward a wooden chair at his small table and taking a seat for himself. "Acurio wrote to me from Bermeo. Your mother is well, Chindarza. When she learned you were alive, she was overcome with joy."

"She is well?" Chindarza stared, then his eyes closed tightly, his head fell into his hands, and single rough sob escaped his lips. For a moment he struggled to master himself. When his face lifted, he smiled and his wet eyes filled with hope. "Will you be heading home too, sir? Perhaps we can travel together, as far as Bermeo, I mean."

Elcano's gaze drifted away but he kept his voice calm. "I am not free to leave yet, Chindarza, but you must not keep your mother waiting. You need to go home and regain your health."

"But you will come soon, sir? You will be our guest?"

Knowing he could keep the truth from him no longer, Elcano took a breath and tried to soften his words, tried to hide the strength it cost to convey his news. "You have someone else that will stay with you from now on, Chindarza. Acurio is waiting for you with your mother."

Chindarza gaped back at him in disbelief. "Acurio and my mother?"

"Yes."

"Acurio?"

"He's a good man, Chindarza."

Chindarza leaned back in his chair, his eyes never leaving Elcano's face. When the silence stretched out too long, he finally said, "He is, sir. A very good man."

"After the *Victoria* arrived in Seville," Elcano said gently, "I was commanded to depart almost at once to meet with the king in Valladolid. I was not given leave to go home, or to Bermeo. I never told Acurio of my intention to meet your mother, or of my hopes. And he never told me that he loved her. As it turns out, he has loved her ever since he was a boy. Acurio sent me letters after he reached Bermeo, and that was the first time he shared what was in his heart. He told me of his joy upon seeing her again, and upon her acceptance of him as a husband. You already know of Acurio's love for you. This is how it was meant to be, Chindarza. Together, the three of you will make a strong family."

Chindarza could not find his voice, so Elcano added what had yet to be said. "I wish Acurio and your mother every blessing. They already have one beyond compare."

Chindarza lowered his gaze until it came to rest upon the candle slowly dripping into a pottery dish in the middle of the table. The flame seemed to capture his thoughts, for he still said nothing.

"Wait now," said Elcano, "I have one thing more to give you." Elcano stood up and went to the bed to pull something from the pocket of Chindarza's new jacket. Upon his return, he sat down and said, "Open your hand, son," and into Chindarza's palm he lowered a long silver chain.

Lifting it up to the candle, Chindarza looked into the cylindrical glass of an amulet nearly identical to Elcano's own. The sliver of wood within it was larger, however, and the scrap of canvas darker in color.

"From the *Victoria*," said Elcano, "although I doubt you'll need it to find your way. You've already come so far without it."

Chindarza's thumb slowly caressed the top of the amulet. "Tiller and sail," he said, reflecting, remembering. His eyes found Elcano's. "I will wear it with gratitude, always."

He looked again at the amulet and after a long moment, abruptly, his thumb stilled. He sat up straighter and his expression lightened. "Sir, did Acurio mention my aunt and cousins in his letters to you? Do you know how they are faring?"

"Yes, Chindarza," Elcano assured him, "your aunt and her sons are doing just fine."

"And is she still living with my mother, sir?"

"Yes, she is."

"Then she has not yet married?"

A dawning awareness crept into Elcano's features. "Why...no."

Letting his mouth soften into a smile, Chindarza lifted the chain over his head and placed his hand atop the amulet where it rested on his chest. "My cousins have much to learn about the sea, sir."

"Is that so?"

"Yes, sir. And my aunt is a fine cook, especially when we have a visitor."

# Epilogue

Two hundred sixty-five men sailed with Ferdinand Magellan from San Lúcar in September of 1519. Only Juan Sebastian de Elcano and thirty men under his command succeeded in completing their mission and making their way back to Spain.

As for the *Trinidad*, more than half of her men died of scurvy while attempting to cross the northern Pacific Ocean. When Gonzalo Gomez de Espinosa turned the flagship back toward the Molucca Islands with the hope of saving what remained of his decimated crew, his ship was captured by a Portuguese fleet. Only Espinosa and three others, after years of imprisonment and anguish, made it back to the shores of their homeland.

In July of 1525, Elcano again sailed from Seville bound for the Moluccas. Journeying with him were three of the Europeans and three of the Bruneians that had served beside him aboard the *Victoria*. The three seamen from Brunei were safely returned to the island of their birth but, after piloting the fleet through the Strait of Magellan, Elcano fell victim to scurvy and never saw his beloved village of Guetaria again.

Before Elcano had set out on his final voyage, however, Holy Roman Emperor Carlos V bestowed upon Elcano and his family a coat-of-arms bearing a gold castle on a field of red. Cinnamon, cloves, and nutmeg lie below the castle, and at its sides stand two kings of the Indies. Above the castle a globe rests on a knight's helmet, and upon the globe is written "Primus cicumdedisti me", "You were the first to encircle me."

# Glossary of Principal Characters

**Juan Sebastian de Elcano** - Master of the *Concepción* and the *Victoria*, and Captain of the *Victoria*

**Ferdinand Magellan** - Captain-general of the fleet

**Gaspar de Quesada** - Captain of the *Concepción*

**Luis de Mendoza** - Captain of the *Victoria*

**Juan de Cartagena** - Captain of the *San Antonio*

**Juan Rodriguez Serrano** - Captain of the *Santiago* and the *Concepción*, and Captain-general

**Juan de Elorriaga** - Master of the *San Antonio*

**Esteban Gomez** - Pilot of the *Trinidad* and Captain of the *San Antonio*

**Juan Lopez Carvalho** - Pilot of the *Concepción*, Captain of the *Trinidad*, and Captain-general

**Gonzalo Gomez de Espinosa** - Master-at-arms of the *Victoria,* and Captain of the *Victoria* and the *Trinidad*

**Giovanni Battista di Polcevera** -Master of the *Trinidad* and Captain-general

**Juan de Acurio** - Boatswain of the *Concepción* and the *Victoria*

**Francisco Albo** - Boatswain of the *Trinidad* and Pilot of the *Trinidad* and the *Victoria*

**Miguel de Rodas** - Boatswain, Pilot, and Master of the *Victoria*

**Pedro de Chindarza** - Cabin boy on the *Concepción* and the *Victoria*

**Juanito Carvalho** - Half-Tupi son of Juan Lopez Carvalho

**Carlos I** - King of Spain and Holy Roman Emperor Carlos V

**Rajah Humabon** - Ruler of Cebu

**Sultan Siripada** - Ruler of Brunei

**Rajah Almanzor** - Ruler of Tidore

# The Author

Christine Echeverria Bender stands in the town square of Guetaria, Spain before a statue of Juan Sebastian de Elcano. Ms. Bender lives with her husband and children in Boise, Idaho. She can be contacted through her website at www.christinebender.com.

# New titles from
# CAXTON PRESS

*Elegant Soul:The Life and Music of Gene Harris*
ISBN 0-87004-445-1
10 x 8, 280 color pages, paper, $24.95

*Our Ladies of the Tenderloin*
*Colorado's Legends in Lace*
ISBN 0-87004-444-3
6x9, 288 pages, paper, $16.95

*Great Meals Dutch Oven Style*
ISBN 0-87004-440-0
6x9, 50 photographs, 220 pages, comb binding
$17.95

*The Lewis and Clark Trail, Yesterday and Today*
ISBN 0-87004-439-7
6x9, 300 pages, photos, paper, $16.95

*Governing Idaho*
*People, Politics and Power*
ISBN 0-87004-447-8
6x9, 250 pages, paper, $16.95

**For a free catalog of Caxton books write to:**

*CAXTON PRESS*
312 Main Street
Caldwell, ID 83605-3299

or

Visit our Internet Website:

www.caxtonpress.com

*Caxton Press* is a division of The CAXTON PRINTERS, Ltd.